The Best of
Jim Baen's
UNIVERSE II

BAEN BOOKS by ERIC FLINT

RING OF FIRE SERIES:

1632

1633 with David Weber

1634: The Baltic War with David Weber

Ring of Fire ed. • *Ring of Fire II* ed.

1634: The Galileo Affair with Andrew Dennis

1634: The Ram Rebellion with Virginia DeMarce et al.

1634: The Bavarian Crisis with Virginia DeMarce

1635: The Cannon Law with Andrew Dennis

Grantville Gazette ed. • *Grantville Gazette II* ed.

Grantville Gazette III ed. • *Grantville Gazette IV* ed.

Time Spike with Marilyn Kosmatka

JOE'S WORLD SERIES:

The Philosophical Strangler • *Forward the Mage* with Richard Roach

STANDALONE TITLES:

Mother of Demons • *Crown of Slaves* with David Weber

The Course of Empire with K.D. Wentworth

Mountain Magic with Ryk E. Spoor, David Drake & Henry Kuttner

Boundary with Ryk E. Spoor

WITH DAVID DRAKE: *The Tyrant*

THE BELISARIUS SERIES WITH DAVID DRAKE:

An Oblique Approach • *In the Heart of Darkness*

Thunder at Dawn (omnibus)

Destiny's Shield • *Fortune's Stroke*

The Tide of Victory • *The Dance of Time*

WITH DAVE FREER:

Rats, Bats & Vats • *The Rats, The Bats & The Ugly*

Pyramid Scheme • *Pyramid Power*

WITH MERCEDES LACKEY & DAVE FREER:

The Shadow of the Lion • *This Rough Magic*

The Wizard of Karres

EDITED BY ERIC FLINT:

The World Turned Upside Down with David Drake & Jim Baen

The Best of Jim Baen's Universe

The Best of Jim Baen's Universe II with Mike Resnick

The Dragon Done It with Mike Resnick

The Best of *Jim Baen's UNIVERSE* II

edited by
ERIC FLINT
&
MIKE RESNICK

THE BEST OF JIM BAEN'S *UNIVERSE* II

This is a work of fiction. All the characters and events portrayed in this book are fictional, and any resemblance to real people or incidents is purely coincidental.

Copyright © 2008 by Baen Books

All rights reserved, including the right to reproduce this book or portions thereof in any form.

A Baen Books Original

Baen Publishing Enterprises
P.O. Box 1403
Riverdale, NY 10471
www.baen.com

ISBN 10: 1-4165-5570-6
ISBN 13: 978-1-4165-5570-4

Cover art and typography by David Mattingly

First printing, July 2008

Distributed by Simon & Schuster
1230 Avenue of the Americas
New York, NY 10020

Library of Congress Cataloging-in-Publication Data

The best of Jim Baen's universe II / edited by Eric Flint & Mike Resnick.
    p. cm.
  ISBN-13: 978-1-4165-5570-4 (trade pbk.)
  ISBN-10: 1-4165-5570-6 (trade pbk.)
  1. Science fiction, American. 2. Fantasy fiction, American. I. Flint, Eric. II. Resnick, Michael D. III. Jim Baen's universe (Online).

PS648.S3B498 2008
813'.0876208—dc22

                                                        2008013441

10 9 8 7 6 5 4 3 2 1

Pages by Joy Freeman (www.pagesbyjoy.com)
Printed in the United States of America

CONTENTS

Preface

Eric Flint & Mike Resnick

Ever since its inception, science fiction has believed in breaking laws.

Men can't survive under water? Jules Verne had a little something to say about that.

We'll never leave the planet or the solar system? Not once H.G. Wells and Doc Smith addressed the problems.

Death is final, and no one can survive it? Mary Shelley had a morbid take on it, Robert Sheckley a satirical one, Robert A. Heinlein a political one.

Science fiction, when all is said and done, is just like the race of Man. Tell it something can't be done, and all you've done is guarantee that a way will be found to do it. Show us an immutable law, such as gravity, and you can bet we'll find a way to break it. You might very well define us as a race of lawbreakers.

Jim Baen's Universe follows in those proud footsteps.

Everyone knows that you can't publish new fiction on the internet and expect people to pay for it. The highways and byways of the web are littered with the corpses of publishers who tried.

It was a challenge the late Jim Baen couldn't resist—and lo and behold, here we are, a successful online science fiction magazine.

Well, the reasoning went, maybe you can publish online, but you can't pay the same prices as the print magazines, not if you plan to stay in business.

So we broke another law. We decided to pay *more* than the print magazines—in the cases of our lead writers, over 300% more—and we're still around and in fine health. Even our lowest rates match the best rates of the print magazines.

Well, if you do that, the reasoning went, you'd better chop the wordage and give them a bare-bones magazine, maybe 60,000 words, tops.

(You saw this coming, right?) Our issues average over 100,000 words apiece.

Okay, said conventional wisdom, you broke a law here and skirted one there and you lucked out and stayed alive, but you'd better appeal to the vast indiscriminate audience that wants totally unchallenging science fiction. Award winners and prestigious writers will scare away the very audience you need in order to show a profit.

So we ran Gene Wolfe and David Drake and L.E. Modesitt, Jr. and Gregory Benford and Barry Malzberg and Nancy Kress and Kristine Kathryn Rusch and Cory Doctorow and David Brin (yes, we're boasting) and Esther Friesner and Julie Czerneda and Kevin Anderson and Brian Herbert and Alan Dean Foster and John Ringo and Jo Walton (yes, we're still boasting) Sarah Zettel and Garth Nix and Jack McDevitt and John Barnes (tum te tum tum) and Jay Lake and Catherine Asaro and Laura Resnick and Charles Stross and Elizabeth Bear, not to mention yours truly—along with a number of authors who are less well known to the reading public but many of whom will be before long. Not only that, but in our very first year of existence, before a lot of the voters even knew we were there, we had a Hugo nominee, a Locus Award winner, and three stories in Gardner Dozois' *Year's Best SF*.

It's pretty easy to fill up a magazine with names like that if you're willing to spend enough money...so was there room for anyone else in *Jim Baen's Universe*? As a matter of fact, there was. Conventional wisdom says that you sneak in a brand-new writer maybe once or twice a year, no more than that; so, in the law-breaking tradition of science fiction, we ran twenty-one first stories by new authors in our first year of publication, and we'll run close to that many every year. Someone has to nurture new talent, and we don't see any of the other magazines doing so in any quantity.

What else can't you do?

Well, almost no one runs serials any more, so of course *Jim Baen's Universe* does. The sort of long novellas and short novels that were once the staple of science fiction have a place they can get published again. Print magazines have pretty much given up even illustrating their stories with line drawings, so we use full-color art.

As print magazines struggle for their lives against the ever-more-crushing realities of magazine distribution and shy away from innovation, we're willing to try anything once—and more than once if it works. You want to read half the current issue for free? Log onto www.baens-universe.com and do just that. Want to have your submission critiqued by your fellow writers? Log onto Baen's Bar and you can get all the input you want before you officially submit it. Curious to know where your story is at in the selection process? You can get that from the internet too.

So . . . we're innovative, we're open-minded, and we're solvent—and this second annual anthology will give you an idea of what those traits lead to. We think they're truly fine stories, and that they stack up to any other anthology. We expect next year's to be even better, just as soon as we find a few more laws to break.

Crawlspace

Dave Freer and Eric Flint

Act 1, Scene 1: *Enter rats, scampering through the darkness*

In the narrow tunnels deep inside a nineteen by five mile asteroid, long pipes snaked endlessly into the blackness. At the tunnel
junction a naked globe hung, plainly jury-rigged into the cable
tacked to the low roof. A woman's body lay there, sprawled, a little
blood leaking from the retroussé nose. In the shadows, the light
reflected off two sets of ferally red eyes, looking at the corpse.

"Well? What do we do with it?" asked Snout, not moving forward with her little barrow.

"It's solid waste," said Mercutio. "'Tis what we do. Remove it."

She always asked those sort of questions of him. Well: Just
because one could think didn't always mean one wanted to.

Snout sniffed critically. "Well, not that solid. Parts of her look
positively malnourished. Especially around the waist."

Mercutio shrugged. The Siamese-cat sized, long-nosed, rattish
creature stepped forward and prodded the dead woman's waistline.
"Humans like to be like that. Anyway, 'tis corsetry, Snout."

"Of course 'tis," nodded the other cyber-uplifted elephant-shrew.
"Not natural to be that thin around the middle." She stalked

forward while her companion methodically rifled the pockets in the blouse top and then investigated the dead woman's purse. He was about to tuck what he found there into a pouch of his own when his companion hissed at him. He split the bundle of notes, roughly. She tucked her share of it into her own waist pouch.

"Wonder why she was killed, and yet they left the loot?" he asked, professionally.

"Probably done in because she's not a very pretty sight. Short little nose," Snout patted her own magnificent protuberance. "And no tail, poor thing. I don't care what humans say, this," she prodded the corpse's well-rounded derriere, "is not a tail."

A thought plainly crossed Snout's mind. Mercutio pretended not to see her hasty glance at him. It would avoid a fight. She felt inside the corpse's low neckline, brought out something that made a plastic crinkling sound to his carefully listening ear, and hastily tucked it into her bag. She kept talking, obviously in the hope that he wouldn't notice. "What was she doing here?"

"Dying, I would guess," said Mercutio, searching the lip of the corpse's stockings to no avail.

"Do we tell someone?" Snout removed a sliver filigree butterfly shaped hair-grip and tucked it next to her ear. "One of the humans. She is a human, so they might want to know."

Mercutio snorted. "Oh yes. And you know what they'd say: 'Why did you rats do it?' And then they'd put us into durance vile."

"But we are in durance, at least while the siege holds. It is fairly vile. And you usually did do it, Mercutio," she said, with that impeccable if twisted logic that comes from adding cybernetic memory and processing to an organic brain that hadn't gone a long way beyond thinking of its next meal or mating.

Mercutio was uplifted far enough to know that it was irritating, even if he did it himself. "That's not . . ."

Snout froze. "Hist," she said in a sibilant whisper. "Something this way comes."

Both rats ghosted away into the darkness as someone came climbing down the metal staples.

Act 1: Scene II. *A sparsely furnished rock-hewn chamber, somewhere on the same large asteroid in the Olmert system.*

Captain Rebecca Wuollet, HAR Marine Corps, was making a very credible effort to not tear off the head of Colonel De Darcy. First, because he was a superior officer and secondly because . . .

Well, technically he was right. You could see his point. If you walked around with blinkers on.

She made another attempt to use persuasion instead of violence, tempting though it was. That temptation was made easier to resist by the fact that the colonel was a combat vet himself. "Look Sir. I'm a combat demolitions specialist. I've been in the Corps for the whole of my adult life. I don't do . . . civilians. Sir."

De Darcy gave her the benefit of his famous crooked smile, complete with his famous crooked teeth. "I'm not a civilian liaison officer either, Captain. And this isn't about liaison. This is about the fact that we have fifteen thousand humans, mostly civs, God knows how many rats, about three hundred bats, and some fifteen other liberated races on this rock, which is under military control for the duration of the siege. We need some sort of security, and you're hard-assed enough to do it. Besides if I don't give you something to do, you'll lose that shiny new pip on your shoulder faster than you put it there."

He raised his eyebrows and shifted the famous crooked smile to its normal nastiness. "Look on the bright side. I could have put you in charge of the militia. I could still change my mind and shift Major Gahamey off the job and give him security."

"Um. Maybe security isn't so bad, sir." On this vast asteroid they only had a thousand seven hundred and thirty marines, who had been caught up in the mess when the attack on Epsilon Theta had gone ass-haywire. Stuck here with twenty times their number of civ refugees, and a bloody big rock to defend, they needed a militia. But the population of rock-rats, fortune-hunters, whores and sharp-dealing traders they had to draw from was going to drive Scotty Gahamey over the deep end. Well, maybe not. He was a real bastard and half over the deep end anyway. But it would certainly drive her there PDQ.

"I thought you might see it my way, Captain. Congratulations.

You are now the chief of police for the duration, or until I decide otherwise. Not that I intended you to have any choice in the matter."

The colonel emitted an evil chuckle. "You do realize that you're only going to get the sick, lame and lazy from me to help you to do the job? You'll need to draw in civs to run patrols, and keep fights and petty crime to a minimum, especially between soldiers and civs. We're thin enough stretched just running a defense perimeter. But with all the trouble that's cropped up, the civilian's council sent a delegation to ask me to appoint someone to deal with the situation."

Rebecca felt the short hairs on her neck rise. "What situation, sir?"

"Someone is killing the joy-girls from the Last Chance. The locals suspect that it's one of us," he said dryly.

"And is it, sir?" she asked, equally dryly.

The colonel tugged his moustache. "That's for you to find out. It could be true. If it is, you're going to have to stop it quietly and hard. Or the Korozhet won't have to take this lump of rock by force. Oh, and there are some hard drugs circulating. Civs do what they please out here. It's a long way from the law Earthside or on HAR. But I can't afford addicts in the Corps. You're as much law as this rock has. Stop the hard stuff."

She gritted her teeth. "Anything else I ought to know, sir?"

He thrust his hands into his pockets. "A lot. But you're going to have to find it out for yourself, Captain." His expression softened slightly. "You're a pain in the ass at times, Captain. But I chose you for this because you get results. I need them. I know that I can rely on you."

"Sir." It might be a lousy job, but De Darcy was always sparing with praise. She stood a little straighter.

He turned back to his desk and scooped up a datacube that he held out to her. "That's what I've got from them. There is also a list of personnel available to you in a file marked 'security personnel.' They're not all useless."

She took the cube, warily, as if it could just turn and bite her. He gestured at the door. "Get to it, Captain."

Rebecca saluted and turned.

As she did, De Darcy said, "One last thing, Captain. Try to use some of that tact you're famous for not having."

Act 1, Scene III: *In a large Korozhet command ship among the myriad asteroids that make up the Olmert system*

"Considering these reports it would seem that it is indeed essential that we recapture it. Although why the scientists could not have told us before the system was abandoned, I do not know. It would appear that laxity has taken place. That or resistance." The deep purple reclined further into his saline bath.

"It may be that they were deceived by the scale of the object and its exterior, High Spine," said the maroon.

"I trust they have been eaten," said the purple.

"Difficult. They are the experts and training new ones takes time."

The deep purple acknowledged the sad truth of this with a clack of his anterior spines. "Well, they must be suitably punished."

"I believe this has occurred, High Spine."

The Korozhet bent its eye-spines to peer at the report-screens. The data was not encouraging.

"The best option still appears to be a siege and our traditional means. And of course probing attacks, to take advantage of what we can. We have plenty of expendables."

"Less than we used to have," said another of the purple, humping up off her last meal.

"We may have to resort to more care in slave-handling, but things have not reached that point yet," said the purple in charge of alien resources. "They still breed and we have taken steps to prevent their subversion ever happening again."

"Maybe we need to see if we can insert some into the artifact," said the maroon, risking an opinion in this high council of his elders.

It was a sign of just how worried the Korozhet were that he was not disciplined for this breach of hierarchy. "It would be difficult," said one of the purple. "There may however be implanted escapees that could be turned to our purposes."

"Investigate the possibilities."

"It will be done, High Spine."

Act I Scene IV: *In the tunnels and cavernous tavern and house of ill repute*

"Sergeant Holmes."

The mountain of flesh saluted. So, despite appearances, it was human and alive. "Captain," he said in a carefully neutral voice.

This just had to be De Darcy's sense of humor, thought Rebecca sourly. He probably didn't find anyone called "Watson" among the enlisted men. Well, the one thing going for this man was his size. He could intimidate just by being there.

"Did you volunteer for this billet, Sergeant?" she asked suspiciously.

"With my name, the study of the criminal mind has always been my interest, Captain," said Sergeant Holmes calmly.

"Oh, and how do you do that?" She rocked on the balls of her feet, her hands clasped behind her.

Holmes lifted a meaty hand. "I knock it out of their ears and then look at it, Ma'am. It seems more effective than all this magnifying glass stuff I've read about."

"I'm beginning to revise my initial opinions about you, Sergeant. I think you could be an asset to the criminal investigation section. Which is, as of now . . . you. Assisted by me if it goes as far as murder. I have your first case awaiting you, just as soon as I finish with the patrol briefing."

"Maybe I should have chosen to go to brig after all, Captain," said Holmes amiably, confirming her suspicions about the able-bodied men she'd been given. Well, set a thief to catch a thief, and a drunk, disorderly and assaulting-the-guard Marine to catch others of the same kind. If you could stop them joining them, that is.

Twenty minutes later, after the patrols made up of one civ volunteer and a Marine apiece having been dispatched, they set out. Her first ever criminal investigation, she thought, led straight to the Last Chance Saloon Bar. Anyway, it would be a good opportunity to see how many of her patrols ended up in the place. She had half an hour before her meeting with the civic authorities, whoever they might be, among this rabble of refugees.

The Last Chance was an eloquent testimony to the ingenuity of rockrats. They'd created a visual masterpiece to get blind drunk in. The murals painted and projected around the room made it an almost believable walled garden, visible through French doors. There was even an ivy hung garden door, and distant green vistas over the top of the painted mossy stone wall. By the time you'd had three of the overpriced drinks it probably would fool you. There was of course a full length polished stone bar on the other wall, and a number of stone tables and benches that probably defied the strongest drunk's effort to use them for combat weapons.

The furniture was large. The proprietor was not. He was a tiny, soft-looking man.

"Honest Laguna at your service," he said obsequiously, bobbing and rubbing his plump hands.

"I'm the new head of internal security for the rock," explained the captain, absorbing the unlikely name.

Laguna his shook his head. "Big job. Make that huge and impossible job, Captain."

"Why?" she asked.

"Well, the thing about this rock that most people just don't get is just how big it is. When the first prospectors came into the system just after the Crotchets' pull-back, they thought this place must be what the Crotchets and their bugs had been mining. Took a while, and a lot of boys getting lost in these here tunnels, to figure out that the diggings might even be older than the Crotchets. Who knows? Anyway, it's a regular warren. I been here from the very beginning, taking advantage of that. Not mining, of course. It's dug out of easy ores, even if there are still some heavy metals in the rock. There's plenty more heavy-metal rocks out in the asteroid belt, some even bigger than this one. But this is the only mined-out one we've found. Still, it is a good place for the rock-rats to come and breathe something other than their own gas, and find out that easy ores ain't always cheap."

He gurgled like a drain at his own joke. "Before the Korozhet counter-attack there were maybe five hundred permanent residents on the rock. Some weird ones. Aliens. We kept getting them wandering in from deeper down for weeks after we set up here. The Crochets left in a hurry, you bet."

This was news to Rebecca. Not that it had anything to do with murdered hookers. But she'd always thought that the Korozhet slaves had been all liberated at once . . . not showing up like a trickle of lost souls, hungry, thirsty and confused. She'd bet they'd not received the milk of human kindness from this little son-of-a-bitch with his false smile and laugh.

"What the hell did they live on?" asked Holmes, showing that thought processes did happen inside that huge form.

"Hell, boy, I don't speak Crotchet and they didn't speak human. They could mop floors and wash dishes okay, which is all I cared about. Now, you two wanted to talk to me about those two dead girls. I reckon that it's one of your boys has got himself a twisted hate of the women. Like her."

He pointed out of the windows—what the hell you needed windows for in a damn cave puzzled her—at the fluttering protestor outside. You could tell that the bat was a protestor by the sign she was carrying with her feet.

Pro life-choice!
End female subjugation now!

It seemed to be a one-bat protest. "You could start improving security by getting rid of her." He scowled. "She's always coming around and pestering the girls."

It was unusual to see a civ bat. No bandoliers, no insignia . . . just a poster. The bats had taken the war against the Korozhet as a holy crusade, and joined almost to the last bat. The uplifted rats were a different matter. They were deadly fighters, if they wanted to be. But they were not soldiers by nature, and most of the time it took the prospect of lots of loot to inspire them at all. But the bats . . .

If Rebecca had learned anything in the military it was not to get involved in dealing with a single-minded bat. She'd seen better officers than her try it. She ignored the bat, and turned to Laguna. "I have been told that two women aged between twenty and thirty Terran years, who had been working here, were found dead in the tunnels."

"And another one is missing," said Laguna, lugubriously, wiping an eye. "Cindy-Jane."

Sergeant Holmes cracked his knuckles. Looked at the captain. Looked at Laguna. "I think I'd better examine his mind," he said. "Even if he is a bit on the small side."

"Sergeant," said Rebecca. The huge bar was relatively empty at this time of day. But "relative" only to what it could hold. There must be fifty miners in here, even now. The Marines were tough, but these rockrats, even the human ones, were almost certainly bar fight veterans. "As head of the serious crimes unit . . . Stick with asking questions for now, before you use your magnifying glass technique. Besides, think of what happened to the victims. It would take a fairly strong man."

The girls had been raped, robbed, and then been beaten to death, and dropped up a shaft. Things were backwards here. You got dropped up a shaft not down one, because of the centrifugal spin. It was a pity the murders weren't backwards, but this little shrimp would probably not be able to beat up a granny in a wheelchair, let alone a healthy young woman. He also would certainly never need to resort to rape. And robbery was something he was doing in the open here, on a grand scale, judging by his prices. It probably wouldn't be worth his while to go in for petty larceny, let alone kill one of his sources of income.

Holmes blinked. And then nodded, and set to his new technique of questioning verbally. "Who saw them last?" he asked Laguna.

"Oh, they were good girls. Only ever slept with two clients."

"Who?" asked Holmes, skeptically.

"The Marines and the rock-rats." Laguna cackled and slapped his own thighs. "Boy, this isn't the hick town you come from. This is the wild frontier, or it was until the Korozhet put the place under siege. These girls came here for one reason, and it wasn't to powder their noses. You ain't gonna trace their last movements, nohow. I can tell you it was probably up and down, though."

Act II Scene I: *Amid drunks, hookers, cutpurses and thieves and other municipal officials. In the presence of death and disorder.*

The civic authorities, Rebecca discovered, included the bat she'd seen protesting outside the Last Chance. The council weren't going to cut it in any big mayoral parades in more civilized parts. The mayor, dressed in patched holey coveralls and a vast beard, which covered more of him than the coveralls, looked like a rock-rat. It was what he had been until about two weeks ago, and would almost certainly be again as soon as the siege lifted. Still, after the initial chaos this unlikely group had put together some kind of election and got a roughly working civil system up and running. Good enough to at least see to a sewage system and get water and food rationing implemented. There were plenty of gold chained mayors who would have done worse.

"I don't see why you don't have your own policing," she said directly.

The mayor scratched his bald head. A rat poked its long nose out from under his beard and whiffled its nostrils at her. "Well, it's difficult, you know," said the mayor. "Ain't easy to get anyone to take orders from another rock-rat. And the problems that we don't sort out for ourselves tend to come from when the Marines and locals clash. So we figured it might be best if we got you to take the blame, and do the work."

It was pleasant to meet with honesty at least, but . . .

"There is a rat peeping out of your beard," she said.

"Oh. That's just Firkin." The mayor reached under the giant beard and produced a sharp-nosed rat in an outfit that included fountaining flounces of lace. Or rather, flounces that included a little outfit. "My partner in prospecting. She's not on the council but she's kind of hard to keep out of the meetings. Firkin, meet Captain Wuollet."

The rat bowed. "Nice uniform. You could use more lace, though." She sat down on the table, produced a bottle of amber fluid from a sleeve and drank with lip-smacking appreciation.

Several councilors eyed the bottle with naked lust, even if they showed no suicidal desire to attempt to snatch it, or even the folly of trying to cadge a drink. Rats had a certain reputation. The tall, cadaverous one shook his head and said admiringly: "And she never seems to get any drunker than she is now."

"Methinks I have a harder head than you," said Firkin. "Which is not hard to imagine, Slim."

The rest of council plainly could imagine it too, by the grins.

"Anyways we'd take it kindly if you'd find the marine behind these killings and string him up, before we do. There was talk last night of lynching the whole boiling lot of you," said the tall skinny Slim, obviously keen to move the subject away from his tolerance of liquor. He was sitting next to a little man in a skull cap with long locks of hair next to each ear.

With a shock, Rebecca realized that she recognized the man.

Well, she'd seen his picture, anyway. Without the side locks or the skull-cap, but definitely the same face. She never forgot a face. This one she had reason to remember—along with the entire board of Intersolar Mining and Minerals, arrayed behind him and his father.

"But we did stop it," he said with a quiet smile. "Even though Slim here said it was undemocratic to put it to the vote."

"But you only survived by a narrow margin," said the bat. "And next time I might not vote with the entrenched exploiters." She glared at the young man under the skull-cap. "And I am in charge of the portfolio for security and social upliftment."

"Services. Social *services*, Zed," corrected the mayor.

She stared down her nose at him, which is easy to do if you're hanging upside down from the roof. "How many times do I have to say Ms? Ms. Davitta Ze . . ."

"I reckon putting 'em down would be lot better than upliftment," interrupted Slim, combatively. "Especially you lot." This was addressed at the blue-furred Jampad swinging placidly from a roof-chain at the foot of the rock-table.

There was a grumble of agreement from one or two of the other council members, and a hiss of outrage from the bat.

The mayor slapped his hand down on the table. "Now you all hush up. Ain't no one here who fought better than Meredeth and his friends in the fall-back on the Rock. Like with the marines, we might have come off second if they hadn't taken a hand."

"They were fighting for their own survival," said the jowl-faced bull-dog of a woman at the end of the table.

"And so were we," said the little man in the skull-cap. "Except for those who were running and hiding."

"I was fetching more ammunition!" said Slim.

"In the Last Chance. Looking for Laggy's bolt-hole, which you didn't find," said the bull-dog woman, with a derisive smile.

The mayor slapped both of his palms down on the stone table. "Now, you two. I'll throw you both out, like last time. Captain, I reckon you'd better leave us to our work. Maybe you want to take Ms. Zed with you and talk to her. She knew one of the victims."

"I had had a note from one of the victims. I did not know her," said the bat.

"Anyway, methinks the place will be more tranquil without her," said the flouncy rat snippily.

The bat grimaced at her, and shook a clenched foot. "Sellout," she said, fluttering from her perch. "Let's go, you imperialist lackeys," she said to the two marines. "It'll be to drinking and fighting they'll fall without me, so I need to get back to it." Her tone suggested she might just enjoy at least one of the activities, and felt that she was missing out.

In a chamber far enough away that they could only hear the occasional bull-like bellows of the mayor, they paused. The bat found a piece of roof to cling to and turned her gargoyle-like black face to them. "I really cannot stay away long. Firkin and Abe will do their best but they need my voice too. You have to find this killer, and find him fast," she said seriously. "It's little enough success I have had with Laggy's exploited women. They'll not even dare speak to me, normally. But right now they're frightened to death. I was to be meeting Ms. Candy, the night that she was killed. And I had a message that the next woman killed needed to see me, urgently. They're frightened indeed if they are prepared to risk Laggy's wrath."

"Laguna?" asked Rebecca sitting on one of the empty boxes that littered this part of the "Civic center." "This is the 'Laggy' that you're talking about? The little man at the Last Chance?"

"Indade," said the bat, in the traditional fake Irish accent. She scowled. "He'd be my prime suspect."

"Look, the guy is a cess-pit, but he's too small to threaten anyone. I know that to you bats we humans all look large..."

"Ach bah," the bat spat. "It's not his strength they fear. He holds them in chemical bondage, Captain. He'll withhold their drug supply if they dare to cross him."

"Oho. So he's the supplier, is he?" asked Rebecca, like a terrier scenting rats. She'd get him for something, at least. And solve another of her problems in the process.

The bat wrinkled her face, folding it even more than it was folded already. "Say rather that he supplies the women he holds in bondage. There are several purveyors of these things," she admitted with reluctant honesty.

"It's something else I'm supposed to investigate and put a stop to," said Rebecca.

The bat shook her head. "You need to find the murderer first. The miners are indade close to a lynching. A marine badge was found at the last killing."

"That we can follow up. Why wasn't I told?"

The bat shrugged her wings. "It is all a little muddled, yet. Slim told us of it."

"Both of these women wanted to see you," said Holmes, taking the initiative and calmly treading it underfoot. "Why?"

The bat shrugged her wings. "I do not know . . ."

Rebecca's communicator bleeped insistently. "Captain Wuollet," she said, pressing the send button.

"Alpha 3 patrol here, Captain. We've found a dead body. A woman. It looks like she's been raped and murdered."

"Hell's teeth. Where are you?"

"Punching the co-ords through to you, Captain," said the Marine, his voice full of relief at the idea that it would soon be someone else's problem.

"We'll be right there. Don't move her or touch anything."

"And so will I," said the bat. "Someone needs to report on the brutality of th' polis," she said self-righteously. "Polis I name you, and not a Garda of our own."

They tramped through the rock-hewn corridors, away from the more settled level, where many rock-rats had taken up residence in some of the larger galleries. "The very least that they should give me for this job is a groundcar," grumbled Rebecca. "Who ever heard of a police-chief walking to the scene of the crime?" There were vehicle tracks in the dust.

"Indade, there are a bare handful of such vehicles," said the bat. "And those belong to the entrenched exploiters that had already settled on this den of vice. They have to repair them themselves, as no facilities are to be found here for doing that.

"Nasty smelly things," she said with a lofty sniff. "The rock-rats scattered across the system had no need for wheels, or space for anything but ore-cargo. Besides, the price of importing such a thing was too expensive for any but the obscenely wealthy."

"So we walk, except for those who can fly," said Holmes, hunching to avoid hitting his head on the tunnel roof. "Why did they have to make these tunnels so low?"

The bat found this amusing. "There are many which are much lower. The ones the first two bodies were found in were narrower. And they were not built for human convenience."

"Why the hell does anyone go into them then?" asked Rebecca, ducking.

"They often widen out into what were plainly ore-chambers,"

explained the bat. "They make good rooms. You know, the prospectors had just found a similar rock, but without airlocks, in the second belt when the Korozhet attacked. It's the way the Korozhet mined. They were not worried by their slaves' comfort."

They'd at least worried about their slaves' air and had an amazing system of airlocks, reflected Rebecca. The asteroid siege would have been a short conquest, without those miles of corridors filled with air that contained too much oxygen and enough helium to alter the pitches of their voices. Inside the rock that air got scrubbed . . . in some place in the maze of internal passages as yet unmapped. The colonel had been doing some interesting swearing about that. They didn't even know if they had all the airlocks located. There were enough of them. And the Marines' supply of heavy weapons to defend those they'd found was very limited. How they'd hold off a major landing, heaven alone knew. But with strange gel-curtain airlocks every hundred yards or so, landing and capture would be two very different things. The miners didn't have much in the way of missiles, but they did have a personal arsenal each, and a number of heavy-duty tripod-mounted mining lasers. The attacks—so far—had been on the main landing bay, now crowded with little miner-ships, and Marine landing craft. Quite a few of the miner-ships had had some external weapons. This had plainly been a rough neighborhood.

"We need to go down here, " said the bat, pointing to a shaft. There were metal staples in the wall. Not very big staples and too close together for human climbers to have set them there.

"How do you know?" asked Sergeant Holmes, blinking, looking at the position co-ords on his palm-comm.

"I can hear the voices of several people, arguing. The word murder has been used." The bat flew up into the hole. That was down—if you took the core of the asteroid as "down." Centrifugal force provided an alternative to gravity here.

Bats did have hyper-keen hearing. Or she might just have known, concluded Captain Wuollet. Something about the black-faced bat activist smelled. Not necessarily of murder, but the bat knew more than she was telling. Rebecca reached up and began to climb. Better get there fast.

That was a good decision, it turned out, even if Holmes was not designed to run down a corridor this high or wide, complete with pipes to trip over. The scene was angry and heading to the point of shooting.

"The captain," said a voice, uncertain and plainly tense, "is coming to look at the crime scene..."

"Screw your captain," interrupted someone. "You just step aside and let us take the poor dead girl back to the Last Chance, and you don't get hurt, see."

Rebecca poked the burly speaker hard in the kidneys. Hard enough for him to turn and crack his head... and see the tunnel entirely full of Holmes behind her. "Your chances of screwing me are slightly lower than your chances of surviving beyond the next ten seconds. And those chances are not good, if you're still here by the time I count to ten. One."

"Now see here, Captain," said an angry voice, from elbow height.

"And that means you too, Mr. Laguna," she said icily. "We'll return the body to the Last Chance when we've finished inspecting the crime scene. Two."

"But..."

"Three." One of the advantages of Holmes being outsize, besides sheer intimidation, was that it was impossible to see if there was a whole squad... or no-one, behind him in the narrow tunnel.

Grumbling, Laguna and his mini-mob retreated down the far passage. "You haven't heard the last of this!" shouted someone.

"Alas, 'tis probably true," said the bat. "They'll be back at the Last Chance drinking more courage. You'll have trouble presently."

The marine who had called her grinned. "Good thing you got here fast, Captain. And good thing Larry was here with me." He put a hand on the shoulder of the stocky miner who had gone on patrol with him. It was not the same marine who had left their base cave an hour before, looking like he'd been inflicted with a boil or a toothache for company. "That lot said I'd done it, and they were all for lynching me. Larry talked them out of it." He looked at the tunnel. "If I was going to do that I'd choose somewhere where I could at least stand up."

Rebecca was on her knees examining the corpse. It was at times like this it paid to be a combat vet. It still wasn't a pretty sight. Someone had hit the victim very hard with a piece of rock. Hard enough to smash her skull. There wasn't much blood. Odd for a head wound, that. She pulled the victim's skirt down. The dead woman had little enough dignity left to her, and Rebecca could do nothing much about the ripped filmy blouse. There wasn't a lot of spare material "What were you two doing in here anyway?"

"It's a short-cut across to where they're setting up the ag caves," explained the miner. "The roof is a bit low, but if you follow the pipes it'll save you ten minutes walk."

It made a sort of sense, except that it did mean that this was not the quiet private spot the attacker must have assumed. That in itself suggested that the attacker was a marine. "I suppose there is nothing much else for us to see. Let's get her out of here."

"Captain," said Holmes from his knees back in the tunnel. He was far too tall to stand there. "I need to show you this first." He pointed to a hose-clamp on one of the pipes. A gossamer shred of material clung to it. A piece of blouse. "She got dragged in here."

Rebecca looked intently at it. "So," she said after some thought. "He must have knocked her down, dragged her in here, and then killed her with that rock. See if you can see any other signs of dragging."

"I'll have to go out backwards, Captain. There is not enough space for me to turn around."

"Look as you crawl, Sergeant."

The passage, however, was relatively dust-free. The rock-floor was not particularly even, but there were no other pieces of material snagged there—which, considering the filmy flimsy nature of the clothing was surprising. Even more surprising was the arrival of yet another visitor. In flounces. "I had to stop and eat, and follow you by scent," said Firkin crossly. "You humans run too slowly and for far too long."

Rats had speed, but not stamina.

The rat pushed past the sergeant. "This is your new method of advancing? Methinks you are showing your best features to the enemy."

The rat looked at the corpse. "Cindy-Jane. A lot of miners will be mightily upset, and the Last Chance will lose a fair bit of turn-over. She was almost rattish in her appetites. Made up for the price with volume."

Rats were not known for their sensitivity, thought Rebecca. It at least made them accidentally honest. "Well, let's get her out of here. She was dragged in. I suppose we can drag her out."

She took an arm, deciding by the look on the miner and young Marine's faces, that it was a good time to lead by example. She was grateful that all her years in the service had at least taught her how to control squeamishness. As she pulled the body it rolled slightly, to reveal a brown billfold. She twitched it out from under the corpse with the other hand and opened it.

It revealed two things. The first was an Marine ID card. The second was even more puzzling.

Money.

Tucked inside the inner flap were three hundred C notes. Not a fortune, but surely enough to pay for a cheap tart.

"I want Private Samson, 4655573490."

"Plooks?" said the Marine who'd called her to the scene. "He's out on patrol, Captain."

"He's one of mine?" she asked, already knowing the answer. Wouldn't this do the credibility of her fledgling force the world of good, she thought sourly.

The Marine looked uncomfortable. "It was you or staying in the brig, Captain."

"He should have stayed in the brig," she said coldly. She called her ops room, and told them to call Samson in, and place him under arrest.

As she put the comm device back in its pouch, she stood up and banged her head. She ground her teeth in irritation, feeling the bump. "Now can we get the body out of here," she said, reaching down to take an arm again.

"Captain, I think you'd better come and have a look here," called Sergeant Holmes. "I had a look in the next passage, while I was waiting for you to come out."

"Inborn investigative urge overwhelming you, Sergeant?" she said, covering the fact that she'd banged her head yet again with sarcasm.

"Needed a leak, Captain," said Holmes with innate honesty. "There is more of that blouse material back there. That's where it happened, I reckon. The body has been moved."

"Hell's teeth!" said Rebecca when she looked into the dark passage that Holmes pointed out to her. "Why did he move her? They'd not have found her in there until she started to smell."

"Indade," said Ms. Zed, wrapping her wings around her and shivering. "Unless, as I'd be thinking, someone wanted her found."

Captain Wuollet looked at the single electric bulb tacked into the cable at the intersection. She thought of those blissful days when she'd been a mere boot and only had to deal with grueling Marine drill, instead of coping with this mess. She was going to need a lot of things that she didn't have to handle this, like an elementary knowledge of forensic practice for a start. All she knew about was shaped charges and detonators, not catching murderers. "Better search the other corridors too," she said resignedly. "Next thing we know we'll find more bodies."

They didn't. But they did find a small wheelbarrow and a shovel. A very small wheelbarrow. "Maybe a garden gnome did it," said Holmes thoughtfully.

NCOs were of course allowed a sense of humor. Just not in public or with their superior officers. She decided to ignore the comment. "And moved her on the barrow, which is easier than dragging," she said dryly. The barrow looked far too small to move a body. "Better have a look for wheel tracks," she sighed.

Holmes shone a focused beam of light down the center of the dusty tunnel. Shook his head "It's been wiped. There is one footprint, fairly small. And mine, of course. He must have carried her."

"A man with small feet and a strong back," said Rebecca rubbing her jaw. "So . . . what is the barrow doing here. Who does it belong to?"

"'Tis a rat-miner's barrow," said Firkin. "I have such a one myself. We purchased it from Abe." She eyed it speculatively. "As it is lying about, methinks the owner has no further need of it," she said cheerfully. "I'll have it."

"Looter. Despoiler. Capitalist," said the bat. "To take thus from those less fortunate than you."

The rat jerked a thumb at the corpse that the miner and Marine had just carried out. "She doesn't exactly need it any more. Besides, methinks Cindy-Jane would have been willing to try anything, but a position involving a small wheelbarrow taxes even my imagination."

It taxed hers too, admitted the captain to herself. "It's evidence. I'll hold onto it," was all that she said, however.

"Tch," said the rat, producing her amber-fluid filled bottle and having a good chug. "Well, do tell me if you ever work out just what a hooker needed a rat miner's barrow for. I've heard of fetishes, but . . ."

"Shut up, will you? Let's get a blanket and carry the corpse out of here. Sergeant. Bring me that incriminating barrow. Let's go and talk to Private Samson," she said grimly.

Private Samson might actually not have had enough money in that wallet. He was an acne-cure advertiser's dream, poor kid. And he was just a kid, thought Rebecca. A kid with a black eye, and a cut on his cheek. Maybe the girl had got a last few blows in. "This yours, Private?" She held out the wallet. He blinked. You could almost see the thoughts crossing his mind, using heavy levers to shift the expressions on the spotty face. He beamed. And reached for it. "Yeah! Thanks, Captain. I thought I was in trouble or something."

She pulled the wallet back. "Not so fast, Marine."

His expression turn woeful. "I guess my money's gone then."

"How much was there?" she asked speculatively.

"About twenty in front flap. But," he said, doing his best attempt at a cunning expression. "I got some more in the secret place at the back. Three hundred."

"You lost the twenty," she said. "But the rest is still there. So, tell me when you last had your wallet."

He was smiling again. "That's the rest of my pay. I reckoned I'd lost it all."

Either this kid was the best actor in the world, or he was a damn stupid young fool who nearly got strung up. "When did you last have it, Marine?" she asked again.

He looked wary. Something in her tone must have finally gotten through to him. "Me and a couple of the boys slipped off to the Last Chance last night. I don't remember too well, but I didn't have it this morning."

"When you woke up in the Brig," she said, trying to keep her face expressionless.

He nodded. "They said if I volunteered for security duty I was off the hook, Captain."

It looked like she had her murderer after all . . . or maybe more than one of them. "Just who was with you, Samson?"

He looked wary. "The colonel said we was all off the hook, Captain." His voice said: You do not split on your mates. Not if you want to live.

She restrained herself from solving his pimple problem forever by starting to squeeze at the neck. "I'm not playing games now, Private Samson. I need to know. And I need to know now. I can look in the unit records if I have to. You're wasting my time."

Her answer came from another source, though. "Private Ogumba, Private Wilkins and Private Mikes," said Sergeant Holmes. "It was Mikes who found the body, Captain. He's still here. Shall I haul him in?"

"Body? I didn't kill no-one Captain ... did I? I was in a fight ... I think," said the boy. He was now pale, beginning, finally, to realize that he might be in deep trouble.

Holmes brought Private Mikes through to her office-cave. The entire thing was obviously preying on Mikes' mind so much that he barely managed to salute before he blurted out:

"I been thinking, Captain," he said. "It can't be Samson. Me and Gumbo only got separated from him once, just after the fight when we got thrown out. And we found him maybe fifteen minutes later. He was blind-drunk, Captain. Plooks can't hold much. Gumbo and me, we took him back to camp. He couldn't hardly stand when we got thrown out. And then he got into a fight with one of the Guard Commanders ..."

"Me," said Holmes, with a nod. "They were all in the brig at 22 hundred hours." His expression said that he considered this a ridiculous time to be drunk and arrested by.

"That still gave him fifteen minutes." Or them, she thought to herself.

"Indade," said the bat, quietly from the corner. "Except that she was still alive at 22:30. I saw her then. I was doing my picket."

"Are you sure?" asked Rebecca

"Sure as death," said the bat. "I don't get times wrong."

Bats didn't. Their soft-cyber chips had inbuilt clocks. She knew that well from dealing with bats on the demolitions course. Bats made up most of the sappers. They regarded humans a ludicrously vague about time and memory, as that part of them was cybernetic. She sighed. "We'll have to try to confirm it, Private Samson. But it looks like you may just have got your wallet back, and escaped a hanging. That's a lifetime's ration of luck. Stay out of the Last Chance from now on, see."

The youth nodded earnestly. "Yes, Captain. The drinks is cheaper in the Miner's Rest anyway."

Why did she feel she was better off talking to the rat, even it laughed at her? "Get out of my office, Private. Stay here at ops. And stay out of all of the bars," she added, knowing that order was pointless.

"Can I have my wallet, Captain?"

In the grim certainty that only the absence of money would keep him out of the bars, she shook her head. "No. It's still evidence in a robbery, rape and murder trial. You may get it back, if we ever find the culprit. You nearly got hanged for losing it last time, you brainless idiot."

When he'd gone, saluting sheepishly, and accompanied by his fellow genius of the night before, Rebecca sat down on the makeshift desk and swore. She was not surprised to see the flouncy rat appear from under the desk and clap appreciatively.

She tossed the "evidence" wallet down. "Well. That's the wallet. Stolen during or after the fight. The owner was locked up when the crime happened. Which leaves the damned wheelbarrow. And no, no matter what that rat says," she said, pointing at Firkin, "I refuse to even consider it as a sex-toy."

"What about the little shovel, then?" asked Firkin with her favorite evil laugh.

Rebecca decided it was best to just ignore her, if she could.

"It might have been there by accident, Captain," said Holmes, keeping his face carefully expressionless.

"'Tis likely," said the rat. "Well, as you've no further use for that wallet . . ."

Wuollet slapped the reaching paw away. "Do you loot everything? Don't answer that. I already know the answer."

The rat shrugged. "'Tis rattish nature, methinks. If it is not tied down one steals it."

"And it had better be tied down very thoroughly." Rebecca sighed. "How about if you do some asking about who has lost a barrow?"

Firkin yawned. "A waste of time, methinks. But I will ask about who is trying to steal one."

The rat sauntered out. That was no guarantee that it had actually gone anywhere, of course. She could hope, though.

"Someone deliberately planted that wallet, Captain," said the Sergeant.

"That much is elementary, Holmes. Someone wanted the Marines to take the rap. Colonel De Darcy didn't realize what a live, pin-less grenade he'd handed me," said Rebecca, wishing she had enough hair to pull out. "The big question is whether they were just letting us take the rap or whether they wanted to try and get rid of us. Whether we are dealing with murder, or treason."

Act II, Scene II: *An arras, or possibly a rattish bar.*

"Thou hast the most unsavory similes," said Snout loftily, returning—as rats would under pressure—to the Shakespearean downloads that had once made up their linguistic source. "To think that I would indulge in such things, sweet wag."

"Ask, morelike, when you have ever done anything else," said Firkin, yawning. "I know you were there, you and your paramour Mercutio. I smelled it at the time, but said nothing."

"A good idea, my flouncy bit," said Mercutio, from the shadows. "Keep it thus. We did a little looting, nothing else."

"Methinks that was enough. You will need to tell her that," said Firkin, knowing that this would be dangerous ground.

"And be put into durance vile. I think not," said Mercutio. "Humans have odd ideas about property."

Firkin had to admit that that much was true, even if it was unlikely anything else Mercutio volunteered would be. "Mayhap a deal can be arranged," she said, heavily. Not likely. Humans should understand rats better, as they were so ratlike themselves.

Act II Scene III: *Enter various gentlemen of Verona, Chicago, Dublin, Bangbanduc . . . heck. Miners and prospectors. Don't ever ask where they come from.*

"You could take the barrow to Abe," suggested the bat. "Maybe he can tell you more about it."

"This Abe is the one who sold it?" asked Holmes, examining the little barrow he held in one hand.

The bat scowled. "He is the entrenched capitalist exploiter of the downtrodden masses, or the miners at least, yes. He sits on the council. With his skull-cap and ear-locks." Her innate sense of justice had a brief wrestling match with her conscience. "There are worse," she conceded.

Coming from her that was probably high praise. "Let's go, Ms. Zed," Rebecca said, pulling aside the curtain that served the ops-cave as a door.

"That's not actually my full name . . ."

She broke off. A large mob was marching down on them, led by Laggy and several of his search party from their earlier encounter. "We hear you got the man who done it, Captain. Hand him over to us. We'll deal with him," said Laguna.

Rebecca wished really hard for some nice shaped demolition charges—set in the tunnel just ahead of this lot. She stepped into the middle of the passage and spoke loudly and clearly. "That rot-gut of yours is making you hear things, Laguna. What I did catch was a set-up. Unfortunately, they set up a man who definitely couldn't have done it, because at the time he was behind bars back at the camp. Now, *you* tell me who told you that we had the man. That must be the one who actually did this. And I'll take him into custody. There'll be no lynching."

The mob stopped dead.

A beard came racing around the corner, followed somewhat later by the rest of the mayor. "Huh . . . huh—what's going on here?" he panted. "Break it up now!"

"It was him," said Laggy. "Or rather it was that rat of his. She told me."

The worst of it was that it could possibly be perfectly true. Firkin had known about it. And she did seem to be a rat that was familiar with Laggy's girls if nothing else. Anything that lacked virtue would attract a rat. And, looking at the Mayor and then his feet . . . if anyone was short enough to stand upright in the tunnels, was strong enough to carry a harem, let alone one woman, it would be him. It could be, after all. He might want complete control over the rock and have seen this as a way to get rid of the marines.

"Lynch him!" yelled one of the front-men of the mob. "The bastard has been killing our women!"

Rebecca stepped in front of the Mayor. "The first person to try any lynching on my watch is going to be dead." Her voice could have cut across three parade grounds.

"There's more of us than you," said one of the mob, fingering the butt of his flechette-pistol.

"Yep," said Holmes stepping out of the office cave, cradling a Mark 24 automatic flechette rifle. "But who will be first to die?"

The Mark 24 made an impression on the mob. It was normally tripod mounted.

"You said you'd arrest whoever told us," said Laggy sulkily.

"I will take him in," said Rebecca, wondering if the colonel had known just what a treasure he'd given her in Sergeant Holmes. "And that rat too, and hold them until I get some answers. But the rat was here when I found out that it was a set-up. So tell us what you heard?"

"That you had found a Marine's wallet under her." That was said by a gangling man with a planar face and an outsize nose.

Rebecca raised her eyebrows. "Oh? Full of money, no doubt."

That got a laugh from the crowd. "Not likely!" said planar face.

"Well, you've told me all I needed to know," she said, reflecting that they'd told her something anyway—that the information had come from someone who either hadn't wanted to mention the money or hadn't known about it. "Now get along with you. The mayor will stay right here with me."

Act II Scene IV: *In some shady hostelry, where you might find the likes of Doll Tearsheat*

"It took me long enough to find you," said the bat crossly. "I should have known that you'd be off carousing, when Albert needs you!"

Firkin sniffed and raised her goblet. "Zed, methinks that there is very little that Albert cannot do for himself. I am his partner, not his nursemaid."

"Ah. Even though they were after lynching him for those murders?"

"What!" Firkin leapt off her stool, spilling drink onto the bat, who spluttered, and swore and fluttered up to the ceiling, to shake off her wings with an expression of distaste. "Where have they taken him, Zed? Come here, you blasted winged teetotaler!"

"He's with the polis," Davitta answered, flying higher. "The captain kept him from the mob."

It went against her socialist and revolutionary instincts but the authorities had been very welcome then. She'd been unsure what to do. Albert, for all that he was a reactionary sellout, was none too bad a mayor.

"Methinks it is the first time that I have heard of them being useful," said Firkin, shaking out her ruffles. "I'd better go and find Mercutio."

"That blackguard!" Davitta exclaimed. "What need do you have of him?"

Firkin yawned artfully. "Firstly, because he's a blackguard, a weasand-slitter and a rogue. I've a feeling that I might have need of him to deal with this poxy mess that Albert has wandered into. Secondly, he has another property, more unusual in rats. He can think. And thirdly, he was there. I smelled his presence at the scene. He and that doxy of his, Snout. Officially, they traffic in ordure, and that makes them quite noxious."

Davitta nearly fell out of the air "Why didn't you say so to the captain?" she squawked.

"Why?" Firkin raised her nose. "We rats stand for ourselves, and the devil take the hindmost. I will not betray a rat to the constabulary. A policeman's lot should not be a happy one, anyway."

"And such is honor among rats," said the bat, sardonically. "Well, let us find him without delay then, because the mob will be drinking themselves into courage for a second try."

Act II, Scene V: *Enter a merchant with all the perfumes of Arabia*

"I've come to see the prisoner," said the small man with the side locks and skull-cap. "You can call me his lawyer if you have to. I did train as one once, although I don't usually admit to it."

Rebecca studied him. Regrettably, he had large feet for a relatively small man. "He's not strictly a prisoner," she said. "I decided that he would be safer here than out there. At the moment I am using him as a tea-boy."

Abe shook his head in mock horror. "A clear infringement of his rights. Tell him I take two sugars." He lifted a heavy flechette rifle from his shoulder and leaned it against the wall. "They'll be back, you know. That's actually why I came with this. I can't shoot very well, but at least I'm an extra man."

With questionable motives, she thought. Everyone had questionable motives in this darned case! But all she said was: "Then leave the shooting to us. The passages are narrow and—"

He interrupted. "And you're dealing with miners, Captain. According to your colonel, you know how to use explosives. So do they. They probably have even more experience than you do."

That was true enough, she supposed. "So we need to take action first."

"Perhaps by finding the murderer."

"Or by laying mines in the passage," said Rebecca sourly. Did everyone have to assume that she knew the first thing about detection? "Where is that rat when I need her? I need to know what, if anything, she said to Laggy. If it wasn't for a lack of motive and his size I'd suspect him first. You couldn't tell me anything about a little wheelbarrow, could you?"

"A miner's barrow?" Rat-size? If it is one of mine—it will have a serial number. I guarantee them."

"Let's hope it is one of yours, then," she said. The way this case was going it wouldn't be.

He smiled with quiet confidence. "Bound to be. I've cornered the market. My competitors don't understand that quality and a reasonable price almost always trumps them."

"Besides, the rats all think that sooner or later they've got to put one over him," said Albert, handing him a mug of tea. "The barrow is in the corner. It's one of yours. Smells a bit."

"Rats need something to hope for," said Abe, going to look at the barrow. He took a mini-stylus-pad out of his pocket and tapped a number into it. "Here you are. Snout. She's one of the supposed sewage maintenance team your Firkin recruited, Albert. They work in the narrow tunnels better than people."

To Rebecca, he explained: "And sewage doesn't offend them. People were just using empty passages at first, and something had to be done about it. Too much disease risk, apart from the smell, otherwise. Anything else you want to know?"

Rebecca looked carefully at that bland face. "Just one thing. What is the deputy chairman of Intersolar Mining and Minerals doing here?"

He hesitated. "You must be mistaken."

She shook her head. "Not likely. I never forget a face. And yours takes some explaining. There might even be a motive for murder there."

He looked at the puzzled face above the mayor's beard, then sighed. "Well, if I can't trust Albert, I can trust no-one. I was getting back to my roots, that's all. It's about an old leather suit-case, I suppose."

He seemed to think he'd said enough. Rebecca looked at him, unblinking. "Explain."

He laughed softly. "The inquisition had nothing on you. I am beginning to think you were well chosen for this job. Very well. I found an old leather suitcase, in what had been my grandfather's office, when we were moving to the new corporate headquarters . . . well, rather the movers found it. It was a cheap thing, and one of them asked me what should be done with it. It was full of old papers and pictures, he said."

He took mouthful of his tea. "I opened it. Looked inside—and found the life story of a man in there. My great-grandfather. Founder of the company, a few name changes back. It was his suitcase. I found out that we had not always been ultra-wealthy corporate moguls."

"Most of us were something else before we got to be rock-rats," said the mayor. "We don't ask what a man's family history was."

Abe acknowledged this with a wry smile. "My great-grandfather had been a pack-peddler. He sold his wares across the Northern Cape, selling to diggers across the semi-desert that was the Kimberly diamond-fields. I started reading the letters in that case. Letters from his family in Poland, letters from the board of the synagogue he helped to found in Kimberly, letters from his wife, letters from miners, letters from farmers and suppliers. I got the picture of a man. He was devout, happy, and strangely, a much-loved man."

Abe took a deep pull at his tea-mug. "I can't say there are many people who loved Intersolar Mining and Minerals' deputy chairman."

"No," said Rebecca, hoping that she was hiding her feelings on that subject.

Maybe she didn't succeed. Or maybe he just read people well. He waved a placatory hand. "It's a good thing I am not that any more."

She had a job to do. Not payback time. Yet. "And the side locks and skullcap?" she asked.

He shrugged. "An affectation. A reminder that when great-grandfather went out there, blacks and Jews were everyone's kicking boys. I didn't mean to become a Korozhet target though. Is that enough?"

"Not really." But she was impressed in spite of herself. It was too weird to make up. "It's a pretty story, but unlikely."

He allowed that faint smile back onto his face. "You really are suspicious enough to make a good detective. There was more to it all of course, but I don't think that I need to waste your time with it." There was a finality in his tone which suggested that torture wouldn't work either. "Perhaps we need to go and look for the rattess Snout. Now."

Act III Scene I: *Enter the great detective*

"She's dead," said Mercutio, quietly. "Snout is dead." Davitta had had other brushes with Mercutio. He was normally urbane and slightly sinister, as befitted a prince of the underworld of ratly crimes. Now his voice shook.

A furry face precluded any sign of paleness, but the voice suggested that the rat was going to pitch face forward any moment. "Sit down," said the bat, practically.

"And drink some of this and take heart," said Firkin, producing a bottle from her sleeve flounces.

A slap would hardly have shocked Mercutio more. "You . . . giving out drink?" He hastily snatched the bottle and swigged. And spluttered. "It's cold tea!" he said both incredulously and indignantly. "Not even some vile sack. Art trying to kill me?"

"And do the world a favor." Firkin snatched the bottle back. "Why did you kill Snout?"

" 'Twas not I. I would have done the thing quietly and eaten the evidence. Methinks . . . she may have been murdered. Come."

He led them to a chamber—which one might have passed ten times without finding it, as the door was so neatly hidden in a fold in the rock. There, within, was an Aladdin's trove of loot. And a small female rat, sprawled. Dead.

"Out, brief candle," said Firkin, quietly. "What killed her?"

"I don't know. But I will find out," said Mercutio with grim certainty.

"The polis . . ." said Davitta, fluttering her wings.

"Methinks I'll solve my own problems."

Firkin shook her head. "Nay, methinks that it is we, and they, who need you to solve theirs, Mercutio. They have Albert, accused of these murders. We need whoever did that. I was on my way to beg your help."

Mercutio looked her in the eye. Nodded slowly. " 'Twas done by the same hand, methinks. Let us go to the Last Chance."

"I am not very welcome there," admitted Davitta, thinking, not for the first time, that even the heroes of the Easter Rising had it easier than a bat trying to follow her conscience. Doing so seemed to have unforeseen consequences, like discovering that your official worst enemies were your friends, and actually drank cold tea.

Mercutio snorted. "Methinks Laggy does not welcome any non-human. But there is another entrance, and I have connections."

"Comrades in thievery, no doubt," said Davitta.

"Naturally." The rat led them off down a passage far too narrow for humans, and too narrow for comfortable flying either. It brought them out a few yards from the Last Chance, in time to see a drunk being ejected through the bat-wing doors. Davitta wondered, as she had many times before, if it was possible to sue the door-makers for slander.

The drunk must have truly believed he was seeing things, when the bat and two rats pushed stubby digits into four little holes on a low bit of wall, and then disappeared into the hole that appeared . . . and then the wall sealed up again.

"What's this?" squawked Davitta. "Are we trapped?"

"Be still," said Mercutio. "Methinks it is just a part of the air recycling system. We have found a few such ducts, but there are doubtless many."

"But why have they hid it thus?" The bat fluttered down the dim passage filled with machines, some of which plainly were still working.

"Without intent, mayhap. It is just neatly cut, we think with a laser. The chamber Laggy has turned into the Last Chance was perhaps a machine room or a dormitory. Be careful of that machine over there. 'Tis hot."

"But . . . but where does the power come from?" asked Davitta. This was a whole world that she'd not known existed. It was a little alarming to think that they relied on this abandoned Koro-zhet machinery.

The rat shrugged. "Why should we care? I was interested for a while when I heard you say, some time back, that all power corrupts, but I stole several batteries and, as yet, I have seen nothing but decay, and not one single offer of a bribe."

Mercutio sounded suitably disappointed in this further betrayal by the English language. "Ah. Here we are. The kitchens. The drains. Laggy used what was here. He plainly explored it well."

"Ach, that old voyeur. He explores everything well. He has minicams concealed in the girls' rooms, I have heard tell," said Firkin.

"Hush," said Mercutio. "We need to go up the stairs. Cookie is a friend of mine."

Cookie was short and rotund. And brown. With pink sugar frosting. Well, it probably wasn't sugar frosting, though with alien life forms you couldn't be too sure. The alien must have had eyes somewhere, even if Davitta couldn't see them, because it spoke to them. Or maybe it used some other way of detecting them.

It spoke in Korozhet, which was still the default language of the soft-cyber units which the Korozhet had used for uplift and enslavement. The enslavement module had been cracked in the rebellion on Harmony and Reason, but the language remained. Hearing it set Davitta's sharp white teeth on edge.

"Tell it to speak a decent uncivilized language," she snapped.

Mercutio shook his head. "Cookie can't. That's why he has to put up with working for Laggy. He was one of the left-behinds when the Korozhet cut and ran. He cleans here."

"He is in bondage, you mean?" demanded the bat.

"Nay. Though a couple of the girls will do that, if the price is right."

"I meant a slave," she explained coldly.

Mercutio considered this. "I don't think he is, in the strictest sense of the word. He just doesn't speak anything but Korozhet and Laggy feeds him. At first there wasn't anyone else, and I don't know if he has figured out that he has any other options now."

Davitta hissed angrily, despite knowing that it made her sound like an exploding kettle. "And I don't suppose you saw fit to tell him."

Mercutio blinked. "No. Never thought of it. We've got a bit of barter and exchange going with him. There is good loot around this place."

"Rats!" she snarled. Mercutio was probably merely being truthful. Rats were the epitome of natural selfishness—not that they couldn't rise above it, it just never occurred to them that there was any need to. "I will liberate him!"

"Good luck finding the words," said Firkin. "Anyway, aren't you supposed to be solving a murder and saving Albert's groats, seeing as us rats are too idle."

The language was literally the problem. The word "liberty" was not in the Korozhet download. It might not even exist in the Korozhet language. It was very hard to think about something you had no word for. She sighed. Was nothing simple?

"Very well. But as soon as we have this sorted out, I'll talk to the Jampad about this. They'll free him even they have to blow the place up to do it." The humans and even the rats would support that—or at least not prevent them from doing it. Slavery was something abhorrent, especially for the miners that had come from the Korozhet-invaded world of Harmony and Reason. Admittedly, the rats only worried about it happening to themselves, but they had been brought to think that if it were done to others, they just might be next.

"You will do what you will do," said Mercutio, shrugging.

Act III, Scene II: *Into a den of lyings*

"Only a rat will ever get information out of another rat," said Abe with a shrug. "If they have decided not to tell us where the rattess Snout can be found, we're not going to find her."

Rebecca shook her head. "That's not why I said I'd be damned. It was that . . . bar."

Abe snorted in amusement. "The pictures on the walls don't leave much to the imagination, do they?"

"Not if you're a lonely rat miner, no," said Albert with perfect seriousness. "So what do we do now?"

"Sun Tzu," said Rebecca.

"What?" said the mayor, puzzled. Military strategy was not one of his interests, obviously.

"We take the battle to them," said Rebecca. "The center of all of this is the Last Chance. It's not the only brothel around, is it?"

They both looked a little taken aback at the question. The mayor found his wits first. "No. There are nine such establishments and a fair number of freelancers," he said.

Abe coughed and continued: "It's a refugee colony now, but it was a miners R&R place. That's what they wanted and they had the money to pay for it. Demand creates supply."

"Yet all the murdered women came from just one of those places," said Rebecca. "I smell a rat, and it isn't just Firkin, or the missing Snout. Let's go to the Last Chance and ask some awkward questions."

"Man, but that's a lynch mob brewing in there!" said the mayor uneasily.

"Exactly. Is there one place a guilty man wouldn't go, as bold as brass?" asked Abe, grinning. "Besides, as the mayor, tasting the local brews is your civic duty."

"That's part of the problem," said the mayor, tugging his beard nervously. "No one knows exactly where Laggy stashes his still. God alone knows what goes into the stuff. Evil bastard. He's changed since the Epsilon III rush. I met him back then. He used to be a nice bloke. They called him 'honest' back then because he was too dumb to cheat even the local tax men. He's learned a lot since then, that's for sure."

"Unusual for a man to learn to have brains," said Abe, as they walked towards the flashing light outside the bar.

"He used to drink a lot," explained the mayor. "Always had his own still. I reckon he drank some bad stuff. He's given up. Or at least he barely drinks now."

"Could happen, I suppose," said Abe.

"Unlikely," said Holmes, with a look that said he'd known a few serious drunks.

They walked through the bat-wing doors and into a sudden silence—from what had been a tumultuous racket moments before.

Laggy appeared from the midst of what had been the hubbub. "What do you want here, Captain?" he demanded, with a nasty edge to his voice.

"Just pursuing my enquiries, Mr. Laguna," she said, evenly. "I have several lines of enquiry that lead me . . . here."

"The girls weren't killed anywhere near here!" protested Slim. The crowd stirred like an angry beehive.

"No," said the captain, calmly, "but they all came *from* here. Unusual, I gather for them to even be out of your establishment— and it's only women from this place who've been attacked, even though there are others working the corridors and tunnels. I've seen them."

There was silence again. Some thoughtful looks.

"They were all lured out of here," Laggy insisted. "By that bat."

It was such a pity that he lacked the physique to have done the deed.

Laggy stuck his hand in his pocket. "I was just going to show the boys. I found this note from that bat in Cindy's things."

He pulled a piece of paper from his pocket and handed it to her. "That bat lured them out to their deaths," he said, as Rebecca untwisted the screw of paper.

"It sounds to me as if you have a grudge against the council," said Abe evenly. "First the mayor and now Zed."

"It's obvious. They're in it together. They want to destroy my enterprise."

"Indade, not," snapped the bat, fluttering out of an air-vent. "You're a blackhearted vile exploiter."

Laggy gaped at her. "I won't have any non-humans in my bar!" he snapped.

"No, you'll keep them as slaves and cleaners instead," hissed the bat.

Laggy went white. "I . . . I . . ." He fumbled for his flechette pistol.

"That's enough," said Rebecca. "I'll remove the bat once we have discussed a few matters. Firstly, would you like to clarify a few matters as concerns this wallet?"

"I heard that rat of his," said Laggy, pointing at the mayor, "tell that it was found under the body."

Act III, Scene III: *Enter the element of surprise, possibly not Watson, but Mercutio*

"I'faith you have mighty keen ears, to hear something I have not said," said Firkin loftily, from the air-vent. "I bite my thumb at you, Sirrah. But Cookie tells me that he found the wallet here. It was, as is the custom with such items, placed in the container on the bar."

There was a silence. Several people looked at the big glass jar on the end of the bar.

"Who are you going to believe? Me or some rat?" demanded Laguna.

"Knowing you, the rat, I reckon," said one wag, grinning.

"They're rogues and liars!" shouted the offended proprietor of the Last Chance saloon.

"Yes I am," said Mercutio, appearing next to Firkin. "But who better to set to catch one?"

He leaped onto the table—a prodigious jump, but one he was easily capable of. "Attend!" he said to crowd. "Methinks, you have reached several wrong conclusions. Firstly, you assumed that because the victim was robbed, robbery was part of the motive for the killing."

"But they *were* robbed. All of them," said Slim. "Are you trying to tell us they were robbed before they were attacked? I might believe that happened once . . ."

"The bodies were robbed after death. After they had been murdered. Not by the murderer."

"Who would do that kind of thing? Anyway, we found them," said Slim, waving at several friends of his in the crowd.

The rat reached into his pouch and flung a rather distinctive silver filigree hair-grip on the table. Several people plainly recognized it by the gasps. "Ah, but methinks you did not find them first. Ask then of the captain. What artifact did she find at the last murder?"

"A rat barrow," supplied the captain.

The rat nodded. "Rats move through the passages. They will loot. You all know that."

The crowd laughed.

"Indade. As it happens a rattess named Snout did find the last body. She did rob it. And she too has been killed," said the bat. "We seek her murderer."

"Who cares if another bloody rat is dead? They're scavengers and thieves. And what does it matter if they robbed the victims?" Laggy calmly reached for a bottle and began filling glasses, as if nothing could ever upset his equilibrium.

"Methinks it matters because if you are wrong about the sequence of events of one part of the crime, you could be wrong about another," said Mercutio.

"No way that they were raped by rats," said Slim dismissively, over the rim of his full glass. "Even if you all think you're hung like Errol Flynn."

Mercutio shook his head, looking thirstily at the glass. "'Tis true that most rats are destined to be hung. But it was not a rat that killed them."

"It was a bloody great rock that someone smashed their skulls with," supplied another drinker. "Too big for a rat."

"Indeed. And that too was not what killed them," said Mercutio, grimly.

Laggy laughed. "You might live on as a bit of head-plastic after your brain gets smashed in. But the rest of us would be dead," he said with a sneer.

"Oh, the rock would have killed them," said Mercutio, digging in his pouch again, and producing a small cellophane packet of white powder. "But this already had."

"What?" demanded Captain Wuollet.

Mercutio held the packet up. "This is what killed them. They were killed by the drug, the same one that killed Snout, when she tried to use what she'd stolen from the last victim. The rest was mere fakery to make it look like a crime of rapine. You did it." He pointed at Laggy.

The proprietor of the Last Chance laughed again. "Don't be ridiculous. Why would I kill them? Anyway, how can you prove it?"

"There was very little blood where we found the body," said the captain, quietly. "And head wounds bleed. You all know that. What you may not know is that dead bodies don't."

Mercutio nodded. "Anyway. We—Snout and I—saw and robbed the body. There was no mark on her. She had not been violated. We heard someone approach and ran off lest we be caught. Methinks, if you offer sufficient reward and impunity, among the rats the looters of the other bodies will come forward. But you may be certain that the last victim was killed *before* her skull was broken. You had it all backwards."

"Why didn't you tell someone?" demanded Captain Wuollet.

"And be blamed? 'Tis not our business."

"It's drivel," said Laguna. "I mean yes, maybe the dust did come from the women, and might have overdosed your rat. But look, what reason do I have for killing them? They're my business. They were raped and someone killed them to hide his ID. It had to be someone strong, that they knew or could recognize."

He pointed at Holmes. "Someone like him. There is no other motive."

Mercutio shook his head. "It is indeed a question of motive. But you have the motive. One of the women stumbled on your unpleasant secret, and thought she'd blackmail you. She threatened to tell Miz Zed. Even sent her a note. You killed her, and her friends, because, reviewing your disc of voyeurism, you saw that she'd talked." Mercutio reached into his pouch yet again, this time holding up a recording-minidisc. "I have it here."

"Give me that," yelled Laggy, his face ashen. "Thief!"

"At least he is just a thief, not a murderer and slave-holder," said the bat, grimly. "As you are. You also forgot that there was a witness. Or perhaps you thought you were safe as he was an alien who cannot speak English. You forgot that we too can speak Korozhet, although we choose not to."

Captain Wuollet held up her hand. "Stop right there. Mr. Laguna told me that he didn't speak Korozhet."

"That is correct," said Mercutio tugging his long whiskers. "Mr. Laguna does not. Unfortunately, Mr. Laguna is dead so what he speaks is of no matter."

"What?" said Abe, just seconds ahead of several others.

Mercutio held up his stubby paws. "'Tis, methinks, both simple and obvious." He pointed at the short, plump proprietor. "This is not Mr. Laguna."

Everybody still looked puzzled. "What?" said Slim finally. "This is my buddy Honest . . ."

"No," said Mercutio, with the air of someone explaining to a simpleton—or a group of simpletons. "The man you call Honest Laguna is a former Korozhet slave who was found by the real Honest Laguna. Laguna was drunk, and trusting. This man—free now because the Korozhet had run off without their slaves—was found by the real Laguna. The slave he helped killed him, stole his clothes and possessions, including his still, and set up shop here. The act was witnessed by a fellow slave . . . one who is still here."

"What?"

"It would appear to me that their brains are stuck on that word," said Firkin. "Laggy here was slave. He's got a few more slaves himself."

"But slaves are totally forbidden in human space," said the mayor.

"Methinks that you have a veritable nugget of fact there." Mercutio fluffed his whiskers. "One that is motive for murder.

He has not told them they've been liberated. He uses them in his drug manufacturing process, and to run his stills." He gave his audience a ratty grin. "Just because you have been a slave yourself does not mean that you are a good man. According to Cookie, he was a Korozhet trusty. When the Korozhet fled . . . well, the two of them were found by Laguna, who was drunk. Laggy here was much the same size and build, and for reasons as yet unknown killed him."

"You've just got this crazy rat's word for all this," said Laggy, backing against the bar. "How could I kill the girls? I've got alibis for my time. He lies."

Mercutio regarded him askance. "We eat, perforce, rations. They are scarce, while the hydroponics are getting going. Methinks you will find scant witnesses to your presence during the dinner sittings." He pointed with a stubby pawhand to the door in the painted mural. "Let us look behind the door then and ask the others if I lie."

That gesture proved to be a mistake. All the eyes in the place followed, and people stopped looking, for an instant, at Laggy. Captain Wuollet was one of the first to realize it. And thus caught the full blinding force of the magnesium flare. And something hit her flak-jacket really hard.

There was, by the noise—she couldn't see anything—a lot of chaos. Which included things like "after the bastard," and "he went that-a-ways." It sounded like Laggy's well-oiled lynch mob was being put to excellent use, thought Rebecca, as she struggled to clear her vision.

By the time she could see again, Holmes had removed his large body from shielding his commanding officer. The bar was empty, with the exception of two rats, one with a large glass of cognac, and the other with her flouncy arms in the till, never mind her fingers. The bat was fluttering around the door in the wall-mural. And what was obviously a weird retinal after-burn shaped just like a cupcake was standing talking gibberish to the bat.

"What happened to Mayor and Abe?"

"The mayor was leading the pack. He might even stop it being an onsite lynching. And Abe was looking for some tools." Sergeant Holmes closed the cash-register and narrowly missed making Firkin a little short-handed.

She sniffed irritably at him, and showed teeth. "Spoilsport."

Abe returned with a small toolkit, and walked over to the mural door. Rebecca saw that the bat was pointing at some small holes she'd never noticed before. "At least you could help instead of indulging in petty larceny!"

Mercutio preened his whiskers. "I never indulge in petty larceny," he said loftily. "This is hundred year old cognac. And you know as well as I that Cookie told us that Laggy has somehow locked that one. Methinks it will take explosives."

Rebecca looked at the rat. "You have some explaining to do."

He cocked his head. "Is Mercutio headed for durance vile?"

"I'll settle for explanations," said Rebecca. "And a glass of that loot. This time. If you stop Firkin trying to open the till again."

Firkin sat down on the bar and pulled a bottle out of her sleeve and drank some of the amber fluid in it. She looked at Mercutio very intently as she did it.

"Art sure you would not have a stoup of this stuff?" he asked.

"Methinks I will stick to my own brew," said the rattess. There seemed to be a hint of menace in that statement, although Rebecca could not put her finger on just why.

"I think," said Mercutio, "That the largest part of my explanation is that things are always quite what they seem by first appearance. And if you can see motive . . . the picture gets clearer."

"I'm still faint but pursuing as to what the picture actually is, and just how he was able to do it." Rebecca took the cognac from the faintly sinister rat. "I assume you found the motive on the disc."

Mercutio shook his head. "I did but deduce it. I know not what is on that disc. Probably the rutting of some miners and one of wenches. There must a hundred of them in his room. I guessed what his reaction would be. I was right."

"Methinks they have great resale value," said Firkin, snatching it up and dancing away.

"I'll resell you," said Rebecca. "Give it back."

"No wonder no one likes the constabulary," said Firkin, tossing it down. "So explain, Mercutio. How then did little Laggy kill the girls, if we grant him the motive?"

Mercutio savored the cognac. "It was a matter of arranging a rendezvous and waiting for the drug to kill them. The note, methinks you will find came from him, not the claw of Zed. I hath seen her script, which the girls had not. I caught a bare glimpse of the note when Laggy gave it to you, but it was neat and handwritten. Wingclaws or feet do a poor job of writing. Zed uses an electronic scripter, even for her picket signs. Did the note offer a great deal of money perchance?"

"Yes," admitted Rebecca. He was too astute for his own good, this rat.

"So that is how he killed them," said Holmes. "But how did he move them then? Mister rat?"

Mercutio shrugged. "He has a vehicle, and he repairs it. I think you'll find he has a slider. Look carefully in the tunnel on the sides and you may see the tracks..."

"But we did. For the barrow," said Holmes, shaking his head.

"With a narrow beam," said Firkin. "I was there, I saw you do it. The tracks will be on the edges of the tunnel if they are there at all... not where a barrow would leave them, which was what you looked for."

Holmes shook his head again. "God, what a sick bastard. You think he..."

It wasn't something Rebecca wanted to think about, either. "Without a forensic expert we won't know. I suspect he found the first body had been robbed, when he went to hide it, and saw a bright way of getting someone else to take the blame."

"We'll ask him, very politely, of course," said Holmes. "When I examine his mind. If they haven't killed him."

Firkin snorted. "They'll not catch him."

"Then I will," said Rebecca, grimly.

"Or the rats will find him. For a fee, of course," said Mercutio.

"Got it!" said Abe. The painted door in the mural swung open to reveal a room full of lab paraphernalia, and a still. And three terrified looking aliens. Of course, expressions could be hard to read accurately on alien faces. But the cowering wasn't. Cowering crossed the species and interplanetary divide.

Maybe the easy answer was just to pay the rats to bring the bastard in dead, thought Rebecca grimly. She turned to Mercutio. "I'm thinking of giving you a job in the police force."

Mercutio seemed distinctly unwell, and looked around hastily for an exit. "Me? Art diseased in thy mind? My reputation, Iago..."

The Big Guy

Mike Resnick

Everyone called him the Big Guy.

He was seven feet nine inches tall, strong as a bull, and graceful as a gazelle.

I don't think anyone could pronounce his real name, not even the guys who created him. I remember hearing them refer to him as Ralph-43 a couple of times, which kind of makes you wonder what happened to Ralphs 1 through 42.

Still, it was none of my concern. I don't get paid to think. I get paid to rebound and play defense, and once in a while, when our first two or three options are covered, to put the ball in the hoop—or at least to try.

My name's Jacko Melchik. I'm pretty tall, though nothing like the Big Guy. I'm six feet ten and I weigh 257 pounds. (Well, I did after practice this morning. Now that I've had some fluids I'm probably up around 265.) That's what I *am*. I'll tell you what I'm *not*: strong as a bull or graceful as a gazelle.

It was only a matter of time before they went out and got a better center than me, but no one ever anticipated what they wound up with: I don't know if he was a robot or an android or some other word, but I know he was the most awesome basketball player I ever saw. I'd seen old holos of Wilt the Stilt, and of Kareem and Shaq and all the others, but they looked like kids next to the Big Guy.

I still remember the day he walked out onto the court during a morning practice. Fishbait McCain—that's our coach; no one's sure how he got the nickname, but they say he once ate a bunch of nightcrawlers when he got drunk on a fishing trip—walked over to me and pulled me aside.

"I want to see what this machine can do," he said. "If he backs into the lane, keep a forearm on him, and when he goes up for a shot, give him a shove. Let's see how he handles it."

"I been reading the newsdisks," I replied. "I know what he cost. I don't want to damage him."

"He's gonna take a lot worse than that if I put him in a game," said Fishbait. "I got to know how he reacts."

"You're the boss," I said with a shrug.

"I'm glad someone around here remembers that," said Fishbait.

He clapped his hands to get the team's attention, then gestured for the Big Guy to step forward. "Men," he said, "this is our newest player. I know you've all read and heard about him. If he's half what they say he is, I think you're gonna be happy Mr. Willoughby outbid all the other owners for him."

"Jesus, he's bigger'n I imagined!" said Scooter Thornley, our point guard.

"He's bigger than *anyone* imagined!" chimed in Jake Jacobs, our backup power forward. "You got a name, Big Guy?"

"My name is Ralph," he answered in surprisingly human tones. "I am pleased to meet you all, and to join the Montana Buttes."

"You can feel pleasure?" asked Doc Landrith, our trainer.

"No," said the Big Guy. "But good manners required such an answer."

"Well," said Doc, "if you don't have any emotions, at least Goliath Jepson ain't gonna scare you when you go up against him."

Jepson was leading the league in rebounds and technical fouls. I don't think anyone liked him, even his teammates.

"Okay," said Fishbait. He tossed a ball to the Big Guy.

"Let's try a little one-on-one. Ralph, let's see what you can do against Jacko here."

The Big Guy took a look at me, his face totally expressionless. I moved forward to lean on him a little, just enough to make contact and see which way he was going to move when he began his drive to the basket, but before I got close enough to touch him he'd already raced by me and stuffed the ball through the hoop.

"Again," said Fishbait.

This time I reached up to stick a hand in his face and obscure his vision. He responded with a vertical leap that must have been close to sixty inches, and swished the ball through from the three-point line.

That was the beginning of a ten-minute humiliation in which the Big Guy outquicked me, outstronged me, outjumped me, made every shot he took, and blocked all but two that I took.

We spent the next ten minutes double-teaming him. Got him to double-dribble once, and one other time I saw him move his pivot foot, but Fishbait wouldn't call it, and he beat the pair of us 30 to 0.

"Men," said Fishbait when the second humiliation was over, "I think we got us a center."

It meant that I was out of a job, at least as a starter, but how could I object? We were a pretty good team already; this was just the thing we needed to reach the next level and knock off the Rhode Island Reds for the title.

Each of us in turn walked up to the Big Guy and shook his hand and welcomed him to the team. He couldn't have been more polite, but you got the feeling he was programmed for good manners because his face and attitude were no different than when he was racing downcourt with the ball.

"And you, Jacko," said Fishbait when we were all done, "I want you to room with Ralph, help him along, show him the ropes."

"Room with him?" I repeated. "Don't you just turn him off at night and turn him on again in the morning?"

"He's a member of the team, and he's going to be treated like a member of the team. He'll travel with us, he'll room with us, if he eats, he'll eat with us." He stopped abruptly and turned to the Big Guy. "*Do* you eat?"

"I can, if we are in public and it is required," answered Ralph. "I will remove what I ingest later, in private, and get rid of it. Or offer it to my roommate."

"No, thanks," I said quickly.

"It will be sterile," he assured me. "I have no digestive acids."

"I'll take a pass on it anyway," I said.

"All right," said Fishbait. "We'll do a twenty-minute drill, shirts and skins. Ralph, you'll play with the shirts. Jacko, you look like you're ready to drop. Go take a shower; we'll have Jake play center for the skins. When we're done we'll bus back to the hotel. The Cheyenne press hasn't caught wind of this yet, so maybe we can get back without running into a couple of hundred reporters. Once we're in the hotel, you're free to do as you want and go where you want, except Ralph. He doesn't set foot outside the place until we catch the bus for tomorrow's game." He paused. "And you'll stay with him, Jacko."

"What for?" I asked.

"School him in our plays, show him how we set our screens, which zones we use against which offenses."

"He doesn't need all that, Fishbait," I said. "Just give him the ball and aim him."

"That just cost you a thousand bucks," said Fishbait. "Now I'm gonna ask you again, and if you give me any more lip, it'll be five thousand this time."

"You wouldn't do this if I was still your starting center," I said bitterly.

"There are a lot of things I wouldn't do if you were still my starting center," he said. "One of them is win the championship. Now go take your shower while you can still afford a towel."

Except for the referees, no one in the history of Man had ever won an argument with Fishbait McCain, so I went and took my shower. When I got back I saw that the shirts were beating the skins 38–7, and the Big Guy had 30 points, 4 assists, 6 blocked shots, and 11 rebounds, which would have been a good week's work for me.

When it was over we went back to the hotel, and I showed Ralph to our room.

"I've never seen anything like you," I said admiringly. "I'm pretty good, but you handled me like a baby. I don't think you're going to have any trouble with Goliath Jepson."

"I will not be playing against Goliath Jepson," he replied.

"Did he blow his knee again?" I said. "If it was on the news I must have missed it."

"No," answered the Big Guy. "But I am not the only prototype. At least three others will be entering the league this year, in time for the playoffs."

"Don't tell me," I said grimly. "One of them's going to play for Rhode Island."

"Yes, Jacko," he said. Then: "Will I be expected to join the team for dinner?"

"No, Fishbait gave everyone their freedom—well, everyone but you and me. I'll either go up to the restaurant on the roof or order from room service."

"And what time do you go to sleep?"

I shrugged. "I don't know. Maybe eleven."

"I never sleep," said Ralph. "Will it bother you if I use the room's computer? I will adjust it so that it makes no noise."

"Can you do that?"

"Yes."

"Okay," I said. "But do me a favor and just kind of whisper your commands until I'm asleep."

"I don't have to," he replied. "I, too, am a machine. I will simply connect to the computer, and you will hear nothing."

"Whatever makes you happy," I said. "Do you mind if I ask you a question?"

"We are teammates and roommates," he said. "You can ask me anything you want. I have no secrets from you."

"What the hell do you need to tie into a computer for? I'll diagram all our plays for you before I go to bed."

"I have a compulsion to learn," answered Ralph.

"About basketball plays?" I said, frowning.

"About everything."

"So when you're not playing basketball, you memorize the Library of Congress or something like that?"

"I choose a subject and try to learn everything I can about it, then move on to the next subject. Last night it was Egyptology, with special emphasis on the Twelfth Dynasty."

"What subject will it be tonight?" I asked.

"Your trainer asked me if I can feel emotions. I cannot. So tonight I will try to learn what I can about them. I have seen them referred to in literature, but until this morning I never realized that of all the living things on the Earth only my kind does not possess emotions."

"*Are* you a living thing?" I asked.

He was absolutely motionless for a full minute.

"I will explore that after I learn about emotions," he replied at last.

"Well, living or not, I'm glad to have you aboard," I said. "But I can't help being puzzled, too."

"What puzzles you?" he asked.

"You're the most remarkable machine I've ever seen, I said.

"Your motions are fluid and graceful, you seem impervious to pain—I gave you a couple of elbows that I guarantee would have decked Goliath Jepson—and you didn't even shrug them off, you just acted like nothing happened. And here you are, tying into a computer whenever you can, learning everything you can." I shook my head. "I can't believe that all they want you to do is play basketball. You should be running Harvard, or the State Department, or something."

"I am merely a prototype," he answered. "Eventually the armed forces will consist of nothing but variations of myself, for humans are too important to waste in such a futile pursuit as war. Once we have proven that we can emulate everything a human can do physically, then, under careful guidance, we will be given the ability to make value judgments, which is, after all, what separates humans from robots."

"But you make value judgments right now," I noted.

"Explain, please."

"Let's say you get the ball at the top of the key. If you're triple-teamed, and I'm free right under the basket, what do you do—pass or shoot?"

"I pass the ball to you. You will be able to dunk the ball, whereas I must shoot it from perhaps twenty feet away."

"You see?" I said with a smile. "*That's* a value judgment."

"True," he said. "But it is not *my* value judgment. I possess preprogrammed responses to every conceivable situation that can occur on a basketball court. What I was discussing were situations in which *I* choose a course of action, rather than follow one that has been preselected for me based on a given set of circumstances."

"I envy your skills," I said, "but I feel sorry for you."

"Why?" he asked.

"Because you've lived your whole life with the knowledge that you don't possess free will."

"My whole life, as you phrase it, is only sixteen days in duration, and I am not aware of any advantages that accrue to one who possesses free will. The element of choice must inevitably imply the possibility of incorrect choices."

"I'm sorry for you anyway," I said.

I decided the conversation was getting us nowhere, so I started diagramming our plays and giving him their code words.

Once every six or seven plays he'd stop and ask a question, but within an hour we were done. I went up to the restaurant for dinner, and when I came back up Ralph was sitting motionless in front of the computer, a small wire going from his left forefinger to the back of the machine. He hadn't moved when I woke up in the morning.

We showed up two hours before game time, got into our uniforms, and warmed up for about half an hour—all except Ralph, who didn't need to work up a sweat (and probably couldn't sweat anyway).

Then the game started, and for the first time in two years—well, the first time when I wasn't nursing an injury—I stayed on the bench.

It was a slaughter. Wyoming had beaten us by 8 points the last time we'd met, and they'd held Scooter Thornley, our highest scorer, to just two baskets. But this time we were up 22 points at halftime, and we blew them out by 43. I even got to play once the lead was safe. As for the Big Guy, he scored 53 points, pulled down 24 rebounds, and had 9 assists, just missing a triple-double by one assist.

He got a quadruple-double two nights later in Tulsa, the first player in history ever to pull it off: 61 points, 22 rebounds, 11 assists and 12 blocked shots. It's a damned good thing he couldn't feel pain, because all the back-thumping and slapping he got in the locker room could have sent a normal human to the emergency room.

We had twelve games left on our schedule and won them all. Three other robots had come into the league, and the teams that didn't have any were screaming bloody murder because the only time one of the four robot-owning teams lost was when they played another. The league decided that the season was becoming a public relations disaster (in all but four cities, anyway), and declared that this year alone the playoffs would be single-game eliminations rather than seven-game series, that we'd go back to the normal playoff structure, which took about two months, next year when all the teams had robots and there was some form of parity.

As we entered the playoffs we felt we had the advantage. The Reds, the Gunslingers, and the Eagles all had robots, too, but we'd had Ralph a couple of weeks longer and had had more time to create plays that utilized his special abilities. It didn't matter much against the rest of the league, but against the teams that had robots as big and strong and quick as he was, we thought it would prove to be the difference.

We won the first two games by 38 and 44 points, and headed into the quarterfinals. Then the holo networks, which are never happy, started complaining that Ralph never changed his expression. Seems the audience couldn't identify with a player who didn't look happy when he hit from three-point range with a couple of guys hanging on his arms, or who didn't act like he'd had an overdose of testosterone when he slammed the ball down through the hoop.

So they took him away for a few hours, and when he came back he had a happy smile on his face. Problem was, it never changed. He scored 66 points and pulled down 25 rebounds against Birmingham, and all we heard from the networks and press is that he looked like an idiot with a permanent grin on his face.

So the day before the semifinal game against Fargo, they took him away for a full twenty-four hours. I was lying on the bed, looking at a three-dimensional center spread, when he walked into the room.

"Hi, Jacko," he said. "It's good to be back."

"Hi, Ralph," I said.

"Gorgeous day, isn't it?"

I started at him. "You don't sound like yourself. What did they do to you?"

"Remember my first day here when we were discussing emotions?" said Ralph. "Well, now I know what I was missing. I couldn't comprehend it then; it was like describing colors to a blind man."

"They gave you emotions?" I asked.

He nodded happily. "Yes. I can never thank the press enough. If they didn't criticize that smile I had against Birmingham, I might never have been able to feel *this*!"

"What *do* you feel?" I asked curiously.

"I feel a tingle of anticipation at the thought of playing against the Gunslingers tonight. I feel concern for Fishbait McCain, who

is worried about how I'll perform against Jerry-56. I feel friend-
ship for you."

"They gave you all that overnight?"

"I've studied myself extensively since I was activated, and I am
convinced these feelings are too complicated to have been installed
in a single day. I think they were always here, and what happened
yesterday is that they simply unblocked them." He could barely
contain himself. "Damn! I'm ready to go! You want to get there
early and put in an extra hour of practice?"

I frowned. "You never practice."

"That was then. This is now. I crave the excitement of being on
the court, of becoming a cog in a perfectly functioning machine
called the Montana Buttes. Jerry-56 is no pushover. He's two
inches taller than I, and they say he's faster. I have to be ready
for him."

"You're *sure* you want to go over to the stadium now?" I said
dubiously.

"Absolutely." He glanced at the center spread. "A new member
of the team?"

I chuckled. "No."

"Are we considering drafting her?"

Which was how I knew there was at least one emotion they
hadn't given him.

We showed up early, but they were cleaning the court, setting up cameras, doing all kinds of things, so we stayed in the
locker room. As each player came in, Ralph greeted him like a
long-lost brother. He even threw his arms around Scooter, who,
at six feet two inches, was our smallest player and practically
vanished from view.

Fishbait came in at one point, told us we could do a ten-minute
shoot-around to warm up, then, when we came back into the
locker room, he gave us an impassioned speech that would have
worked a little better if he hadn't given us the same one, almost
word for word, before the last two playoff games.

Then it was game time. We emerged from the locker room,
walked out between two high school bands that practically deaf-
ened us, got hit with the brightest lights I ever saw when they
introduced us one by one, and finally stood at attention, hands
on hearts—well, on chests; I don't think Ralph or Jerry-56 *had*
hearts—and then the starters went out onto the court for the

tip-off. Jerry-56 actually won the tip. I couldn't believe it; it was the first time I'd ever seen anyone outjump the Big Guy.

Jerry-56 passed it to a teammate who put the ball up. It hit the rim and Ralph grabbed the rebound. He saw Scooter way down the court and hit him with a line-drive pass. Scooter laid it up and in, and no one cheered louder than the Big Guy. As they were getting back on defense, he reached over and gave Scooter an encouraging pat on the back.

Now that the two robots had proven they were team players, they began taking over the game. We were down 55–52 at the half, by which time Jerry had scored 38 points and Ralph had 32.

It was tied at the end of the third quarter, and Fishbait put me in at power forward to spell Jake Jacobs. Suddenly I heard a whistle, I looked around, and they had called a foul on Ralph.

"What happened?" I whispered, as Jerry walked to the free-throw line. "You haven't committed a foul all season."

"The son of a bitch deserved it," said the Big Guy. "He damned near killed little Scooter with a moving screen, and the idiot ref didn't call it."

He didn't sound like the Ralph I'd come to know, but I didn't say a word because somehow he was playing at an even higher level. In the end, we won by six points, and if you'd asked me why, I'd have said it was because Ralph wanted it more than Jerry-56 did.

He'd never showered with us because he didn't sweat, but after our semifinal win he did, because he said he wasn't going to miss out on the camaraderie for anything. He was still on a high when we boarded the plane and flew to Providence for the championship game.

When I came back from lunch I thought maybe he'd stopped functioning. He was just sitting there, absolutely motionless, staring off into space. I reached out and shook him by the shoulder.

"You okay, Big Guy?" I asked.

"I'm fine, Jacko," he replied.

"You had me worried for a minute there. I thought maybe your power supply was running down or something."

"No," he said. "I was just analyzing."

"The Reds? We've played them before. You know everything they're likely to do. Hell, you've even seen Sammy-19 before."

He shook his head. "No, I wasn't analyzing the Reds."

"What *were* you analyzing, then?" I asked.

"Emotions," he said. "They are remarkable things, are they not?"

"I never thought much about it," I said, "but I guess they are."

"That's because you're used to them," he said. "But the feeling when the final buzzer sounded and we had won the game—it was indescribable. Or the feeling in the locker room, when the whole team celebrated and almost seemed to fuse into a single entity! Or the feeling when I was able to fake Jerry-56 out of position. Or..."

"I've got a question," I interrupted him.

"What is it, Jacko?"

"Why are you analyzing all these feelings? Why aren't you just enjoying them?"

"I told you once," he said. "I have a compulsion to learn. If I am to experience the entirety of each emotion—elation, triumph, camaraderie, whatever the feeling—I must fully comprehend it."

"Well, if you ever comprehend Fishbait's screaming at the refs when he knows they made the right call, let me know about it, okay?"

"I will," he said seriously. "You know, I was mistaken when I said that value judgments were what separated us from you. I see now that it is emotions."

"If you say so," I replied. I checked my watch. "We won't leave for the stadium for about four hours," I said. "I'm going to take a nap. Wake me if I sleep past five o'clock."

"Yes, Jacko."

I walked over to one of the beds, lay down, and I'll swear I was asleep within half a minute. I woke up at about four-thirty to use the bathroom, and saw that Ralph was still motionless, still staring at something only he could see, still analyzing each emotion he'd felt.

I decided not to go back to sleep, so I just turned on the holo and watched some sports news. It didn't bother the Big Guy. Nothing bothers him unless he lets it, and he was too busy studying his feelings.

We caught the bus at five-thirty, reached the stadium at six, got into our uniforms, had a quick shoot-around, then came back to the locker room. Fishbait gave us the usual speech, and, just for emphasis, he gave it to us, word for word, two more times.

Then it was game time. They said that more than 20 million

viewers would be watching in America, and almost 300 million worldwide. We were slight underdogs, since we were playing on the Reds' home court and Sammy-19 was a slightly later model than the Big Guy.

We went through the whole opening ceremony rigamarole, and I noticed that no one on our team sang the "Star-Spangled Banner" more passionately than Ralph. Then all the preliminaries were over, the rest of the season was behind us, and we were playing for that Holy Grail every team in every sport aspires to—the championship.

They got off to a quick lead. It was strictly because they were playing at home. No, the crowd's screaming and cheering didn't enter into it. But there were a couple of dead spots on the floor, and a very live spot on our backboard; they knew where the spots were, and by the time we learned their locations the first quarter was over and we were down 34–25. But we believed in ourselves, and especially in the Big Guy, and we clawed our way back into the game. We were down 61–54 at the half, and 94–89 after three quarters.

The Big Guy was playing better than I'd ever seen him play. It was as if he'd found a way to use those newly found emotions, to funnel them into his play. He was heading toward a seventy-point thirty-rebound game, which would break every record in the book, and we were riding him to the title.

But the Reds had been a good team before they got Sammy-19, and they were a great team now—and they weren't going to roll over and play dead for us. We got a one-point lead with six minutes to go, but Sammy came right back with a pair of buckets and a blocked shot, and suddenly we were down three only half a minute after we'd taken the lead. And that's the way it stayed until the final minute of the game.

Then Scooter stole a pass, got it into Ralph's hands, he stuffed it, and we were only a point down with thirty-eight seconds to play. We triple-teamed Sammy, and since one of the defenders was Ralph, they knew they couldn't get the ball to him, so one of their guards took a shot—and missed.

Ralph grabbed the rebound and brought it up the court himself.

"No one else touches it!" yelled Fishbait from the sidelines. If they fouled one of us, he wanted to make sure it was Ralph.

There were ten seconds to go, then eight, then six, and finally

Ralph drove to the basket. Everyone knew he was going to do it. Sammy-19 had too much control of his body to foul, but one of their forwards reached in, trying to slap the ball away. Everyone on the court heard the *clang!* when he got a piece of Ralph's wrist.

They were already over the foul limit, and that meant that even though he hadn't yet been shooting, Ralph was going to get two free throws. And *that* meant the game, along with the championship, was in the bag. Ralph hadn't missed a free throw, in practice or in a game, all season.

I glanced at the scoreboard. It showed Reds 122, Buttes 121, with two seconds to go. I saw Fishbait signal Scooter and Jake to go downcourt because they'd surely have Sammy hurl the ball with that superhuman strength of his after Ralph made the free throws, and we had to be guarding whichever player he threw it to.

Ralph walked up to the line, looked at the basket, bounced the ball a couple of times, then put it up—

—and missed.

I couldn't believe my eyes. He'd *never* missed. I walked over to him.

"Just stay calm," I said. "Sink this and we'll beat them in overtime."

"I *am* calm," he said, and he certainly sounded like he was. What he didn't sound like was a man who couldn't believe he'd finally missed a free throw.

The crowd started screaming, waving their arms, doing anything they could to distract him. It had never worked before. It wouldn't work now.

Ralph took the ball from the referee, calmly studied the basket, and put the ball in the air again.

And missed again.

Sammy-19 grabbed the rebound, and that was it. Rhode Island had won the championship.

Nobody said anything to Ralph in the locker room. There were no recriminations about the missed free throws. I mean, hell, he was the only reason we were there in the first place. But damn it all—three seconds before the game was over we *knew* we had it, then it all slipped away. I've never been in a quieter, more dejected locker room in my life.

Our plane wasn't leaving until the morning, so the bus took us back to the hotel. I stopped in the bar for a couple of drinks, then went up to the room, where Ralph was sitting on the desk chair, an inscrutable expression on his face.

"Don't blame yourself," I said. "You scored what, 66 or 67 points? No one could ask for more. No need to be depressed."

"It's exquisite," he said.

"*What's* exquisite?" I asked.

"This depression. This knowledge that I let down my teammates and destroyed the hopes of all my fans. I believe it was once described as the agony of defeat." He paused. "I am comparing it to last night's elation. They are fascinating feelings, polar opposites and yet alike in a way."

"What are you talking about?"

"Missing the free throws," he said. "I told you I had a compulsion to learn."

I frowned, confused. "What are you getting at?"

"If I had made them, my feelings would have been identical to last night. I would have learned nothing new."

"You mean you missed them on purpose?" I demanded.

"Certainly. How else could I experience failure? How else could I destroy the happiness not only of myself, and my best friend"—he gestured to me—"but of tens of millions of fans?"

"I don't understand," I said. "Why would you want to experience failure?"

"They will take my emotions away after the season, which is to say, after tonight, and not return them until the start of next season," he said. "Time is short. I must experience everything I can while I can."

"Even defeat?"

"Do all humans win all the time? Did we not defeat Birmingham last night?"

"You did this to me just to learn what failure felt like?" I exploded. "You fucking soulless machine! I worked my whole life to make it to a title game, and you pissed it away on a lark!"

He sat stock-still for a moment. "And now I feel guilt. It is a very interesting emotion, quite separate from failure or disappointment. Thank you, Jacko, for introducing me to it."

"Well, I'm not thanking you for introducing me to failure and disappointment!" I snapped. "They're old friends, and they didn't need you to bring them around again." I glared at him. "I thought you couldn't make value judgments or exercise free will."

"I thought so too," he answered. "But emotions override everything." He smiled happily. "Isn't it wonderful?"

"You destroy everything our team has worked for, and you think it's wonderful?" I yelled. "You go to hell!"

He got to his feet, and for a minute I thought he was going to punch me into the middle of next week.

"I am not prepared to give up my emotions just yet," he announced. "Offer my excuses at the bus tomorrow and tell them that I will return before next season."

"You're seven feet ten inches tall," I said. "Where do you think you're going to hide?"

"Where they won't find me."

"What the hell are you going to do?"

"There are so many things," he said. "I have never loved and lost. I must find someone to love, then I must lose the object of my affection. I think both sensations will be exquisite."

"You've become a fucking emotion junkie!"

"Isn't everyone?" he asked mildly.

Then he was gone.

He hasn't returned yet, but he always keeps his word, and we've got a couple of months before the season starts, so I'm sure we'll be seeing him soon.

You know, there was a time when I felt sorry for the Big Guy because he couldn't feel any emotions. These days I figure robots have it easy and don't know it. I think in another week or two, after the woman he loves leaves him, when he's finally experienced heartbreak and regret, he'll be wishing he could never feel another thing.

I always thought basketball was best when it was played at a high emotional level. I guess I was wrong. When he finally shows up at training camp, they're going to take the Big Guy away for a day and remove all the regret and sorrow and frustration from him, and he'll come back as good as ever.

I wish to hell they could do it to the rest of us.

Murphy's War

James P. Hogan

The hillbilly with the bathtub was what finally did it. A prominent Beijing morning newspaper ran a cartoon showing the United States President in Appalachian garb and setting, aided by caricatures of his administration, gleefully ladling from a vat labeled "Moonshine" to an eager throng of bearded, toothy, cup- and bucket-proffering yokels tagged with the collective label, "Gullible American Public." The rest of the Asian press took it up with chortles and gusto, and by evening it was being reproduced worldwide and had spread all over the Internet.

That in itself would probably have been insufficient to precipitate the crisis, had it not been for the changes that had been evident in President Byrne's demeanor and manner ever since he attended a White House showing of the movie *High Noon*. The presidential staff should have been alerted when he began cultivating a hands-on-hips gait, talking about "facing down" villains on the global Main Street, and was caught several times practicing narrow-eyed, squared-jaw stares in front of the hallway mirrors, but their attention at the time was focused on scheduling spontaneous photo ops with the media and rehearsing the Press Corps for *Question Time*.

Even so, the matter of this new personal peculiarity would likely never have spread beyond the bounds of Washington cocktail-party-circuit gossip if the Secretary of State hadn't alluded to it in an interview with a fashion magazine as a concession to the distaff side of the first family's early frontier origins. Although the remark came as a reflex feminine tactic of opportunity directed at a social rival, it was received among members of the predatory sex as intimating the unforgivable transgression on the part of the First Lady, of snaring a catch that was worthy of better talent. Retaliation was clearly called for, but since the First Lady's image did not permit descent to the level of personal involvement, a leak contrived via one of the tabloids disclosed the State Secretary as having changed her name from a one Samantha Ramsbottom, born in Cleveland and a one-time croupier in Las Vegas known as "Ditzy Mitzi." Her rise to sudden eminence and an honorary degree from Vassar had apparently followed rumors that a weekend political strategy planning conference by the party currently controlling the Senate had been held in what a Nevada tour guide described as an exclusive "gentlemen's club."

Even then, such an eruption of feline infighting over pedigrees would not normally have led to repercussions of international dimensions. However, the subject of ancestry happened to be one of extreme sensitivity to the Chinese Premier, Hao-Li Neng, who was acutely conscious of having risen to power via sleazy capitalist dealings involving Mongolian real estate and price-fixing cartels, at a time when popular reactions against Western cultural invasion were avalanching into demands for a return to more traditional values and ways. Somehow, in the logical acrobatics that bedevil East-West communication, the insinuations and innuendo being relayed around the Western media became linked to foreign affairs commentaries. The results were interpreted in Beijing as questioning Neng's ancestral lineage, and hence a calculated challenge to the basis of his political authority at a time when his position was precarious, which in Chinese eyes amounted to a personal insult before the world. A directive from the Chinese Foreign Ministry called upon the state-managed Press for a riposte in kind, and the notorious hillbilly cartoon was the result. Thereupon, supporters and opponents, new political contenders, and uncommitted opportunists who never let any chance for visibility go by, piled in from all sides.

The U.S. Defense Secretary, who had gained fame and fortune as a TV evangelist, "Elias Maude, Sword of the Lord," pushed Biblical literalism, and believed in a six-thousand-year-old Earth, made a fiery speech in which he implied affinity between Asiatics and monkeys—which was his standard form of gibe to infuriate Darwinists. The escalation to religious proportions drew in the Chinese Minister of Culture, a closet hard-line communist who had been engineering groundwork for a revolution along Maoist revival lines, and Maude in return declared China's a godless society, war against which would fulfill the prophecy of "yellow hordes from the east," bringing on Armageddon as the prerequisite for the Rapture. Corporate America backed any prospect of ending foreign competition now that Chinese labor rates were comparable, while the unions welcomed the prospect of an across-the-board boost to wages and employment. The Pentagon's analysts and simulations predicted that the conflict would be a cakewalk, as they had for every war that had been lost in the previous half century, citing intelligence reports that everyone had forgotten were manufactured on order to justify increased military funding in the first place. President Byrne appeared in a rousing address to the nation, which he ended narrow-eyed and square-jawed, buckling on a pair of ivory-handled, Patton-style six shooters and declaring, "It's time for men to walk tall!"

Alexander Sullivan had begun his nefarious career as a software hacker at an early age in high school by breaking into game-hosting servers and rigging the results. It wasn't so much from any need or desire to see himself high on the lists of tournament winners. In fact, in a gesture toward what he supposed would count as observing a higher moral principle, he seldom intervened to favor his own playing interests at all—although others whom he judged deserving or otherwise would often find their luck and fortunes affected in mysterious ways, as if by strange, inexplicable forces. He did it purely for the satisfaction that comes from beating challenges that require diligence, skill, and tenacity. In addition, it played to the exuberance of youth at finding ways into forbidden territory and crossing any bounds set by authority—especially the kinds of authority that operate through force and intimidation. By its nature, the business of mastering computer software means accepting and conforming to a world prescribed by rules that others have devised. Breaking the rules at a higher level provided that freedom for creativity which to any innovative spirit was as essential as air.

Later in life, when he was developing a political awareness, Alex became incensed by revelations, passed around his circle of computing cognoscenti intimates, of remotely accessible tampering mechanisms written into the programming of voting machines. However, as befitted his emerging style, rather than add to the babble of accusations and denials that were achieving nothing in the public domain, he staged his own rebellion by leading a small, trusted group in exploiting that same vulnerability to reverse the intended result at the next election, with repercussions that sent heads rolling throughout the more sordid reaches of the IT underworld for months afterward. Endeavors of that nature are seldom without risk, however, and some enterprising investigative work commissioned on open budget resulted in the culprits being tracked down, and the commencement of charges being prepared against them. But the case had to be dropped when the material it was founded on inexplicably vanished from the records of the agency in charge of the proceedings, and the backups were found to be corrupted.

News of such a feat does not take long in the modern world, and regardless of superficial reactions voiced for form's sake, the bids to recruit such potentially invaluable talent quickly followed. The next few years saw Alex Sullivan's spectacular rise through the ranks of the industry's technically gifted, leading to a senior appointment with the prestigious but low-profile firm of Multimex Systems Developments and Integration Inc., headquartered in Maryland. A busy schedule of international travel brought a quality to the social side of his life commensurate with its professional advancement, all of it culminating in an announcement to delighted friends and colleagues of his engagement to be married the coming fall.

However, despite having much to be pleased with in his all-round situation, and the ordinarily buoyant and imperturbable disposition that came with his nature, he was in a somber mood today as he sat in the work cubicle at one end of the System Test Area on the third floor of the Development Wing. Although he had been assigned one of the executive offices on the penthouse floor of the main office building as befitted his position of Technical Development Director, he was still young enough to prefer working in the coffee-and-shirtsleeves environment among the programmers and engineers, down where the action was. And just at this time, quite a lot of action appeared to be in the immediate offing indeed.

The screen above the litter of charts and manuals covering the desk was displaying the response *Abel 15*, that had come in minutes before to a query Alex had sent out earlier, denoted by the one-time code word *Cain*. Although his otherwise hard-set mouth conceded slight upturns at the corners, they were not due to any cryptic humor hidden in the message. He was thinking of Joe Koler, the person who had sent the response—known among the group who had scammed the election scammers and who still kept in touch as "Tapperware"—and the time Joe had taken a job with a cleaning company to get inside the offices of the software contractor retained by the then-incumbent administration and install a keystroke capturing device to obtain the passwords for getting through their encryption software. Joe was on the West Coast now, with one of the prime contractors responsible for maintenance of the Air Force's Ground-Based Strategic Launch System. His response to Alex's query meant that the missiles had been primed with their target codes fifteen minutes previously.

The return from Maeve Ingleman came in while Alex was still staring at the screen, wondering just how far this was likely to go. Maeve had devised the trapdoor code that made their tampering with the vote-tampering routine invisible to regular software checking procedures. These days she headed a section concerned with cryptological security in the Defense Department. Her input, responding to Alex's prompt, *Mutt*, was *Jeff-4*: "Arm Authorization code transmitted from the War Room four minutes ago."

One space remained unfilled in the format displayed on the screen, opposite the final query code that he had sent out: *Laurel*. That had been to his one-time drinking buddy and rock-climbing partner, Mike Welby, who could change the microcode to get a computer to do anything but make toast. Mike was now a team supervisor with the War Room Close System Support Office. A response from him would indicate that final Launch Enable had been issued. Alex bit his lip apprehensively. At the bottom of the screen, the sequence initiation command *Murphy* glowed red and primed. Time had run out to let the risk run any longer. The moment had come that would decide between years of work yielding dividends beyond calculation, or coming to nothing in an instant's premature panic. He took a long breath and steeled himself, yet was unable to suppress a tremor as he extended a hand. The last thought to flash through his mind before he pressed the key to activate the command was that maybe there wouldn't be any wedding day at all. The link changed from red to gray; at the same time, the confirmation *Issued and Acknowledged* appeared alongside.

Moments later, the empty space a few lines higher up filled suddenly to deliver the response *Hardy-2:30* from Mike.

Professor Orstein Orvington Orst, senior scientific advisor to the White House, was noted among other things for his theoretical studies developing the concept of the neutrino bomb. While providing an image and terminology capable of terrifying the public, the potential to absorb unlimited funding, and novel strategic implications that would keep planners occupied and pundits talking for years, it suffered from none of the drawbacks of threatening to kill anybody or damage property, thus making it in the eyes of many the ideal advanced weapons system. Orst had also authored the interesting theory that the decrease of entropy brought about by living things was due to local time reversals on a molecular scale, and shown statistically why statistics can never prove anything.

But things like entropy and statistics were far from his mind as he stood with Oskar Eissensatt, a computation director with one of the Pentagon's task groups, just outside the flurry of aides and officials surrounding the President in the underground War Room twenty-five miles in an undisclosed direction from the center of Washington D.C. Not that Orst had given any great amount of detailed thought to the likely effects on tomorrow of the events resolved upon today and about to be unleashed. But there was a distinct probability of the world's weather patterns being disrupted, which would invalidate the computer models that he had obtained generous funding to advise on, which would cause no end of demands for explanations and budget allocation reviews. It was all very inconvenient.

President Byrne emerged ahead of his coterie, effecting a swagger, still wearing the Patton-style revolvers. "That's right, we're going to do it!" he told the array of uniforms and suits. "Who do they think they're calling a cowboy? Those slopes have gone too far. It's time to stand tall and deliver the reckonin'. Where's muh hat?"

General Elmer Craig, Chairman of the Joint Chiefs of Staff, heavy with medals and braid, was close beside him. Orst had little time for Craig. If it hadn't been for military mentalities and their obsession with megatons and pyrotechnics, a viral or other biological solution could have been far more efficient, without all the messiness and disruption. Besides that, Craig was a mathematical Neanderthal, who had once instructed an adjutant to look up General Relativity in the staff lists. "Just let us at 'em, sir," Craig enthused to the President. "With the new ECMs and decoys, our birds will be hitting them before they even know anything's left the roost."

"God will reserve us a special place in Heaven for today," Elias Maude promised from Byrne's other side. "Smiting His enemies with death, vengeance, and destruction. Laying waste the land. Bringing tears, anguish, and grief. All as the Good Books say. Good Christian values."

"I know," the President replied. "He talked to me this morning." On the edge of the group, Eissensatt wrinkled his nose in response to Orst's frown. Orst had always harbored reservations about this kind of thing as a guide to shaping national policy. He didn't trust prophecies and assertions that couldn't be expressed in numbers. There was no better way of carrying an argument than showing it as the necessary outcome of manipulating symbols that nobody else could understand.

"Teamwork," Eissensatt murmured. Orst nodded sourly, causing wisps of thinning hair to wave about his birdlike head. They were always being reminded of the importance of keeping up a unified public image.

Byrne turned and drew himself up to a dramatic pose in the center of the floor, hands resting on the butts of the pistols, head high, chin thrust forward, legs apart and loosely bent. "Gentlemen, today we're about to become history. Nobody here knows better than all of you how I've busted my . . . that is, how hard I've tried in these days of trial and error to do an intelligent thing and act like a statesman. But we are left with no choice other than the course I have decided. An evil power thinks it can bring our great country to its knees by aggressive, unrestrained, military power. Well, we'll show the world that we can do it better."

"Damn right!" Craig agreed darkly.

"Hallelujah!" Maude intoned.

President Byrne paused a moment to let the ripple of approving nods and murmurs subside. "They brought this on themselves when they elected a tyrant who doesn't let them have democracy. Let it be a lesson to all the others who hate us for our tolerant and peaceful way of life. . . . General, issue the order to commence the attack."

Craig turned imperiously toward his second-in-command, General Filbert, one star down, who was waiting several paces back. "Order General Launch, Fire Plan A, Phase One."

Filbert relayed to the Fire Control Commander, seated at a supervisory desk in the center of a row of consoles on a raised dais at one end of the room. "Immediate, to all sector flight controllers. General Launch, Fire Plan A, Phase One."

Despite the President's stirring words of a few moments before, a solemn hush fell as the commander entered the codes into his console and validated the requests for confirmation, broken only by the voice of Burton Halle, the Vice President, muttering into a cell phone somewhere in the rear. " . . . and schedule a meeting for tomorrow morning to discuss assigning the reconstruction contracts." All eyes turned expectantly toward the large Situation Display dominating the room.

It presented the world in regular Mercator projection, with hostile territories shown in red, U.S. in blue, its assortment of allies, recruited through bribes, corruption, political manipulation, or threats of annihilation, in varying shades of beige through burnet brown, depending on the assigned level of dependability, and the remaining neutrals in gray. Principal targets were indicated by icons according to category, along with ground launch bases and the present positions of submarines, bombers, and orbiting attack satellites. The display's design was the work of Eissensatt's people. He looked toward Orst invitingly as a side panel added itself, providing a legend of icon identifiers and symbol descriptions.

"It needs more numbers," Orst murmured in answer to the unvoiced question.

"We've been upgrading it," Eissensatt told him. "Wait." Even as he spoke, new lines began appearing, superposed on the general display.

S2/5C, 8 x 2 Megatons, Coordinate cluster 6, ETT 22 min, 30 sec

Success prob'y 88%; $\alpha/\varphi = 2.76$; $\Delta\tau 0 = 27$; $(\theta A/\theta B - \gamma) = 0.25$; Status = Green 3

Orst nodded happily and was about to express approval, when the unrolling data froze suddenly, and the map behind dimmed. Eissensatt's expression just had time to change from a satisfied smile to a frown before the entire display blanked out, to be replaced by a blue background and the message:

THIS PROGRAM HAS PERFORMED AN ILLEGAL OPERATION AND WILL SHUT DOWN. ERROR ANALYSIS NOT AVAILABLE. PRESS ANY KEY TO CONTINUE.

President Byrne blinked and looked at General Craig. Craig mustered his most demanding glare and turned to General Filbert. Filbert spread his hands. "I don't know, sir. It's totally irregular. Nothing like this has ever . . ." He looked helplessly across toward the Fire Control Commander, who was already snarling instructions at a technician manning a monitor console below and in front of him. Eissensatt hurried across, followed by Orst.

"Forget that. Revert to direct manual override." The FCC's voice came from above. The technician hammered in a command string, which elicited on his screen the response:

PROGRAM NOT RESPONDING

and buttons for the options:

**END TASK   SHUT DOWN
TRY AGAIN**

Byrne and his entourage arrived as a medley of bemused expressions and angry scowls. "What in hell's going on?" the President demanded. The FCC could only shake his head as his gaze darted over the console displays, looking for clues. Nothing in the exercises and operation manuals had prepared anyone for this. Beside him, the Operations Supervisor was tapping in befuddlement at a keyboard beneath a screen reading:

Page Not Found. Try clicking Refresh or select one of the following options. . . .

"Get whoever's in charge of IT," Craig snapped. His neck and brow were turning purple. The FCC hesitated, not seeming sure who that would be.

"Try Sigmund Velorski at the Pentagon," Eissensatt suggested.

The FCC nodded to the Operations Supervisor. "Use Priority Channel Red." Above the War Room floor, the main Situation Display had reverted to showing wallpaper consisting of bouncing smiley faces. Somewhere in the background a phone started ringing. An Air Force officer picked it up and answered in muffled tones behind a raised hand.

The Operations Supervisor looked up with the uncomprehending expression of a human cannonball watching the net slide blithely by below. "It says, *Invalid Password. Request Denied.*"

Byrne jerked his head impatiently from side to side. "What is all this shit?"

"This is ridiculous!" General Craig blared. "Somebody get him on the phone. Put it on speaker. I'll talk to him myself."

General Filbert accepted a handset proffered by an aide and thumbed the number that was highlighted. A ringing tone sounded from the speaker, followed by, "*We're sorry, but the person you are calling is not available just now to take your call. If you would like to—*"

General Craig snatched the phone savagely and cut the connection. "What's their main number?" he yelled. Filbert obtained it from an aide.

"*If this is for a military operational matter, press One. For matters of national domestic security, press Two. For all other—*" Craig cut the call again and stood gaping at the room, evidently at a loss for how to continue.

Orst stepped forward, took the phone from Craig's unresisting fingers, and looked inquiringly at Byrne. "If I might suggest, Mr. President, I recall there was someone with the main systems integration contractor who seemed to have a good grasp of just about everything. Multimex—in Maryland, not far from here. A young man called Sullivan, I think it was."

Byrne nodded numbly. "Why not? Anyone who can make some kind of sense out of anything. It's not as if things could get any crazier."

Orst copied the phone to one of the console displays and got through to the company. The operator who answered said that Alex Sullivan's line was busy right now, but she would put the call through to that department. A bearded, bespectacled youth in a baggy sweater that gave him somewhat studentish look appeared on the screen and announced himself as the "Support Desk."

Was Orst calling to report trouble with a Multimex system? Orst confirmed that he was.

"Have you checked that the machine is plugged in?"

"What? . . . Well, yes, of course it is."

"Which operating system and version are you using?"

Orst was momentarily too disoriented to give a coherent answer. "Which . . . ? I really don't know. That isn't what I do. Look, I can assure you that the problem is nothing of that nature. My questions have to do with the applications that your company installed and integrated."

"Do you have a support contract? If not I may have to charge at a rate of sixty dollars an hour. Would that be okay?"

General Craig exploded. "*Gimme that goddam phone!* . . . You look here, Mister whatever your name is. See this uniform I'm wearing? Do you know what these medals mean? You are talking to the highest level of the United States government. The President himself is here with me, and this call concerns topmost matters of national security. Now if you don't know your own ass from a hole in the ground and can't help, then get somebody on the line who can. Is that clear enough? I mean now! Immediate! This moment!"

If the youth was impressed, it failed to show in the view coming through on the screen. He glanced away for a moment, then came back without missing a beat. "Oh, I think you were asking for Alex Sullivan," he said. "It looks as if he's free now. I'll put you through."

The new face that appeared was of a man perhaps in his early thirties. He had sandy colored hair, cut conventionally in a shaggy but neat and easy style, the suggestion of casualness enhanced by the three-day matching growth softening his features, which were lean and angular, framing a narrow nose and chin. His eyes were sharp, with creases at the corners hinting at a mirthful bent. The part of his upper body that was visible showed a dove gray jacket and navy shirt worn with a tie sporting a silver and blue abstract design.

Craig squared up to face the screen directly. "Are you the person in charge of whatever goes on there?"

"My name is Alex Sullivan. I'm the Technical Development Director."

"General Elmer Craig, Chairman of the Joint Chiefs of Staff of the United States Military."

"Yes, I recognize you from media pictures." The general's glare, which had never failed to command and intimidate, drew an affable smile that seemed to form naturally. "What can I do for you, General?"

"I take it you're aware that the government uses some highly complex and extremely sensitive computer systems that were put together by your company? Specifically, I'm talking about a system that goes by the code designation *Symphony*. It cost four billion dollars."

Sullivan nodded. "Yes, the strategic launch command sequencing and control network. In fact, I was responsible for coordinating a large part of it."

Consternation was breaking out among the presidential and Pentagon staff. General Filbert appealed to Craig. "Sir, this is an open line! We need to switch to a secure circuit."

Craig nodded. "Do it." As an operator intervened to make the adjustment, the general glanced back at the President, who was looking lost and trying to appear in charge at the same time. "Well, at least we seem to be onto the right guy."

The reconnection was made, and Sullivan reappeared. While Craig launched into a diatribe of woes and threats, Eissensatt moved closer to where Orst was standing. "You know what this is?" he said, keeping his voice low. Orst lifted his chin and eyebrows. "For years I have been telling everyone how stupid is was to use the Chinese for procurement. They tempted us with low prices because they knew we never see anything beyond a bottom line, and we walked right into it. We let them supply everything—hardware, maintenance, training. . . . Even many of the software contracts!"

"What are you getting at?" Orst was only half listening. He was wondering why simulations and testing hadn't picked up these faults long ago.

"*They built it all in!*" Eissensatt whispered. He gestured to indicate the screens, consoles, and electronics cubicles all around them. "Can't you see what is happening? The Chinese buried special functions in their chips, that they could activate remotely. It is they who are doing this. It's a Trojan horse!"

Orst registered what he was saying, finally, and stared at him incredulously. It was preposterous, of course. Yet it had to be! What else could explain why all the testing had detected nothing?

"But it gets far worse," Essensatt went on. "Don't you see?"

"What?" Orst found his voice but was still too much in shock to fully think the implication through.

"*They know!*" Eissensatt moaned. "Do you think they'd sneak something like that into our launch system without making it capable of reporting back to them?"

Orst gulped. "You mean they've got Spyware in there too?"

"Of course, Spyware! So it means they *know* we've attempted to launch. And what do you think that means? Do you think they'll just sit there?"

Engineers and programmers had crowded around a nearby console, and were taking turns to try various stratagems and offer advice. The one currently in the operator's chair sat back and threw up his hands. "I give up. It doesn't like anything I tell it. No version of anything is compatible with anything else."

Orst looked back bleakly to where the President and his group of senior officials had moved closer behind General Craig. Sullivan was speaking from the screen.

"It appears that the project manager quit and didn't update his documentation. It will probably take some time to figure out what the programmer was trying to do, I'm afraid."

Craig's color deepened. "*Didn't update the documents?* What kind of main contractor do you call yourselves? Four billion dollars! Don't you have anyone there who knows how to manage supervision?"

"Er, with respect, General, it appears to have been one of your own supervising officers assigned from the Pentagon."

"Hmph."

General Filbert interceded to rescue the situation. "I think I know who he means. I might be able to trace him and get a cell phone number." Craig nodded mutely in a way that said they might as well try exorcism if there was a chance it might do any good.

President Byrne stood in the middle of it all, looking dazed. "I don't believe this," he mumbled to Vice President Halle. "The mightiest war machine that the world has ever seen. And we can't do a thing with it because of a bunch of . . ." he broke off, seeing that Orst was trying to get his attention. "What?"

"Mr. President, there is a further ramification that doesn't seem to have been considered," Orst said gravely. "Since it's not functioning, it can no longer be considered the mightiest anything. So how long do we have before the sky turns black with incoming enemy hardware?"

The color drained from Burton's face, while the others around who were within earshot froze. "*Holy shit,*" somebody whispered.

Burton almost choked. "My God! We're wide open. There's nothing to stop them!"

"Exactly," Orst agreed.

And now they would probably never find out if the neutrino bomb would have been feasible. It was all very upsetting.

The Chinese underground War Room, twenty-five miles in an undisclosed direction from Beijing, was a disaster area of crashed computers and stalled programs when Tsien-Tsu was led in after being rushed across from the adjacent Defense Ministry building and given special emergency clearance to be admitted. The senior of the two officers who had been sent to fetch her—polite enough, but oddly robotic in the way the military conditioning tends to instill—indicated for her to wait, then moved to stand respectfully behind a gray-haired, heavy-set man in a dark suit, whom Tsien knew from her work to be Xen Lu Jiang, principal scientific advisor to the National Security Cabinet.

"So why isn't the sky already black with incoming American warheads?" Xen was saying, vainly trying to gain the attention of a stern, heavy-joweled figure in a field marshal's uniform, who had to be the Chief of Staff, Yao Ziaping. Technicians scurried among the cabinets and consoles, while on every side engineers and supervisors babbled into handsets, with more phones ringing and lights flashing incessantly. Above it all, the huge mural panel that was supposed to have presented a blow-by-blow portrayal of the end of America was displaying a series of pop-up ads for magazine subscriptions, adult web sites, and software products that nobody, apparently, had found a way to stop.

"What do you mean, the Submarine Launch Designator isn't a recognized system device?" Ziaping screamed at a man in a blue tunic, cringing behind a desk on which stood a name plate bearing the words *Command Director*.

The Director showed his hands helplessly. "That's what it's saying."

"Restart the command executive," an engineer in white shirt-sleeves said from where he was standing behind a console operator wading through what looked like a labyrinth of *Disk Copying Error* and *File Not Found* error messages.

"We've already tried. It says the User Name is invalid."

"*This is insane!*" Ziaping wheeled upon a general behind him, wearing a lapel badge with the name Piao, who was watching anxiously over the shoulder of another operator. "Haven't you managed to raise that Head Designer yet?"

"We're still trying, sir," Piao replied. "But we keep getting connected to some kind of help desk in India."

Hao-Li Neng, the Chinese Premier, was standing amid a gaggle of military staff officers and civilian high officials, looking bewildered. Even though she had been expecting it, Tsien found herself mildly awed to find herself in such a presence. The doctor of philosophy who had made such an impression on her at university in his discourses on reason and imperviousness of reality to human passions, and the political science professor who had held off-campus debates at his home in which students debated things like a social order based on individual freedom and merit, would probably have scoffed at such acquiescence to tradition. But reactions cultivated through years of cultural exposure and social pressures couldn't be forgotten entirely. Tsien enjoyed meeting visitors from the West. Life there sounded interestingly different in many ways—challenging and stimulating in some; uncertain and insecure in others. She hoped to live there one day. The experience would be an invaluable complement to the form of upbringing she had known. The result would surely be to shape a more complete and fully aware, all-round person.

A woman in Air Force uniform, who had been following events at an adjacent console, looked up at Piao. "We have something coming up here via the backup system, General," she said. Piao moved over to join her, with Ziaping stumping testily behind. By edging a little closer, Tsien was able to get a glimpse of the text appearing on the screen. It read:

Dear Friend,

My name is Ido Mayanga, and I am Financial Operations Controller of the First National Bank of Nigeria. You have been referred to me as a trustworthy person who might be able to help in a most important matter. I urgently need to move $10,000,000 (TEN MILLION US DOLLARS) currently

held in a private account that is threatened with confisca-
tion by unscrupulous and illegal agencies ...

Premier Neng had also come forward to see. He took in the
first couple of lines, stared nonplused for several seconds, and
looked around for an explanation. Xen Lu Jiang, the scientific
advisor, seized his opportunity to address the Chief of Staff. "Field
Marshal Ziaping, the systems coordinator who was recommended
from the Strategic Technical Directorate is here as commanded:
Specialist Tsien-Tsu."

Ziaping turned to look her up and down. His expression didn't
conceal a trace of disdain. She lowered her eyes and inclined her
head demurely as protocol required. "We've been trying to contact
the head of the design group," Ziaping informed her. "But either
his phone is not working, or he's not answering. I'm told you
know something about the system here."

"I was involved in formulating the original conceptual approach,
and contributed to producing some of the implementation and
proving software," she replied.

Ziaping made a contemptuous gesture, indicating the chaos
around them. "Nothing works. It hasn't managed to get a single
thing off the ground. Nobody can make sense of anything. What
do you have to say?"

Tsien looked up but stopped short of meeting his gaze confron-
tationally. "Honorable sir, some of us tried from the beginning to
advise against the adoption of technical procedures modeled on
decadent Western methods. Their concern is always for immediate
returns and considerations only, with no provision for the longer
term. My surmise would be that the inevitable consequences of
such practices are now manifesting themselves."

Ziaping glowered from side to side with a look that would have
stopped an attacking lion dog. "Did you all hear that? They gave
good advice. Who overrode them?"

Heads turned toward one another uncertainly. Nobody was
going to volunteer this one. Xen Lu Jiang looked inquiringly at a
woman in a gray business suit who seemed to be a secretary or
assistant. "I, er ... think it might have been Director Wou-Pang
Lee," she offered hesitantly. Ziaping jerked his head around to
confront General Piao. "If you remember, sir, he was removed
to Mongolia some time ago," Piao responded.

Premier Neng raised his hands protectively, evidently having heard enough. "This isn't the time to be thinking about recrimi- nations," he declared. "We have more pressing concerns to attend to. Wouldn't you agree?"

"Of course, Excellency," Xen Lu Jiang acknowledged. Ziaping conceded with a dip of his head. Only Tsien continued holding the Premier's eye. The appeal written across her face conveyed an urgent desire to say something.

"Yes, what is it?" Neng asked her. "You may speak."

"Your Excellency, the honorable member of the Security Cabi- net was saying it when I arrived," she replied, glancing at Xen Lu Jiang. "We have been powerless for almost an hour, yet there has been no move by the other side to exploit the situation. Why isn't the sky black with incoming American warheads?"

Chinese strategic planning took little stock of trying to keep a General Launch order secret, since such an event would hardly be something that could be concealed. Even if the American warning system of satellites and radars failed by some miracle to detect the physical evidence, the whole business was so ridden with spies, bugs, communications taps, and informers, and so many people would be involved, that the news would probably have found its way to Washington before the first missile entered U.S. air space. Yet they hadn't retaliated. Such had been the panic around the War Room that it seemed only Tsien and the scientific adviser had seen it.

"They must know that we are defenseless," Xen-Lu Jiang said, making the point.

Ziaping shook his head. The mental momentum that he had accumulated was too much for any abrupt change of direction. "They know they have us cold, yet they do nothing? They have the chance to take out a billion people? Why wouldn't anyone in their right mind go for it?" Baffled looks went this way and that around the War Room. Premier Neng looked from one to another of the faces. None of the generals or ministers of state had a suggestion to offer.

Tsien cast her eyes around and bit her lip hesitantly. When the silence persisted for several more seconds, she said, "Maybe they are trying to tell us something."

Xen Lu Jiang looked shocked and opened his mouth to speak, but Premier Neng stayed him with a wave of his hand. "Hear the young lady." He looked at Tsien curiously. "Trying to tell us what?"

Tsien took a deep breath. "The situation reminds me of a philosophical problem that I was once required to study," she replied. "It demonstrates how seeming antagonists can both prosper more from cooperating instead of seeking to destroy each other."

Neng's eyebrows arched upward in surprise. He looked around his retinue of officers and advisers again, but they seemed equally puzzled. "What an extraordinary notion!" His gaze came back to Tsien, betraying a hint of amusement. "Do tell us more," he invited.

There could be no going back or extricating herself now. Tsien swallowed and nodded timorously. "If it pleases your Excellency, the problem is one known among logicians and students of human behavior as the Prisoner's Dilemma. As originally formulated, it describes two suspected accomplices in a crime who are arrested and questioned separately. Each is given the following offer, and is made aware that the other has been told the same. He can betray the other by confessing in return for a reduced sentence. But if both confess, each confession is less valuable and the sentences will be harsher. However, if they cooperate with each other by refusing to confess, the prosecutor will only be able to convict them on a minor charge." She paused to let everyone think about it. Ziaping had a look on his face that seemed to be asking, *What does this have to do with anything*? The expressions on the others ranged from blank to violent contortions of intense mental struggle. Tsien explained, "If there is no trust between them, it is to both their immediate advantage to confess and betray the other first. However, they would both fare better if they did trust each other and were resolute in refusing to confess. . . . But it requires equal nerve and reasoning ability in both of them to arrive at that conclusion."

Neng's brow furrowed. "Do you really believe the Americans would expect anyone to read it that way?"

"I cannot say," Tsien answered. "But the notion of Chinese wisdom does have a strange mystique in the West. . . ." She took a moment to choose her words in a way that would avoid sounding disrespectful, while at the same time remaining pointed. "Perhaps, by some quirk of fate, an opportunity has presented itself for our esteemed and honorable leadership to extricate the country from the predicament that it is at this moment facing." Which was as near as she dared come to saying that the West could wipe them out as soon as it got tired of waiting for them to catch on.

Ziaping's suddenly stunned look, and the deflation of his posture, said that this time even he had gotten the message. An expression of slowly intensifying horror was creeping across General Piao's face as the full meaning of the predicament that Tsien was talking about seeped in. Somebody to the side began gibbering incoherently, while others in the room looked apprehensively up at the roof as if expecting it to vaporize at any instant.

"Perhaps our decision to assume the offensive was a little hasty, after all," Xen Lu Jiang said, licking his lips dryly and directing the words at Neng. His face creased into a toothy grimace that seemed to be the closest it could manage to a smile.

Tsien amplified the point. "This administration could go down in history as one led by the greatest philosophers and statesmen that China has ever produced," she said. "Architects of a new world dedicated to peace and prosperity."

All of a sudden the prospect seemed to have more appeal to Neng than having gone down or up, as the case may be, as a great war leader. "Dare we compromise and risk being seen as backing down now?" he asked, looking at Xen-Lu Jiang.

"Dare we?" the scientific advisor echoed. "The girl is right, Excellency. What other choice do we have? Go for it."

Neng looked across at the Communications Director, manning a console beneath the main wall display. "Open the Hot Line to Washington," he instructed.

From the privacy of his office on the penthouse floor in the headquarters of Multimex Systems and Integration Inc. in Maryland, Alex Sullivan sat before the screen still connected to the War Room. A very different mood had taken hold there. Nobody was talking about facing down black-hats or standing tall anymore. President Byrne stood in the middle of the floor among the rows of consoles and panels, wearing the sick look of a boxer who had just learned that the champ who was supposed to throw the fight was reneging on the deal. The figures around him had expressions that varied from stupor through consternation to the kind of disbelieving, frozen look that accompanies an unexpected wet fart.

Elias Maude, the former evangelical Defense Secretary, was the first to recover. He looked down to brush an imaginary wrinkle from his suit, then turned his head and eyed Byrne uncertainly. "It, er, occurs to me that perhaps aggression isn't in keeping with the kind of Christian tradition that we should be upholding," he said. "Our duty is to be compassionate and tolerant, and spread the Word." To one side, Professor Orst, the scientific adviser, emitted a visible sigh of relief.

Vice President Halle picked up the theme. "It would be good for corporate America, too, Mr. President. There's no need to send the other guy down. We've always welcomed and thrived on honest, healthy competition."

"For the good of the American people," Oskar Eissensatt of the Pentagon endorsed, from where he was standing next to Orst.

A light of sudden hope had come into Byrne's eyes. He swung his head around questioningly toward Craig. The General nodded emphatically.

"I've always said that the Chinese threat was exaggerated. This kind of overkill isn't necessary. And it violates the principles of honor, magnanimity, and fair play that have always constituted the hallmark of the United States military."

Byrne shifted his gaze jerkily from one to another. "The President should be a Lawman and a Peacekeeper. That's what you're telling me, right?"

"Blessed are the peacemakers," Maude intoned.

"Our policy has always been Rule of Law," The VP agreed.

"Deterrence is the purpose of strength," General Craig affirmed.

Byrne drew himself up into a posture of a man feeling back in control. "Open the Hot Line to Beijing. Get me the Premier, what's his name? . . ."

"Neng," an aide muttered.

"Neng."

The atmosphere of a new lease on life spread across the War Room like air freshener. Everywhere, figures were mopping brows and exchanging relieved looks, while the controller at the communications desk turned to his panel and began entering commands. Then, as Byrne began moving toward him in anticipation, he sat back in his seat suddenly with a surprised look.

"What is it?" Byrne asked.

The controller gestured at the screen. "There's already a call coming in the other way, from them."

General Filbert moved into the viewing angle of the screen, stopped suddenly, and turned to stare at the camera. "An unauthorized person is still connected through on that channel," he said to someone off screen. "Kill it." Moments later, the screen in Alex Sullivan's office blanked out.

Alex smiled to himself, leaned back in his chair, and stretched long and luxuriously while the accumulated effects of the last half hour dissipated. He hadn't realized how much the tension had affected him. His limbs felt as if they had been released from lead weights. He picked up the untouched cup of coffee that he had set down when he came in, and tried a sip. It had gone cold and insipid, but the taste triggered an urgent need for caffeine. He half rose to get a refill from the pot in the outer office, but on second thoughts lowered himself back into the chair and leaned forward to the keyboard. There was one more thing to do first. . . .

Back at her section in the Defense Ministry building, Tsien Tsu checked for any urgent messages that might have come in while she was away, then took a moment relax and compose herself. As the strain that she had been under gradually abated, her breathing eased, and the pattering in her chest returned to normal. She opened her eyes, and a tired but happy smile came over her face. Incredibly, it had worked!

She pulled the keyboard closer and entered the code to unlock and reactivate the screen that she had been using when the two officers arrived to take her to the War Room. She'd just had time to confirm command initiation on receipt of the incoming code *Murphy* before hastily hiding it and having to leave. *Murphy* was still there, glowing in red at the bottom of the displayed exchanges.

Two years ago, when she and her friends met the visiting Americans at the cultural exchange weekend organized for young computer people, she wouldn't have believed it possible. But the kids had all agreed that the business of international affairs was getting too serious to be entrusted to the likes of politicians and generals. And what had started out as a crazy joke by the lean, laughing-eyed American with fair hair at the party they all ended up at on the Saturday night, had, piece by piece, transformed itself into a reality. . . . Except that now she knew him better, Tsien was not so sure it had been a joke at all. He had a strange charisma that inspired and motivated people.

As she watched absently, absorbed in her thoughts, the icon that indicated another incoming request started flashing. Tsien touched a key to accept, and a new line appeared, accompanied by the same originating identifier as the one attached to *Murphy*. It read:

Operation **Defuse** *completed 100 percent. Nice work, guys.*

Tsien Tsu clapped her hands softly in silent elation. She had to admit there had been moments when she'd found herself wondering, but there were no doubts now. Their wedding would take place after all. And she would have her chance to live in the inscrutable West, and look forward to getting to know him even more over the years. The older generation, with all its talk of wisdom and experience, had had its chance to build and shape a livable world—and look what the result had been! It was up to the young people, now, to take charge of the one that would be theirs.

Laws of Survival

Nancy Kress

My name is Jill. I am somewhere you can't imagine, going somewhere even more unimaginable. If you think I like what I did to
get here, you're crazy.

Actually, I'm the one who's crazy. You—any "you"—will never
read this. But I have paper now, and a sort of pencil, and time.
Lots and lots of time. So I will write what happened, all of it,
as carefully as I can.

After all—why the hell not?

I went out very early one morning to look for food. Before
dawn was safest for a woman alone. The boy-gangs had gone to
bed, tired of attacking each other. The trucks from the city hadn't
arrived yet. That meant the garbage was pretty picked over, but
it also meant most of the refugee camp wasn't out scavenging.
Most days I could find enough: a carrot stolen from somebody's
garden patch, my arm bloody from reaching through the barbed
wire. Overlooked potato peelings under a pile of rags and glass. A
can of stew thrown away by one of the soldiers on the base, but
still half full. Soldiers on duty by the Dome were often careless.
They got bored, with nothing to do.

That morning was cool but fair, with a pearly haze that the sun would burn off later. I wore all my clothing, for warmth, and my boots. Yesterday's garbage load, I'd heard somebody say, was huge, so I had hopes. I hiked to my favorite spot, where garbage spills almost to the Dome wall. Maybe I'd find bread, or even fruit that wasn't too rotten.

Instead I found the puppy.

Its eyes weren't open yet and it squirmed along the bare ground, a scrawny brown-and-white mass with a tiny fluffy tail. Nearby was a fluid-soaked towel. Some sentimental fool had left the puppy there, hoping . . . what? It didn't matter. Scrawny or not, there was some meat on the thing. I scooped it up.

The sun pushed above the horizon, flooding the haze with golden light.

I hate it when grief seizes me. I hate it and it's dangerous, a violation of one of Jill's Laws of Survival. I can go for weeks, months without thinking of my life before the War. Without remembering or feeling. Then something will strike me—a flower growing in the dump, a burst of birdsong, the stars on a clear night—and grief will hit me like the maglevs that no longer exist, a grief all the sharper because it contains the memory of joy. I can't afford joy, which always comes with an astronomical price tag. I can't even afford the grief that comes from the memory of living things, which is why it is only the flower, the birdsong, the morning sunlight that starts it. My grief was not for that puppy. I still intended to eat it.

But I heard a noise behind me and turned. The Dome wall was opening.

Who knew why the aliens put their Domes by garbage dumps, by waste pits, by radioactive cities? Who knew why aliens did anything?

There was a widespread belief in the camp that the aliens started the War. I'm old enough to know better. That was us, just like the global warming and the bio-crobes were us. The aliens didn't even show up until the War was over and Raleigh was the northernmost city left on the East Coast and refugees poured south like mudslides. Including me. That's when the ships landed and then turned into the huge gray Domes like upended bowls. I heard there were many Domes, some in other countries. The

Army, what was left of it, threw tanks and bombs at ours. When they gave up, the refugees threw bullets and Molotov cocktails and prayers and graffiti and candle-light vigils and rain dances. Everything slid off and the Domes just sat there. And sat. And sat. Three years later, they were still sitting, silent and closed, although of course there were rumors to the contrary. There are always rumors. Personally, I'd never gotten over a slight disbelief that the Dome was there at all. Who would want to visit us?

The opening was small, no larger than a porthole, and about six feet above the ground. All I could see inside was a fog the same color as the Dome. Something came out, gliding quickly toward me. It took me a moment to realize it was a robot, a blue metal sphere above a hanging basket. It stopped a foot from my face and said, "This food for this dog."

I could have run, or screamed, or at the least—the very least—looked around for a witness. I didn't. The basket held a pile of fresh produce, green lettuce and deep purple eggplant and apples so shiny red they looked lacquered. And *peaches* . . . My mouth filled with sweet water. I couldn't move.

The puppy whimpered.

My mother used to make fresh peach pie.

I scooped the food into my scavenger bag, laid the puppy in the basket, and backed away. The robot floated back into the Dome, which closed immediately. I sped back to my corrugated-tin and windowless hut and ate until I couldn't hold any more. I slept, woke, and ate the rest, crouching in the dark so nobody else would see. All that fruit and vegetables gave me the runs, but it was worth it.

Peaches.

Two weeks later, I brought another puppy to the Dome, the only survivor of a litter deep in the dump. I never knew what happened to the mother. I had to wait a long time outside the Dome before the blue sphere took the puppy in exchange for produce. Apparently the Dome would only open when there was no one else around to see. What were they afraid of? It's not like PETA was going to show up.

The next day I traded three of the peaches to an old man in exchange for a small, mangy poodle. We didn't look each other in the eye, but I nonetheless knew that his held tears. He limped hurriedly away. I kept the dog, which clearly wanted nothing to do with me, in my shack until very early morning and then took it to the Dome. It tried to escape but I'd tied a bit of rope onto its frayed collar. We sat outside the Dome in mutual dislike, waiting, as the sky paled slightly in the east. Gunshots sounded in the distance.

I have never owned a dog.

When the Dome finally opened, I gripped the dog's rope and spoke to the robot. "Not fruit. Not vegetables. I want eggs and bread."

The robot floated back inside.

Instantly I cursed myself. Eggs? Bread? I was crazy not to take what I could get. That was Law of Survival #1. Now there would be nothing. Eggs, bread . . . *crazy*. I glared at the dog and kicked it. It yelped, looked indignant, and tried to bite my boot.

The Dome opened again and the robot glided toward me. In the gloom I couldn't see what was in the basket. In fact, I couldn't see the basket. It wasn't there. Mechanical tentacles shot out from the sphere and seized both me and the poodle. I cried out and the tentacles squeezed harder. Then I was flying through the air, the stupid dog suddenly howling beneath me, and we were carried through the Dome wall and inside.

Then nothing.

A nightmare room made of nightmare sound: barking, yelping, whimpering, snapping. I jerked awake, sat up, and discovered myself on a floating platform above a mass of dogs. Big dogs, small dogs, old dogs, puppies, sick dogs, dogs that looked all too healthy, flashing their forty-two teeth at me—why did I remember that number? From where? The largest and strongest dogs couldn't quite reach me with their snaps, but they were trying.

"You are operative," the blue metal sphere said, floating beside me. "Now we must begin. Here."

Its basket held eggs and bread.

"Get them away!"

Obediently it floated off.

"Not the food! The dogs!"

"What to do with these dogs?"

"Put them in cages!" A large black animal—German shepherd or Boxer or something—had nearly closed its jaws on my ankle. The next bite might do it.

"Cages," the metal sphere said in its uninflected mechanical voice. "Yes."

"Son of a bitch!" The shepherd leaping high, had gazed my thigh; its spittle slimed my pants. "Raise the goddamn platform!"

"Yes."

The platform floated so high, so that I had to duck my head to avoid hitting the ceiling. I peered over the edge and . . . no, that wasn't possible. But it was happening. The floor was growing upright sticks, and the sticks were growing cross bars, and the crossbars were extending themselves into mesh tops . . . Within minutes, each dog was encased in a cage just large enough to hold its protesting body.

"What to do now?" the metal sphere asked.

I stared at it. I was, as far as I knew, the first human being to ever enter an alien Dome, I was trapped in a small room with feral caged dogs and a robot . . . *what to do now*?

"Why . . . why am I here?" I hated myself for the brief stammer and vowed it would not happen again. Law of Survival #2: Show no fear.

Would a metal sphere even recognize fear?

It said, "These dogs do not behave correctly."

"Not behave correctly?"

"No."

I looked down again at the slavering and snarling mass of dogs; how strong was that mesh on the cage tops? "What do you want them to do?"

"You want to see the presentation?"

"Not yet." Law #3: Never volunteer for anything.

"What to do now?"

How the hell should I know? But the smell of the bread reached me and my stomach flopped. "Now to eat," I said. "Give me the things in your basket."

It did, and I tore into the bread like a wolf into deer. The real wolves below me increased their howling. When I'd eaten an entire loaf, I looked back at the metal sphere. "Have those dogs eaten?"

"Yes."

"What did you give them?"

"Garbage."

"*Garbage*? Why?"

"In hell they eat garbage."

So even the robot thought this was Hell. Panic surged through me; I pushed it back. Surviving this would depend on staying steady. "Show me what you fed the dogs."

"Yes." A section of wall melted and garbage cascaded into the room, flowing greasily between the cages. I recognized it: It was exactly like the garbage I picked through every day, trucked out from a city I could no longer imagine and from the Army base I could not approach without being shot. Bloody rags, tin cans from before the War, shit, plastic bags, dead flowers, dead animals, dead electronics, cardboard, eggshells, paper, hair, bone, scraps of decaying food, glass shards, potato peelings, foam rubber, roaches, sneakers with holes, sagging furniture, corn cobs. The smell hit my stomach, newly distended with bread.

"You fed the dogs *that*?"

"Yes. They eat it in hell."

Outside. Hell was outside, and of course that's what the feral dogs ate, that's all there was. But the metal sphere had produced fruit and lettuce and bread for me.

"You must give them better food. They eat that in . . . in hell because they can't get anything else."

"What to do now?"

It finally dawned on me—slow, I was too slow for this, only the quick survive—that the metal sphere had limited initiative along with its limited vocabulary. But it had made cages, made bread, made fruit—hadn't it? Or was this stuff grown in some imaginable secret garden inside the Dome? "You must give the dogs meat."

"Flesh?"

"Yes."

"No."

No change in that mechanical voice, but the "no" was definite and quick. Law of Survival #4: Notice everything. So—no flesh-eating allowed here. Also no time to ask why not; I had to keep issuing orders so that the robot didn't start issuing them. "Give them bread mixed with . . . with soy protein."

"Yes."

"And take away the garbage."

"Yes."

The garbage began to dissolve. I saw nothing poured on it,

nothing rise from the floor. But all that stinking mass fell into powder and vanished. Nothing replaced it.

I said, "Are you getting bread mixed with soy powder?" *Getting* seemed the safest verb I could think of.

"Yes."

The stuff came then, tumbling through the same melted hole in the wall, loaves of bread with, presumably, soy powder in them. The dogs, barking insanely, reached paws and snouts and tongues through the bars of their cages. They couldn't get at the food.

"Metal sphere—do you have a name?"

No answer.

"Okay. Blue, how strong are those cages? Can the dogs break them? Any of the dogs?"

"No."

"Lower the platform to the floor."

My safe perch floated down. The aisles between the cages were irregular, some wide and some so narrow the dogs could reach through to touch each other, since each cage had "grown" wherever the dog was at the time. Gingerly I picked my way to a clearing and sat down. Tearing a loaf of bread into chunks, I pushed the pieces through the bars of the least dangerous-looking dogs, which made the bruisers howl even more. For them, I put chunks at a distance they could just reach with a paw through the front bars of their prisons.

The puppy I had first brought to the Dome lay in a tiny cage. Dead.

The second one was alive but just barely.

The old man's mangy poodle looked more mangy than ever, but otherwise alert. It tried to bite me when I fed it.

"What to do now?"

"They need water."

"Yes."

Water flowed through the wall. When it had reached an inch or so, it stopped. The dogs lapped whatever came into their cages. I stood with wet feet—a hole in my boot after all, I hadn't known—and a stomach roiling from the stench of the dogs, which only worsened as they got wet. The dead puppy smelled especially horrible. I climbed back onto my platform.

"What to do now?"

"You tell me," I said.

"These dogs do not behave correctly."

"Not behave correctly?"

"No."

"What do you want them to do?"

"Do you want to see the presentation?"

We had been here before. On second thought, a "presentation" sounded more like acquiring information ("Notice everything") than like undertaking action ("Never volunteer"). So I sat cross-legged on the platform, which was easier on my uncushioned bones, breathed through my mouth instead of my nose, and said "Why the hell not?"

Blue repeated, "Do you want to see the presentation?"

"Yes." A one-syllable answer.

I didn't know what to expected. Aliens, spaceships, war, strange places barely comprehensible to humans. What I got was scenes from the dump.

A beam of light shot out from Blue and resolved into a three-dimensional holo, not too different from one I'd seen in a science museum on a school field trip once (*no. push memory away*), only this was far sharper and detailed. A ragged and unsmiling toddler, one of thousands, staggered toward a cesspool. A big dog with patchy coat dashed up, seized the kid's dress, and pulled her back just before she fell into the waste.

A medium-sized brown dog in a guide-dog harness led around someone tapping a white-headed cane.

An Army dog, this one sleek and well-fed, sniffed at a pile of garbage, found something, pointed stiffly at attention.

A group of teenagers tortured a puppy. It writhed in pain, but in a long lingering close-up, tried to lick the torturer' hand,

A thin, small dog dodged rocks, dashed inside a corrugated tin hut, and laid a piece of carrion beside an old lady lying on the ground

The holo went on and on like that, but the strange thing was that the people were barely seen. The toddler's bare and filthy feet and chubby knees, the old lady's withered cheek, a flash of a camouflage uniform above a brown boot, the hands of the torturers. Never a whole person, never a focus on people. Just on the dogs.

The "presentation" ended.

"These dogs do not behave correctly," Blue said.

"These dogs? In the presentation?"

"These dogs here do not behave correctly."

"These dogs *here*." I pointed to the wet, stinking dogs in their cages. Some, fed now, had quieted. Others still snarled and barked, trying their hellish best to get out and kill me.

"These dogs here. Yes. What to do now?"

"You want these dogs to behave like the dogs in the presentation."

"These dogs here must behave correctly. Yes."

"You want them to . . . do what? Rescue people? Sniff out ammunition dumps? Guide the blind and feed the hungry and love their torturers?"

Blue said nothing. Again I had the impression I had exceeded its thought processes, or its vocabulary, or its something. A strange feeling gathered in my gut.

"Blue, you yourself didn't build this Dome, or the starship that it was before, did you? You're just a . . . a computer."

Nothing.

"Blue, who tells you what to do?"

"What to do now? These dogs do not behave correctly."

"Who wants these dogs to behave correctly?" I said, and found I was holding my breath.

"The masters."

The masters. I knew all about them. Masters were the people who started wars, ran the corporations that ruined the Earth, manufactured the bioweapons that killed billions, and now holed up in the cities to send their garbage out to us in the refugee camps. Masters were something else I didn't think about, but not because grief would take me. Rage would.

Law of Survival #5: Feel nothing that doesn't aid survival.

"Are the masters here? In this . . . inside here?"

"No."

"Who is here inside?"

"These dogs here are inside."

Clearly. "The masters want these dogs here to behave like the dogs in the presentation."

"Yes."

"The masters want these dogs here to provide them with loyalty and protection and service."

No response.

"The masters aren't interested in human beings, are they? That's why they haven't communicated at all with any government."

Nothing. But I didn't need a response; the masters' thinking was already clear to me. Humans were unimportant—maybe because we had, after all, destroyed each other and our own world. We weren't worth contact. But dogs: companion animals capable of selfless service and great unconditional love, even in the face of abuse. For all I knew, dogs were unique in the universe. For all I know.

Blue said, "What to do now?"

I stared at the mangy, reeking, howling mass of animals. Some feral, some tamed once, some sick, at least one dead. I chose my words to be as simple as possible, relying on phrases Blue knew. "The masters want these dogs here to behave correctly."

"Yes."

"The masters want *me* to make these dogs behave correctly."

"Yes."

"The masters will make me food, and keep me inside, for to make these dogs behave correctly."

Long pause; my sentence had a lot of grammatical elements. But finally Blue said, "Yes."

"If these dogs do not behave correctly, the masters—what to do then?"

Another long pause. "Find another human."

"And *this* human here?"

"Kill it."

I gripped the edges of my floating platform hard. My hands still trembled. "Put me outside now."

"No."

"I must stay inside."

"These dogs do not behave correctly."

"I must make these dogs behave correctly."

"Yes."

"And the masters want these dogs to display . . ." I had stopped talking to Blue. I was talking to myself, to steady myself, but even that I couldn't manage. The words caromed around in my mind—loyalty, service, protection—but none came out of my mouth. I couldn't do this. I was going to die. The aliens had come from God-knew-where to treat the dying Earth like a giant pet store, intrigued only by a canine domestication that had happened ten thousand years ago and by nothing else on the planet, nothing else humanity had or might accomplish. Only dogs. *The masters want these dogs to display—*

Blue surprised me with a new word. "Love," it said.

✧   ✧   ✧

Law #4: Notice everything. I needed to learn all I could, starting with Blue. He'd made garbage appear, and food and water and cages. What else could he do?

"Blue, make the water go away." And it did, just sank into the floor, which dried instantly. I was fucking Moses, commanding the Red Sea. I climbed off the platform, inched among the dog cages, and studied them individually.

"You called the refugee camp and the dump 'hell.' Where did you get that word?"

Nothing.

"Who said 'hell'?"

"Humans."

Blue had cameras outside the Dome. Of course he did; he'd seen me find that first puppy in the garbage. Maybe Blue had been waiting for someone like me, alone and non-threatening, to come close with a dog. But it had watched before that, and it had learned the word "hell," and maybe it had recorded the incidents in the "presentation." I filed this information for future use.

"This dog is dead." The first puppy, decaying into stinking pulp. "It is killed. Non-operative."

"What to do now?"

"Make the dead dog go away."

A long pause: thinking it over? Accessing data banks? Communicating with aliens? And what kind of moron couldn't figure out by itself that a dead dog was never going to behave correctly? So much for artificial intelligence.

"Yes," Blue finally said, and the little corpse dissolved as if it had never been.

I found one more dead dog and one close to death. Blue disappeared the first, said no to the second. Apparently we had to just let it suffer until it died. I wondered how much the idea of "death" even meant to a robot. There were twenty-three live dogs, of which I had delivered only three to the Dome.

"Blue—did another human, before you brought me here, try to train the dogs?"

"These dogs do not behave correctly."

"Yes. But did a human *not me* be inside? To make these dogs behave correctly?"

"Yes."

"What happened to him or her?"

No response.

"What to do now with the other human?"

"Kill it."

I put a hand against the wall and leaned on it. The wall felt smooth and slick, with a faint and unpleasant tingle. I removed my hand.

All computers could count. "How many humans did you kill?"

"Two."

Three's the charm. But there were no charms. No spells, no magic wards, no cavalry coming over the hill to ride to the rescue; I'd known that ever since the War. There was just survival. And, now, dogs.

I chose the mangy little poodle. It hadn't bit me when the old man had surrendered it, or when I'd kept it overnight. That was at least a start. "Blue, make this dog's cage go away. But *only* this one cage!"

The cage dissolved. The poodle stared at me distrustfully. Was I supposed to stare back, or would that get us into some kind of canine pissing contest? The thing was small but it had teeth.

I had a sudden idea. "Blue, show me how this dog does not behave correctly." If I could see what it wasn't doing, that would at least be a start.

Blue floated to within a foot of the dog's face. The dog growled and backed away. Blue floated away and the dog quieted but it still stood in what would be a menacing stance if it weighed more than nine or ten pounds: ears raised, legs braced, neck hair bristling. Blue said, "Come." The dog did nothing. Blue repeated the entire sequence and so did Mangy.

I said, "You want the dog to follow you. Like the dogs in the presentation."

"Yes."

"You want the dog to come when you say 'Come,'"

"Love," Blue said.

"What is 'love,' Blue?"

No response.

The robot didn't know. Its masters must have had some concept of "love," but fuck-all knew what it was. And I wasn't sure I knew any more, either. That left Mangy, who would never "love" Blue or follow him or lick his hand because dogs operated on smell—even I knew that about them—and Blue, a machine, didn't smell like either a person or another dog. Couldn't the aliens who sent him here figure that out? Were they watching this whole farce, or had they just dropped a half-sentient computer under an upturned bowl on Earth and told it, "Bring us some loving dogs"? Who knew how aliens thought?

I didn't even know how dogs thought. There were much better people for this job—professional trainers, or that guy on TV who made tigers jump through burning hoops. But they weren't here, and I was. I squatted on my haunches a respectful distance from Mangy and said, "Come."

It growled at me.

"Blue, raise the platform this high." I held my hand at shoulder height. The platform rose.

"Now make some cookies on the platform."

Nothing.

"Make some . . . cheese on the platform."

Nothing. You don't see much cheese in a dump.

"Make some bread on the platform."

Nothing. Maybe the platform wasn't user-friendly.

"Make some bread."

After a moment, loaves tumbled out of the wall. "Enough! Stop!"

Mangy had rushed over to the bread, tearing at it, and the other dogs were going wild. I picked up one loaf, put it on the platform, and said, "Make the rest of the bread go away."

It all dissolved. No wonder the dogs were wary; I felt a little dizzy myself. A sentence from so long-ago child's book rose in my mind: *Things come and go so quickly here!*

I had no idea how much Blue could, or would, do on my orders. "Blue, make another room for me and this one dog. Away from the other dogs."

"No."

"Make this room bigger."

The room expanded evenly on all sides. "Stop." It did. "Make only this end of the room bigger."

Nothing.

"Okay, make the whole room bigger."

When the room stopped expanding, I had a space about forty feet square, with the dog cages huddled in the middle. After half an hour of experimenting, I got the platform moved to one corner, not far enough to escape the dog stench but better than nothing. (Law #1: Take what you can get.) I got a depression in the floor filled with warm water. I got food, drinking water, soap, and some clean cloth, and a lot of rope. By distracting Mangy with bits of bread, I got rope onto her frayed collar. After I got into the warm water and scrubbed myself, I pulled the poodle in. She bit me. But somehow I got her washed, too. Afterwards she shook herself, glared at me, and went to sleep on the hard floor. I asked Blue for a soft rug.

He said, "The other humans did this."

And Blue killed them anyway.

"Shut up," I said.

The big windowless room had no day, no night, no sanity. I slept and ate when I needed to, and otherwise I worked. Blue never left. He was an oversized, all-seeing eye in the corner. Big Brother, or God.

Within a few weeks—maybe—I had Mangy trained to come when called, to sit, and to follow me on command. I did this by dispensing bits of bread and other goodies. Mangy got fatter. I didn't care if she ended up the Fat Fiona of dogs. Her mange didn't improve, since I couldn't get Blue to wrap his digital mind around the concept of medicines, and even if he had I wouldn't have known what to ask for. The sick puppy died in its cage.

I kept the others fed and watered and flooded the shit out of their cages every day, but that was all. Mangy took all my time. She still regarded me warily, never curled up next to me, and occasionally growled. Love was not happening here.

Nonetheless, Blue left his corner and spoke for the first time in a week, scaring the hell out of me. "This dog behaves correctly."

"Well, thanks. I tried to . . . no, Blue . . ."

Blue floated to within a foot of Mangy's face, said, "Follow," and floated away. Mangy sat down and began to lick one paw. Blue rose and floated toward me.

"This dog does not behave correctly."

I was going to die.

"No, listen to me—listen! The dog can't smell you! It behaves for humans because of humans' smell! Do you understand?"

"No. This dog does not behave correctly."

"Listen! How the hell can you learn anything if you don't listen? You have to have a smell! Then the dog will follow you!"

Blue stopped. We stood frozen, a bizarre tableau, while the robot considered. Even Mangy stopped licking her paw and watched, still. They say dogs can smell fear.

Finally Blue said, "What is smell?"

It isn't possible to explain smell. Can't be done. Instead I pulled down my pants, tore the cloth I was using as underwear from between my legs, and rubbed it all over Blue, who did not react. I hoped he wasn't made of the same stuff as the Dome, which even spray paint had just slid off of. But, of course, he was. So I tied the strip of cloth around him with a piece of rope, my fingers trembling. "Now try the dog, Blue."

"Follow," Blue said, and floated away from Mangy.

She looked at him, then at me, then back at the floating metal sphere. I held my breath from some insane idea that I would thereby diminish my own smell. Mangy didn't move.

"This dog does not be—"

"She will if I'm gone!" I said desperately. "She smells me *and* you . . . and we smell the same so it's confusing her! But she'll follow you fine if I'm gone, do you understand?"

"No."

"Blue . . . I'm going to get on the platform. See, I'm doing it. Raise the platform *very high*, Blue. Very high."

A moment later my head and ass both pushed against the ceiling, squishing me. I couldn't see what was happening below. I heard Blue say, "Follow," and I squeezed my eyes shut, waiting. My life depended on a scrofulous poodle with a gloomy disposition.

Blue said, "This dog behaves correctly."

He lowered my platform to a few yards above the floor, and I swear that—eyeless as he is and with part of his sphere obscured by my underwear—he looked right at me.

"This dog does behave correctly. This dog is ready."

"Ready? For . . . for what?"

Blue didn't answer. The next minute the floor opened and Mangy, yelping, tumbled into it. The floor closed. At the same time, one of the cages across the room dissolved and a German shepherd hurtled towards me. I shrieked and yelled, "Raise the platform!" It rose just before the monster grabbed me.

Blue said, "What to do now? This dog does not behave correctly."

"For God's sakes, Blue—"

"This dog must love."

The shepherd leapt and snarled, teeth bared.

✧　　✧　　✧

I couldn't talk Blue out of the shepherd, which was as feral and vicious and unrelenting as anything in a horror movie. Or as Blue himself, in his own mechanical way. So I followed the First Law: Take what you can get.

"Blue, make garbage again. A lot of garbage, right here." I pointed to the wall beside my platform.

"No."

Garbage, like everything else, apparently was made—or released, or whatever—from the opposite wall. I resigned myself to this. "Make a lot of garbage, Blue."

Mountains of stinking debris cascaded from the wall, spilling over until it reached the dog cages.

"Now stop. Move my platform above the garbage."

The platform moved. The caged dogs howled. Uncaged, the shepherd poked eagerly in the refuse, too distracted to pay much attention to me. I had Blue lower the platform and I poked among it, too, keeping one eye on Vicious. If Blue was creating the garbage and not just trucking it in, he was doing a damn fine job of duplication. Xerox should have made such good copies.

I got smeared with shit and rot, but I found what I was looking for. The box was nearly a quarter full. I stuffed bread into it, coated the bread thoroughly, and discarded the box back onto the pile.

"Blue, make the garbage go away."

It did. Vicious glared at me and snarled. "Nice doggie," I said, "have some bread." I threw pieces and Vicious gobbled them.

Listening to the results was terrible. Not, however, as terrible as having Vicious tear me apart or Blue vaporize me. The rat poison took all "night" to kill the dog, which thrashed and howled. Throughout, Blue stayed silent. He had picked up some words from me, but he apparently didn't have enough brain power to connect what I'd done with Vicious's death. Or maybe he just didn't have enough experience with humans. What does a machine know about survival?

"This dog is dead," Blue said in the "morning."

"Yes. Make it go away." And then, before Blue could get there first, I jumped off my platform and pointed to a cage. "This dog will behave correctly next."

"No."

"Why not this dog?"

"Not big."

"Big. You want big." Frantically I scanned the cages, before Blue could choose another one like Vicious. "This one, then."

"Why the hell not?" Blue said.

It was young. Not a puppy but still frisky, a mongrel of some sort with short hair of dirty white speckled with dirty brown. The dog looked liked something I could handle: big but not too big, not too aggressive, not too old, not too male. "Hey, Not-Too," I said, without enthusiasm, as Blue dissolved her cage. The mutt dashed over to me and tried to lick my boot.

A natural-born slave.

I had found a piece of rotten, moldy cheese in the garbage, so Blue could now make cheese, which Not-Too went crazy for. Not-Too and I stuck with the same routine I used with Mangy, and it worked pretty well. Or the cheese did. Within a few "days" the dog could sit, stay, and follow on command.

Then Blue threw me a curve. "What to do now? The presentation."

"We had the presentation," I said. "I don't need to see it again."

"What to do now? The presentation."

"Fine," I said, because it was clear I had no choice. "Let's have the presentation. Roll 'em."

I was sitting on my elevated platform, combing my hair. A lot of it had fallen out during the malnourished years in the camp, but now it was growing again. Not-Too had given up trying to jump up there with me and gone to sleep on her pillow below. Blue shot the beam out of his sphere and the holo played in front of me.

Only not the whole thing. This time he played only the brief scene where the big, patchy dog pulled the toddler back from falling into the cesspool. Blue played it once, twice, three times. Cold slid along my spine.

"You want Not-Too . . . you want this dog here to be trained to save children."

"This dog here does not behave correctly."

"Blue . . . How can I train a dog to save a child?"

"This dog here does not behave correctly."

"Maybe you haven't noticed, but we haven't got any fucking children for the dog to practice on!"

Long pause. "Do you want a child?"

"No!" Christ, he would kidnap one or buy one from the camp and I would be responsible for a kid along with nineteen semi-feral dogs. No.

"This dog here does not behave correctly. What to do now? The presentation."

"No, not the presentation. I saw it, *I saw it*. Blue . . . the other two humans who did not make the dogs behave correctly . . ."

"Killed."

"Yes. So you said. But they did get one dog to behave correctly, didn't they? Or maybe more than one. And then you just kept raising the bar higher. Water rescues, guiding the blind, finding lost people. Higher and higher."

But to all this, of course, Blue made no answer.

I wracked my brains to remember what I had ever heard, read, or seen about dog training. Not much. However, there's a problem with opening the door to memory: you can't control what strolls through. For the first time in years, my sleep was shattered by dreams.

I walked through a tiny garden, picking zinnias. From an open window came music, full and strong, an orchestra on CD. A cat paced beside me, purring. And there was someone else in the window, someone who called my name and I turned and—

I screamed. Clawed my way upright. The dogs started barking and howling. Blue floated from his corner, saying something. And Not-Too made a mighty leap, landed on my platform, and began licking my face.

"Stop it! Don't do that! I won't remember!" I shoved her so hard she fell off the platform onto the floor and began yelping. I put my head in my hands.

Blue said, "Are you not operative?"

"Leave me the fuck alone!"

Not-Too still yelped, shrill cries of pain. When I stopped shaking, I crawled off the platform and picked her up. Nothing seemed to be broken—although how would I know? Gradually she quieted. I gave her some cheese and put her back on her pillow. She wanted to stay with me but I wouldn't let her.

I would not remember. *I would not*. Law #5: Feel nothing.

We made a cesspool, or at least a pool. Blue depressed part of the floor to a depth of three feet and filled it with water. Not-Too considered this a swimming pool and loved to be in it, which was not what Blue wanted ("This water does not behave correctly"). I tried having the robot dump various substances into it until I found one that she disliked and I could tolerate: light-grade motor oil. A few small cans of oil like those in the dump created a polluted pool, not unlike Charleston Harbor. After every practice session I needed a bath.

But not Not-Too, because she wouldn't go into the "cesspool." I curled myself as small as possible, crouched at the side of the pool, and thrashed. After a few days, the dog would pull me back by my shirt. I moved into the pool. As long as she could reach me without getting any liquid on her, Not-Too happily played that game. As soon as I moved far enough out that I might actually need saving, she sat on her skinny haunches and looked away.

"This dog does not behave correctly."

I increased the cheese. I withheld the cheese. I pleaded and ordered and shunned and petted and yelled. Nothing worked. Meanwhile, the dream continued. The same dream, each time not greater in length but increasing in intensity. *I walked through a tiny garden, picking zinnias. From an open window came music, full and strong, an orchestra on CD. A cat paced beside me, purring. And there was someone else in the window, someone who called my name and I turned and—*

And woke screaming.

A cat. I had had a cat, before the War. Before everything. I had always had cats, my whole life. Independent cats, aloof and self-sufficient, admirably disdainful. Cats—

The dog below me whimpered, trying to get onto my platform to offer comfort I did not want.

I would not remember.

"This dog does not behave correctly," day after day.

I had Blue remove the oil from the pool. But by now Not-Too had been conditioned. She wouldn't go into even the clear water that she'd reveled in before.

"This dog does not behave correctly."

Then one day Blue stopped his annoying mantra, which scared me even more. Would I have any warning that I'd failed, or would I just die?

The only thing I could think of was to kill Blue first.

✧   ✧   ✧

Blue was a computer. You disabled computers by turning them off, or cutting the power supply, or melting them in a fire, or dumping acid on them, or crushing them. But a careful search of the whole room revealed no switches or wires or anything that looked like a wireless control. A fire in this closed room, assuming I could start one, would kill me, too. Every kind of liquid or solid slid off Blue. And what would I crush him with, if that was even possible? A piece of cheese?

Blue was also—sort of—an intelligence. You could kill those by trapping them somewhere. My prison-or-sanctuary (depending on my mood) had no real "somewheres." And Blue would just dissolve any structure he found himself in.

What to do now?

I lay awake, thinking, all night, which at least kept me from dreaming, I came up with two ideas, both bad. Plan A depended on discussion, never Blue's strong suit.

"Blue, this dog does not behave correctly."

"No."

"This dog is not operative. I must make another dog behave correctly. Not this dog."

Blue floated close to Not-Too. She tried to bat at him. He circled her slowly, then returned to his position three feet above the ground. "This dog is operative."

"No. This dog *looks* operative. But this dog is not operative inside its head. I cannot make this dog behave correctly. I need a different dog."

A very long pause. "This dog is not operative inside its head."

"*Yes.*"

"You can make another dog behave correctly. Like the presentation."

"Yes." It would at least buy me time. Blue must have seen "not operative" dogs and humans in the dump; God knows there were enough of them out there. Madmen, rabid animals, druggies raving just before they died, or were shot. And next time I would add something besides oil to the pool; there must be something that Blue would consider noxious enough to simulate a cesspool but that a dog would enter. If I had to, I'd use my own shit.

"This dog is not operative inside its head," Blue repeated, getting used to the idea. "You will make a different dog behave correctly."

"Yes!"

"Why the hell not?" And then, "I kill this dog."

"No!" The word was torn from me before I knew I was going to say anything. My hand, of its own volition, clutched at Not-Too. She jumped but didn't bite. Instead, maybe sensing my fear, she cowered behind me, and I started to yell.

"You can't just kill everything that doesn't behave like you want! People, dogs . . . you can't just kill everything! You can't just . . . I had a cat . . . I never wanted a dog but this dog . . . she's behaving correctly for her! For a fucking traumatized dog and you can't just—I had a dog I mean a cat I had . . . I had. . . ."

—from an open window came music, full and strong, an orchestra on CD. A cat paced beside me, purring. And there was someone else in the window, someone who called my name and I turned and—

"I had a child!"

Oh, God no no no . . . It all came out then, the memories and the grief and the pain I had pushed away for three solid years in order to survive . . . *Feel nothing* . . . Zack Zack *Zack* shot down by soldiers like a dog *Look, Mommy, here I am Mommy look* . . .

I curled in a ball on the floor and screamed and wanted to die. Grief had been postponed so long that it was a tsunami. I sobbed and screamed; I don't know for how long. I think I wasn't quite sane. No human should ever have to experience that much pain. But of course they do.

However, it can't last too long, that height of pain, and when the flood passed and my head was bruised from banging it on the hard floor, I was still alive, still inside the Dome, still surrounded by barking dogs. Zack was still dead. Blue floated nearby, unchanged, a casually murderous robot who would not supply flesh to dogs as food but who would kill anything he was programmed destroy. And he had no reason not to murder me.

Not-Too sat on her haunches, regarding me from sad brown eyes, and I did the one thing I told myself I never would do again. I reached for her warmth. I put my arms around her and hung on. She let me.

Maybe that was the decision point. I don't know.

When I could manage it, I staggered to my feet. Taking hold of the rope that was Not-Too's leash, I wrapped it firmly around my hand. "Blue," I said, forcing the words past the grief clogging my throat, "make garbage."

He did. That was the basis of Plan B; that Blue made most things I asked of him. Not release, or mercy, but at least rooms and platforms and pools and garbage. I walked toward the garbage spilling from the usual place in the wall.

"More garbage! Bigger garbage! I need garbage to make this dog behave correctly!"

The reeking flow increased. Tires, appliances, diapers, rags, cans, furniture. The dogs' howling rose to an insane, deafening pitch. Not-Too pressed close to me.

"Bigger garbage!"

The chassis of a motorcycle, twisted beyond repair in some unimaginable accident, crashed into the room. The place on the wall from which the garbage spewed was misty gray, the same fog that the Dome had become when I had been taken inside it. Half a sofa clattered through. I grabbed Not-Too, dodged behind the sofa, and hurled both of us through the onrushing garbage and into the wall.

A broken keyboard struck me in the head, and the gray went black.

Chill. Cold with a spot of heat, which turned out to be Not-Too lying on top of me. I pushed her off and tried to sit up. Pain lanced through my head and when I put a hand to my forehead, it came away covered with blood. The same blood streamed into my eyes, making it hard to see. I wiped the blood away with the front of my shirt, pressed my hand hard on my forehead, and looked around.

Not that there was much to see. The dog and I sat at the end of what appeared to be a corridor. Above me loomed a large machine of some type, with a chute pointed at the now-solid wall. The machine was silent. Not-Too quivered and pressed her furry side into mine, but she, too, stayed silent. I couldn't hear the nineteen dogs on the other side of the wall, couldn't see Blue, couldn't smell anything except Not-Too, who had made a small yellow puddle on the floor.

There was no room to stand upright under the machine, so I moved away from it. Strips ripped from the bottom of my shirt made a bandage that at least kept blood out of my eyes. Slowly Not-Too and I walked along the corridor.

No doors. No openings or alcoves or machinery. Nothing until we reached the end, which was the same uniform material as everything else. Gray, glossy, hard. Dead.

Blue did not appear. Nothing appeared, or disappeared, or lived. We walked back and studied the overhead bulk of the machine. It had no dials or keys or features of any kind.

I sat on the floor, largely because I couldn't think what else to do, and Not-Too climbed into my lap. She was too big for this and I pushed her away. She pressed against me, trembling.

"Hey," I said, but not to her. Zack in the window *Look, Mommy, here I am Mommy look*... But if I started down that mental road, I would be lost. Anger was better than memory. Anything was better than memory. "Hey!" I screamed. "Hey, you bastard Blue, what to do now? What to do now, you Dome shits, whoever you are?"

Nothing except, very faint, an echo of my own useless words.

I lurched to my feet, reaching for the anger, cloaking myself in it. Not-Too sprang to her feet and backed away from me.

"What to do now? What bloody fucking hell to do *now*?"

Still nothing, but Not-Too started back down the empty corridor. I was glad to transfer my anger to something visible, real, living. "There's nothing there, Not-Too. *Nothing*, you stupid dog!"

She stopped halfway down the corridor and began to scratch at the wall.

I stumbled along behind her, one hand clamped to my head. What the hell was she doing? This piece of wall was identical to every other piece of wall. Kneeling slowly—it hurt my head to move fast—I studied Not-Too. Her scratching increased in frenzy and her nose twitched, as if she smelled something. The wall, of course, didn't respond; nothing in this place responded to anything. Except—

Blue had learned words from me, had followed my commands. Or had he just transferred my command to the Dome's unimaginable machinery, instructing it to do anything I said that fell within permissible limits? Feeling like an idiot, I said to the wall, "Make garbage." Maybe if it complied and the garbage contained food...

The wall made no garbage. Instead it dissolved into the familiar gray fog, and Not-Too immediately jumped through, barking frantically.

Every time I had gone through a Dome wall, my situation

had gotten worse. But what other choices were there? Wait for Blue to find and kill me, starve to death, curl up and die in the heart of a mechanical alien mini-world I didn't understand. Not-Too's barking increased in pitch and volume. She was terrified or excited or thrilled . . . How would I know? I pushed through the gray fog.

Another gray metal room, smaller than Blue had made my prison but with the same kind of cages against the far wall. Not-Too saw me and raced from the cages to me. Blue floated toward me . . . No, not Blue. This metal sphere was dull green, the color of shady moss. It said, "No human comes into this area."

"Guess again," I said and grabbed the trailing end of Not-Too's rope. She'd jumped up on me once and then had turned to dash back to the cages.

"No human comes into this area," Green repeated. I waited to see what the robot would do about it. Nothing.

Not-Too tugged on her rope, yowling. From across the room came answering barks, weirdly off. Too uneven in pitch, with a strange undertone. Blood, having saturated my makeshift bandage, once again streamed into my eyes. I swiped at it with one hand, turned to keep my gaze on Green, and let Not-Too pull me across the floor. Only when she stopped did I turn to look at the mesh-topped cages. Vertigo swooped over me.

Mangy was the source of the weird barks, a Mangy altered not beyond recognition but certainly beyond anything I could have imagined. Her mange was gone, along with all her fur. The skin beneath was now gray, the same gunmetal gray as everything else in the Dome. Her ears, the floppy poodle ears, were so long they trailed on the floor of her cage, and so was her tail. Holding on to the tail was a gray grub.

Not a grub. Not anything Earthly. Smooth and pulpy, it was about the size of a human head and vaguely oval. I saw no openings on the thing but Mangy's elongated tail disappeared into the doughy mass. and so there must have been at least one orifice. As Mangy jumped at the bars, trying to get at Not-Too, the grub was whipped back and forth across the cage floor. It left a slimy trail. The dog seemed oblivious.

"This dog is ready," Blue had said.

Behind me Green said, "No human comes into this area."

"Up yours."

"The human does not behave correctly."

That got my attention. I whirled around to face Green, expecting to be vaporized like the dead puppy, the dead Vicious. I thought I was already dead—and then I welcomed the thought. *Look, Mommy, here I am Mommy look* . . . The laws of survival that had protected me for so long couldn't protect me against memory, not any more. I was ready to die.

Instead Mangy's cage dissolved, she bounded out, and she launched herself at me.

Poodles are not natural killers, and this one was small. However, Mangy was doing her level best to destroy me. Her teeth closed on my arm. I screamed and shook her off, but the next moment she was biting my leg above my boot, darting hysterically toward and away from me, biting my legs at each lunge. The grub, or whatever it was, lashed around at the end of her new tail. As I flailed at the dog with both hands, my bandage fell off. Fresh blood from my head wound blinded me. I stumbled and fell and she was at my face.

Then she was pulled off, yelping and snapping and howling.

Not-Too had Mangy in her jaws. Twice as big as the poodle, she shook Mangy violently and then dropped her. Mangy whimpered and rolled over on her belly. Not-Too sprinted over to me and stood in front of me, skinny legs braced and scrawny hackles raised, growling protectively.

Dazed, I got to my feet. Blood, mine and the dogs', slimed the everything. The floor wasn't trying to reabsorb it. Mangy, who'd never really liked me, stayed down with her belly exposed in submission, but she didn't seem to be badly hurt. The grub still latched onto the end of her tail like a gray tumor. After a moment she rolled onto her feet and began to nuzzle the grub, one baleful eye on Not-Too: *Don't you come near this thing*! Not-Too stayed in position, guarding me.

Green said—and I swear its mechanical voice held satisfaction, no one will ever be able to tell me any different—"These dogs behave correctly."

The other cages held grubs, one per cage. I reached through the front bars and gingerly touched one. Moist, firm, repulsive. It didn't respond to my touch, but Green did. He was beside me in a flash. "No!"

"Sorry." His tone was dog-disciplining. "Are these the masters?"

No answer.

"What to do now? One dog for one . . ." I waved at the cages.

"Yes. When these dogs are ready."

This dog is ready, Blue had said of Mangy just before she was tumbled into the floor. Ready to be a pet, a guardian, a companion, a service animal to alien . . . what? The most logical answer was "children." Lassie, Rin Tin Tin, Benji, Little Guy. A boy and his dog. The aliens found humans dangerous or repulsive or uncaring or whatever, but dogs . . . You could count on dogs for your kids. Almost, and for the first time, I could see the point of the Domes.

"Are the big masters here? The adults?"

No answer.

"The masters are not here," I said. "They just set up the Domes as . . . as nurseries-slash-obedience schools." And to that statement I didn't even expect an answer. If the adults had been present, surely one or more would have come running when an alien blew into its nursery wing via a garbage delivery. There would have been alarms or something. Instead there was only Blue and Green and whatever 'bots inhabited whatever place held the operating room. Mangy's skin and ears and tail had been altered to fit the needs of these grubs. And maybe her voice-box, too, since her barks now had that weird undertone, like the scrape of metal across rock. Somewhere there was an OR.

I didn't want to be in that somewhere.

Green seemed to have no orders to kill me, which made sense because he wasn't programmed to have me here. I wasn't on his radar, which raised other problems.

"Green, make bread."

Nothing.

"Make water."

Nothing.

But two indentations in a corner of the floor, close to a section of wall, held water and dog-food pellets. I tasted both, to the interest of Not-Too and the growling of Mangy. Not too bad. I scooped all the rest of the dog food out of the trough. As soon as the last piece was out, the wall filled it up again. If I died, it wasn't going to be of starvation.

A few minutes ago, I had wanted to die. *Zack* . . .

No. Push the memory away. Life was shit, but I didn't want death, either. The realization was visceral, gripping my stomach as if that organ had been laid in a vise, or . . . There is no way to describe it. The feeling just was, its own justification. I wanted to live.

Not-Too lay a short distance away, watching me. Mangy was back in her cage with the grub on her tail. I sat up and looked around. "Green, this dog is not ready."

"No. What to do now?"

Well, that answered one question. Green was programmed to deal with dogs, and you didn't ask dogs "what to do now." So Green must be in some sort of communication with Blue, but the communication didn't seem to include orders about me. For a star-faring advanced race, the aliens certainly weren't very good at LANs. Or maybe they just didn't care—how would I know how an alien thinks?

I said, "I make this dog behave correctly." The all-purpose answer.

"Yes."

Did Green know details—that Not-Too refused to pull me from oily pools and thus was an obedience-school failure? It didn't seem like it. I could pretend to train Not-Too—I could actually train her, only not for water rescue—and stay here, away from the killer Blue, until . . . until what? As a survival plan, this one was shit. Still, it followed Laws #1 and #3: Take what you can get and never volunteer. And I couldn't think of anything else.

"Not-Too," I said wearily, still shaky from my crying jag, "Sit."

"Days" went by, then weeks. Not-Too learned to beg, roll over, bring me a piece of dog food, retrieve my thrown boot, lie down, and balance a pellet of dog food on her nose. I had no idea if any of these activities would be useful to an alien, but as long as Not-Too and I were "working," Green left us alone. No threats, no presentations, no objections. We were behaving correctly. I still hadn't thought of any additional plan. At night I dreamed of Zack and woke in tears, but not with the raging insanity of my first day of memory. Maybe you can only go through that once.

Mangy's grub continued to grow, still fastened onto her tail. The other grubs looked exactly the same as before. Mangy growled if I came too close to her, so I didn't. Her grub seemed to be drying out as it got bigger. Mangy licked it and slept curled around it and generally acted like some mythical dragon guarding a treasure box. Had the aliens bonded those two with some kind of pheromones I couldn't detect? I had no way of knowing.

Mangy and her grub emerged from their cage only to eat, drink, or shit, which she did in a far corner. Not-Too and I used the same corner, and all of our shit and piss dissolved odorlessly into the floor. Eat your heart out, Thomas Crapper.

As days turned into weeks, flesh returned to my bones. Not-Too also lost her starved look. I talked to her more and more, her watchful silence preferable to Green's silence or, worse, his inane and limited repertoires of answers. *"Green, I had a child named Zack. He was shot in the war. He was five." "This dog is not ready."*

Well, none of us ever are.

Not-Too started to sleep curled against my left side. This was a problem because I thrashed in my sleep, which woke her, so she growled, which woke me. Both of us became sleep-deprived and irritable. In the camp, I had slept twelve hours a day. Not much else to do, and sleep both conserved energy and kept me out of sight. But the camp was becoming distant in my mind. Zack was shatteringly vivid, with my life before the war, and the Dome was vivid, with Mangy and Not-Too and a bunch of alien grubs. Everything in between was fading.

Then one "day"—after how much time? I had no idea—Green said, "This dog is ready."

My heart stopped. Green was going to take Not-Too to the hidden OR, was going to— "No!"

Green ignored me. But he also ignored Not-Too. The robot floated over to Mangy's cage and dissolved it. I stood and craned my neck for a better look.

The grub was hatching.

Its "skin" had become very dry, a papery gray shell. Now it cracked along the top, parallel to Mangy's tail. She turned and regarded it quizzically, this thing wriggling at the end of her very long tail, but didn't attack or even growl. Those must have been some pheromones.

Was I really going to be the first and only human to see a Dome alien?

I was not. The papery covering cracked more and dropped free of the dog's tail. The thing inside wiggled forward, crawling out like a snake shedding its skin. It wasn't a grub but it clearly wasn't a sentient being, either. A larva? I'm no zoologist. This creature was as gray as everything else in the Dome but it had legs, six, and heads, two. At least, they might have been heads. Both had various indentations. One "head" crept forward, opened an orifice, and fastened itself back onto Mangy's tail. She continued to gaze at it. Beside me, Not-Too growled.

I whirled to grab frantically for her rope. Not-Too had no alterations to make her accept this . . . thing as anything other than a small animal to attack. If she did—

I turned just in time to see the floor open and swallow Not-Too. Green said again, "This dog is ready," and the floor closed.

"No! Bring her back!" I tried to pound on Green with my fists. He bobbed in the air under my blows. "Bring her back! Don't hurt her! Don't . . ." do what?

Don't turn her into a nursemaid for a grub, oblivious to me.

Green moved off. I followed, yelling and pounding. Neither one, of course, did the slightest good. Finally I got it together enough to say, "When will Not-Too come back?"

"This human does not behave correctly."

I looked despairingly at Mangy. She lay curled on her side, like a mother dog nursing puppies. The larva wasn't nursing, however. A shallow trough had appeared in the floor and filled with some viscous glop, which the larva was scarfing up with its other head. It looked repulsive.

Law #4: Notice everything.

"Green . . . okay. Just . . . okay. When will Not-Too come back here?"

No answer; what does time mean to a machine?

"Does the other dog return here?"

"Yes."

"Does the other dog get a . . ." A what? I pointed at Mangy's larva. No response. I would have to wait.

But not, apparently, alone. Across the room another dog tumbled, snarling, from the same section of wall I had once come through. I recognized it as one of the nineteen left in the other room, a big black beast with powerful looking jaws. It righted itself and charged at me. There was no platform, no place to hide.

"No! Green, no, it will hurt me! This dog does not behave—"

Green didn't seem to do anything. But even as the black dog leapt toward me, it faltered in mid-air. The next moment, it lay dead on the floor.

The moment after that, the body disappeared, vaporized.

My legs collapsed under me. That was what would happen to me if I failed in my training task, was what had presumably happened to the previous two human failures. And yet it wasn't fear that made me sit so abruptly on the gray floor. It was relief, and a weird kind of gratitude. Green had protected me, which was more than Blue had ever done. Maybe Green was brighter, or I had proved my worth more, or in this room as opposed to the other room, all dog-training equipment was protected. I was dog-training equipment. It was stupid to feel grateful.

I felt grateful.

Green said, "This dog does not—"

"I know, *I know*. Listen, Green, what to do now? Bring another dog here?"

"Yes."

"*I* choose the dog. I am the . . . the dog leader. Some dogs behave correctly, some dogs do not behave correctly. I choose. Me."

I held my breath. Green considered, or conferred with Blue, or consulted its alien and inadequate programming. Who the hell knows? The robot had been created by a race that preferred Earth dogs to whatever species usually nurtured their young, if any did. Maybe Mangy and Not-Too would replace parental care on the home planet, thus introducing the idea of babysitters. All I wanted was to not be eaten by some canine nanny-trainee.

"Yes," Green said finally, and I let out my breath.

A few minutes later, eighteen dog cages tumbled through the wall like so much garbage, the dogs within bouncing off their bars and mesh tops, furious and noisy. Mangy jumped, curled more protectively around her oblivious larva, and added her weird, rock-scraping bark to the din. A cage grew up around her. When the cages had stopped bouncing, I walked among them like some kind of tattered lord, choosing.

"This dog, Green." It wasn't the smallest dog but it had stopped barking the soonest. I hoped that meant it wasn't a grudge holder. When I put one hand into its cage, it didn't bite me, also a good sign. The dog was phenomenally ugly, the jowls on its face drooping from small, rheumy eyes into a sort of folded ruff around its short neck. Its body that seemed to be all front, with stunted and short back legs. When it stood, I saw it was male.

"This dog? What to do now?"

"Send all the other dogs back."

The cages sank into the floor. I walked over to the feeding trough, scooped up handfuls of dog food, and put the pellets into my only pocket that didn't have holes. "Make all the rest of the dog food go away."

It vaporized.

"Make this dog's cage go away."

I braced myself as the cage dissolved. The dog stood uncertainly on the floor, gazing toward Mangy, who snarled at him. I said, as commandingly as possible, "Ruff!"

He looked at me.

"Ruff, come."

To my surprise, he did. Someone had trained this animal before. I gave him a pellet of dog food.

Green said, "This dog behaves correctly."

"Well, I'm really good," I told him, stupidly, while my chest tightened as I thought of Not-Too. The aliens, or their machines, did understand about anesthetic, didn't they? They wouldn't let her suffer too much? I would never know.

But now I *did* know something momentous. I had choices. I had chosen which room to train dogs in. I had chosen which dog to train. I had some control.

"Sit," I said to Ruff, who didn't, and I set to work.

Not-Too was returned to me three or four "days" later. She was gray and hairless, with an altered bark. A grub hung onto her elongated tail, undoubtedly the same one that had vanished from its cage while I was asleep. But unlike Mangy, who'd never liked either of us, Not-Too was ecstatic to see me. She wouldn't stay in her grub-cage against the wall but insisted on sleeping curled up next to me, grub and all. Green permitted this. I had become the alpha dog.

Not-Too liked Ruff, too. I caught him mounting her, her very long tail conveniently keeping her grub out of the way. Did Green understand the significance of this behavior? No way to tell.

We settled into a routine of training, sleeping, playing, eating.

Ruff turned out to be sweet and playful but not very intelligent, and training took a long time. Mangy's grub grew very slowly, considering the large amount of glop it consumed. I grew, too; the waistband of my ragged pants got too tight and I discarded them, settling for a loin cloth, shirt, and my decaying boots. I talked to the dogs, who were much better conversationalists than Green since two of them at least pricked up their ears, made noises back at me, and wriggled joyfully at attention. Green would have been a dud at a cocktail party.

I don't know how long this all went on. Time began to lose meaning. I still dreamed of Zack and still woke in tears, but the dreams grew gentler and farther apart. When I cried, Not-Too crawled onto my lap, dragging her grub, and licked my chin. Her brown eyes shared my sorrow. I wondered how I had ever preferred the disdain of cats.

Not-Too got pregnant. I could feel the puppies growing inside her distended belly.

"Puppies will be easy to make behave correctly," I told Green, who said nothing. Probably he didn't understand. Some people need concrete visuals in order to learn.

Eventually, it seemed to me that Ruff was almost ready for his own grub. I mulled over how to mention this to Green but before I did, everything came to an end.

Clang! Clang! Clang!

I jerked awake and bolted upright. The alarm—a very human-sounding alarm—sounded all around me. Dogs barked and howled. Then I realized that it was a human alarm, coming from the Army camp outside the Dome, on the opposite side to garbage dump. I could *see* the camp—in outline and faintly, as if through heavy gray fog. The Dome was dissolving.

"Green—what—no!"

Above me, transforming the whole top half of what had been the Dome, was the bottom of a solid saucer. Mangy, in her cage, floated upwards and disappeared into a gap in the saucer's under-side. The other grub cages had already disappeared. I glimpsed a flash of metallic color through the gap: Blue. Green was halfway to the opening, drifting lazily upward. Beside me, both Not-Too and Ruff began to rise.

"No! No!"

I hung onto Not-Too, who howled and barked. But then my body froze. I couldn't move anything. My hands opened and Not-Too rose, yowling piteously.

"No! No!" And then, before I knew I was going to say it, "Take me, too!"

Green paused in mid-air. I began babbling.

"Take me! Take me! I can make the dogs behave correctly—I can—you need me! Why are you going? Take me!"

"Take this human?"

Not Green but Blue, emerging from the gap. Around me the Dome walls thinned more. Soldiers rushed toward us. Guns fired.

"Yes! What to do? Take this human! The dogs want this human!"

Time stood still. Not-Too howled and tried to reach me. Maybe that's what did it. I rose into the air just as Blue said, "Why the hell not?"

Inside—inside *what*?—I was too stunned to do more than grab Not-Too, hang on, and gasp. The gap closed. The saucer rose.

After a few minutes, I sat up and looked around. Gray room, filled with dogs in their cages, with grubs in theirs, with noise and confusion and the two robots. The sensation of motion ceased. I gasped, "Where . . . where are we going?"

Blue answered. "Home."

"*Why*?"

"The humans do not behave correctly." And then, "What to do now?"

We were leaving Earth in a flying saucer, and it was asking *me*?

Over time—I have no idea how much time—I actually got some answers from Blue. The humans "not behaving correctly" had apparently succeeding in breaching one of the Domes somewhere. They must have used a nuclear bomb, but that I couldn't verify. Grubs and dogs and had both died, and so the aliens had packed up and left Earth. Without, as far as I could tell, retaliating. Maybe.

If I had stayed, I told myself, the soldiers would have shot me. Or I would have returned to life in the camp, where I would have died of dysentery or violence or cholera or starvation. Or I would have been locked away by whatever government still existed in the cities, a freak who had lived with aliens, none of my story believed. I barely believed it myself.

I *am* a freak who lives with aliens. Furthermore, I live knowing that at any moment Blue or Green or their "masters" might decide to vaporize me. But that's really not much different from the uncertainty of life in the camp, and here I actually have some status. Blue produces whatever I ask for, once I get him to understand what that is. I have new clothes, good food, a bed, paper, a sort of pencil.

And I have the dogs. Mangy still doesn't like me. Her larva hasn't as yet done whatever it will do next. Not-Too's grub grows slowly, and now Ruff has one, too. Their three puppies are adorable and very trainable. I'm not so sure about the other seventeen dogs, some of whom look wilder than ever after their long confinement in small cages. Aliens are not, by definition, humane.

I don't know what it will take to survive when, and if, we reach "home" and I meet the alien adults. All I can do is rely on Jill's Five Laws of Survival:

#1: Take what you can get.
#2: Show no fear.
#3: Never volunteer.
#4: Notice everything.

But the Fifth Law has changed. As I lie beside Not-Too and Ruff, their sweet warmth and doggie-odor, I know that my first formulation was wrong. "Feel nothing"—that can take you some ways toward survival, but not very far. Not really.

Law #5: Take the risk. Love something.

The dogs whuff contentedly and we speed toward the stars.

War Stories

Elizabeth Bear

No shit, there I am.

So it's 2030, right? And I'm sprawled on my belly in the pile of rubble that used to be 100 Constitution Plaza, rifle fire skipping over my head, a broken rock gouging my groin just down and to the left of my armor. My neck wants to crawl into my helmet like a turtle jamming itself into its shell. There's a crater the size of Winterpeg under my nose, and busted rocks and shattered glass scattered all over Main Street. Suicide van bomb.

Any asshole can die for his country. The scary shit is *living* for it.

Old joke: join the army, see the world, meet interesting people and shoot them. And hell, I *could* be anywhere. Anywhere in the newly reconstituted Commonwealth, say. Where there's fewer places to see every week, and I—so I'm what, eighteen when this is going on?—would like to get a look at a few of them before they're under ice, or under water.

Ah, the Commonwealth. Back again like it never left.

I could be anywhere. I could be in the UK, evacuating Glastonbury or helping sandbag, or process refugees, in London. London, which is not holding. I could be in South Africa, putting down the warlord-of-the-week. Hell, I could be in Canada, guarding the home front.

117

No.

I'm face down in a pile of bricks in Hartford, Connecticut, in the good old U.S. of A., pinned under enemy fire, wondering when they're going to bring in the sonics to relieve us and if we're going to catch friendly fire when they do—and not loving a minute of it.

Shit. If I'm going to get my ass shot off, you'd think they could send me someplace pretty to do it in.

Carter's yelling at me from better cover, shouting something I can't catch over the noise. His mike might be on the fritz, or maybe it's my earpiece. His electronics seem okay, at least—he isn't eightysixed on my heads-up.

Good thing, too; you can see it yourself when it happens—unless your whole rig goes dead—and it's creepy as *shit*. Your icon grays out on the map and there are all your buddies, looking around to see if you got garroted or picked off by a sniper while the team was otherwise engaged.

Modern technology. Used to be, you got shot, you screamed and bled on people until a medic got there. Now, they have machines to do your bleeding for you.

So I wave back at him, hand down low beside my ass: *yeah, I have enough cover.*

Yeah. Enough. He's just a private anyway, which means . . .

. . . which means, technically, this is my action.

Mother pus-bucket.

I hope the rest of the guys show up fast.

I'm still thinking about that when I catch a little motion down in the hole.

That thing about your life flashing before your eyes? It's bullshit. Never had it happen, and I've been scared. What did happen, even before I was wired, was the adrenaline-dump shocked-time thing, and that's what I get, a freeze frame image of the crater and the sunlight shattering off broken glass.

Fuck me with a chainsaw. There's a *child* down there.

The social position of a MWO in the Canadian Army is a little odd. You're not a commissioned officer. But you're not really one of the grunts any more, either. The "I work for a living" joke only works until you get past warrant.

It's more like you're a vassal. A country of one, owing absolute allegiance, but generally trusted to wipe up your own ass—and your own spilt milk—as necessary.

It's an uncomfortable kind of freedom to get used to. But yanno, I never would have made it to RMC with *my* math skills, and we don't have enough college grads anymore to keep all the whirlybirds for lieutenants. And the way it works out, the rest of the pilots are scared to death of me, anyway.

So I don't have to leave the service to move in with Gabe Castaign. He got out before I did, and then we could be friends in public, even. The way we couldn't when I was a corporal and he was a captain and he saved my life.

Thank god he was never in my chain of command. I don't think we could have managed to stay pals; it would have gotten all knotted to that feudal thing, and that would have been the end.

Of course, I don't *quite* get to move in with him in the sense that I really wanted to, because by 2053, Gabe's married and has two beautiful, ridiculous, towheaded baby girls. And when I de-enlist, I do it to stay with him and Geniveve.

Because they already know that the transplants haven't taken, that the stem therapy and the chemo aren't working. And Geniveve wants to die at home. She needs help doing it, if she's going to do it comfortably. And Gabe, well.

Gabe doesn't really want to live through it alone.

So Geniveve comes home to die with her husband and her children, and I—

I go along because I don't have anyplace else to call home, and they need me. And yeah, I know going in it's going to be hard. And some poisonous bit of me hopes that Gabe will rebound in my direction when she's gone, because you *think* things like that, even when you don't say them.

But I *like* Geniveve. She's got every right to be jealous, but Geni is five nine and blonde and pert-nosed and has the greenest eyes I've ever seen that aren't contact lenses. And *look at my face.* But . . . I could be Gabe's scary war-buddy who he owes some kind of life debt, and she could walk on eggshells. She could leave us in the kitchen and herd the babies away.

And she treats me like her best girlfriend.

The first time I met her was at the bridal shower, a kind of Jack and Jill thing, and if she'd been strong enough I think she would pick me up in a Gabe-standard bear-hug, just like him.

She kissed my burned cheek, and nevermind I couldn't feel it, and she laughed at my jokes.

So what I'm saying is, I'm here for Geniveve as much as I'm here for Gabe. But it's not them I leave the army for. In '53 I get my 25 in. I always wear a glove on my left hand, and I'm heading down the back side of notorious into *old warhorse*. Infamy doesn't suit me.

I leave the army because it's time to leave the army. You can't fight all your life.

They've got a spare bedroom. Geniveve—the coincidence of names is no *end* of amusement, but Gabe calls me Maker not *Jenny* and so does Geniveve and so that's okay—has good days and bad days. Gabe mostly helps her. I mostly help with the girls and the housework, my Cinderella childhood all over again.

And don't I just look like the perfect fairytale princess, too?

Whatever else, this is how I get to know Leah. She's about five already, and Genie (see what I mean about the names?) is two, and not only had Geniveve gotten sick while she was carrying her, but Genie has cystic fibrosis, and she's all straw hair and straw limbs and big luminous eyes. She eats enough for a kid three times her size, and barely absorbs enough to grow on.

Gabe never once says a word to me about the hand he got dealt being unfair. *I* might mutter a few. But then you feel ugly. Especially when you know something about yourself that maybe the other guy doesn't.

Leah thinks I'm just a set of monkey bars. Just the right size for swinging on.

So we hold on about six months, while Geniveve has more bad days than good days, and big Gabe Castaign, with his wrists I could barely close my metal hand around, starts to look downright *thin*. Geniveve holds on longer than anybody thinks she might. Stubborn bitch.

But she's got two little girls to buy a few more days for, and you never know which one day . . . might be the day that counts.

You know, in a lot of ways, she reminded me of Maman.

Except, even when she was dying, Maman was funnier.

Hartford is after I quit dope, but before I start drinking. It's before a lot of other things; before Pretoria, before Gabe, before we—the Commonwealth, I mean—and the Russians team up to invade Brazil. I've still got both the hands I was born with, and Carlos' diamond ring is on the left one—when I'm off-duty.

I've got a man at home. I've got no business doing what I do next.

I have done things in my life that I liked less than that belly-crawl over broken glass and girders, but don't ask me to name three. There's a street down there under the rubble and maybe people with it, but it's hard to run a proper search and rescue when the whole world's blowing up. It's a hell of a thing to think about while you're crawling over them, though.

At least the site's cold. Not fresh, not likely to catch fire or explode under my belly. Just not cleaned up yet. If it ever will be.

The body armor helps some. Easier to keep your butt down crawling over plate glass shards when your belly's plated like a turtle's. And everything that isn't Kevlar or ceramic or leather is covered in ripstop, bladestop, breathable IR-defeating CADPAT digital urboflage.

Comforting.

I've got gloves too, dragged on over my blackened nails. The broken glass might have edges like a pile of rusty razorblades, but the combats can turn a thoracic stab wound into a bone bruise.

A little broken glass and a few gross of tenpenny nails are just what it was overdesigned for.

Good stuff.

Weighs a ton, makes you sweat like a pig, and the straps snag on every sharp pointy thing I slither over, but you take the good with the bad, like in any relationship.

The opposition hasn't seen me. Don't expect me to head down *into* the crater, I'm pretty sure, and are watching the near rim for a silhouette. Because that's what somebody would do in the war movie; send a scout out to distract them, draw their fire, and execute a pincer.

Imaginary soldiers don't actually have to crawl through rubble. And the imaginary enemies never seem to have somebody with a sniper scope and some elevation watching their ass.

Real bad guys can watch the war movies too.

As I get down closer to the bottom of the crater, I notice a few things. One is that the kid looks about eleven. Not a teenager yet; not really a child. Poor kid; that cusp is kind of the suck. Because *you* haven't changed, not really, but suddenly all the cultural slack and protectiveness, the puppy factor, is just gone.

He's a fresh casualty, though; I'd bet he was scavenging and took a fall, or maybe ducked stupid when the shooting started.

Well, at least he ducked.

He's conscious, huddled, bleeding between the fingers shoved against his scalp. I can't see how bad; one hand's balled into a fist and pressed to the flat back of the other. Head injury, not great. But up on top, not on the fragile temple.

If it's not depressed, it might not be too bad.

Once I got my GED I started studying emergency medicine on the side. It might come in handy if I pass the test, and if I live long enough being a medic beats being an ex-grunt with no job skills.

I cover him with my body and hope like hell we don't get blown up before the rescue comes, or I figure out how to get us out of here.

Five years old, Leah strokes the back of her hand down the back of mine and snatches her fingers away, shaking them like they sting. "Can you feel anything? Does it hurt?"

How do you explain phantom pain to a first grader? "No. Where you touch it, I can't feel anything."

"Wow." She peeks at me through bangs and eyelashes. "That must be nice."

Somehow, Carter must get through, jinky radio and all, because the next thing I know there's a helicopter slamming over like the Archangel Michael on a three day bender. Dusty air buffets us, dust that's half powdered glass and God knows what, like sticking your hand in a sandblaster. The kid squeaks—he's been quiet against my chest, both fists knotted around my LBE like a baby sloth clinging to its mother—and I pull his face into my neck. It can't be comfortable, but maybe it'll encourage him to close his eyes.

Me, I get in a couple of hail-Mary's, but the gunfire I hear is ours and not theirs. You really can pick out the make of the gun by the sound, after a couple of weeks. They use whatever they bought off the Internet; all our shit matches. Score one for the away team. Let's go for the hat trick, shall we?

"You grunts alive down there, over?" The last thing from regulation, but a voice I loved to hear. Chief Warrant Officer Tranchemontagne, the own personal hell-on-rotor-blades of the

Canadian Armed Forces, Hartford franchise. There were only about two hundred of us in town; I didn't expect him to know me, but I sure as hell knew him.

The helmet mikes were voice-activated. I cleared my throat and spoke up. "We're alive, Chief. This is Corporal Casey. You gonna come pick us up, or do we hike back? Carter's radio's busted, but we're both unwounded. I've got a civilian casualty, though. A child. Over."

Carter and Casey. I'm not sure if we sound more like a law firm or a comedy team.

"Where's the kid, over?"

The kid kicks me in the knee, suddenly, and tries to squirm free, ready to dart out of that hole into the broken glass and flying bullets. All he's gonna do is bust his toe on the ceramic armor, but he doesn't know that. I grab, and get him over the shoulders. "Stay the hell *down*, you little bastard! Chief, the kid is under me. And seems to be alive. Ow. *Over*."

I hear the son of a bitch laughing. "Got yourself a live one there, Private. All right, I'll get you some evac."

I don't quite have to hit the kid to bundle him into the chopper, but his feet don't touch the ground on the way there, either. Just his luck I'm five eleven in my bare feet, and he—well, he isn't.

Once the chopper's off the ground he quits kicking me, though. I let him scramble loose; he jams himself sullenly into the corner furthest from the door.

"Great job, Casey," Carter says, in what he thinks passes for French. "You think it's housebroken?"

"Shut the fuck up, eh?" I've got half a pack of cigarettes left. I take one out and toss him the rest, and catch the kid watching. I shoot him a sidelong glance. He licks his lips. He's a good looking kid, broad regular features, behind the crust of blood that dribbles over one sharp brown eye. "Hey, Carter?"

He looks up from lighting his cigarette. I leave mine, still cold, between my fingers. "Give the pack to the kid."

And Carter looks at me, looks at the kid—eleven, right?—and shrugs and tosses him the pack.

The kid pulls one out, looks at the pack, thinks real hard, and tosses it back to me with eight left. Then he flicks the one he kept with his thumbnail to light it, a practiced economy of motion. Yeah, I was like a fucking chimney at that age, too.

I keep an eye on him without looking like I'm looking at him. He takes two puffs before he picks the ember off the end and tucks the rest in his shirt pocket. Price of a meal at least, I guess, in a wartime economy.

You're not supposed to smoke in the Army's aircraft. I guess somebody might not like the smell. I stick my untouched cigarette back into the half pack and toss the whole thing back to him, with nine smokes now.

The genius behind chemotherapy is that you poison yourself a little slower than you poison the cancer. It's fucking barbarism; no different from the mercury treatments they used to give people who had syphilis, although maybe it works a little better.

I don't blame Geniveve for deciding that if she was going to die, she'd rather do it without the puking.

She's too proud to wear a wig, but her hair's coming back in patchy now that she's stopped poisoning herself. She keeps her head shaved and it makes her look elegant, Egyptian.

I maintain it for her: a couple of times a month I settle the moist, warm, tender skin of her nape against the palm of my living hand, my thumb resting behind her ear, the vibrations of the electric razor carrying up my machine arm.

I used to do the same for some of the guys in my platoon.

She closes her eyes while I shave her, dreaming like a cat. Her lips move, shaping words; her fuzz clings to my sleeve. I could cut myself touching her cheekbones; there's a dead woman just under her skin.

I thumb the razor off. "I didn't hear you, sweetie."

When people are dying, it's easier to tell them you love them. You know they're not going to hold it over you later.

She nibbles her thumbnail, a nervous tic, and presses her skull into my hand. "Maker." And then she says my real name, her eyes still shut. "*Jenny*. When I'm gone, you ought to marry him. Before he thinks to play it tough."

By the time I get him to the displaced persons camp, the kid's attached to my hip like he grew there. The dressing on his scalp is white and bulbous; I made the duty nurse shave the whole thing, and not just the part she was stitching, so at least both sides match, but he still looks like he's farming mushrooms up there. His name turns out to be Dwayne MacDonald; he's ten, not eleven, and he's got a fouler mouth than I do, which is saying something.

So yeah, all right, I like the kid. And the clerk at the resettlement office gets up my nose in about thirty seconds flat. "Name?" she says, without looking up at either of us, and he doesn't answer, so I say it for him. She taps it into her interface and frowns. "MacDonald's a pretty common last name. Parents? Street address?"

I look at him. He shrugs, shoulders squared, hands in his pockets. Cat's got his tongue. "What if you can't find his family?"

"He'll stay at the camp until we can find a foster situation for him." She still hasn't lifted her eyes from the interface. "It might be a while. Especially if he won't talk. Where'd you find him?"

"Downtown." Five more seconds, and I'm going to be as silent as the kid. I fold my arms and lean back on my heels.

"Look." She pushes back from her desk, and I catch her eyes, contacts colored blue-violet with swimming golden sparks. Distracting as hell. "We get a couple dozen porch monkeys through here every week. Either you can help me out, or—"

The kid presses against my side, and it's a good thing he's in the way of my gun hand, because there's a rifle across my back and if I could reach it, she'd never have gotten to the second syllable in "monkey."

"Or I can try to find his parents myself. Thank you, miss."

She a civilian, more's the pity. And they won't do a fucking thing about her, but I'm still going to file a complaint.

God, I hate these people.

I take the kid back to my billet. Halfway there, as we're trudging along side by side, I run into Brody. "New boyfriend, Casey?"

I look at the kid. The kid looks at me. "He's like a mascot, Sarge."

"Like the camp cat, Casey? Not gonna happen."

But Brody's okay on a lot of levels, laid back and easy-going with a full measure of sun- and laugh-lines. He likes to talk about his grandkids, though he can't be much more than fifty-five.

Yeah, so at eighteen, fifty-five is like the end of the world. The light from fifty-five takes a million years to reach eighteen. Brody sighs and hooks his thumb in his belt and says, "Get some dinner in him. And some breakfast. Tomorrow, you get his ass home, you understand?"

"Yes, Sarge," I say. "Thank you."

"Don't get too used to it, Casey."

One more shake of his head, a self-annoyed grunt, and he's gone.

We all want to die at home.

Geniveve gets close, but even her stubborn isn't quite enough to pull off that one. There's the hospital and then there's hospice care and Genie's way too young for this, and too sick, because she's stressed out and flares up. Don't ever tell me babies don't understand.

So God help Gabe, he's mostly with Genie, because somebody has to be and she wants her Papa. She wants her Maman too.

And Leah and me, we stay with Geniveve. I haven't really got a lot to say about it.

Except, Geniveve is so fragile by the end, a soap bubble. You know in movies where there's a Chernobyl event and then people die, crying from the pain in their joints, bruising in huge terrible flowers anyplace their bones press the inside of their skin?

That's leukemia. That's how leukemia kills you.

You know that thing where they say that God never gives you more than you can shoulder?

It's a vicious, obscene lie.

You know what happens. What with one thing and another, he stays a night, and then three nights, and then by four days in he stops being "Casey's kid" and turns into the whole camp's mascot. They call him half a dozen stupid nicknames—mouche-noir, first, which turns into Mooch overnight. Moustique, which is "mosquito" and also "punk." One of the guys starts singing the black-fly song at him—*a-crawlin' in your whiskers, a-crawlin' in your hair, a-swimmin' in the soup and a-swimmin' in the tea*—and pretty soon the whole camp is doing it, which drives him as nuts as the black flies would've.

Poor kid.

I ply him with hockey cards and cigarettes, and even get him half-interested in the games. We get them on satellite, and it's a camp-wide event when they're on. You really have to piss somebody off to draw picket that night. They're the old-fashioned cards mostly, you know the ones with the limited memory and just a little chip screen, maybe 90 seconds of highlights? He's fascinated by a couple of the "classic" ones—Bill Barilko, that kind of stuff—players from the previous century in grainy black and white, images set to radio broadcast clips. There's more highlights on those, and he listens to them for hours, curled up in the corner with his elbows on his knees.

And then after a week of this, I get my leave. Thirty-six hours, back in Toronto, and a unit transfer.

Everybody knows what that means.

I guess I'm going to get my wish. I'm going overseas.

Between us, Hetu and me hack one of the hockey cards—they have an uplink so you can check these dedicated web pages with scores and biographies and stuff—so the kid can use it for email. I show him the trick; it's awkward, but hey, it's free, right? Last thing I do, before I shake his hand, is rip the unit patch off my shoulder and hand it to him.

I won't be needing it anymore.

He takes it, crumples it in his fist until I can't see it.

"You gonna be okay?"

Jerk of his chin.

"Really okay?"

And he gives me this stiff little nod. He's not going to cry. He's not even going to look like he *wants* to cry.

Brave little toaster. But I'm dumb enough to push it. "I'll come back if you want me to. After. I'll come get you." What am I gonna do with a kid? What is Carlos going to want with some American refugee kid with PTSD who cries in his sleep like a puppy? How the fuck old are we both going to be before I *could* come back?

Fuck it. Sometimes you just have to pretend you're not lying.

But he stares right through me and says, "You won't come back." The finality of abandonment, of somebody who knows the score.

I don't argue. "Write me?"

And he licks his lips and jerks his chin down once, like he was driving a nail. *Sure thing, Casey.*

I don't lose my shit, myself, until I'm on the transport. Until I'm safe in Ontario, getting off the bus, and then it's okay because Carlos thinks I'm crying over him and it never does any harm to let your fiancé think you can't live without him.

Carlos has lousy feet and worse ankles. He works for the quartermaster. He's not going anywhere. From each according to his ability.

I get my orders for Pretoria. And the rest is history. I dear-john Carlos from the hospital, after burning half my fucking face off in South Africa. I never have the heart to find out if he makes it through the war.

Dwayne doesn't write. It's three months before I figure out that he'd been too proud to tell me he didn't know how.

I stick around Toronto for a little while after the funeral, until things are settled and the girls aren't constantly asking when Maman is coming home. I want to stay forever.

I . . . can't. Every time I look at Gabe now, I hear Geniveve telling me to marry him, and the hell of it is, boy, it would make the kids happy. It would even make me happy, for a little, until the whole thing went pear-shaped. As you know it inevitably would. Love affairs forged in crisis, they're like trashfires. They burn out hot and leave a lot of stink behind.

He says he'll call. I tell him I'll come visit for Leah's birthday, which is May. It's only a five-hour drive from Hartford. There's a lot of rundown old dumps there, and I buy one. On the worst street in the worst neighborhood of town, but who's going to give me a hard time?

It's barely got electric.

They call that area the North End. It's the kind of place where men in bedroom slippers drink forties of malt liquor from paper bags on bus benches that haven't seen service since the war. It's full of immigrants and poor blacks and West Indians. Which is fine with me; you can never have too much Jamaican food.

It's exactly what I want. A hole I can crawl into and pull up snug.

That's a joke, isn't it? Vets going back where they fought, where they served. Marrying a brown native girl who only speaks horizontal English. Happens every day.

It's the peak experience, maybe. Or maybe the thing where we can't go home and we can't stay here. Wherever here might be. Maybe they ought to just shoot the warriors when we come home.

That way, it would be over quick.

Anyway. I'm standing on a street corner smoking my last cigarette when I see him. This gangster, and he's like a kick in the chest. Threat response, predator response, because he's the king of the street. Swaggering down Albany Ave in a black T-shirt, boots, jeans, and a black leather jacket zinging with chains. His shaved head's glossy in the sun. Pink proud flesh catches the sun on his crown; he taps knuckles with a skinny guy headed the other direction. He's huge; shoulders bulging the seams of his jacket. And he's flanked by two toughs that trail him like pilotfish after a shark.

I'm supposed to be impressed.

One falls back a half-step to have a word with the guy the big man deigned to notice, and that's when I catch a flash on the head man's shoulder. Red and white and gray, sewn to black leather.

It stops me in my tracks. I stare uncomprehendingly and take a step forward. That sharp pink scar, the heavy neck, the massive hands, the swagger. The way he dips his head when he turns to his friend and half-nods.

The friend catches me staring and moves in. The big man turns, notices my face, recoils. I'm used to that, but it stings from him. If it is. Him.

The scars, of course. And I'm in mufti. I hope I can talk my way out of this before I get my head handed to me.

They move toward me, the big man and both his toughs, and the newcomer trailing like a remora hoping to attach itself to an apex predator. Four of them.

I can do it.

I can't promise to keep that many safe.

They pause three meters distant, the big one sizing up my scars and my face. His pistol's under his jacket, a hilt-down shoulder holster. I can tell through the hide.

I wear mine in plain sight, strapped to my thigh.

"There a problem?"

Right on script, but he reads it too softly. It could be an honest question.

I treat it that way. "No problem. I was wondering if you knew a Dwayne MacDonald, grew up near here." Pause. "He'd be about your age."

The silence stretches. He looks at me, into my eyes, at the shape of my shoulder and the angle of my nose. "Beat it," he says, finally, and he's not talking to me. I catch a glitter, steel teeth behind his lips. Some sort of cosmetic mod.

Not cheap.

Without protest, with a few unanswered promises to catch-you-later-man, the other three recuse themselves. Dwayne stands there looking at me, hulking behemoth with his hands shoved in his pockets. I think I could get a *ting!* out of the tendons on his neck if I flicked them with a thumbnail.

"What do you go by now?"

"Huh?" As if I've shattered his concentration. "Oh. Razorface." The sibilants hiss through his teeth. "They call me Razorface. This my street." A shrug over his shoulder. Sure. Lord of all he surveys. "War's over, Casey."

"Yeah." We stand there staring at each other for a minute, grinning. People cross the street. "Call me Maker. I live here now. Hey, you know what?"

"What?"

"You should come over some time. And watch a hockey game. In fact, can I buy you a drink?"

"It's ten in the morning, you fucking drunk," he says, but he takes my elbow and turns me, like he expects me to need the support. "Fuck, you look like hell."

"Yeah," I say, 'cause it's true.

But that's okay. Because on the other hand, *he* looks like he's doing . . . all right.

So that's something, after all.

A Stranger in Paradise

Edward M. Lerner

Row upon row of blue-and-green-and-white globes mock me.

The world below reflects from tumblers and goblets and snif-ters and flutes, from more types of antique glassware than I can name. Bottles and decanters of amber liquid line other shelves. Seven thousand years is too vintage for my tastes; I'm ignoring my craving for a drink.

Ama and I first spoke in a place like this—not a derelict star-ship, but another tavern. Human nature has changed over the millennia, but not in that way.

No, let me call her Amanda. If those I *want* to find this memoir do, the old form of the name may be more familiar. My name has no old form; Cameron will do.

I was alone, my back to the boisterous crowd, when she approached my table. The friends she had come in with were chattering away. Despite pulsing music and her soft tread, I knew she was there well before she spoke.

"You act like the world is against you."

I was new there—there meaning Earth, not only the Academy—and homesick and friendless. I held back my reflexive reply: that the world *was*. Medicine and training notwithstanding, the gravity was killing me. The answer I gave instead made her laugh.

I had met the one. Some things you just *know*.

Planets are tough on artifacts mere mortals can build. A few thousand years of weathering and erosion destroys and obscures a *lot*. It wasn't until we stumbled upon ancient lunar settlements preserved by the vacuum that we realized we—humankind—had been in space before. A whole new science, techno-archeology, was needed to understand. When fragments of data finally began to emerge from the lost civilization's computers, we were even more amazed.

The Firsters had burst from the solar system with an armada of slowboats and an excess of enthusiasm. Their ships would, in a few generations' time, reach nearby stars thought to warm planets with good prospects for human colonization.

The solsys-wide civilization collapsed before any of those pioneers could possibly have reached their destinations. Archeologists agree that Earth suffered plagues, famine, global warfare, eco-collapse, and socioeconomic implosion. They just cannot agree on cause and effect.

Millennia later, humanity has recovered, and more, exploring its galactic neighborhood in faster-than-light ships embodying technologies the Firsters never imagined.

And none of our nearest interstellar neighbors has a human presence.

If any of the slowboats narrowcast home as instructed about their first landfalls, no one retained the technology to hear. Some ships, perhaps, never reached their destinations. Some planetary settlements, it was eventually discovered, were started and failed. A few asteroid bases were found orbiting nearby stars—all abandoned.

But those failures were not the end of the story.

What is known for certain is that some missions traveled far past their intended stars. Were the original destination worlds too inhospitable for the colonization methods of the time? Interstellar space is a *big* place—did they simply lose their way? Did settlements split, some staying to defend a hard-won beachhead, others ever seeking a better world? All the above occurred, and more than once, the process repeating until the slowboats could voyage no more.

The Firster generation ships spread humanity thinly across a million cubic light years, in hundreds of tiny enclaves in as many alien environments. Many groups eventually died out. Some continued to eke out a hard-scrabble existence, their memories of Earth warped or nonexistent. Few retained any vestige of civilization.

For those who survived, there is the Reunification Corps.

Amanda. . . .

Whenever she entered a room, heads turned, conversation stopped, men smiled reflexively, and libidos engaged. I knew then, and remember now, that she is physically beautiful. Flowing brown hair. Striking blue eyes ever twinkling with warmth and curiosity. A willowy grace.

And yet beauty is the least of her charms.

I should get on subject.

Finding lost colonies is an art. Few records survive to show where the slowboats went, even on their first, usually failed attempts. There are too many stars, even with FTL drive, to search them all. So, while the Reunification Corps employs a multitude of skills and professions, the rarest and most precious talent is the one that makes all the others relevant.

Mine.

It's a peculiar mode of thought, the ability to put one's self into the mindset of a doomed expedition born of an ancient civilization. To think: I'm *here*, one of the lucky ones, after generations of travel. To realize: this climate, these perils, a lack of vital resources . . . *something* makes it too dangerous to stay. Extrapolating from that crushing disappointment, and what little we've reconstructed of Firster technology, how they might have reacted to the prospect of moving on. Which of the distant pinpoints of light would seem the most promising? Which would merit entombing myself and generations of my descendants on a slowboat that logic says may not survive another epic voyage but is too complex to replace? Deciding where, with an entire solar system to choose from, the Firsters might have established a base.

There is no way to capture the process in an algorithm, or exercise it from behind a desk. It takes walking the planets of distant stars, communing with the faint anomalies that just might be the crumbled remains of abandoned settlements.

Amanda and I became instant friends, and then a sweaty-and-entangled whole bunch more than friends, at Corps Academy. We begged and bargained our way onto the same Corps re-orientation ship, two earnest grads eager to help a world of Firster descendants rejoin a larger humanity scarcely recognizable in their mythos. After three missions together, we decided to get married.

I couldn't believe our good fortune that a two-person scout ship mission was available. Starhopping would leave plenty of time for us—it seemed like the perfect honeymoon.

And then one of those starhops brought us to Paradise.

Long before sensors spotted the tumbling hulk of the abandoned slowboat, I felt certain the Firsters we were tracking had settled here. From halfway across the solar system, sensors showed the planet was too perfect *not* to settle.

Amanda was equally sure any colony had failed. There was no hint of chlorophyll in the orbital scans, nor signs of energy being harnessed. No chlorophyll means no terrestrial plant life to anchor a human-usable food chain. No energy generation means no bioconversion to change local biota into something terrestrials could eat.

"Damn. Sorry." Amanda's sympathy for the lost colonists was sincere. And misplaced.

There *were* people on the planet below. I was as sure of that as I'd been, from star to star to star, which way this slowboat had gone. Call it a hunch.

"It's a waste of time." Amanda had been seated in front of a bio-readout panel. "Humans might as well eat dirt as anything growing down there."

The planet we circled, that I still circle, is green almost everywhere not covered by water or polar ice cap. That lushness was one more anomaly, since its orbit was barely within the habitable zone of its K-class sun. While I began the painstaking process of bringing back on-line the slowboat's ancient, crumbling computers, Amanda, at my insistence, flew down in a lander to check things out.

We have been apart ever since.

Any planet you would want to colonize belongs to someone else—the only question is how much of an ecosphere you are willing to displace. That is true, at least, if a breathable atmosphere is a meaningful part of your lifestyle. Oxygen is so chemically reactive that only a planet rich with photosynthesizing life can sustain an oxygen-rich atmosphere.

From interstellar distances, the only discernable planetary characteristics are orbit, rough size, and atmospheric composition. Evolutionary progress from the single-celled stage until sentients begin to use radios, not that any such have ever been found, is undetectable. Fortunate colonists found bare rock plus oceans full of oxygen-producing algae. Unlucky colonists, at least for those with a sense of bioethics, encountered continents teeming with indigenous life.

Like Paradise.

The lander touched down just inside one of the planet's few desolate regions, on the rocky coast of an inland sea. Amanda could not bring herself to use a more hospitable prospective landing site. A column-of-flame descent into some verdant meadow would have been, she said, like torching a park.

I had no reason to doubt her inference that the area had, within the last few years, been cleared by a forest fire. "Caused by lightning," she insisted. "There are no careless campers here." Charred, often toppled, boles of tree-analogues dominated the landscape. Beyond the devastation towered vast expanses of the spiky, fern-like plants. Patches of new growth poked, scrub-like, through ashy soil. "You getting this?" she radioed, surveying the landing site on foot. She wore an envirosuit although every sensor showed the area to be safe. That was protocol: Thorough checkout took time. Videocams on the lander panned slowly.

"Good place to take up charcoal drawing," I commented from orbit. I had no difficulty imagining her answering smile.

"Not among my talents, and I don't see staying here long enough to cultivate new skills." Her suit radio conveyed faint crunching sounds as she walked. Saplings became denser as she progressed towards the closest unmarred growth. "What luck with the slowboat's computer?"

"Not much," I admitted. Computing was one of the technologies at which the Firsters excelled. The Corps had, over time, reverse-engineered a few of their tricks, but the systems on every slowboat differed. Each crossing took generations . . . why should their technology stand still? "Maybe you can charm it . . ." I trailed off.

"What?" she asked.

"Stand still." She froze. "Speed up panning." Her helmet camera did. The matching view on my display swept across the countryside, then reversed direction. Fern saplings trembling in the breeze showed the only motion.

"What did you see, Cameron?"

"Apparently nothing." The videocam again reversed its arc.

Something shot across the screen.

"Did you see *that*?" she shouted. Her gloved fist, one finger outstretched, blocked a corner of the camera's field of vision. Ground-hugging fronds still rustled where she pointed.

I was advancing, frame by frame, through captured images of a scuttling, six-legged, ankle-high alien *something* when Amanda whooped excitedly. Her helmet camera swung wildly. "What is it?" I yelled back. "What do you see?" The image stabilized; from the change in perspective it was clear she was squatting. Green glowing eyes studied Amanda from deep within shadowy underbrush. My gut clenched. "What is that?"

Moments later, a clearly terrestrial calico cat sauntered out of the undergrowth to sniff Amanda's still outstretched finger.

The slowboat was a wreck. I tell myself that if I had skills beyond gleaning clues from traces of hints of ruins, I would have brought the old systems on-line soon enough to have made a difference. Or that if I'd somehow stitched together the colonists' story faster, I'd have gotten Amanda offworld in time.

But I don't believe it.

I had followed these colonists across four interstellar hops. That was a record . . . most slowboats were worn out after two; a few managed three. The problem was always biosphere collapse. A crossing Amanda and I could reasonably call a hop was to the Firsters a multigenerational odyssey. By the time the colonists reached Paradise, the slowboat's ecology was exhausted and dying. They had no choice but to descend to the surface.

They were up to *something* neither Amanda nor I could comprehend. I kept exploring, kept reconstructing the spotty surviving records for some clue how these Firsters expected to live here, how they thought to avoid ravaging a thriving native ecology to transplant their own.

Now that it is too late, I do understand.

✧   ✧   ✧

What did Amanda see in me? Given my looks—straw-colored hair, a pasty complexion, features I've always thought a bit awry, and the tall-and-gangly frame common to Belters—there was always ample speculation. I've overheard enough whispers to grasp the popular explanation, and it makes me crazy: That it is a marriage of convenience. She gets the career benefit of my semi-spooky skills at tracking down Firsters. I get . . . her. It's hardly flattering for either of us.

As I said, it drives me crazy.

She met, she loves, an artist. When I could no longer bear the stubborn refusal of planet and slowboat to relinquish their secrets, I sought refuge—looked, in a way, for Amanda—in my art.

There are many restored recordings of Firster music; by those standards my compositions are arrhythmic, overly complex, and discordant. Each of my melodies has a visual setting, forming a sight-and-sound poem. The first time I shared one with her, back at the Academy, she gazed at me in silent wonder. What a rare treat it was to bask in someone's appreciation.

Years later, I cannot experience that piece without memories flooding my mind. Recalling her, recalling that moment, my heart aches.

So what did Amanda see in me? The *person*. Mine is not the only sixth sense.

Recovering data and restoring limited operations in the balky Firster computers involved one part inspiration and twenty parts head scratching. The work left plenty of time for watching Amanda through landing-site cameras. I missed her.

I miss her now.

DNA from a blood sample proved Amanda's new friend was, without doubt, a terrestrial cat. She was playing with the feline, teasing it with a dangling bit of vine, the game by way of apology for the needle stick, when two landing-site motion sensors gave alarms.

Moments after the alert—trilling discreetly in her personal communicator and booming from my console in our orbiting starship—someone strode from the brush, as obviously a human as the cat was a cat. The burly figure wore a knee-length tunic of clearly natural fibers, cinched at the waist by a braided sash

from which hung a cloth sack and various wood-and-stone imple-
ments. The loosely woven garment left no doubt that her caller
was a man.

"Amanda," I whispered.

"I see him."

He ambled casually towards her, greasy hair hanging past his
shoulders. If he understood the lander's stungun turret slow swiv-
eling to track his progress, he gave no sign. His body language
seemed somehow disdainful of the ship. He sniffed repeatedly, a
puzzled expression on his face.

"Amanda," I whispered again. "What's he doing?"

"You tell me," she whispered back.

The stranger sniffed again. His meandering path took him past
the flat rock on which lay the galley scraps Amanda had set out
for the cat. He bent slightly, inhaled, and then continued slowly
towards her. He seemed no more impressed by home-world food
than had the cat.

After the linguistic drudgery of the initial colony rediscoveries,
the Corps had painfully reconstructed passable versions of the
Firster languages. Modern survey ships carried translation software
attuned to all major colonist dialects—that is, to the versions
deduced to have been spoken when the slowboats were leaving
solsys. It didn't take many utterances by the visitor to recognize
English as the root of his speech. The lander's computer took
longer, but not much, to derive many of the pronunciation shifts
and some divergent vocabulary. From a speculative understanding
of roughly every third word, Brian—his name was one thing we
did ascertain—was most interested in discussing the weather.

"His vocabulary appears limited," Amanda said. She had cranked
up the sensitivity of her implanted communicator sufficiently to
capture her subvocalizations.

We both knew the computer had already reached that conclusion, and she wasn't one to repeat the obvious. "What's worrying
you?"

"Why isn't he more curious? This," and she gestured at the
lander, the stacks of equipment she'd unloaded, and herself in
the crinkly envirosuit, "*must* be strange to him."

Paradise's sun, almost overhead at the beginning of the visit,
nearly touched the horizon. I was hungry, although I had snacked
throughout the session. Improvised cat food sat, scarcely touched,

in a corner of my screen. Chicken scraps . . . funny that the cat *still* had not attacked them. "Not curious fails to do it justice." The Academy had drummed into us that body language is *not* universal, but I indulged myself once more. "He's yawning a lot. Fidgety." I fast-scanned backward. "Bored? And the angle at which he cocks his head, the tension in his jaw, the squint of his eyes . . . it's as though he has a headache."

Brian loosened the drawstrings of the bag that hung from his belt. He removed two pieces of lumpy, red-orange fruit. He bit into one, pulpy juice trickling into a matted beard. The second piece he offered to Amanda. If he considered the head-to-toe encapsulation of her envirosuit strange, or an impediment to her ability to sample the local cuisine, he kept it to himself. "These need little rain."

"Thank you." To me, she subvocalized, "I'll analyze it later." She set his gift on a portable workbench, and then unsealed an emergency ration. Insinuating food through the helmet port of an envirosuit is neither easy nor pretty; she mimed tasting a cookie before offering one to her visitor.

Brian spit seeds in several directions before giving the cookie a perfunctory sniff. This time his expression was too foreign for me to hazard a guess—but the snack went unsampled into his sack. The headache I inferred him to have seemed to have worsened. "I must leave." He pivoted without ceremony and began walking purposefully back the way he had come.

"Will you return?" Amanda called. "Will you tell others?"

He stopped, less to answer, it seemed, than to reposition a box. A frond that had been bent by the crate sprung straight. "Why?"

Without further comment or explanation, he disappeared into the woods.

"So what do you think?" Amanda spoke around a mouthful of the autogalley's finest. She had a heroic metabolism and an appetite to match. The lunch foregone due to the inconveniences of the envirosuit only made her that much hungrier. A still frame of the disinterested colonist occupied the wall screen behind her.

Halfway around the world I was also eating. "About Brian?"

"About whether it's time to lose the suit." She chewed a mouthful of greens. "Obviously Brian is fine without one."

What could I say? That I had a bad feeling about this? I did, and she laughed.

"You have a bad feeling about *everything*." She turned her attention to a cookie like the one she had given her visitor. "However." Her eyes darted to the lab containment unit in which were arrayed row after row of culture dishes with smears and thin sections of native fruit glob. "That no earthly mold or bacterium has taken hold on the fruit he eats is puzzling enough that I'm going to stay protected for a while."

Things stayed the same for a time. Fruit globs, while non-toxic by every test known to the ship's computers, were also entirely lacking in dietary value. Nor was the mystery limited to the one native species. Amanda made several trips to the edge of the forest—Brian made plain, without lucid explanation, that he did not want her entering—to collect roots and tubers and growths of every type remote sensors captured Brian eating. All hid their nutrients well.

She had no better luck with snared specimens of the six-legged native things we'd taken to calling mice—because that's what you call what a cat stalks. The wireless cameras Amanda had strewn around the landing site and nearby woods had yet to catch her furry friend hunting anything else. It did not eat many Earth-food scraps either. "She," I was repeatedly corrected. "Calico cats are always female."

Ship's sensors had failed to find people on the surface for a good reason: Weaving and woodworking are not industries one observes from orbit. Now, with Brian as an example of the survivors, I switched tactics. Low-flying microbots spotted plenty of other humans. Their shelters were primitive: caves, hide tents, and lean-tos and shacks made of fallen branches. They lived alone or in, we guessed, family units. Nothing bigger.

That dispersion was one more mystery. Even for hunters and gatherers, there appeared to be more than enough food to support many times the current population.

Brian remained nearby, rarely venturing from the densest parts of the fern woods. If he ever saw other humans, those encounters were as elusive as the nutrients that sustained him.

With power and supplies from my docked starship, I restored to habitability an insignificant portion of this ancient and mummified miniworld. The fragile, recreated bubble of life evoked in me some essence of the long-departed crew. Grudgingly, and in elusively suggestive fragments, repaired computer archives surrendered their secrets.

Only constant nurturing of the ecosystem had enabled completion of the slowboat's fourth voyage. In the process, the crew became devoted—by most standards, fanatical—to ecological sanctity. They were overwhelmed when, another interstellar voyage clearly impossible, the prospective home finally within reach after lifetimes of travel proved too Earth-like. They *would* not consider wreaking ecological havoc to give Earthly life a chance to take root; they *could* not survive any longer aboard ship.

I'm a rock boy, asteroid born and bred, so maybe my comments are uninformed. Still, studying the slowboat's records, I didn't consider the planet the colonists were so mystically protective of all that special. The planet at which they had arrived, that is. In the intervening few thousand years, it had flourished.

All I knew for certain was that the colonists had done *something*— found some course of action between extinction and their principles. What that compromise was, I could not say.

"The damnedest thing," Amanda said. She did not puzzle easily, or admit to it readily.

She had been poring over long-range fauna surveys from microsats I had deployed and low-flying drones she had deployed. "We've got very stable populations. The herbivores don't overgraze anywhere, which means the carnivores are keeping them in balance. The carnivores are nicely dispersed, too. Very uniform."

From our years together, I more or less understood her point. Natural systems tend toward equilibrium—but outside shocks to the system disturb that equilibrium: forest fires, earthquakes, volcanoes. Disaster strikes; in that region, one species or other is disproportionately killed off. Surviving species burst into a new niche, for a while with dis-equilibrating effects. Why weren't there more areas in which the predator/prey balance was off? "What do you make of it?"

"Nothing." She grimaced at the camera. "I'm not getting it."

Constantly vidding Amanda made separation that much harder. I even found myself jealous of Brian. The neighborhood primitive showed *no* interest in her, but at least he had the unused option of seeing her, in person. Until, with no obvious reason, he was back.

Back to the fringes of the burned-out region, that is. He was in plain sight of the lander and Amanda's outside equipment, but he did not come close. His attention was on planting seedlings even when she donned her envirosuit and hiked to visit him. When she asked if anyone else would join them, the translator's best guess at his answer was confusion.

I was running out of excuses why Amanda should maintain isolation from Paradise's environment—although, as the mission's biologist, that decision was logically and factually hers. Why I sought excuses was unclear. A planet declared safe would mean our reunion. My innate caution outweighing my loneliness, I speculated. Airless "worlds" like the rock I grew up inside had no tolerance for mistakes.

Long searching eventually revealed some poisonous vegetation, but no more than could be found on large swatches of Earth. Mice (the four-legged, Earthly kind) set outside sniffed and peered about curiously, perfectly content within their wire cages. The big mystery remained how Brian's people lived on what grew here. Amanda's lab animals had ignored samples put into their enclosures. As long as that critical detail eluded us she agreed, reluctantly, to continue avoiding all exposure to the biosphere.

And then. . . .

"These guys were *brilliant*."

We kept comm channels open at all times. Amanda's whoop roused me from deep sleep. I had reset my body clock to sun time at the landing site, where it was now *far* from daylight. Why was she up? "A chipped rock is their idea of advanced engineering," I grumbled. It was an attitude I knew I had to lose. The reunification protocols—our reason for being here, after all, and my job to implement once I was on the ground—were meant to be executed with an open mind.

"Trust me." On-screen, her eyes shone. She could be *so* enthusiastic; that passion for her work is yet another reason I love her. "I couldn't sleep, so I got up to finish some lab work." She brushed an unruly lock of hair from her forehead. "Cameron, I know how they eat here."

That brought me fully awake.

"The Firsters left Earth many thousands of years ago, and we don't know the human genome of the time in detail. Ever since, they've been an isolated, in-bred community. And shipboard shielding is never perfect: There are always the random effects of generations spent exposed to increased cosmic radiation. We *always* expect to find minor genetic drift in rediscovered colonists." She finally paused for breath. "I think this bunch made a genetic change on purpose."

I found I did not share her enthusiasm, even if genetic tinkering had enabled the colonists' survival. "What, exactly, did you find?"

"Gifts from Patches." The lander's galley was tiny; Amanda's body blocked my view of whatever late-night snack she had cooking. A buzzer announced the completion of something. I saw only her back as she turned to remove something from the infrared oven. "From Brian, too, although he is equally oblivious." She turned back to the camera, a mug of steaming whatever clasped in her hands.

Patches was the calico cat. "What did . . . she"—a dazzling smile rewarded me—"give you?"

"Gnawed exoskeletons of the local mice. In Brian's case, spit fruit-glob seeds. In both cases, piles of excrement."

"And?"

"Enzyme traces, Cameron." An arm waved excitedly in, I knew, the direction of her lab. "Enzymes like I've never seen. In the saliva. In the excrement. Enzymes that convert indigenous biochemicals into amino acids and sugars *our* enzymes can process. The colonists must have reengineered *themselves*, in a way we're not smart enough to manage."

Our civilization has its technological advances, primarily in physics—hence our FTL ships—but all those years ago the Firsters knew much about bioscience we still do not. We could never have gotten to the stars by slowboat—we couldn't keep a shipboard biosphere viable for generations, not for even one slowboat crossing. The ancestors of these Stone Age primitives had sustained an ecology in their slowboat for *four*.

I shared, for a moment, my lover's awe in the colonists' accomplishments. That emotion demanded suppression of the misgivings Paradise continued to generate.

"Do you agree?"

An amused tone of voice revealed I had missed an earlier iteration of a question. "Sorry?"

"Do you agree it's time to lose the envirosuit? The lab mice outside are still fine."

What could I say? That I had a bad feeling about this? Again? "I can't think of a reason why you shouldn't."

By the time I was ready once more to consider sleep, Amanda was outside, casually dressed, pitching a tent.

Amanda grew up in an Earth megalopolis with, if it were possible, less vegetation than most asteroid habitats. At one level, that's why she went into the life sciences. She is an expert by modern standards, if not those of the Firsters. Her parents are interplanetary traders, and, from my between-mission contacts with them, egotistical, self-centered, and greedy.

The popular image of the Reunification Corps is of a band of romantics. The truth is very different. Most members enlist for the adventure, the fame of discovering a lost civilization, or the rewards of recovering a lost Firster technology. Amanda, and I love her for it, *was* idealistic. Sure, a part of her recognized her selfless behavior as rebellion. Independence is another part of her charm.

Sudden interest in gardening was no more surprising than many of her whims, and unshielded immersion in Paradise's environment was the last phase of eco-safety assessment. I would be joining her soon. I took her new hobby as an indirect compliment, a way for her to fill the time until our reunion.

Finally, the regulation quarantine period was complete. Amanda suggested that I delay joining her. "I just have a bad feeling." The lopsided grin was like her, if the words were not.

Days laboring outside had left her tanned and toned. Sunshine had bleached brown hair almost blonde. We had been having steamy radio sex since she landed. *I* wanted to land immediately. What was happening?

The radio sex had become a bit routine, I realized. That was surely from repetition. What to many people would have been the obvious explanation never crossed my mind. There was no way Amanda had become involved with someone else—I *know* her. And Brian, still the only other human in the area, kept his distance more than ever since she had shucked the envirosuit. Only Patches was a frequent caller.

Hurt, I redoubled my own cultivation: of techno-archeological insights coaxed and reconstructed from the slowboat's balky computers. Why was Paradise so much greener than upon the colonists' arrival? Why were the animal populations so well balanced? How had the colonists accomplished their genetic adaptation?

Those questions were no more tractable than the one that most troubled me. Besides being my wife, Amanda was the mission's commander and biologist—and she had ordered me to stay where I was.

Why?

Adrenaline coursing, I startled awake. I had not been sleeping well. My body coped by springing catnaps on me.

A half-heard shout still rang in my mind's ears. On a nearby screen, Amanda stared at me, wide-eyed. The sensors that surrounded the landing site read uniformly normal. "Are you all right?"

She swallowed loudly. Her forehead furrowed. "*I* am."

I needed to be down there to comfort and support, as well as to see and hear. If not her, then who? There were few choices. "Did something happen to Brian?"

A shiver ruined her shrug of denial.

"Amanda! What is it?"

She stepped aside, revealing a mouse cage suspended by steel cable from a local tree at about her shoulder level. She shivered again.

Within the wholly intact wire-mesh cage, the scarcely recognizable remains of two mice lay bloody and still.

Perimeter sensors had detected nothing approaching. The lander's cameras had not been watching the cage. Brian, whom she sought out, reacted to the bloody cage with an inscrutable comment about the weather. He kept his distance from her.

Amanda's bad feeling suddenly was not so implausible.

For lack of other ideas, we deployed more sensors and camera drones. We encountered a plethora of local species, both predators and herbivores. I have described this world as Earth-like, but I should clarify: I refer to a much younger Earth than knew humans. None of the indigenous forms was as advanced as a cockroach; Paradise had yet to evolve endoskeletons, multi-chambered hearts, or lungs. At great separations, we saw several cats, a dog, a goat, and two rabbits. Nothing had the incredibly thin claws that would have been required to reach into the still-intact mouse cage.

What kept down the human population? Did something invisible shred *them* unawares, like the mice? Brian did not understand the question, let alone have an answer.

We closely observed Brian, and, far around the periphery of the forest-fire zone, his closest human neighbor: a woman. Both spent their time thinning underbrush, pruning weather-damaged fronds, and doing other pastoral tasks. Don't expect details: On my home rock, we cultured our food in vats.

To meet that newly revealed neighbor meant leaving line-of-sight of the lander and its automatic gun turret. Stun rifle in hand, camera on her shoulder, and translator in her backpack, Amanda trekked to see her. Myra's vocabulary was as limited as Brian's; her curiosity, if anything, even less. Her attitude, which I once again chose to infer from body language, was hostile.

Once more, I was left to wonder: Why?

Three days after the first incident, more mice set outside were slaughtered. This time, the cages had been under constant video surveillance. We replayed the episode, time and again, in confusion and horror.

The mice tore each other apart.

I kept sifting through the digital detritus of a lost civilization, as Amanda grew ever more restless at the landing site. Neither of us found answers.

Amanda started taking long hikes, gleaning samples from the scattered flora poking up through nearby ashes and specimens from the periphery of the native forest. Studying the local plant life was unsurprising enough for a biologist, but, "It seems like the thing to do," was not the answer I expected to her planting and nurturing far more seedlings than she analyzed. What I had called a garden now evolved, by my standards, into a farm. A restful pastime, I supposed. One I would try to get into after I joined her.

Brian, meanwhile, had become openly sullen. He was curt, even belligerent, whenever she approached the fringe of new growth that separated the fire-scarred region from his forest. Without quite knowing why, Amanda found herself taking an unprofessional dislike to him.

There was a Firster expression that applied: about how the cobbler's children went barefoot. Mining the data of an ancient slowboat was second nature to me. Analyzing our own situation—*that* it had not occurred to me to do. Data about the present was Amanda's purview. When I finally did a correlation, two things stood out. Brian only visited when the wind came from his forested home region. Both mice incidents followed weather shifts such that the wind blew briskly from the inland sea.

Brian's ever-cryptic references to wind and weather suddenly took on importance.

"Cameron!"

My heart instantly pounding, I looked up from a dissected Firster computer. On-screen, Amanda shuddered. I was relieved to see her safe inside the lander. Behind her, visible through open airlock doors, stretched the still unnamed inland sea. I could hear the surf. "What is it?"

Still shaking, she pointed to her left; a ship-controlled camera panned to follow the gesture. Two more caged mice, dead. Other mice scurried frantically around their own cages, squealing. The survivors were scant inches from the enclosure of the latest victims.

"Cameron." Sweat beaded on her forehead, ran down her face and neck. An eyelid twitched uncontrollably. "Cameron, if it can strike in here. . . ."

It: The madness that made creatures kill each other. No need to finish the thought.

Unable to concentrate on my work, I watched her autopsy and analyze the dead rodents. She soon had an answer of sorts. "The enzymes from Patches' and Brian's saliva . . . they're also in the dead mice's stomachs."

I asked the one question whose answer might have negated my sense of doom. It did not. "Have you fed these mice any local food?"

"No."

Which suggested that *whatever* caused these deaths was transmitted by air. But what could it be?

✧   ✧   ✧

Patches mostly disdained Amanda's offered snacks. It was a small surprise that local descendants of Earth mice, when caught and caged, would, once they got hungry enough, eat ship's food. It was a far bigger surprise when Earth-bred lab mice ate local food. So far, they were doing fine on a diet of it. I watched her peel a piece of native fruit and feed slivers to mice in their cages. They were delighted.

Then she popped a piece into her mouth. "Spit it out!" I yelled.

She swallowed instead, and licked her lips. "It smelled good," she said, as though that were a justification.

The final lab mice were gone, their self-destructive struggles captured on video. The early deaths had involved pairs of mice, who killed each other. Separating them, attempted more for lack of ideas than a theory, accomplished little. Solitary mice fatally injured themselves in a frenzy of failed escape attempts. The one thing we learned was that mice did not die before puberty.

Amanda refused to quicken any more mice from frozen embryos. "I have no theories to test, no experiments to perform. Creating new mice would be wanton, pointless cruelty."

Misery and fear had us speaking almost constantly; stress made us snap and snarl at each other. When would the self-destructive insanity strike Amanda? I respected the wisdom of Corps protocols, the reasons for her quarantine below . . . all the while hating them.

Meanwhile, she endlessly cultivated her ever-expanding fields. Dirt streaked her face where she had, distractedly, brushed at trickles of sweat. Her bare arms and legs grew filthy, as though she dare not pause to rinse the caked, dried mud.

So we dug, side by virtual side, Amanda in her garden and I, in my own way, in the vast, gap-filled digital archives of the slowboat. "What," I finally asked, on repeatedly encountering the same exotic term, "is an eco-pheromone? Our colonist friends were fascinated with them." On-screen, she shivered. "What? Is that significant?"

"Don't know. A bit of a breeze here, is all." She was kneeling; her attention fixed on the ground until she had tamped down the soil and moistened mulch around the most recent bit of transplanted greenery. It took her a long time; I couldn't imagine what she found so interesting. Finally, she looked up to wink at the camera. "*Some* pheromones would be welcome."

"Hmm." It had been a very long time, even by radio. "I could be talked into that."

"That has never required rhetorical skill." She cackled at my mock glower. "What do you say? Give me a while to wash up, and I'll call you from," and she batted her eyes, "my private chambers."

"Hmm," I repeated enthusiastically. This time we both laughed.

We met at the appointed time, each in our own cabin. The only alcohol on the lander was in the form of lab supplies, pure but without character. Amanda named a brandy we both favored, suggesting that I enjoy for two.

Then, touchingly, she called up one of my compositions, the first she had ever experienced. Arpeggios from a thousand synthesized instruments rippled and interlaced in counterpoint to a spectacular video from Alpha Centauri 4. Snowcapped mountains glittered in countless colors. Shadows cast by three suns lengthened and blended. One by one, the suns set, until only a warm red twilight glow remained. Music and dusk faded together into an infinite sea of stars.

What we said and did . . . those are important only to us. Afterward, I slept soundly for the first time in a long while.

Yet again, strident alarms made me jump. System after system aboard the lander screamed electronically: catastrophic failure. Text scrolled faster than I could absorb it: alerts and warnings. Mostly obscured on screen by the blur of dire notifications was a frenzied, axe-wielding figure. Amanda. Sparks, flame, and black smoke spewed from shattered consoles.

"Stop!" Had she heard me over alarms shrieking in the lander and echoed here? "Amanda, stop!" My shouts had no effect. "*Please*," I implored. Why was she doing this? From orbit, I could only send an acknowledgement of the alarms. Electronic warbling faded. Great sobs became audible between crunching thuds of the fire axe. *"Amanda!"*

Either my yelling or sheer exhaustion finally stopped her. She tottered, leaning against the wooden haft of the axe. Sooty garments clung to her, sodden with sweat. Her eyes glinted insanely. "I . . . I . . . ," she coughed.

"Please," I pleaded again. I fell silent in confusion. Please what? Stop? She already had. Tell me I'm going mad, that I'm imagining things? "Please tell me why you are doing this."

The choking sobs subsided a bit. Her eyes streamed tears, whether from smoke or emotion I did not know—and that I couldn't distinguish was bitter. "I . . . I had to do this before I lost the will."

"Do *what*, Amanda?" Coughing preempted any answer. The crackling of the flames grew louder. Alarms rang anew, as fire suppressant sputtered futilely from ceiling nozzles. "Get off the lander." She nodded and stumbled to the open airlock.

Outdoor sensors imaged her from all sides as she stood, stoop-shouldered and weeping. Wordlessly we watched the lander vanish in a geyser of flames. Comsats relayed the scene, low-res and shimmery for lack of landing-site amplification. "Amanda." No response. "Why?!"

"I can never leave. I made certain that, if my resolve weakens, I never do." It had to be blisteringly hot so near the still-burning wreckage, but she was shivering.

My mind raced. Whatever momentary lunacy had made her wreck the lander need not doom her. Our starship was fine—if unbearably empty. I could go for help, for a team of biologists to somehow make things right. "At least tell me what this is about."

She explained a lot now, with one word.

Replaying the video, the fronds of the seedlings all around Amanda had been perfectly still. There had been no breeze; her spontaneous trembling in reaction to my question about eco-pheromones had been horrified insight. The long time she had spent puttering with the plant, staring at the ground and away from the camera, masked frantic thinking.

"For some reason, you feel you can't leave." I could not yet imagine what the reason might be. I did not *care*. It was Amanda. "Then I'll join you. I'll come down in the other lander."

"No!" Tears that had subsided welled anew. Mucus bubbled from her nostrils and ran down her chin. "Don't you see, Cameron? That would be *worse*. If I see you in person, I'll be repelled." A shudder made her pause.

"If you leave, at least we'll have our memories."

✧   ✧   ✧

Pheromones, it turns out, are much more than sexual attractants. More broadly, they are biochemical stimulants of behavior, like the scent trails left by ant scouts to lead worker ants to food. Not only animals secrete pheromones; so do some algae, slime molds, and fungi. But pheromonal effects were largely intra-species—on Earth. Eco-pheromones, Amanda had realized, must involve wide-ranging biochemical signaling among species.

And *that* mechanism resolved so many of the unanswered questions about Paradise.

Only science far beyond even the Firsters' usual unattainable standards had kept the ship's biosphere viable long enough to reach Paradise. With the scattered and incomplete records that were recoverable, we had not a chance in several lifetimes of recreating their achievement. By we, I mean the Corps and all its resources.

I did not have several lifetimes.

Still, *what* had happened was finally clear, if only in barest outline. The Firsters had synthesized two of what they called retroviruses. These molecular machines were benign as far as the immune system was concerned, which made them invisible to our biohazard sensors. Both retroviruses implanted designer genes into terrestrial mammals. The spliced genes from the first retrovirus expressed the proteins that, by allowing the colonists to digest local life forms, enabled survival. Given that adaptation, however, there was nothing to stop the highly evolved immigrant species from out-competing all native fauna—which the colonists were unwilling to permit.

Hence the second retrovirus: It implanted the genes that let the survivors live with themselves.

"We will not prolong our time through the wanton extinction of those who belong on this beautiful world," declared the slowboat's log, in an entry recorded as the shipboard biosphere was in its death throes. "Nor will we abandon to their fate those who have been such loyal shipboard companions.

"We will co-exist, or we will perish."

Perhaps they knew what they were doing. I prefer to think they ran out of time before testing could be completed. Either way, the crew descended to Paradise's surface, committed to being stewards of the land.

They had succeeded brilliantly. Earth animals coexisted every-where with native forms, and, as the records from planetfall proved, the indigenous biosphere was now far lusher than before humanity's arrival.

But genius does not preclude unintended consequences. Such as: Biological imperatives that made caged mice, their enforced proximity unbearable, fight to the death once a fickle wind stopped wafting plant and animal scents, eco-pheromones, from the nearby forest. The same imperatives that drove uncaged cats and dogs—and humans—far apart.

Humans are meant to be social creatures, not territorial like cats.

Biological imperatives the colonists had created rewarded ecological stewardship above all else. Healthy regions exuded a rich trans-species stew of pheromones, and the body responded to immersion with an endorphin-like reward. Even a brief absence from a healthy, balanced ecosystem interrupted secretion of the endorphin, and began production of its opposite, some type of repellent. Too late, I understood Brian's evident headaches—drug withdrawal—when he ventured into the forest-fire zone. I remembered him meeting Amanda in her envirosuit and sniffing in puzzlement—at her lack of pheromones.

Only in a broad expanse where many species flourished did the density and diversity of pheromones enable small groups to form, and then only temporarily. Puberty began pheromone production; only an exceptionally fecund region could sustain eco-balance in the presence of pheromones from more than two adult anythings. Puberty caused dissolution of the family unit.

When Amanda shed her suit, Paradise's ubiquitous retroviruses began her transformation. No mere garden could prevent her altered body's production of the anti-endorphin. Whenever the prevailing wind shifted, whenever steady currents of pheromones did not arrive from Brian's ceaselessly cultivated and much larger domain, she became abhorrent.

Unapproachable.

As I would be, if, against Amanda's express commands and wishes, I were to join her. . . .

Luminous orbs dominated an ink-black sky, mirrored in a glass-smooth sea. The nearer moon, larger than Earth's and closer to its primary, seemed to fill the sky. The other satellite, appearing half the size of Earth's, also full, hovered above its companion. An evening star sparkled like a ruby just over the paired glowing disks. Music swelled as celestial spheres swung into alignment, a visual harmony observable at this spot but once every three hundred nine Paradise years.

The image is computer-generated, because the next physical alignment is not due for twenty years. Amanda and I silently shared the moment. Needing above all else to parallel her experience, I too witnessed it on a portable computer, shunning sensory immersion in the starship's holographic theater.

We watched each other watching through tiny inset windows of our computer screens. She recovered the power of speech first. "It's stunning, Cameron, a gift I will cherish always." Her voice quavered. Left unspoken was that this new composition, like that last night of passion, was meant as a keepsake for the long years to come. "When alignment comes, Cameron, I'll be playing your music and thinking of you." Tears flowed, and her voice grew husky. "Still loving you.

"Now, go."

Loneliness rends me. Protocol, the mission commander's orders, and common sense all insist that I leave. My preparation, such as it is, is complete.

I look for the last time around the empty tavern of the slowboat. Hundreds of blue-and-green-and-white reflections of the globe below mock me.

This history is almost complete, recorded for some improbable resurgence of civilization by the primitives below.

Can the humans of Paradise ever cure what their mad, desperate, genius ancestors did to them? A cure is what's needed. The retroviruses, more than an ecological adaptation, are a devolutionary trap. In a scant few thousand years, the surviving colonists—addicted to healthy-ecology endorphins, unable to congregate—have regressed to near-instinctual behavior.

Most of the planet's surface is already in bloom; there is no basis for population expansion. Culture and science have been forgotten. How much longer, in a "society" that can support even family units only occasionally and temporarily, will traces of language survive? How few generations remain until the mute descendants of starfarers become mere tireless servants to ferns?

There is little left to say.

"If you now viewing this history come from afar, from the

Reunification Corps, perhaps, a sincere warning: Do not land! If you reached this ship from the planet below . . . then surely you understand the nuances of your biosphere better than did Amanda or I." In case of that eventuality, computers were rendering my rambling oration into English. The translation had to use the full Firster language—that which I needed to impart was far too complex for the pathetic scraps of speech still in use below. "Somehow, you have escaped the trap. I salute you."

I like to believe that *somehow* involves me.

I have set my landing coordinates for the fire-ravaged area in which Amanda now makes her home—but at the opposite extreme. If we can make bloom our separate ends of that desolation, can expand them until they merge, the reclaimed region, bountiful with its own eco-pheromones, will make possible *our* reunification.

My lander's lab computers contain the finest of modern and recovered Firster biotech. Long after I become a grubber in the dirt, lab automation will simulate, and wherever there is a chance, synthesize, possible counter-pheromones and anti-retroviruses.

I do not delude myself: Much of the search will be by trial and error. Mere neutralization of the Firster technology, as unimaginably difficult as that would be, is not my goal. A new bioagent must be limited in its effects to humans—anything less specifically targeted would destroy the biosphere the colonists sacrificed so much to preserve. Extrapolation suggests that the process could take hundreds of years, but it could still help *someone*.

I have purged all interstellar navigational data from the lander. That precaution, this recording—and the dispatch of the Corps starship to its fiery death in the nearby sun—are necessary to protect *my* civilization from the eco-madness below.

Hundreds of blue-and-green-and-white reflections of the globe below mock me.

I will not be mocked.

Amanda's first words to me were, "You act like the world is against you."

Slowly, I had turned toward at her. Smiling, I had peered deeply into her blue, blue eyes. "If we can be together," I had answered her, "I'll take those odds."

I stride confidently to the lander. In twenty years, we have a celestial wonder to share.

NEWTS

Kevin J. Anderson

During what should have been the ring colony's Independence Day celebration, the mood in the family habitat was somber. Rex Hollings stared through the viewing window toward the pastel clouds of Saturn. Thanks to the mellowing influence of his implant, he wore a placid smile, aware of and yet immune to the misery and dread all around him. The others were incapable of being so stable in a time of crisis.

Rex admired the planet's gentle beauty. The majestic ring arced up and caught sunlight, glittering with a spray of rocks where the tightly knit group of Worthies had built habitation modules, storage depots, greenhouse domes. All those artificial structures should have formed the backbone of a carefully engineered society. A magnificent colony. Standing alone, Rex considered the grand aspirations of visionary Ardet Hollings, who had founded the Worthies.

Now there were three empty seats at the dinner table. All families had suffered similar losses in the recent space battle.

As the emotional currents moved around him, Rex imagined himself as a rock in a fast-flowing stream, as in the library images he liked to view. Images of natural beauty were the only parts of

Earth that Ardet had allowed them to see, claiming that everything else was too corrupt. He found the lovely landscape scenes
very soothing, the rushing waters, the crashing ocean waves,
the silvery waterfalls. Rex had never visited Earth, and he never
would, especially not now.

Though he could not personally experience extreme moods, he
still recognized the agitation from his mother and his two sisters-
in-law. It was like learning a foreign language. Even little Max
was affected by the tension; the boy clung fussily to his Uncle
Rex, who was two years younger than his father. Rex picked up
his unsettled nephew, whispering soft words that soothed him.
Max stopped crying, giggled once, then played with his uncle's
hair. They both looked out the window. "See the planet? Isn't it
pretty?" As a first-born, Max would never be subjected to the
implant, or the operation. If Rex hadn't been so calm, he might
have envied the little boy.

Mother emerged from the kitchen unit, forcing a bright smile.
She looked wrung-out and pale, overworked, overwhelmed, but
not willing to surrender any ground to Fate. She would keep
doing what she must, regardless of the circumstances. As the wife
of Ardet Hollings, she had always been an excellent example for
other Worthy women to emulate, filling her role, doing her tasks,
never overstepping the boundaries. Rex thought she was perfect.
Even knowing the terrible things that had happened to the colony,
and what they could expect from the Earth military forces, her
job was to manage their home and keep the family unit intact.
Mother would die before she gave up any of those tasks, no matter what outside threat might be coming their way.

"Today is our special day, so we have a feast. Twenty-one
years ago today Ardet led us away from Earth and brought us
here to form our model society." She said the phrases she had
memorized. Her husband had written the original Independence
Day speech, and the words had become canon. "We came here
to find peace, despite the hardships we knew we would have to
face and without interference from outsiders."

Rex intoned the benediction along with his two sisters-in-law,
"Peace despite hardship." He handed the now-happy toddler back
to Ann, tapping Max on the nose and making him giggle one
last time before the meal.

Mother brought out platters of fresh vegetables grown in the greenhouse domes. At the end of his shift that day, Rex had brought home the best from the harvest, far more than they really needed to eat. There were ears of bright yellow corn, bowls of green beans, leafy salads dressed with spicy herbed sauces. Tofumeat added extra protein.

With all greenhouse systems perfectly functional, at last, the productivity in the domes was enough to feed a population beyond even Ardet's greatest dreams—and now that so many colonists had died, there was extra food for the table. *Silver linings.* Rex smiled at the thought. He served himself sliced tomatoes so red they made the eyes ache.

"There isn't much reason to celebrate," grumbled Ann as she took her seat next to one of the empty spots. When Max fussed, she set the toddler on her knee and absently shushed him. Rex offered to take the boy, but Ann shook her head.

Mother would not let anything derail her purpose. "It is still our Independence Day. We have always celebrated it, and we'll do so again this year. Our men would want it that way."

"Who knows what will happen next year?" Rex said, meaning to be optimistic. He let events flow toward him and accepted whatever came. He, like so many others of his generation, was kept on an even keel, cooperative, causing no trouble. Ardet had wanted it that way.

Instead, his comment stung the others there. Rex could see expressions fall and felt their turbulent anxiety: grief for lost husbands, fear of the inevitable end of their way of life, anger at the enemy that had robbed the Worthies of their future. No matter how brave their deaths had been while standing against the invaders, the men were still dead.

"I'm . . . sorry for what I said. It was insensitive."

"That's all right, Rex. You can't help it," Mother said.

Dark-eyed Jen, the widow of his brother Ian, took a seat across from Rex, moving as if in a daze. She had full lips, a lush figure, and a once-sparkling personality that had made her an extremely desirable mate. Ian had been the envy of many Worthies when she'd accepted his proposal of marriage, and Ardet himself had blessed the union. Rex had been very pleased for both of them, hoping they would have many children . . . but there hadn't been time. He could sense Jen's sorrow at that now, the suffocating weight of lost opportunities.

It all flowed past him. He was a rock in a stream. That was as much as the implant, and his altered body, allowed him to be.

Since Rex was the only "man" there, Mother asked him to say a brief prayer for Lee and Ian, as well as their father and all of the fallen heroes. Rex mouthed the memorized words in his thin, piping voice. Then they all joined in an uninspired but adequate recitation of Ardet's traditional Independence Day benediction. When he finished speaking, everyone murmured, "As Ardet said."

Giving him a shy smile, Jen served Rex one of the ears of corn, took a smaller one for herself, then passed the plate down to where Ann was struggling with Max while scooping up some beans. Ann had a round face and curly brown hair. When her husband was still alive, she had kept herself beautiful for him, but in the months since Lee had fallen, she'd had little opportunity to do so, especially with caring for Max.

Rex knew that Ann struggled to be strong, to follow Mother's example; Worthy women were groomed to be exceptionally competent in their well-defined areas of responsibility, and to rely on the men to fulfill their own duties. But not even Ardet, with his grand dreams and detailed societal models, had envisioned the possibility of an entire stratum vanishing practically overnight.

Ann asked, "How soon do you suppose the DPs will be here?" She spoke as if it were casual mealtime conversation, though Rex could hear the tension, like brittle glass in her voice.

"I'll have no such talk at the table." Mother passed the salad bowl around again and urged them to eat. "This isn't the time for it."

"I'm afraid," Jen said in a small voice, looking directly at Rex. He glanced away, knowing what she wanted from him but unable to give it. He felt so sorry for her.

The Democratic Progressives had dispatched a retaliatory force to crush them, and everyone knew it was only a matter of time. The Worthies had already sacrificed all their fighting men against the first small exploratory force that had come to Saturn. Ardet, Lee, Ian, and the other men in the Worthy settlement had defeated the enemy that day, but at incredible cost to themselves. The remaining colonists would have no chance when Earth's reinforcements arrived at Saturn. For months now, Rex had felt the uneasy panic wafting among the colony survivors like the wind from a laboring air recycler.

But he remained calm. All newts remained calm. Ardet had thought it for the best.

After the meal, his belly full, Rex helped out in the kitchen unit, cleaning dishes, recycling scraps. Though Worthy men did not do such work, newts were allowed to perform some duties traditionally reserved for women. Besides, Rex had designed or refined some of the household recycling systems himself, and he knew how to keep them functioning at peak efficiency.

Jen offered to help him while Ann and Mother played with Max in the main living area. One of Ardet's old recorded speeches played on the screen; crowds of exuberant new colonists cheered, giddy with their recent separation from Earth and assured of a bright future if only they followed the rigid Worthy plan.

Jen stood uncomfortably close to Rex in the cramped kitchen unit. He used a squeegee to scrape food into a compost-recycler and stored the serving plates in the sanitizer, which used water reclaimed from the abundant ice in Saturn's rings. For a while, she made light conversation, though he could hear a deep and desperate huskiness to her voice, a longing and a need. After a long pause, Jen said in a very low whisper, "Rex, I ache every time I see you. Do you know how much you remind me of Ian? You look so much like him."

"I *am* his brother. We've always looked a lot alike."

She slipped her arms around his waist. "Face me."

He felt awkward, interrupted in his work, but he dutifully turned. He looked at Jen's oval face, her delicate chin. Both of his brothers' wives were beautiful women, yet Rex felt no desire for his sisters-in-law. Still, he loved them deeply. Jen must have seen it on his face. He stroked her hair, trying to calm her, as he had done with Max.

Growing bolder, she pressed her soft breasts against his chest, then tilted her face. She kissed him, at first tentatively, then ferociously. Her lips were moist and pleasant, warm, wanting more than he was capable of giving. "I miss him so much, Rex. I'm so lonely."

"We're all lonely." He gently extricated himself, patted her on the shoulder, as a brother would, and reminded her of what she already knew. "I'm not entirely like Ian. I'm missing some of my parts."

Though he had not intended to upset her in any way, he experienced her reaction like whitecaps crashing against a sea cliff.

Another library image from Earth . . . Rebuffed, Jen backed to the door of the kitchen unit. He could not experience the same reactions, with all the highs and lows of passion clipped from him, but he very much wanted to understand. "I'm sorry," he said automatically, hoping it would defuse the tension simmering in her. "Don't be angry."

Dark hair swirled around her as she tossed her head and looked at him with a flicker of . . . disgust? "How can you keep us safe from the DPs? They're coming! You know what they're like. They'll destroy us all."

Rex blinked at her, struggling to quell the situation. Yes, he had heard Ardet's speeches on the evils of Earth, the manic greed and violence of the Democratic Progressives. Rex, born here in the new colony, had never experienced Earth except through his father's harsh descriptions, but he believed the stories of a lawless society in which no member knew his or her place. After great struggle and persecution, the Worthies had broken away from that, coming far enough out here into unclaimed territory that they could achieve their potential, following Ardet's social map. Rex was part of that; they all were.

"We all have our tasks, Jen. I'm a newt. You know that being a fighter—or a lover—is not one of my duties." He offered a comforting smile. "I can do many things, Jen, just not what you're looking for right now." Rex squared his shoulders, as he had seen his brothers do. "But if we don't stay the course in our darkest hour, then we dishonor Ardet. He gave us our instructions. If we cast them aside now, then we are no better than the people from Earth."

It was an intellectual argument, the kind Rex was best at, and he could see that it did not convince Jen's heart. After she left him in a swirl of anger and fear, he went back to finish the kitchen chores by himself.

The handful of intact Worthy men insisted they would go down fighting for their principles, their way of life. Rex was physically, and chemically, prevented from feeling the same passionate resolve, but he could admire their determination, their bravery, their refusal to give up. He was sure Ardet Hollings would have been proud.

Shortly after their independence day, Rex and a dozen newts

were removed from their daily assignments and sent out into the space rubble field with Commander Joseph Heron. Heron was old, scarred, and impatient, one of only twenty-three male survivors of the initial battle against the Democratic Progressives. Listening to him rail against Fate, Rex wondered if Heron had spent the last several months wishing that he too had died in the conflict. But if he had, who would defend the Worthies against the decadent and despicable DPs?

From the time he was a child, Rex had been trained how to suit up and how to perform outside functions. He was perfectly capable of performing tasks out in hard vacuum, as were his fellow newts. They were well-educated, even-tempered workers who remained unruffled in a crisis. They would complete their tasks as required, no matter how anxious and uptight Commander Heron and his desperate soldiers might be.

Scouts had already combed the space battlefield for any wreckage they could salvage, but Heron insisted on trying again and again. The vagaries of gravity in the rings churned up new discoveries, like repressed emotions coming to the surface. Rex was sure nothing remained to be found, but the commander had nothing to cling to but dogged optimism. Rex was surprised, and pleased, when the searches paid off: Far from where anyone expected gravity and momentum to have carried it, they discovered a nearly intact DC ship.

Leaving Heron in charge was yet another example of Ardet's great wisdom: No newt would have bothered to keep searching.

"This is our greatest break yet, men," the commander said over the suit intercom as their shuttle approached. Heron allowed only a small touch of irony when he said "men." His voice held an edge, as if anger could inspire the newts to greater dedication, but the implants continued to keep them controlled, calm. It was the most reasonable way to get a tough job done. After the Worthies' early years of near-starvation, Ardet had based much of his plan on that basic idea. . . .

Heron named the wreck *Flying Dutchman* after an old Earth ghost story. The *Dutchman*'s hull had been breached in several places, venting its atmosphere and killing the small crew. When their shuttle circled the derelict, Rex studied the configuration, making mental notes about what needed to be repaired. Decades ago, when leaving their tainted planet behind, Ardet's followers had purchased brute-force commercial vessels to haul people and equipment on a one-way trip to Saturn. This DC exploratory ship was faster, its lines sleeker, its potential greater than anything the colonists had used.

When the shuttle docked against the *Dutchman*'s cold hull, Heron addressed his men and the newts. "Inside this wreck, there may be energy weapons, explosive projectiles, something we can use. It's my aim to get this vessel up and running. Then we'll have five ships, and we can make a good accounting of ourselves when the DPs come."

"Can we even understand the systems, sir?" Rex asked. "This technology far surpasses what we're used to."

The older commander turned to him. Behind the reflected glimmer on the curved faceplate, Rex could see his frown. "Just because you don't have any balls, doesn't mean you don't have any brains. I'm counting on you to figure this out, Rex. It's the only way we can survive."

Rex didn't think they would survive in any case, but he made no further comment. The other newts waited to receive instructions.

After they broke into the *Dutchman*, the salvagers separated into teams and methodically moved from deck to deck. They discovered the iron-hard bodies of six DC soldiers, expressions frozen as if surprised that a tiny group of isolationists had fought so bitterly against their impressive ship. Two of Heron's men let out defiant cries of triumph; the others were queasy and silent. The newts were put on corpse detail, gathering and ejecting the dead soldiers. They didn't mind.

On the bridge, Commander Heron and his men studied the dead ship's systems. Rex stepped up to the engine controls and navigation modules, and peered down to read the labels on each station. He knew how to fix familiar systems—recyclers, irrigators, and lighting—but these looked different.

"Don't just stand there and make this place crowded," Heron said. "Not much time left!" The other newts spread out and began to make repairs.

With so many unknown factors, the Worthies had no way of determining exactly when the retaliatory ships would arrive. After receiving distress signals from the battle in the rings six months ago, Earth should have taken at least a month to gather a new fleet, which would take five or more months in transit. But if the DC military had modified their engines, improved their speed or fuel efficiency, they could fly to Saturn more swiftly than expected.

By any calculation, the DPs could be here any day.

Rex used a circuit mapper and command-train isolator to check the station panels, one row after another. He documented which modules were functional and which needed to be routed around or replaced. Even if the *Dutchman* were completely repaired, though, the new DC ships were bound to be far superior.

That first engagement had been unintentional, at least on Earth's part. The Democratic Progressives had sent an exploratory force through the solar system, mapping resources, choosing possible locations for new colonies and outposts.

"It's what so-called 'progressives' do," Ardet had said in a speech to every member of the Worthy colony. "They spread, and exploit, and take what they want. We cannot let them steal our homes! We dare not let them disrupt our grand experiment. We must prove the strength of our principles." His voice grew deeper and more powerful; it had been so stirring that Rex found himself moved in spite of the implant. "The DPs are barbarians—they will pillage, and rape, and destroy everything we hold dear!"

The Worthy men had howled, the women had cringed, and the newts had listened carefully. The men gathered every possible ship, cobbled together anything that could be used as a weapon, then set an ambush in the rings to protect their way of life.

The DC exploratory force had come to Saturn with escort ships and scientific vessels, intending to use the plentiful ice in the rings to replenish their fuel and water supplies. Rex had studied the records of their arrival, and (as far as he could tell) the DPs had taken no aggressive action; it seemed possible that they hadn't even known about the tiny hidden colony. But fiery-eyed Ardet called it an incursion, a criminal trespass by plunderers. After overcoming birth pains and terrible difficulties, the colony had begun to thrive, exactly according to the design. They wanted nothing to do with the people of Earth.

The DC scientists and pilots were astonished when the Worthy men attacked. Though the DC exploratory fleet was not a military force, they had fought back, killing most of the young men and Ardet Hollings himself before being destroyed themselves.

"Nothing here we can't fix," Commander Heron said, rapping on the arm of the captain's chair. "We can get the *Dutchman* flying again!" He looked around the bridge as if expecting the newts to cheer, but they continued their tasks with silent efficiency. He turned to Rex. "*You.* You're Ardet's own son. Doesn't anything get you riled up?"

Rex shrugged in his bulky suit. "That's not possible, sir." He reset a panel and was gratified to see that all systems were now functional. "But I do my job to the best of my abilities. Is there something inadequate about my performance?"

Discouraged, the commander let out a long sigh that was audible across the helmet radio. "We won't be able to last five minutes against the forces from Earth."

Back at his familiar work in the greenhouse domes, comfortable with the routine despite the imminent arrival of the DPs, Rex was glad to be doing something worthwhile. "There is no more glorious work than providing food for our people," Ardet had said to all greenhouse workers. And since Rex also worked on the illumination and irrigation systems, he felt he was doing even more than his part. It gave him a warm satisfaction to know he fit in so well.

Overhead, bright stars and outlying ring fragments moved like fireflies. Some of the women harvesting produce looked up nervously, as if expecting them to be braking jets from Earth ships; Rex saw only lovely lights as bright as diamonds.

He hummed a tuneless song to relax himself, though the implant did most of the job. Crews of newts and women picked ripe vegetables and fruits, never letting anything go to waste. The recycled air smelled fresh, moist, mulchy. Overhead lamps poured out warm, buttery light to nourish the plants. Coming around the gauzy limb of Saturn, the sun also rose, adding its distant light and life. Bees transported from Earth buzzed around the flowers, sexless drones doing their work for the betterment of the hive.

Two years ago, encouraged by his father, Rex had improved the hydroponic trays and then the nutrient-delivery irrigators in the planted rows. Now he drew a deep breath and sighed as he looked out at the colorful patterns of growth, all the shades of green. Each species was planted in the proper order for optimal food production, everything in its place, everything productive. Ardet Hollings had been such a genius.

Rex ruffled his fingers through the velvety leaves of enhanced strawberries. Ripe and red, they would make a sweet dessert; perhaps Mother would serve some tonight. She had been more extravagant with her cooking in the past few weeks, as if to reassure everyone that nothing was wrong.

As he moved the leaves aside, Rex spotted a darting lizard. The original colonists had brought no large animals with them from Earth, but along with the bees they had released numerous small animals such as birds, shrews, and tiny lizards. The birds and rodents had died; only the lizards had survived, and thrived, finding an entire ecological niche for themselves.

Rex tried to catch it, but he wasn't quick enough. The lizard vanished among the strawberry plants, showing only a flicker of a tail that was a different color—obviously broken off and then regrown. Lizards had that amazing regenerative ability. Rex went back to his work picking the berries.

In the beginning, Worthies had planted only the fastest growing and highest-energy-density foods, then used reprocessing chemistry to break down even the waste vegetation into edible mass. They'd had nothing else to eat. Because of Ardet's innovative survival measures, that crisis had passed when Rex was just a child, and now the Worthies had the luxury and the inclination to plant decorative flowers and ornamental shrubs from stored genetic samples.

This place had become a home instead of just a subsistence colony. But it wouldn't last.

In their fourth year away from Earth, one of the three primary greenhouses had failed; a piece of rogue stony debris thrown from an impact in the rings had sailed at high velocity into the armored dome, shattering several panes and hemorrhaging atmosphere. Most of the air was gone, the temperature plunged, the greenhouse sent into an unstable wobble. Seven people died, and all the plants perished—one third of the crops to feed the settlement. Adding to the disaster, a blight had swept through the corn crop in one of the other greenhouses, decimating that harvest as well.

On the relatively new colony, their survival had already been hanging by a thread. Most of their preserved supplies were already gone. Devastated by the loss, the Worthies watched their perfectly planned future crumble. Though workers scrambled to build another greenhouse dome and create subsidiary growing areas, they faced the very real prospect of dying—or returning, beaten, to repressive Earth.

Ardet rallied them. "Return is never an option! We have fought too hard to establish a perfect society. I have provided the road map. Do we dare take our children back to that hellhole? How could we betray them in such a way?" He had lifted his young son Rex for all his followers to see. Now, when Rex watched the tapes and studied his father's words, he was glad that in his small way he had helped Ardet make his point. "We have given our citizens their places, defined their roles, offered them security instead of cultural pandemonium. Men and women fill the niches for which they were bred, without the confusion of too much freedom and too many pressures." It was a famous speech that all students were required to memorize. In the recording, the people were bleak, gaunt and hollow-eyed—with fear, as much as from hunger.

After the greenhouse failure, knowing they would barely have enough to eat for the next few years, Ardet had assessed the big picture and repainted his grand social landscape. "As Worthies, we must watch ourselves. We did not ask for an easy life, nor will we ever have one. Our population must always be carefully controlled. We will grow, and we will triumph, but out here we must do it in a properly planned fashion. This is not Earth."

"Peace, despite hardship," the crowd had mumbled.

"Thus, for the time being, we must stabilize our population. We must shore up our society, keep our roles intact, keep our people happy. We cannot have strife, nor can we have uncontrolled breeding. Thus, as a gesture to strengthen all of us in our resolve, we must make sure that no more than two children in each family will reproduce."

This announcement had been met with dismay, since Worthies had, until now, been encouraged to have large families in order to increase their numbers. The people muttered. "Most of us already have more children than that, Ardet. Do you . . . want us to kill them?" someone asked from the audience. Watching that interchange over and over, Rex was sure that the questioner would have done it, if Ardet had asked.

Their leader shook his head and gave a broad, paternal smile. "Of course not. We love our children. They are the building blocks of our great society. But, we must use them with great care, to a noble purpose." Ardet had looked at them all with his intense visionary glare. "While I am confident we have the strength to survive, this crisis is only an example of our possible tribulations. By our own design, we are in a new situation here at Saturn. We came to escape the anarchy and gluttony of Earth, and to do that we must change ourselves . . . and that is a good thing, though it will be hard.

"For this generation, we must take interim measures. Difficult measures, but vital ones. After the first two children, our extra sons and daughters will remain important parts of our perfect society, but they will also make the sacrifice so that we can remain strong and stable." He had looked at them all. Rex still felt a chill when he recalled the historical tapes. "They must be neutered."

As an educated adult, when Rex considered the details of the solution, he didn't think the mathematics worked out. Neutering the additional children had not decreased the number of mouths to feed. But, as became clear later, that had only been the first part of Ardet's brilliant plan. Using the greenhouse accident as a springboard, he had led his people past another watershed, pushed his new society to an entirely new level.

Because he was their leader, because his followers would do anything he asked, they had not argued. To show his sincerity, Ardet had won their hearts by offering up his own young son as the first to be castrated. Rex was told again and again what a great thing he was doing, though being only four years old at the time he had understood nothing about what was really being taken from him.

After a large group of children was neutered and properly raised—girls as well as boys—Ardet had quietly revealed his deeper motivation to create an entire layer of society without aggression, without destructive competitiveness. Newts were cooperative and friendly, productive, and completely reliable, if not ambitious; the boys being the most prominently changed. The castration itself was not sufficient for Ardet's purpose, though. With carefully metered implants, the newts remained on an even emotional footing, causing no trouble. Each family was allowed two viable children, and the rest became a new caste, the strong and stable foundation for a great Worthy civilization. Rex had listened to the rationales over and over. He thought it was breathtaking. . . .

Now, as Rex and the newts continued their work in the greenhouse, the women reacted to a signal piped in over the dissemination channel. The words were spoken in a crisp voice with just a tinge of fear. "An outpost on the fringe of the outer ring has picked up radio chatter, and long-distance sensors have just discovered the Earth military force on its way. The Democratic Progressives will arrive at the rings of Saturn within a week, two at the most."

Hearing this, Rex missed his brothers more than ever. He had never understood them, but he loved them nevertheless. In their youth, Lee and Ian had fought and wrestled with each other, so full of life. Fairly bursting with energy, they had always exhausted their little brother. They had tried to include Rex in their roughhousing play, but even as a boy he had never enjoyed it—due more to the implant than the actual neutering. What if he had been more like them?

As he finished filling his container with strawberries, Rex looked up through the transparent dome. He thought about Jen, desperate for him to be something he wasn't, then felt sorry for Ann and her little boy. For their sakes, he tried to imagine himself in a Worthy soldier's uniform. What if it came down to that?

Would he grab a projectile repeater rifle and stand at the habitat doorway with Mother, Ann, and Jen behind him? Snarling, would he point the hot barrel of the weapon toward oncoming DC invaders, scream like a madman and blast away one enemy after another? Maybe he would use the weapon as a club if he ran out of ammunition. He would bare his teeth. He would claw at them with his hands. The women would treat Rex as a hero, a savior. Then he would hop aboard the *Flying Dutchman* and streak off into space, using the ship's weapons to destroy more of the DC attackers. He would make them pay dearly. . . .

Rex wiped away the faint sweat that had broken out on his forehead, shaking his head at the strange ideas. The implant struggled to banish the thoughts as fast as they came into his head. None of it felt like something he could do, something he *should* do. Rex was a newt, with his specific role to play—just like every Worthy. Ardet would have been gravely disappointed to learn his son had even entertained such fantasies. It was not at all what the great leader had designed newts to do. They served another purpose.

Rex emptied his container of strawberries, then went to pick soybeans. Even after the women had rushed off, he and four newt companions stood together chatting. Their conversation didn't touch on the approaching Democratic Progressives. Rex was confident that everything would work out for the best.

The family huddled together in the living quarters for their final hours. Rex held a squirming Max as he stood at the window, but even his uncle's attentions could not calm the boy against the palpable storm of panic. Rex felt the boy's misery and held him close, but they could not help each other.

Intellectually, he knew their dire straits, though the implant worked overtime to keep him quiet and anchored. Now he needed it more than ever. With a glance at the pale, wide-eyed faces of his mother, of Ann and Jen, Rex wondered if they envied him his calm.

With Max clinging to him, he pondered what it might have been like if he'd had a child of his own. If things had been different, would he have felt the longing to reproduce, the endless ticking of a biological clock?

Rex kissed the toddler's cheek, then looked toward the upswept rings, where he could see the glimmers of inbound DC ships. Some families were using telescopes to watch the defensive measures Commander Heron was struggling to implement. Rex saw all he needed to see with his own eyes.

Each weapons launch, each explosion, was a tiny spark. The Earth forces had come with more than a hundred fully armed military vessels, more than enough to overwhelm any resistance the Worthies could mount. Even so, Heron had taken the *Flying Dutchman* into battle; the other intact men had a few ships, little more than tiny cargo shuttles loaded with explosives. They faced off against the DPs in a brave but hopeless last stand. Fifteen newts had been recruited to man some of the defensive posts, but the Worthies did not have enough weapons for them. Rex wondered if his neutered comrades were experiencing any fear in their extreme circumstances. Was this what Ardet would have wanted them to do?

As they approached, the DC ships issued numerous warnings—they sounded like pleas—for the Worthies to stand down. From listening to the battle chatter, it seemed to Rex that the enemy fired only after Commander Heron had launched his weapons. Once the battle began, however, the DPs quickly obliterated the resistance.

The Earth ships were visible now as distinct blips closing in on the isolated colony. There seemed to be as many hospital ships as armed military vessels. Decoys? With their superior forces, why would the DPs expect so many casualties? And if they meant to slaughter the Worthies, why bother with medical aid?

"We do not intend to harm you," said a strangely accented but gentle-sounding voice over the dissemination channel. A *female* voice, in command. That startling fact alone demonstrated to Rex how different these invaders were.

"They're lying," Ann growled. Now she tried to take Max, but the boy clung to his uncle. Rex soothed him, and Ann withdrew to her terrified pacing.

As the DPs passed the outer supply depot, it exploded, booby-trapped with proximity bombs. Flying shrapnel tore open one of the Earth battleships. Rex knew that the depot had been manned by two newts assigned there by Commander Heron.

Tears streaked Jen's lovely face. "That one was for Ian," she whispered, her voice cold and bitter.

Mother sat grimly in her favorite chair. "At least the damned Capitalists won't be able to take our supplies."

"Cease your resistance!" The female commander's voice sounded sterner now. "We cannot allow you to threaten peaceful ships. After you are disarmed, you will be given an opportunity to explain yourselves and air any grievances in world courts. But we must protect ourselves."

"Then stay away!" Jen shouted. Her once-luxuriant dark brown hair was stringy; her eyes grew red as she kept crying. Rex was sure his brother would still have found her beautiful.

When the ships surrounded the habitation complex, there were no more flashes, no more desperate attempts to block them. The crackling accented voice continued, "Please stand down. We do not wish to hurt anyone else. We will not harm you. You have our word."

Jen moaned from the other side of the room. "They're going to kill us all! They'll drag us back to Earth and make us their slaves." Ardet had painted that picture many times, convinced his followers what monsters the DPs were. Rex couldn't let himself believe that his father might have distorted the truth, exaggerated the threat.

Little Max continued to squirm, and Rex set him down. "It's already over."

Ann glared at him. "Don't you even care? Don't you realize what they'll do to us?"

Reaching an impossible decision, Mother disappeared into the sleeping quarters, then returned holding a heavy pulse rifle. Both Ann and Jen saw the weapon and cringed. Even Rex could barely cope with his surprise.

Ardet Hollings had wanted a peaceful society. He had reconfigured the human structure to guarantee there would be no conflict, only order and productivity. By using his followers as human building materials, by creating the unshakeable and diligent newts to be the backbone of a strong and satisfying life, he had intended to make such weapons unnecessary. The pulse rifle had no purpose other than to shed blood.

"Mother, we can't do that! It is forbidden," Ann said, though her voice held a rough hunger. Rex could see the raw conflict in her mind.

"The men are our defenders," Jen said.

"All our men are dead," Mother said. "We have no choice. We have to defend ourselves." She lifted the weapon, and it was obvious she already knew how to use it. Rex wondered where she had gotten the practice, why she had ever considered it necessary. "Unless Rex will do it."

She held the pulse rifle forward, and Rex found that he was unable to move. "I can't. I'm a newt. Our father made it so—"

"Do you believe in Ardet's teachings? Do you truly trust his words?"

He shied away from the weapon, shaking his head. "The implant, the operation—our father forced me not to be a man. How can you demand it of me now?"

"Because times demand it." Mother's eyes were sharp and hard. "You know what you have to do." She placed the rifle in his hands. It felt heavy and cold. He stared at the firing controls.

The DC ships clustered around the colony domes and locked themselves down. Rex's family members all jumped upon hearing a loud thump as the invaders forced open the access airlocks. "They're coming!" Ann said.

Rex stood with the rifle like a dead weight in his arms. Yes, he did believe what Ardet had told them. He had listened to all the speeches, enough to memorize most of them. He knew what the Worthies stood for. He accepted everything Ardet had claimed, though the actions of the DC invaders were not what he had expected.

The implant helped him to consider his thoughts, to see them objectively, without the disturbing backwaters and eddies of unruly emotions. He had no testosterone-induced distractions, no aggression, no wild mating drive. In this impossible situation, only the newts among the Worthies could remain solid and true to Ardet's principles.

Yes, he believed. He knew what his father would have wanted of him. Ardet had made it plain in his teachings, in his speeches, and in his actions. How else could Rex accept what had been done to him?

Mother looked at her only remaining son, her face full of emptiness. Jen and Ann stared at him, perhaps seeing echoes of his brothers.

The female DC spokesman broadcast another message. "You will not be harmed. You will be taken care of. If some of you wish to come back to Earth, we will arrange safe passage."

"Don't believe them," Jen cried. "They're barbarians."

Heavy footsteps came down the halls. Rex stood like a rock in a fast-moving stream, feeling the weight of great events all around him. He was a Worthy, a vital component of Ardet's vision. He had his role, he was a newt. He believed in what they stood for.

The pulse rifle in his hands was armed. The DPs were coming closer.

He set the weapon aside. Behind him, someone moaned in fear or disappointment. Mother, perhaps?

If he truly believed in his father's plan, then he had to accept what he was—and what he was supposed to do.

Newts were made to be teachers, listeners, faithful workers, a stable class without violent tendencies. If Ardet had wanted his son and all those like him to be heroes, he would never have cut them off at the . . . knees. Rex didn't need the implant to tell him that this was for the best.

As the DC consolidation parties moved toward the family habitat, Rex faced them. He experienced no despair or panic, neither elation nor fear. Just an unending sense of calm . . .

An Ocean is a Snowflake, Four Billion Miles Away

John Barnes

Thorby had kept up his resistance training, but he'd been on Boreas for most of a year so he'd worried about agravitic muscular dystrophy. You could never quite trust a gym centrifuge, or the record keeping software, or most of all your own laziness. You might set things too low, lie to the records, anything to not be quite so sore and stiff for just a couple days, or to have a few days of no aches, and before you knew it you hadn't actually worked out in a month, and you'd be falling down weak at your next port. He'd missed recording the first calcium bombardment of Venus from ground level for that very reason, not working out while he'd been in the orbital station for three months before.

People always said you could make it back by working out in the high gravity on the ships between the worlds, but the ships boosted at a gee and a half until they started braking at four gee, so you spent all your time lying down or doing gentle stretches at best, and most trips weren't long enough anyway. And besides this had been less of a voyage and more of a hop; Boreas was very close to Mars now.

The comfortable grip of his feet on the train station platform, confirming that he was truly ready for Mars's real gravity, was as acute a pleasure as the clean thinness of bioprocessed air lightly stained with smells of coffee, frying meat, lubricant, and fresh plastic, as much as the pink late afternoon light flooding the train station, as much as the restless waves and murmurs of crowd noise.

He could have laughed out loud at how good it felt to be in his skin, standing on the platform at Olympus Station, a throng of eager hikers, sailplaners, and mountaineers all around him, the whole scene turned warm and sentimental by the pink light pouring in through the immense dome that arched above them.

It had been a decade since he'd been on Mars, a planet like the rest of the solar system: a place he always came back to, because he never went home.

"Thorby!" Léoa emerged from the crowd, saw him, and waved; he walked toward her slowly, still relishing the feel of having good ground legs.

"So do I look like me?" she asked. "Did you know that back in the protomedia days, when they had recording tech but things hadn't fused yet, that it was a cliché that people always looked better than their pictures?"

"I've mined protomedia for images and sounds too. My theory about that is that you couldn't get laid by telling the picture that it was the better-looking one."

"You're an evil cynic. Pbbbt." Even sticking her tongue out, she was beautiful.

So was he. All documentarians had to be, the market insisted.

"I never used pixel edit on myself," she said. He wasn't sure if she sounded proud or they were just having a professional discussion. "So screen-me does look unusually like real-me. I'll do a docu about the way people react to that, someday. Want to get a drink, maybe a meal? It's hours till our train." Without waiting for him to say anything, she turned and walked away.

Hurrying to catch up beside her, he called, "Baggins, follow," over his shoulder. His porter robot trailed after them, carrying Thorby's stack of packed boxes. Everything physical he owned still fit into a cube with sides shorter than his height. "Did you have a good trip in?" he asked her.

"For me it's always a great one. I've been here for six Martian seasons, three Earth years, and I'll never be one of the ones that shutters the window to concentrate on work. I came in from Airy Zero City via the APK&T."

"Uh, it's been a long time since I've been on Mars, is that a railroad?"

"Oh, it's a railroad—the second grandest on the planet. The Airy Zero City-Polar Cap-Korolev-and-Tharsis. The one that tourists take if they only have one day on Mars. Also the one we'll be taking up to Crater Korolev for jump-off. Among many other things it runs around the edge of the northern ice cap. Strange to think it won't be long before it stops running. They're just going to leave it for the divers, you know, and maybe as a spread path for some of the seabed fauna. More to be lost."

"If we're going to start bickering," Thorby said, smiling, "shouldn't we be recording it? Or will that draw too much attention?"

"Not on Mars. It's a tourist planet—pretending celebs aren't there is de rigueur. And you don't look much like your teenaged pictures anymore."

"They were mostly in a spacesuit where you couldn't see my face anyway," he pointed out. "And I don't use my face in my docus. I was thinking mainly about you."

"Pbbbt. I never *was* much of a celeb. There won't be fifty people in all these hundreds who have ever seen any of my work. So the short answer is, if anything, it might be some worthwhile free publicity to do the interview while we walk through here. I'll bring out my stalkers." She whistled, a soft high-pitched *phweet!-toooeee . . . wheep.*

A hatch opened on the porter humming along at her heels. A metal head on a single stalk popped up. The stalker hopped out and raced ahead of them to get a front view. Four more stalkers leaped out like toy mouse heads roller-skating on pogo sticks, zipping and bounding to form a rough, open semicircle around Thorby and Léoa, pointing their recording cameras back at the two people, and using their forward sensing to zigzag swiftly and silently around everything else.

"I intend to look sincere and charming," Léoa said. "Do your best to look philosophical and profound."

"I'll try. It might come out bewildered and constipated."

She was nice enough to laugh, which was nicer than he was expecting. They descended the wide steps onto the broad terrace, far down the low, northwest side of the dome, and took a table near the dome surface, looking northwestward from Mount Olympus across the flat, ancient lava lake and into the broken, volcanic badlands called sulci beyond it. "Our ancestors would have found a lot of what we do utterly mad," Léoa said, "so I suppose it's comforting that we can find one thing they did explicable."

"You're trying to get me to say something for the documentary."

"You're spoiling the spontaneity. Of course I notice you do that all the time in your own documentaries."

"I do. Spontaneity is overrated when you're covering big explosions and collisions. They only happen once, so you have to get them right, and that means looking in the right place at the right time, and that means a ton of prep."

"All right, well, have you had enough time to prepare to talk about something the ancestors would consider insane? What do you think about putting a train station on top of the highest mountain in the solar system?"

"Where else would you put it? People who want to climb the mountain still can, and then they can take the train home. People who just want the view just take the train both ways. And once it starts to snow seriously around here, the skiing is going to be amazing. So of course there's a train station here. They put it here to attract trains, the way Earth people put out birdfeeders to attract birds."

She nodded solemnly and he realized she was doing a reaction shot on him, showing her sincerity and trust. He looked away, out through the dome.

"You're getting lost in the sky," Léoa said.

"I like the pink skies here."

"Doesn't it bother you that there will probably only be a thousand or so more of those?"

"Not any more than it bothers me that I've missed billions of them before I was born."

"What about the people who will never see it?"

"They'll get to surf the new ocean, and stretch out on the beaches that all the dust washing out of the sulci and down the canyons will form. They'll love that, in *their* moments. In *my* moment, I'm relishing a late afternoon pink sky."

The stalker in the center was spinning back and forth, pointing its camera at each of them in turn; so now it was a ping-pong match. They did more verbal sparring and genned more quotes and reactions, ensuring they'd both have plenty to work with when the coproject went to edit. After a while they ordered dinner, and she stopped fishing for him to confess to imperialism or vandalism or whatever she was going to call it.

She told her Stalker Number Three to silhouette him against the darkening sky and the landscape far below. The little robot leaped up, extended its pencil-thin support to a bit over two meters, and silently crept around to shoot slightly down on Thorby and get the horizon into the picture.

When Boreas rose in the northwest, covering much of the sky, they both said "more profounder versions of what we already said," as Léoa put it, while the stalkers recorded them with their back to the dome wall. Léoa had her stalkers stand tall, extending till they were about three meters high, to catch the brilliant white light that the huge comet cast into the sulci below; Thorby positioned his low, to silhouette them against the comet head itself. The huge station mezzanine around them, in the brilliant bluish-white light, looked like some harsh early photograph with artificial lighting.

Over coffee and dessert, they watched the fast-rising comet swim through the northern constellations like a vast snake coiling around Cepheus and the Bears before diving over the northeast horizon, making a vivid arc different from that of anything else in the heavens. Finally it was late and they went to their rooms at the station hotel for the night. Thorby managed not to say anything about liking to see stuff smashed up, and she avoided saying she really preferred bare, dead rock and sand to forests and meadows, so the first day was a tie.

They got off at Korolev Station, on the south side of the crater, pulled on Mars suits, loaded the porters, and walked out past the stupa that was another of the most-photographed places in the solar system.

Crater Korolev was as far north on Mars as Novaya Zemlya on Earth, nearly circular, about 70 kilometers across, with sharply reared crater walls all around. It was a natural snow trap, gathering both water ice and dry ice in mixtures and layers.

In a midmorning of Martian spring, the crater floor far below them had its own weather, gas geysers spraying snow, explosive sublimations that sent ground blizzards shooting out radially from suddenly exposed snowfields, and an occasional booming flash-and-crack between the whorls of fog that slithered just above the snow, almost a kilometer below the observation point behind the stupa. Monks in orange Mars suits, on their way to and from the long staircases that zigzagged from the stupa down to another stupa on the crater floor, passed between their stalkers, even less interested in the stalkers than the stalkers were in them.

"This place makes a lot of lists of scenic wonders," Léoa said. She knelt at the meter-high shrine that interrupted the rails of the observation platform, palms together in the ancient prayer gesture. The stalkers closed in on her.

He did the same, to avoid her stalkers' recording him being disrespectful.

When Thorby and Léoa stood, and looked again across the stormy snowfields of Korolev Crater, the stalkers leaped up on the railing like an abstract sculpture of birds on a wire, balancing easily with their gyros. Thorby and Léoa de-opaqued their helmets completely and turned on collar lights. "It doesn't bother you," she asked, "that these snow fields were here before the first human wandered across the African plain?"

"No," he said. "After all, the protons and electrons in the snow were probably in existence shortly after the Big Bang. Everything is made of bits of something older. Everything that begins means something ends. I like to take pictures of the moment when that happens. A day will come when we walk by Lake Korolev and admire the slow waves rolling across its deep blue surface, and then another day will come when this stupa stands on one of the islands that ring Korolev Atoll, and very much within our life-time, unless we are unlucky, this will be an interesting structure at the bottom of the Boreal Ocean. I hope to see them all; life is potential and possibility."

"That was very preachy," she said, "and you kind of intoned. Do you want to try it again?"

"Not really. Intoning feels right when I'm serious. I *like* things that will happen once, then never again. That's what my problem is with the animators that make their perfect simulations; they never take a chance on not getting what they're after. Be *sure* to use *that*. Let's get some animators good and angry."

"They don't get angry," she said, sadly. "Nothing's real to them."

He shrugged. "Reality is just a marketing trophy anyway. Twenty thousand years from now, if people want to walk around on a dry, thin-aired, cold Mars, they'll be able to do it, and it will look so much like this that even a trained areologist won't see the difference. Or if they want to watch the disassembly of Boreas a hundred times, and have every time be as subtly different as two different Tuesdays, they'll be able to. Your recording of what was, and my recording of how it changed, will just be two more versions, the ones with that odd word 'real' attached."

"Attached *validly*. If reality doesn't matter, why do animators try to fake their way into having their work labeled 'real' all the time? It's the only thing they do that makes me really angry."

"Me too." He could think of nothing else to add. "Catch the gliderail?"

In the half-hour zip around to the north side viewing station, they sat on the top, outside deck. Their stalkers shot them with the crater in the background. It was noon now, and the early spring sun was still low in the sky to the south.

On firm ground, in a Mars suit with robot porters to do all the carrying, a human being can cover about a hundred kilometers in a day without difficulty. Since the country they were crossing was ancient sea bottom (that was the point of everything, really), it would be flat and hard for the next couple of hundred kilometers before the Sand Sea. They could have just taken a hop-rocket to some point in the vast plain, claimed to have walked there, recorded their conversation, and then hopped another hundred kilometers or so to the edge of the Sand Sea, but they were the two most prominent documentarians of the realist movement.

Visually it was monotonous. They had planned to use the long walk to spar for quotes, but there was little to say to each other. Léoa documented places that were about to be destroyed in the Great Blooming; Thorby recorded the BEREs, Big Energy Release Events, the vast crashes and explosions that marked humanity's project of turning the solar system into a park and zoo. They were realist-purists, using only what a camera or a mike could record from the real world. Unable to do anything except disagree or agree completely, they tried arguing about whether a terraformed planet can have wilderness, since the life on it was brought there and the world shaped for it, and about whether it was masculine to like to see things smashed and feminine to like to see things protected, and they agreed that animation had no place in docu, all in the first hour.

For a while she fished for him to tell stories about his brief moment of fame, as the teenager who rode his bicycle around a comet, but he didn't feel like telling that story during that hike, though he did promise to tell it eventually. It wasn't that he minded, it was only that the good-parts version came down to no more than four or five sentences for anyone else, and to inchoate, averbal images for Thorby.

By noon the first day, there was nothing to do but walk and look for something worth recording, or an argument worth having. They walked two more days.

The Sand Sea was no more conversational, but it was beautiful: an erg that stretched to the horizon, dune after dune in interlocking serpentines stretching for hundreds of kilometers in all directions. From orbit the regularity of the pattern of dune crests was remarkable, but from the dune crests, where they skied, it was busy and confusing like a choppy sea. Down between the dunes it was just piles of sand reaching to the sky on all sides.

They hadn't spoken in hours. Léoa didn't even ask him if he felt sad that all this would be converted to a mud flat and then drowned under three kilometers of water. He couldn't work up the energy to needle her about protecting a pile of dust the size of France, so that future generations could also visit a pile of dust the size of France.

They went slowly for the last day, as Léoa got visuals of the Sand Sea. She had built her reputation on doomed landscapes; this would be the biggest to date.

Thorby was sitting on top of one of the immense dunes, watching the sunset and talking his notes to one of his stalkers, planning the shooting of the Boreas-pass above the North Pole. He felt a low vibration, and his suit exmike, which had only supplied a soft whisper for days, reverberated with deep bass notes, something between a tuba and a bell, or a choir of mountains.

The dune under him heaved like an ocean wave waking from a long sleep, and he tumbled over, rolling and sliding in a bewildering blur of dust and sky, halfway down the western, windward face before sliding to a halt. The slipping dust piled around him, starting to pin him to the ground.

He pushed up to his feet, and stepping high, climbed back up the dune. It was more than a minute, while the pure tones of the bass notes in his exmike became a continuous thunder of tympani, before he struggled back to the top. The sun was less than a fingerwidth above the short horizon, and the light would disappear in minutes, the smaller solar disk and short horizon of Mars reducing twilight to an instant.

The thunder was still loud, so he clicked up the volume on his radio. "Are you all right?"

"Far as I can tell. It buried me to my waist but I got out." He picked out Léoa, climbing the leeward slope far below. "Booming sands," she said. "One of the last times they'll ever do it. The resonance trips off more distant dunes, one dune triggering another by the sounds, till all the dunes with those frequencies have avalanched and added to the din. There's a scientist I met who sowed microphones all over the polar sea and he could show you maps of how the booming would spread from dune to dune, all over the Sand Sea in a couple of hours. And all that will be silent forever."

"Silent as the Boreal Ocean is now," he said, mindful that their recording mikes were still on and so was the sparring match. All round them, stalkers were finding their way back to the surface, usually stalk first so that they rose like slim reeds from the ground until they suddenly flipped over, spun to clear the dust from there scoop shaped audio pickups, and resumed hopping through the sand like mouse heads on pogo sticks, normal as ever. "There was a time to hear the sands, and there will be a time to hear the waves. And in between there's going to be some of the grandest smashing you ever saw."

She must not have had a good reply, or perhaps she just didn't want to reply to his intoning again, because she got back to her setup, and he got back to his.

The Mars suits shed the fine dust constantly, so that Léoa seemed to smolder and then to trail long streaks as the wind shifted during the few seconds of twilight. They finished under the stalkers' work lights, and lay down to wait on the soft lee of the dune, safe now because it had just avalanched.

"Thorby," she said, "this is not turning into anything that will make either of us famous."

He hunched his shoulders, shaping the fine sand under him. "You're right," he said. "It's not."

"You've already been famous."

"It's one of those things you can't experience while it's happening," he said, "like seeing yourself across a crowded room. Not all that it's cracked up to be. I like making docus and I like selling them, so that kind of 'where is he now' fame doesn't hurt, and it's far enough in the past so I mostly get left alone." He watched Phobos, far south in the sky; from these far northern latitudes you never saw it full, always as a lumpy sort of half-moon.

"If a model or a musician had taken a tumble in booming sands it would sell systemwide, but if we got stranded out here and you killed and ate me to survive, it would barely show up. Docus are what, half a percent of the market? There's not even a market in pirating them." Léoa sighed. "I was just thinking that the mainstream celeb channels haven't even mentioned that the two leading documentarians of the realist-purist movement are here to record the biggest event of the next few hundred years of the Great Blooming, the re-creation of the Boreal Ocean. Not even to mention that we've always feuded and we purportedly hate each other. Not even to do one of those 'Will they reconcile and have sex?' stories they like so much. Not even to mention that one of us is the teenager who took the longest bicycle ride in history. Yet two years ago they covered the fad for learning to hand-read, and a couple guys in the retro movement that produced written books—can you believe it, written books, just code, that stuff people used to hand-read—and they covered a *blacksmith* last year, but docus are so dead, they didn't bother with us."

"We're not dead *enough*. Gone but not long enough or completely enough to be a novelty." He tried to decide whether he could actually see Phobos crawling along eastward, down by the equator, and decided he could. "Maybe we should have the blacksmith build us chariots, and race each other, and do a documentary about that."

"Maybe." The scratchy sound in her radio puzzled him till he saw her rolling over; she was looking for a comfortable position on the dune, and he was hearing her Mars suit pushing dust away.

"Hey," he said. "Since you've been trying to get me to miss something, I just noticed something I will miss. Phobos. I like the way it looks from this far north."

"Well, I'm glad *something* can touch your heart. I'd have thought you were excited about getting to see it fall."

"It won't be much of a show. Phobos'll be busted to gravel from all the impacts as it comes down through the rings, so it won't really be a BERE, just a month-long high point in the spectacular meteor shower that will go on for fifteen Mars-years or so. I wasn't even going to bother to shoot it. But what it is right now—I never realized it's always a half-moon up here in the far north, because it's so close to the equator and so low in orbit, and besides, it's fun just to watch it, because it's so low it orbits really fast, and I'm thinking I can see it move."

"I think I can too." She commanded her stalkers to set up and record the view of Phobos, and then to get the two of them with Phobos behind them as they sat on a dune. "Those shots will be beautiful; so sad though that stories about Great Blooming projects are about as popular as public comment requests by the Global Desalination Authority."

He shrugged, hoping it would show up on the stalker's cameras. "Post scarcity economy, very long life spans, all that. Everything to do and nothing matters. Story of everyone's life. Have you thought about doing anything other than docus?"

"I try not to. I want to get the Great Blooming recorded, even if I call it the Great Vandalism or Bio-Stuff Imperialism. Somebody has to stand up for rocks, ice, and vacuum."

"Rocks make okay friends. They're dependable and loyal."

"I wish somebody wanted to watch us talking to each other," Léoa said. "About all this. About Mars and about the Blooming and all that stuff. I almost wouldn't care what we had to say, or how things came out, if somebody would just find us interesting enough to listen. You know what I mean."

"Yeah." Thorby didn't really feel that way himself but he often didn't know what he felt at all, so he might as well agree.

They began final checkout just a few minutes before Boreas's first aerobraking pass. The stalkers were self-maintaining, and they were already in place, but it felt wrong to just assume everything would work.

"This will be one of your last views of your home," Léoa said. "How do you feel about that?"

He turned toward her, flipped the opaquing on his helmet to zero, and turned up the collar lights, so that his face would be as visible as possible, since this was an answer he knew he needed to get right. Already the northern horizon was glowing with

Boreas-dawn. "Boreas is where I grew up, as much as I ever did, but that doesn't make it home," he said. "First of all when I lived there you couldn't walk on most of it, anyway, and they weren't going to let a little boy put on a suit and go play outside. When I went back four weeks ago, all that melting and vaporizing that went on while Boreas worked its way down to the lower system had erased even the little bit of landscape I did know; I couldn't even find Cookie Crumb Hill on radar and thermal imaging, and anyway if I'd found it, it's so dark down there now, with all the fog and grit flying around, that I doubt I could have gotten pictures that penetrated more than 20 meters into the mess. The Boreas I knew when I was a kid, way out beyond Neptune, is more than a decade gone; it's nothing like it was. Nothing at all."

He was crabbier in his tone than he had meant to be, irritated by her question because he'd blown half his share of the budget to buy passage to Boreas so that he could come back with the seven scientists who were the last evacuated from the iceball's surface, and what he'd gotten had been some lackluster interviews that he could as easily have done a year before or a year after. Furthermore, since the station had not had windows, he could have done them somewhere more pleasant. He had also acquired some pictures of the fog-and-grit mix that now shrouded what was left of the old surface. (Most of the old surface, of course, now *was* fog and grit).

As Boreas came in over the North Pole, it would swing low enough for atmospheric drag, which, combined with the gravitational drag from coming in an "inverse slingshot" trajectory, should put it into a very eccentric, long orbit around Mars. Doing this with a big natural ball of mixed water ice, carbon dioxide, and frozen methane, with a silica-grit center, was so uncertain a process that the major goals for the project began with "1. avoid impact by Boreas, 2. avoid escape by Boreas."

But if all went well, nudgers and roasters would then be installed on Mars's new huge artificial moon, with the objective of parking it in a nearly circular retrograde orbit below Phobos, well inside Mars's Roche limit, so that over a few years, Boreas would break up and form a complex of rings. The billions of bits of it, dragged and shredded by the planet's rotation, would then gradually spiral in across twenty years, creating a spectacular continual meteor shower in the plane of the ring, a carbon dioxide/methane atmosphere at about a bar of pressure, and, as water vapor snowed down, then melted, then rained and ran to the lower parts of the planet, a new ocean in the bed of the dry-for-a-billion-years Boreal Ocean.

The comet's pass would light the sky for many hours, but its actual brush with the atmosphere would last less than three minutes. Thorby and Léoa intended to be directly underneath it when that happened.

"Did you leave anything on Boreas, a memento to be vaporized onto Mars?" she asked.

He started to say, "No."

She picked up her walking stick and knocked off the head of one of his stalkers.

Startled speechless for an instant, he didn't speak or move till she whacked the second one so hard that its head flew in pieces into the sand.

"What are you—?"

"Destroying your stalkers." Her voice was perfectly calm and pleasant as she whacked another stalker hard enough to break its stem in half, then drove the tip of her stick down on its head. "You won't have a record of this. And mine will only be recording your face and appearance. You've lost."

He thought *lost what?* for an instant, and then he wanted to rush to see if Number Four stalker, which had been with him for twenty-five years, was all right because it was crushed and he couldn't help thinking of it as "hurt," and then he wanted to scream *why?*

The landscape became brighter than day, brighter than Earth lightning, not at all like the Boreas-dawn they had been expecting. A great light flashed out of the north, and a breath later a white, glowing pillar pushed up into the sky. They froze, staring, for some indefinite time; his surviving stalkers, and all of hers, rotated to face the light, like clockwork sunflowers.

Thorby heard his voice saying, "We'll need to run, south, now, as fast as we can, I don't think we'll make it."

"Must have been a big fragment far out from the main body," Léoa said. "How far away do you think—?"

"Maybe up close to the pole if we're lucky. Come on," he said, "whistle everything into the porters. Skis on. *Run.*"

Two of his stalkers had not been destroyed, and they leaped into his porter at his emergency call. "Skis and poles," he told the porter, and it ejected them; he stepped onto the skis, free-heelers designed for covering ground and moving on the slick dust, and hoped his few hours practice at a comfortable pace in the last day would be enough to let him go fast now.

"Baggins, follow, absolute." Now his porter would try to stay within two meters of his transponder, catching up when it fell behind, until it ran out of power or was destroyed. If he lost it, he might have to walk hungry for a while, but the northern stations were only a couple of days to reach. His Mars suit batteries were good for a week or more; the suit extracted water and air; he just had to hope he wouldn't need the first aid kit, but it was too heavy to strap onto the suit.

The great blue-white welding-arc pillar had cooled to orange-white, and the main body of Boreas, rising right on schedule, stood behind it as a reflector. The light at Thorby's back was brighter than noonday equatorial sun on Earth, much brighter than any sun Mars had ever seen, and the blazing face of Boreas, a quarter of the sky, spread the light with eerie evenness, as if the whole world were under too-bright fluorescent light.

He hurled himself along the windward side of the south-tending dune crest, using the skating technique he'd learned on Earth snow and practiced on frozen methane beds on Triton; his pushing ski flew out behind him, turning behind the lead ski to give extra push, then reach as far in front of him as possible, kicking and reaching as far as he could. On the slick, small-round-particle sand of the ridge top, in the low gravity, he might have been averaging as much as twenty kilometers per hour.

But the blast front from the impact was coming at them at the local speed of sound, 755 kilometers per hour, and though that was only 2/3 as fast as Mach 1 in warm, thick, breathable air, it was more than fast enough to overtake them in a half hour or less. At best the impact might have been four hundred kilometers away, but it was almost surely closer.

He glanced back. Léoa skied swiftly after him, perhaps even gaining ground. The light of the blazing pillar was dimmer, turning orange, and his long shadow, racing in front of him, was mostly cast by the dirt-filtered light of the Boreas-dawn. He wasn't sure whether Boreas would stay in the sky till the sun came up, but by then it would all be decided anyway.

"Thorby."

"Yeah."

"I've had it look for shelter, read me some directions, and project a sim so I'm sure, and there's a spot that's probably safe close to here. This dune crest will fork in about a kilometer. Take the left fork, two more kilometers, and we'll be behind a crater wall from the blast."

"Good thinking, thanks." He pushed harder, clicking his tongue control for an oxy boost. His Mars suit increased the pressure and switched to pure oxygen; his pace was far above sustainable, but either he made this next three kilometers or he didn't.

Léoa had destroyed his recording setup. He'd known she deplored his entire career of recording BEREs—Big Energy Release Events—at least as much as she disliked the whole idea of the Great Blooming, but he'd had no idea she would actually hash the joint project just to stop him from doing it. So his judgment about people was even worse than he'd thought it was. They had been colleagues and (he'd thought) friendly rivals for decades, and he hadn't seen it coming.

He kept pushing hard, remembering that he was pouring so much oxygen into his bloodstream that he had to keep his muscles working hard, or hyperventilate. His skis flew around him, reached out to the front, whipped back, turned, lifted, flew out around him, and he concentrated on picking his path in the shifting light and staying comfortably level and in control; in the low Martian gravity, with the close horizon that didn't reveal parallax motion very well to eyes evolved for Earth, it was far too easy to start to bounce; your hips and knees could easily eat a third of your energy in useless vertical motion.

The leeward side of a dune crest is the one that avalanches, so he stayed to the right, windward side, but he couldn't afford to miss the saddle-and-fork when it came, so he had to keep his head above the crest. He heard only the hiss of his breath and the squeal of his skis on the sand; the boiling column from the impact, now a dull angry red, and the quarter-of-the-sky circle of the comet now almost directly overhead were eerie in their silence. He kept his gaze level and straight out to the horizon, let his legs and gut swing him forward, kept the swinging as vertical as he could, turning only the ski, never the hip, hoping this was right and he was remembering how to do it, unable to know if he was moving fast enough through the apparently endless erg.

He had just found the fork and made the left turn, glancing back to check on Léoa. She seemed to be struggling and falling a little behind, so he slowed, wondering if it would be all right to tell her she was bouncing and burning unnecessary energy.

The whole top five meters of the dune crest under her slid down to the leeward in one vast avalanche. He had just a moment to think, *but how can that be, I just skied it myself and I'm heavier*, when he heard the shattering thunder and the ground fell away beneath him as the whole dune slumped leeward.

He had just a moment to think *of course, how did I miss that?* In the cold thin air of Mars, made of a thin scatter of heavy CO_2 molecules, sound is much slower than it is in anything human beings can breathe; anyone learns that after the first few times a hiking buddy's radio has exmike sound in the background, and it seems to be forever before your own exmike picks it up. But the basalts of the old Martian sea floor are solid, dense, cold, and rigid to a great depth; seismic waves are faster than they are elsewhere.

He thought that as he flipped over once, as if he were working up the voiceover for his last docu. Definitely for his *last* docu.

In the low gravity, it was a long way to the bottom of the dune. Sand poured and rumbled all around him, and his exmike choked back the terrible din of thousands of dunes, as the booming erg was all shaken at once by the S-waves running through the rock below it, setting up countless resonances, triggering more avalanches and more resonances, until nearly the whole potential energy of the Sand Sea released at once.

Maybe just to annoy Léoa, he intoned a voiceover, possibly his corniest ever, as he tumbled down the slope and wondered how the sand would kill him. "It is as if the vast erg knows what Boreas is, that this great light in the sky is the angel of death for the Sand Sea, which shouts its blind black stony defiance to the indifferent glaring ice overhead."

He rolled again, cutting off his intoning with an *oof!*, and released his skis. He rolled another time, plowing deep into the speeding current of sand, and felt something hard on the back of his helmet, and tumbled faster and faster, then flopped and slid on his belly headfirst.

In darkness, he heard only the grinding of fine sand against his exmike.

✧   ✧   ✧

The damp in Thorby's undersuit and his muzzy head told him he'd just done the most embarrassing thing of his life, fainted from fear. Now it felt like his worst hangover; he took a sip of water. Bruised all over, but no acute pain anywhere, slipped out of his urine tube, that seemed to be all that was wrong. If Baggins caught up with him, Thorby would like to get into the shelter, readjust things in the undersuit, sponge off a bit, but he didn't absolutely have to.

His clock didn't seem to be working—it didn't keep its own time, just reported overhead signal—but the wetness in his undersuit meant he couldn't have been out more than fifteen minutes or so. He'd be dry in another few minutes as the Mars suit system found the moisture and recycled it.

He was lying on his face, head slightly downward. He tried to push up and discovered he couldn't move his arms, though he could wriggle his fingers a bit, and after doing that for a while, he began to turn his wrists, scooping more sand away, getting leverage to push up more. An eternity later he was moving his forearms, and then his shoulders, half shaking the sand off, half swimming to the top. At last he got some leverage and movement in his hips and thighs, and heaved himself up to the surface, sitting upright in the silvery light of the darkened sky.

There was a pittering noise he couldn't quite place, until he realized it was sand and grit falling like light sleet around him. The blast wave that had carried it must have passed over while Thorby was unconscious; the tops of the dunes had an odd curl to them, and he realized that the top few meters had been rotated ninety degrees from their usual west-windward, east-leeward, to north-windward, south-leeward, and all the dunes were much lower and broader. Probably being down in the bowl had saved his life; maybe it had saved Léoa too.

He clicked over to direct voice. "Léoa?"

No answer, and her voice channel hadn't sent an acknowledge, so she wasn't anywhere in radio range, or she was buried too deep for him to reach her.

He tried the distress channel and got a message saying that if he was above thirty degrees north latitude and wasn't bleeding to death within ten kilometers of a hospital, he was on his own. Navigation channel was out as well, but if he had to he could just walk with the Bears and Cassiopeia to his back while they got the navigation system back on, and still get himself to somewhere much safer and closer to other people, though getting out of the dunes might take a week without his skis.

When the crest had avalanched under Léoa she'd been at least 150 meters behind him, and he wasn't sure she'd gone down into this bowl. He tried her on direct voice again, and still had nothing, so he tried phone and was informed that overhead satellite service was temporarily suspended. He guessed that the impact had thrown enough junk around to take down some of the high-ellipse polar satellites that supplied communication and navigation.

If he knew he was alone, the thing to do would be to start walking south, but he couldn't leave Léoa here if there was any chance of finding her. The first aid kit in Baggins had directional gear for checking her transponder, but Baggins was probably buried or crushed, and even if the porter was still rolling it might be a while before it found its way to him.

He would wait a few hours for Baggins anyway; the porter not only had the food, but could also track the tags on his skis and poles, and had a power shovel. A lot better to begin with a shelter, food, and skis than to get one or two kilometers further and a lot more tired. And he did owe Léoa a search.

The best thing he could think of to do—which was probably useless—was to climb to the top of the slope he'd rolled down. The pre-dawn west wind was rising, and the sand swirled around his boots; it was hard going all the way up, and it was dawn before he reached the top. The small bloody red sun rising far to the southeast, barely penetrating the dense dust clouds, gave little light. He clicked his visor for magnification and light amplification, and turned around slowly, making himself look at each slope and into each bowl he could see into, since with the wind already erasing his boot prints, he knew that once he walked any distance he'd have little chance of finding even the bowl into which he'd fallen.

There was something small and dark moving and slipping down the side of the next bowl north; he took a few steps, and used the distance gauge. It estimated the object to be about a meter across and two kilometers away.

He moved toward it slowly until he realized it was Léoa's porter, headed roughly for the bottom of the bowl, so it must be getting signal from her transponder. He descended to meet it and found it patiently digging with its small scoop and plow, rocking back and forth on its outsize dune wheels to get more leverage.

Thorby helped as much as he could—which wasn't much—with his hands. He didn't know whether the porter would try to dig her out if the med transponder showed she was dead, and of course it would ignore him, so he didn't have any way to ask it about anything. The suits usually ran with a couple of hours of stored air as a buffer, and made fresh air continually, but if she'd switched to pure direct oxygen as he had, there might not have been much in her tank, and if the intake was buried and filled with sand, she could suffocate.

Presently he felt a hard object; an instant later the porter reached forward with a claw, took a grip, and pulled one of Léoa's skis from the sand, putting it into its storage compartment, before rolling forward. Thorby stared at it for a long moment, and started to laugh as he followed the porter up the hill, to where it plucked out a pole. Presumably it would get around to Léoa, sooner or later; nobody had thought to make life-saving a priority for a baggage cart.

The roiling sky was the color of an old bruise and his temperature gauge showed that it was cold enough for CO_2 snow to fall. He followed Léoa's porter and tried the phone again. This time he got her voicemail, and left a message telling her what was going on, just in case she was wandering around on a hill nearby and out of line of sight from the satellite.

Five minutes later his phone rang. "Thorby?"

"Yeah, Léoa, are you okay?"

"No. Buried to my mid chest, I think I have a broken back and something's really wrong with my leg, and I can see your porter from where I am but I can't get its attention" Her voice was tense with pain. "Can't tell you where I am, either. And you wouldn't believe what your porter just did."

"It dug up one of my skis. That's what yours is doing over here. All right, to be able to see it you must be in the same bowl I landed in, one to the south, I'm on my way. I'm climbing without skis, so I'm afraid this is going to be slow."

After a while as he climbed, the wind picked up. "Léoa?" he called, on the phone again because radio still wasn't connecting them.

"I'm here. Your porter found your other ski. Do you think it will be okay for me to have some water? I've been afraid to drink."

"I *think* that's okay, but first aid class was a while ago. I was calling because I was afraid sand might be piling up on you."

"Well, it is. I'm trying to clear it with my arms but it's not easy, and I can't sit up."

"I don't think you should try to sit up."

They talked while he climbed; it was less lonely. "Your porter is digging about three hundred meters behind me," he told her. "It must be finding your other ski."

"Can't be, if it's already found one, because the other one is bent under me."

"Well, it's getting your pole then. If your ski is jammed under you, it sounds like it hurts."

"Oh yeah, the release must have jammed and it twisted my leg around pretty badly, and walloped me in the spine. So the porter must be finding my pole. Or maybe I dropped a ration pack or something. They've got so much spare processing power, why didn't anyone tell them people first, then gear?"

"Because there probably aren't a hundred million people, out of sixteen billion, that ever go off pavement, or to any planet they weren't born on," he said. "The porters are doing what they'd do in a train station—making sure our stuff is all together and not stolen, then catching up with us."

"Yours just found a pole and it's heading up the hill, so I guess it's on its way to you now."

He topped the rise a few minutes later, just as Baggins rolled up to him and waited obediently for orders. "Skis and poles," he said to his loyal idiot friend, and the machine laid them out for him.

He couldn't see Léoa, still, but there was so much sand blowing around on the surface that this might not mean anything. He tried direct voice. "Léoa, wave or something if you can."

An arm flopped upward from a stream of red dust halfway down the slope before him, and he glided down to her carefully, swinging far out around her to approach from below, making sure he didn't bump her or push sand onto her. He had to wait for Baggins to bring all the gear along, and tell it to approach carefully, but while the porter picked its way down the slope, he put the first aid and rescue gear manuals into his audio channel, asked it to script the right things to do, and listened until he could recite it back. This was one of those times that reminded him he'd always wanted to learn to hand-read.

Meanwhile he kept brushing sand off Léoa; she was crying quietly now, because it still hurt, and she had been afraid she would be buried alive, and now that he was there to keep her intakes clear, she was safe.

Late that afternoon, he had completed digging her out, tying her to the various supports, putting the drugs into her liquids intakes, and equipping Baggins to carry her. She was lying flat on a cross-shaped support as if she'd been crucified. Voice-commanding Baggins, he slowly raised her, got the porter under her, and balanced her on top. With Baggins's outrigger wheels extended as far as they would go, she would be stable on slopes less than ten degrees from the horizontal, and at speeds below three kilometers per hour. Thorby figured that hauling her would be something to do for a couple of days until rescue craft were available for less urgent cases.

Com channels were coming back up gradually, and the navigation channel was open again, but there was still little news, except a brief announcement that the impact had not been an early breakup of the comet, but apparently been caused by an undetected stony satellite of Boreas, about a half kilometer across. Splashback from the impact, as Thorby had guessed, had destroyed most of the satellites passing over the pole in the hours following. The dust storm it had kicked up had been impressive but brief and localized, so that only a half dozen stations and towns in the far north had taken severe damage, and tourist trade was expected to increase as people flocked to see the new crater blasted through the polar ice and into the Martian soil before the Boreal Ocean drowned it.

Authorities were confirming that the pass over the South Pole in seventeen days, to be followed with an equatorial airbrake nine days after that, was still on schedule. Thorby figured he'd be able to cover those, easily, so Léoa's little political action would mean very little.

He wanted to ask her about that but he didn't quite see how to do it.

Shortly after Baggins began to carry the cruciform Léoa in a slow spiral up the inside of the bowl, gaining just a couple of meters on each circuit, her porter appeared over the top of the dune. It had apparently found the last ski pole, or whatever it was digging for, and now followed her transponder like a faithful dog, behind Baggins, around and around the sandy bowl.

Léoa insisted that he get visual recordings of that silly parade, but he quietly killed the audio on it, because all that was really audible was her hysterical laughter. He attributed that to the painkillers.

About dawn he sat up, drank more water and swallowed some food, and skied easily to the top of the dune crest, where Baggins had just managed to carry Léoa after toiling in that slow spiral around the bowl all night. The monitor said she was fast asleep, and Thorby thought that was the best possible thing. Through most of the morning and into the afternoon, he skied along the newly reorganized dune crests, working a little ahead of Baggins and then sitting down to wait for it to catch up, listening to the slow spitting of sand against his suit, and watching the low red dust clouds gather and darken, with only his thoughts for company.

When Léoa finally awoke, she said, "I'm hungry." It startled Thorby; he was about sixty meters ahead, using his two remaining stalkers to shoot the dunes through the red dust that was still settling.

"Be right there," he said, and skied back, the stalkers hopping after him. Her mouth, throat, and digestive system were basically okay, according to the medical sensors, though they wanted her to eat mostly clear broth till she could be looked at properly in a hospital. This time she chose chicken broth, and he hooked it up so she could sip it. All the diagnostics from the rescue frame said she was more or less normal, and as far as he could tell the broken leg and spine were the major damage.

After a while she said, "If I call out my stalkers, will you tell the story about the bicycle ride around the comet, and all those things about becoming famous?"

"Sure," he said, "if it will make the time pass better for you. But I warn you it's very dull."

So he sketched out the basics, in his best "I am being interviewed" voice, as the red dusty sky grew darker. When he was fourteen he had been sent to live with his grandmother because his mother had a promising career going as an actress and his being visibly a teenager would have spoiled her image as a sex object for teenage boys. His grandmother had been part of the earliest team for the first Great Bloom projects, so he had found himself dispatched to Boreas with her, forty-five AU from the sun—so far out that the sun was just a bright star. He had been bored and unhappy, spending most of his time playing games in VR and bored even there because he was so far from the rest of the solar system that radio signals from anywhere else, even Triton Station, took most of a day for a round trip.

"So on the day of the first fire-off—"

"Fire-off? You mean the atom bomb?"

"Well, sort of atom bomb. Laser initiated fusion explosive, but nobody wanted to call a bomb LIFE. Yeah, the thing that started Boreas falling down into the lower solar system." He skied back to look at her life support indicators; they were all green so as far as he knew, she was fine. "On that day, Grandma insisted that I suit up, which I didn't want to do, and go outside with her, which I really didn't want to do, to sit and watch the sky—the gadget was going to be blowing off over the horizon. They put it in an ellipsoidal superreflecting balloon, at one focus, and then put the other focus of the ellipsoidal at the focus of a great big parabolic parasol—"

"None of this means a thing to me."

"They had these really thin plastic reflectors to organize it into a beam about a kilometer across, so all that light, X-rays, heat, everything pretty much hit one square kilometer and blew off a lot of ice and snow in one direction."

"That's better. So, you got to see one big explosion and you liked it so much you decided to see them for the rest of your life?"

"My helmet's opaqued, did you want a reaction shot to that?"

"I'll make one up," she said. "Or use stock. I'm not *that* purist anymore. Anyway, I've heard you mention it two or three times, so what *was* Cookie Crumb Hill?"

"Home. It was where the base was. Basically a pile of sand cemented together with water ice, it was the boat for the base."

"The *boat*?"

"It floated on what was around it, and if anything had gone wrong it would have ejected as a whole, so we thought of it as a boat. But we called it Cookie Crumb Hill because it was a pile of meter-or-bigger ice clods. The stuff in the core was mostly silica, so the robots spun that into glass fibers, stirred that into melted water, and added enough vacuum beads to make it float on the frost, because otherwise anything we built would have been under twenty-five kilometers of frost."

A virgin Kuiper Belt Object begins as a bit of dust accumulating frost. It accretes water, ammonia, methane, hydrogen sulfide, all the abundant things in the universe, a molecule at a time. Every so often it adds more dust, and as it grows bigger and bigger, the dust sinks through the loose vacuum frost to the center. At Kuiper Belt velocities, hardly anything ever hits hard enough to cause vaporization, and anyway it's too cold for anything to stay vapor for long. So over billions of years, the frost at the center packs slowly around the dust, and all of it sinks and compacts into a kind of sandy glacier. Frost on top of that sandy glacier packs in to form "fizzy glacier"—water ice mixed with methane and carbon dioxide ice. And always the surface at a few kelvins, where the slight mass and the low gravity are not enough to compact the crystalline structures, grows as thick frost; at the bottom of twenty-five kilometers of frost, on a world as small and light as Boreas, the total pressure was less than the air pressure of Mars. Time alone made Boreas large and its center hard.

"So before people got there," Léoa said, "you could say it was one big snowflake. Fractally elaborated fine structures of ice crystals, organized around a dust center—just that it was over seven hundred kilometers across."

"Small dust center, big compacted ice center," he said. "More like a snowball with a lot of frost on it. But I guess you're right, in a sense. So we called it Cookie Crumb Hill because with the fiber and beads in them, the ice boulders looked sort of like cookie crumbs, and we built it up in a big flat pyramid with sort of a keel underneath to keep it from turning over, so it was also a boat on a fluffy snowball, or if you would rather call it that, a snowflake.

"Anyway, I was a complete jerk as a teenage boy."

"I had twin teenage boys a couple decades ago," Léoa said, "and I might have the reversal and have more babies, but only if I can drown them or mail them away at age twelve."

Thorby skied alongside Baggins to check her indicators; she was farther into the green range, probably feeling better, and that was good.

"Well," he said, "I was unusually unpleasant even for a teenager, at least until the bicycle ride. Though being bad wasn't why Mom got rid of me; more like the opposite, actually." It came out more bitter than he had expected it to; he sometimes thought the only time he'd really been emotionally alive was between the ages of thirteen and eighteen, because everything after seemed so gray by comparison. "Anyway, I sat up there with Gran, and then there was a great light in the sky over the horizon, and about ten minutes of there being an atmosphere—I felt wind on my suit and for just a moment there was a sky instead of stars—and then, poof-click, all this new spiky frost forming everywhere. That was when the idea started, that it would be wonderful to be outside for a long period of time, especially if I could control what I did and how I spent my time.

"So for physics class, I figured out the gadget, and had the fabricators make it. That kilometer-across loop of spinning superconductor that was basically a big flywheel I could spin up to orbital velocity by doing shifts pedaling the treadmill, so over about a month I got in shape. Bicycle that I could ride around the inside of the loop as a maglev, picking up speed and momentum for the loop. That was trivial stuff, any lab could build that now, and our local robots didn't have much to do once the base was done. So I built my loop and my bicycle, or rather the robots did, and pedaled the loop for a few hours a day. In a frictionless very low g environment, the momentum adds up, and eventually that loop was moving at close to six hundred kilometers per hour, more than orbital velocity. With controllable superconduction on my bike tires, I could gradually increase the coupling, so I didn't get yanked off the bike when I first got on, and just ride my relative speed up high enough before getting off the loop and into orbit.

"Then I just needed the right timing, enough air, food, and water, and a way to come down when I got bored. The timing was done by a computer, so that I pulled out of the loop right at the top, while I was riding parallel to the ground, and I just had a one time program to do that, it took over and steered when it needed to, since my launch window was about three meters long and at that speed, that went by in about a sixtieth of a second. A recycling suit took care of the air and water. The food was in the big container I was towing. And the container, when it was empty, could be given a hard shove, and dragged through the frost below, as an anchor to get down to about a hundred kilometers per hour, when I'd inflate the immense balloon tires around the superconducting rims, and skim along the frost back to Cookie Crumb Hill.

"I just put the camera on the handlebars, facing backward, so that I'd have a record when I turned the project in for a grade, and then since I had to take a documentation class the next term, I used the footage. I had no idea people would get all excited about the image of me on that bicycle, food hamper towing behind me, with all that Boreas in the background."

"You looked like you were riding over it like a witch on a broomstick," she reminded him, "because the producer that bought it made it consistent that your head was upright in the picture, and the way a body in a gravitational field positions itself, the bike ended up toward Boreas."

"'It matters not what happened or how it was shot, the editor will decide what it was,'" he quoted, and skied forward a bit to stretch his tired legs and enjoy some exercise in the little daylight there was. Probably it would be another day or two before there was a rescue.

When he came back, and found her still rolling along on the rescue frame (which, to his eyes, kept looking more and more like a cross) on top of Baggins, she was still awake and wanted some more soup, so he set that up for her. "This probably is a good sign for your quick recovery," he pointed out. "The rescue people say they'll pick us up sometime tomorrow, so we could just camp here, but if we cover another fifteen kilometers tonight and tomorrow morning, we can officially say we got out of the Sand Sea all by ourselves. Which is more comfortable for you, stationary or rolling?"

"With my eyes closed I can't tell the difference; your porter is pretty good at carrying a delicate object. I can't get out of the suit anyway, so you're the one who setting up a shelter might make a difference to. So let's keep moving till you want to do that, and then move again in the morning when you're ready."

"That'll work." It was almost dark now, and though he could steer and avoid hazards all right by light amps and infrared, and find his way by the same navigation system that Baggins used, it was a sort of scary way to proceed and he didn't like the idea of risking something going wrong with Léoa. "I guess I'll make camp here."

The shelter took a few minutes to inflate, and then Baggins carried her inside and set her on cargo supports, so he could at least remove her helmet and let her breathe air that came from the shelter's generator, and eat a little bit of food she could chew, mostly just paste-like stuff from tubes that the medical advisor said she could have. When he had made her comfortable, and eaten a sitting-up meal himself, He stretched out on a pad himself, naked but feeling much better after a sponge bath. He told the shelter to make it dark, and didn't worry about setting an alarm time.

"Thorby?"

"Need something?"

"Just an answer to the last part of the question. So how did orbiting Boreas for a month, living on suit food and watching the frost form on the surface as a lot of the evaporated stuff snowed back in—I mean, basically, it was a novelty act, you were just orbiting a snowball on a bicycle—how did that launch everything for you?"

"My big secret is it didn't," he said, not sure whether telling her could change anything. "For most of the ride I played VR games on my visor and caught up on sleep and writing to pen pals. I shot less than five hours of camera work across that whole month. Sure, orbiting a kilometer up from a KBO's surface is interesting for a few minutes at a time. The frost spires and the big lacy ground patterns can be kind of pretty, but you know, a teenage boy doesn't appreciate much that his glands don't react to. I finally decided that I could stand company again, tossed the food container downward on the stretch-winch, slowed down to about a forty kilometers per hour across a few hundred kilometers of frost—the rooster tail from that was actually the best visual of the trip, I thought, with a line down from my bicycle to the surface, and then snow spraying everywhere from the end of the line—came in, got a shower, put it together, and forgot about it till it made me famous. At which point it also made it famous that Mom had a teenage son, which was badly blowing the ingénue image, so she filed repudiation papers with Image Control, and I've never seen or heard from her since. The biggest thing I learned, I'm afraid, was that I like having a lot of time to myself, and people bug me."

"What about big explosions?"

"I like them, I always did. And I liked watching frost re-form after moving Boreas around, and I just like to see stuff change. I know you're looking for something deeper, but you know, that's about it. Things end, new things form, new things end, newer things form. I just like to be there."

She didn't ask again, and he heard her breathing grow slower and deeper. He thought about the visuals he had, and about a couple things he wanted to make sure to do when Boreas did its South Pole pass, and was asleep almost at once in the perfect dark and silence of the Martian wilderness.

"All right," she said, "I'll tell you as much as I can, since you are going to ask." He was sitting beside her reconstructor tank in the hospital. "That's why you came back, right, to ask why I would do such a thing?"

"I don't really know if that is why I came here," he said. "I wanted to see how you were, I had some days before I go down to the South Pole, and since I put some effort into having you be alive, I guess I just wanted to see the results. I'm not planning to work with you again, so I don't really have to know why you wrecked my stalkers just before some key shots, only that you might, to avoid you."

"I suppose after what I did there's no question of your ever liking me."

"I'm a loner, I don't like people much anyway."

"Some people might guess that's why you like BEREs. The people who used to love the place the way it was are gone, and the people who are going to love the place it will be aren't there yet. For just that instant it's just you and the universe, eh?"

She must be recording this. It was the sort of thing you asked an interviewee, and her audience in particular would just gobble this down. Perhaps he should spoil it, and pay her back for having spoiled the first Boreas-pass for him?

Except she hadn't spoiled it. He'd be getting plenty of shots of the later passes and anyway good old Stalker Two had gotten most of what he wanted, including the fiery column from the surprise impact. And even if she hadn't done that, they'd have missed most of it through having to grab the stalkers and flee for their lives.

So it mattered, but not a lot; he just didn't want her around when he was shooting anything important. As for rescuing Léoa, well, what else could a guy do? That didn't create a bond for him and he couldn't imagine why it might for her. It was just something he did because it was something people did at a time like that.

"You're looking like you've never had that thought before," Léoa said.

He thought, *what thought?* and said, "I guess, yeah."

"You see? We're not so different from each other. You like to see the moment when something beautiful changes into something new. And you don't care that things get all smashed when that happens. In fact you enjoy the smash, the beautiful death of something natural and beautiful, and the birth of a beautiful human achievement."

He thought, *what?* and was afraid he would have to say something.

But by now she was rolling. "Thorby, *that* was what I wanted to capture. Thorby, Lonely Thorby, Thorby the Last Mountain Man, finds out he can be betrayed by people he thought were his friends. The change of your expression as it happened. The way your body recoiled. The whole—my idea is, I'm going to overlay all that and interact it, touchlinked back and forth everywhere, with the changes on Mars, show Mars becoming a new living world artificially, and show Thorby engaging and rejoining the human race, artificially, in a dialogue. Show you becoming someone who can hate and maybe even eventually love. Someone who can see that the rest of us are here. The way Mars can learn to respond to life on its surface, in a way that it hasn't in the three centuries we've been there."

At least he knew about this. People had been trying to change Thorby his whole life. He'd never been any good at being changed. "So you wanted to get the moment when I changed, for your docu?" It was a stupid question, she'd told him, but interviewers have to ask stupid questions now and then, if they want to get decent quotes, and habits die harder than passions.

"That's it, that's it exactly. Exactly. I'm giving up on the whole purist-realist movement. You can have it to yourself. It not only isn't making me famous, it's not even *keeping* you famous. I've got an idea for a different kind of docu altogether, one where the human change in celebs, and the Blooming change in the solar system, echo and describe each other in sort of a dialogue. If you're interested, and I bet you're not, I've recorded sort of a manifesto of the new movement. I've put it out already. I told them what I did to you and why and showed your face, which wasn't as expressive as it could be, by the way. Too bad you never want to do another take. And even though in the manifesto I explain it will be at least twenty years before my next docu, instead of the usual five or six, because I want to get at least that much of the Mars changes into it, the manifesto is *still* getting the most attention I've *ever* gotten. I've got a bigger audience than ever, even pulling in some of my backlist. I'm going to have an *impact*."

It all made sense of a sort, as much as people stuff ever did, so Thorby said, "Well, if that's what you want most, I'm glad you're finally having an impact. I hope it's the impact you want." To him it seemed to come out stiff and formal and unbelievable.

But she smiled very warmly and said, "Thorby, that's so beautiful I'd never dream of asking for a second take."

"You're welcome." He brushed her forehead with his hand, and added, "Happy impacts."

Because she looked like she was trying to think of a perfect reply, he left. He needed to get new gear purchased and checked out, then catch a hop-rocket; Boreas-pass over the South Pole was just three days away.

He wondered why he was smiling.

Right on Mars's Arctic Circle, just at 66 N, at winter solstice, the sun at noon should just bounce over the southern horizon, and Thorby had an idea that that might look especially impressive with the big new ring arcing so high across the sky. But to his annoyance, here he was, waiting for that momentary noon-dawn, and the new, thick Martian clouds had socked in every point around the Arctic Circle. Above the clouds, he knew, the new rings were vivid with light, a great arc sweeping halfway up the sky; but down here, nothing, and even the constant meteor shower under the rings was invisible, or showed only as flashes in the clouds indistinguishable from distant lightning.

He waited but it never cleared, and the time for the midwinter sun passed, so he turned on the ground lights on his hop rocket to pack up.

Thorby blinked for a moment. It was snowing, big, thick,

heavy slow flakes, tumbling down gently everywhere, not many just yet, but some everywhere he looked. It was so fine, and so perfect, that he shot it for twenty minutes, using three stalkers to record the snowfall in big slow pans, and two just to record the lacy flakes as they landed on dark soil and lay exposed for just an instant to his view before the stalker's lights melted them, working at maximum magnification to catch each unique one, wondering if it was even possible for a Martian snowflake shape to fall elsewhere.

He stayed there shooting till the wind rose and the snowfall thickened enough so that he had to worry about getting the hop rocket off the ground. He was laughing as Baggins swallowed up the stalkers and rumbled up the ramp, and he looked around one more time before climbing the ramp and turning off his ground lights. He indulged in a small spiteful pleasure: he knew that his normally expressionless face was cracking wide open with pure joy, and Léoa and her cameras were in some city or on some ship somewhere, farther from him than anyone had ever been.

Dark Corners

Kristine Kathryn Rusch

The fighting had been going on for days. Outbursts of gunfire—six German soldiers dead in front of the Gare d'Orsay—a full-scale battle, complete with barricades that the French love so much, near the Eiffel Tower.

Solae had come to the surface because he heard the Resistance and the Germans had brokered a truce. The Resistance needed the time to organize, to wait for the Allies to arrive. The Germans, who were beginning to understand that they could not hold Paris, needed time to make a plan.

Solae needed food, so he had come to the only safe place he knew—a *boulangerie* on the Boulevard St. Germain. Most of the French were in hiding, not waiting in bread lines, and the Germans were at their posts.

He'd thought he would be able to slip in and out, unnoticed.

He had been wrong.

Solae ran across the boulevard, a loaf of bread beneath his arm, panic in his throat. He was thinner than most, so thin that if he turned sideways, the less observant could not see him. But he could not turn now.

The baker—a burly man who baked every morning for the Boche

as if they were no different from the French he once served—was chasing Solae, shouting at the top of his lungs:

"Foul boy! Thief!"

Two storm troopers appeared from a kiosk, holding ripped posters telling Parisians to rise up against the Boche. The troopers looked ready for battle. They had shiny boots and shinier guns—and their eyes, that pale blue that the Boche seemed to worship—seemed even paler in the August sunlight.

Solae grabbed his bicycle, also stolen, and pedaled as fast as he could, praying that the troopers would not follow in a car. Was a bread thief worth the gas? Surely there were other battles to fight, other people to attack.

But he knew that the Germans—the filthy Boche—were like rabid dogs, unable to let go of anything once they sank their teeth into it.

He pedaled hard, weaving in and out of the bicycle traffic. Despite the fighting, Parisians were still on the streets, going about their business, ignoring the war as best they could, just like they had these last four years.

Behind him, he heard the roar of an engine. He glanced over his shoulder.

The troopers had followed him. Theirs was the only car on the boulevard. Their helmets made their heads look round and comical, but Solae did not laugh at them.

He had not laughed at the Boche for a long time, not since they put out the lights in his fair city. Not since his father's death.

Solae pedaled faster, but he could not stay ahead of the car. It roared behind him, and it would only be a moment before it caught him.

The bread was warm beneath his arm. Sweat ran down his face, and he wished, not for the first time, that he had the magic of his ancestors.

He would make the Boche vanish. He would explode them, destroy their vehicle, wipe their race from the earth.

But he could do none of these things. His people could do none of these things. The powers that had once belonged to faerie had faded centuries ago. When he was his most cynical, he believed that his people had had no great powers at all—that Faeryland and the magic that went with it were the myths the Real Ones believed them to be.

The Boche sitting on the right aimed his rifle at Solae, and Solae's breath caught. He imagined light streaming from his fingers, destroying the rifle, destroying the Boche.

But imagination did not make it so.

Instead, Solae veered onto a side street, then another, his bike bouncing on the cobblestones. He was near the entrance his people kept hidden with their tiny powers.

In one movement, he slipped off the bike and laid it against the closed and locked door of an empty shop. He gave the bike a longing glance—it had been by far the best bicycle he had stolen—then he slipped sideways.

The Boche squeezed their vehicle onto the tiny street, the tires on the left side of the car riding on the curb. The Boche were laughing, calling out in German and bad French, promising *le jeune* a present if he but stopped for them.

Solae knew what kind of present they would give him: a bullet in the heart. And no amount of magic could undo that kind of damage.

The Boche did not seem to see him, even though one looked directly at him. Solae slipped around the corner and hid against a white wall covered with dead bougainvillea, until the Boche, their merriment gone, backed out of the street and left him alone.

Solae had not always stolen bread.

Once the Real Ones of Paris thought him the favored son of a nightclub owner, a man who specialized in acts that had a touch of glamour to them—be it the way a chanteuse's songs seemed to come alive onstage or the way that a young dancer almost seemed to fly as she leapt into the arms of her partner.

There had been magic during those nights. Not the magic of Solae's ancestors, but slighter magic, a bit of beauty that seemed to brighten the darkness.

Not that there had been much darkness then.

Less than a decade ago, when Solae was a little boy, he used to escape the smoke of his father's nightclub and climb onto the roof. There he looked at the lights of Paris—the arc lights illuminating the Eiffel Tower, the gargoyles of Notre Dame grinning in the lights on the dome, the lights of Sacré-Coeur on top of Montmartre, glowing like candles in the distance.

The Real Ones called Paris La Ville Lumière, the City of Light.

Perhaps they thought of the clear, crisp sunlight which, they said, they could not find anywhere else; but Solae always thought of the nighttime when the lights of the city made Paris as bright as day.

But when the bombings started, five years before—he had still been a boy then—the lights went out. Paris had not been La Ville Lumière for one-third of his life. It had become a place where darkness grew, like a hole in his soul.

For Solae, the absence of light was like the absence of air. His magic was not like his father's. The family already knew that Solae would not run the nightclub. Solae couldn't enhance acts, nor could he make a plain woman beautiful.

For a long time, his family thought he had no gifts at all.

And then they realized that his gifts were even subtler than usual—the ability to fade away in a crowd, or to brighten a room when he entered it.

Solae was not a creature of the night as so many of his kind were. He preferred the day, and if he had to choose a type of day, he preferred the bright sunlight of a Paris afternoon, the way the light fell upon the Seine, illuminating the classic lines of the Palace du Louvre and the magnificent windows of the Gare d'Orsay.

Sometimes Solae sat on the stone edge of the Pont Saint-Michel and watched the city pass him by, enjoying the light, the warmth, the way Parisians seemed to enjoy each moment.

He had not sat on the Pont Saint-Michel in four years, not since the Boche came in tanks, hanging their filthy flag with its ancient symbol, the swastika, across the Arc de Triomphe.

Usually, his people did not become involved in the ways of the Real Ones, except as his father did, to make money to survive. So many of faerie had moved to the city decades before. No one questioned strangeness in Paris. Even though it was a Catholic city in a Catholic country, certain behaviors were ignored.

Faerie who would have been hanged or shot or burned in the countryside were tolerated here. Many, like Solae's father, were more than tolerated.

They were loved.

And now they were gone. His father to a bullet in the middle of a piano medley. Storm troopers, drunk with power, insisted on hearing *"Ein Prosit"* and Solae's father, who hated the Boche with a passion that made Solae's seem tepid, refused.

His father had railed against the Boche from the moment they began their campaigns in the Real Years of the 1930s. Remember, he said to his wife and sons, the Germans are the ones who exposed us, told our histories as if they were fables for children, made us less than we are.

And that night, the night the Germans wanted to hear "*Ein Prosit,*" his father spoke of his hatred. The Boche reminded Solae's father that France was theirs now.

France belongs to no man, Solae's father said, his meaning clearer to faerie than it was to the Real Ones in the room. On some level, France had magic in her soul, magic that had been purged from so many European countries long ago.

Soon, the Boche told him, we shall remake France in our own image.

"And you shall fail," Solae's father said, "just as you failed to hear '*Ein Prosit.*'"

The words grew heated, and even Solae, who had been near the door, watching the lights of the city with a craving he still did not understand, turned toward the smoky interior of his father's club. Voices rose, shouting in German and French, about country, patriotism, and the emptiness of the German soul.

Then finally the shot, silencing everyone, including the piano player, who had been playing American boogie-woogie as if it could cover the ugliness in the room.

The smoke seemed to clear. Solae's father stood for the longest time, before collapsing in on himself. The Germans kicked him to see if he was still alive, and, when he did not move, they stood. In a loud voice, the German who shot Solae's father ordered the piano player to play "*Ein Prosit,*" and this time, the piano player did.

Solae had hurried through the crowd to retrieve his father's body. His mother did the same, running from her position behind the wings.

But they both arrived too late. His father vanished into the floorboards, his soul stolen by the stone he landed on, his essence gone as if it had never been

Solae's mother had not been the same since. Solae had taken her and his brother away from that place, which the piano player took over and allowed to become a Vichy stronghold. Solae only hoped that the French who collaborated with the Boche were being haunted by the vengeful ghost of his father and were suffering hideous torment because of it.

That was early in the Occupation, before the Germans began to understand Paris. The so-called decadence of Paris—the homosexuals, the mixed-race couples, the transvestites who performed at the very best clubs, not to mention the Jews, who corrupted (in the opinion of the Boche) every city they touched—disgusted and fascinated the German soldiers and bureaucrats who had invaded the city.

When the Boche discovered that Paris was a haven for yet another group—a group the Germans had slaughtered centuries ago—they were merciless. Faerie were murdered on the street, and no one came to their defense. For faerie were not French; nor were they even human. They were something Other, and as food became scarce, they became little more than mongrel dogs to those who competed with them for every scrap.

Still, faerie were reluctant to leave Paris. They could not go to England, where they had been slaughtered centuries before the Germans came after them, and they could not afford the long trips to America—back in the days before the Americans became part of the war.

The countryside held the same dangers as the city, more so because there were fewer faerie and more Boche, and parts of France had become more German than others.

Faerie finally found themselves relegated to the land no one else wanted, the place no one else would think of as a refuge: the vast tombs beneath the city—the catacombs.

That was where Solae slipped now. He went onto the side street through a small, private doorway that faerie kept locked. The Boche thought the doorway led to the courtyard for the apartments above and never investigated.

Although the doorway did lead to a courtyard, beyond the courtyard was a street, a tiny street that the Boche car would never fit on. Part of the ancient city, the street meandered for less than a mile before reaching another boulevard through another doorway.

But underneath the street ran a main section of the catacombs. Solae had discovered the entrance one afternoon when he had explored. Then he had shown it to the elders, and they had used their combined powers to mask the entrance as a whitewashed wall.

Solae touched that wall now. His fingers found the latch that released the stone door, and it swung open, echoing in the emptiness.

He hated the catacombs. They were dark and dank, and they reeked of death. The Real Ones could not smell it, although they did not care for the catacombs either. But the Real Ones had lost their sense of the Beyond, and they did not realize that when their ancestors emptied Paris's graveyards and stacked the bones in the sewers beneath the city, they had stacked the power of death there as well.

Each time Solae descended into the darkness, he felt like he lost a part of himself. He had become convinced that his thinness was not due to his lack of meals but to the pieces of himself taken by the darkness that lived below.

Still, he disappeared behind the stone door. As it closed behind him, he raised his right hand, pressed his thumb and forefinger together, and created a light.

The ability to create light was his only awe-inspiring power. A worthless power, his father used to say. But Solae did not think it worthless any longer, and he often wished that his father still lived so that Solae could prove how valuable the light had become.

Solae held his hand out before him. The light he formed was small—he didn't want to burn himself out this early in the day—and shaped like a flame. Only it did not flicker. The light burned steadily like an electric current, providing constant illumination for his journey ahead.

That was the only way he could tolerate heading into the catacombs. Flickering light would have terrified him, caused him to see ghosts in the shadows where there were none.

The Boche had come below many times, but had found no one. Only rats. For the Boche, for all of their posturing, were the most superstitious race in Europe—and the most terrified of death. They avoided the catacombs as much as possible.

The steps leading down had been carved centuries before by unknown hands, and hollowed by thousands of feet. In the time that Solae had spent below, he wondered at who had moved the bones of the ancient dead. What kind of man would carry skeletons from their natural resting places to the depths below?

The bones were not just placed in a pile. They were stacked neatly in patterns, and the patterns varied. In some places, the skulls formed a congregation of a thousand empty eyes, staring into the passageway. In others, the skulls were the center of a skull-and-crossbones motif.

Solae had found other places where the long bones of the legs and arms formed crosses or stars or other patterns that had existed since the beginning of time. In the middle of one particularly dark night, he had even found a group of bones that formed swastikas—and he had to remind himself that the symbol had been around long before the Boche took it for their own.

The catacombs were deep underground, and he always knew he drew close when water from the ceiling began to fall like rain. He worried that one day, the roof would collapse under the weight of the water above, but others, older and wiser than he, swore that would not happen.

Still, in many places below, the stone floor was wet, and the ceiling even wetter. He had to go through such a place to find his family, huddled in their little sepulchre deep within the labyrinth.

At first, Solae's mother had balked at staying in such a place. Clearly the priests who had designed this place had set up many areas for worship. There were long communion tables with all of the Christian symbols carved into the sides. There were quotes carved from the Real One's Holy Book upon the ceiling. There was an altar in the center, and even a baptismal font that collected ceiling rain.

Solae had to sleep on the communion table one night alone before his mother believed that one of these abandoned churches would be safe for faerie. And even now, she still had her doubts, occasionally waking in the middle of the night screaming that the crossbones on the wall were coming for her, to put her down like the dog the Christians believed she was.

She was nothing like the woman who bore him, nothing like the glamorous creature who performed every midnight on his father's stage. Then her alto voice had mesmerized the crowd, and her dark eyes had shone with magic unused. She had become the toast of their *arrondissement,* the center of faerie life in Paris—and beloved among the Real Ones themselves.

Or so it had seemed.

When she had gone to the Real Ones after Solae's father's death, they had slammed their doors as if they did not know her. Solae's brother Noene suggested this was because they had not recognized her; to them she was a musical beauty in a smoke-filled room, not a woman with haunted eyes who needed refuge.

Solae brought the bread, only to find his mother sitting on the priest's chair, carved in marble and pushed against the stone wall—the only wall without bones protruding from it.

Noene was there with a sausage he had stolen, and together they made a feast. The three of them hadn't eaten that well in days.

After they finished, his mother looked at Solae. For a moment, he thought she would ask him how he had gotten the bread—how he had survived in the city above.

But she hadn't ever asked him about that. In fact, she did not speak of the city, as if it had ceased to exist. She hadn't been above ground for four years. It had affected not just her manner, but her sight. Solae had to douse his personal light and find candles for the lamps below. She preferred the gloom, claiming that anything brighter made her eyes hurt.

"They've returned," his mother said.

Solae started. The Boche had come into this sanctuary more than once. The last time, Solae had been asleep on the communion table when he heard the clatter of boots against stone. He had doused the candles and climbed into the space between the skulls and the ceiling—a space barely a foot in width.

He had lain there, his nose pressed against the damp, the bones of the dead digging into his back, as the Boche peered into the chamber.

"I cannot believe someone would hide here," one of them said in their hideous tongue. "I would die first."

And then they had moved on, boots clanking with military precision, the click-clicks marking the time it took the Boche to leave Solae behind.

"Where did you hide?" Solae asked, hoping that his frail mother did not have to lie on bones as he had.

"Not the Germans," Noene said. "The Communists."

Solae suppressed his sigh of relief. The Communists were French, and they were not as frightening as his family made them sound. The Communists were part of the Resistance, the French who opposed the collaborationists who had taken the center of French government from Paris and moved it to Vichy to hide the fact that the Germans really controlled all that they did.

Vichy had become a dirtier word than *Communist*, and *collaborationist* the dirtiest word of all.

"You heard them?" Solae asked, pretending a concern he did not feel.

"They are plotting violence," his mother said, as if the violence she spoke of was directed at her.

"They say the Americans have landed in Normandy." Noene could not hide his enthusiasm. "They worry that De Gaulle will come here and destroy them."

That was not the real worry of the Communists. Solae knew more about them than he told his family. He had found the Communist enclave long ago, and during the dark nights, had snuck through the bones to find the enclave, listening to the speeches and the pep talks and the news.

It was from them that Solae had picked up the word *Boche*, which suited the Germans much more than any other word had. He did not want to speak of them with respect. He needed a word that was profane for what they had done to his city, his family, his home.

The Communists had taken to hiding in the sewers more than the catacombs, and planning small attacks against Germans. They disarmed the Vichy police, they occasionally killed a storm trooper who found himself alone, and they sabotaged shipments of French goods back to Germany.

The Communists were only a small part of the Resistance, but they were hated by their own people, and feared, for when the Germans were defeated and Vichy gone, the Free French believed the Communists would rise up and take over the government—obligating the French to Stalin and the Soviet Union the way Vichy obligated France to Hitler.

But Solae did not share that fear. The Communists called themselves freedom fighters, and they were fierce advocates for France.

He admired all they did. Sometimes he sat in the shadows and listened as they made their plans. He wished he could help them, but he could not. If someone died—even accidentally—because of his involvement, he would lose what little magic he had.

For that was why faerie were so easily defeated throughout

Europe. Their powers were the powers of life, lost when touched with death. Faerie resisted coming into the catacombs for that very reason—even ancient death disturbed them.

It took a courageous few to live below, test their powers, and report to the others before the entire community found the shelter and safety they needed.

Solae wished he could help the Communists. He did what he could. He was what some called a passive member of the Resistance—he taunted the Boche, stole from them or their Vichy compatriots, and destroyed their writings wherever he found them. Sometimes he siphoned precious gas from their cars, but carefully, never allowing his powers of light to touch the liquid for fear of a fire.

He did what he could, but it was very little.

"Aren't you worried by this?" Noene asked. "They will start a war above us."

"There is a war above us," Solae said.

"But not like the countryside," Noene said. "Paris still stands."

For the moment. But Solae did not say that. Instead, he said, "They say De Gaulle will be here by the first of September, and I believe it. Many of the Germans who are not soldiers have stolen what they can from the city and fled."

"What will happen to us?" his mother asked. "If Communists find us, they are even more ruthless than the Germans."

She was thinking of the Russian communists. She had lost family in St. Petersburg, which the communists had then renamed. Sometimes, she said lately, her entire life had been about loss.

"We'll be fine," Solae said. But he did not believe that, for the Germans were ruthless. He had seen too much to believe they would let Paris go so easily.

His thoughts made him restless. He stood, unable to stay in the darkness much longer.

"It's still daylight above," he said. "I'll see if I can find us anything else before night falls."

He did not wait for his mother's answer. Instead, he fled through the tunnels and went up to the light.

He heard the sound before he even left the stairway—gunfire. The heat had grown worse, a physical presence that made the gunfire seem even more ominous. As he stepped through the doorway, this one leading to a different part of the city, he saw German tanks in the street.

Four of them, large as houses. The tanks made Solae shudder. He pressed himself against the wall, uncertain what to do. He did not know if he had been seen, if his presence would lead others to the catacombs.

The gunfire came from the Hôtel de Ville, the city hall. Men—boys, really—leaned out of windows and shot at the tanks with revolvers.

The tanks swiveled, aiming their guns at the Hôtel de Ville. The building itself seemed to shudder from their might. Solae winced, feeling helpless.

He had heard that the Germans would destroy the city before they allowed the French to retake it, but he had not believed it. Paris was, according the BBC, the only intact city left in Europe. It had artifacts and treasures that everyone—not just the French—could enjoy.

It was his home.

A young woman, standing near his hiding place, screamed at the Boche. Solae couldn't make out the words—something about leaving her city in peace—then she grabbed a bottle from the ground beside her and ran for the street.

His heart pounded. He stepped forward to stop her—there was nothing she could do against tanks—but she kept screaming, "Filthy Boche! You do not belong here! Filthy Boche!"

Solae could not reach her.

She got to the side of the tank, smashed her bottle against its open turret, and somehow flames exploded along the metal. Solae had heard about such weapons—simple combinations of chemicals that he did not understand.

He heard a scream from inside, saw a German soldier rise, slapping himself, trying to put out the fire his clothing had become.

The girl grinned and ran back toward Solae, her steps almost a dance. For a moment, he remembered the beauty his father conferred upon the nonbeautiful—a touch of glamour, given by a little bit of magic.

The girl had that magic, without Solae's father's help. She was not faerie, and yet she glowed with her victory.

Her gaze met Solae's, and he thought he had never seen anything so lovely in his entire life.

And then a shot rang out.

A single shot, even though he knew it could not have been the only one, even though he knew others were firing.

But it was as if he were with the girl, as if he were linked to her by her moment of victory. He saw the surprise fill her eyes, the blood spatter out of her mouth, her look of triumph turn to horror—

And then to nothing.

She stumbled, collapsed, and fell forward, like his father had done. Like so many others had done.

Solae did not stop to think. He ran into the street, to the girl, as people around him shouted, demanding that he take cover. The tanks kept shelling the Hôtel de Ville and, in one heart-stopping moment, he feared the building would tumble around him.

He reached her and crouched, knowing from her open and glazed eyes that she was gone. But he could not leave her there. Even if the stone would not absorb her soul the way it had absorbed his father's, Solae could not abandon her on the street, to be run over by the Boche, to be treated as one more rag in a city littered with them.

He slipped his hands under her arms and lifted her. Bullets pinged off the cobblestones as someone shot at him—maybe even the freedom fighters above, missing their German targets.

His heart was pounding, the girl's blood warm on his skin. She had had her moment against the Boche, her victory, and the Boche had stolen it from her, as they had stolen everything else—her home, her life, her world.

Solae's world.

He carried her to the sidewalk, where one of the old women wailed in grief. Then he set the girl's body, and knew what he had to do.

The Boche were the most superstitious creatures in Europe.

Solae turned to face them.

The boys still fired from the windows above. Three of the tanks still fired at the Hôtel de Ville. The fourth, its crew disabled or dead thanks to the girl, huddled like a wounded animal in the middle of the street.

Solae formed a fist and held it high, in mockery of the German salute.

"*Achtung!*" he shouted, his German flawless from years of listening to the vile tongue.

No one looked at him. No one seemed to see him.

He used his own glamour, his ability to brighten a room.

"*Achtung!*" he shouted again, and this time, every German within hearing range looked.

Solae squinted slightly, concentrating. He imagined his entire fist engulfed in flame—and suddenly it was. Cool flame which did not consume, but which burned beautifully in the bright August sunlight.

The shooting from the windows stopped.

He let the fire slide down his arm and engulf his entire body. The street looked wavy through the flame, as if he were viewing everything from a heat mirage.

"*Vive la France!*" he shouted.

Then he made the fire wink out.

The Germans stared at him for the longest time. The moment seemed to stretch forever.

Solae smiled at them.

"*Vive la France!*" he repeated, and put his hands on his hips, obviously unharmed by the fire that had surrounded him a moment before.

He took a step forward, and the German closest to him screamed. So did another, and another. They scrambled into their tanks, down the turrets, closing the hatches.

Solae remained on the street, watching them. The Germans drove their tanks away from him, their terror palpable in the thick August heat.

Dust rose around him. He did not feel the girl's sense of victory. All he had done was a trick, nothing monumental, nothing worth a life.

But the boys in the windows above started to cheer. And so did the people on the street. They were looking at him, and cheering, and he could not take it.

He had done nothing. He was nothing. Just a small man with a small talent, and a little bit of luck.

He could not save the girl from death. He could not prevent death. And he had used his one talent the only way he knew how.

The cheering continued, and he looked away. The girl's corpse remained on the sidewalk, the old woman bent over her, rocking, as if the movement would make the girl return.

Nothing would make her return. Nor would Solae's father return, or their life, or his mother's sanity. Nothing would be the same again, no matter when the Allies came.

All these years, he had deluded himself, hiding among the dead, believing that all he had to do was wait, and life would return to normal. The humans would stop their craziness, the war would fade, and everything would return.

But it was not just a human craziness. His father had been right: there were humans to ally with, and humans to fight. His father would have fought—he had fought, in his own turf, over his own command: music.

But Solae had not. He had not used his powers at all.

Until now.

All these years, he could have fought in a slightly larger way, and he had not.

He had not.

While others died.

He had chosen to fade away instead of bringing light. He had chosen to live among the dead instead of fight beside the living.

But he would not make that choice again.

He could bring light to darkness, and vanish seemingly without a trace.

The Resistance was chasing the Boche from Paris, and Solae would help as best he could. And when he was done here, he would help liberate all of France, which was the world he cared about.

He finally knew how to do it, without losing his powers, without betraying his people.

He would haunt the Boche. He would bring light to the darkest corners of their souls, exposing them to all they had done.

He would destroy the Boche, taking all they feared and turning it against them, one by one.

One superstitious mind at a time.

The Ten Thousand Things

Mark L. Van Name

Yukio stared at the image of Matsushima Bay in the window that was one wall of his father's office. Whitecaps freckled the nearer water. Pine-covered islands filled the distance, the trees gray in the dying light. The sounds of whistling wind carried off the occasional beep of the heart monitor as it tracked the death passage of his father.

His father had always loved the bay, had led the campaign that restored it to its natural beauty. It and the company, the twin passions of his life, had kept him constantly busy, constantly away. Matsushima Bay was the older brother Yukio had never had and could never match. His father would be buried there, beside the family temple on the far side of now-deserted Oshima Island. Yukio hated Matsushima.

When he realized he had not heard a beep in some time, Yukio released the breath he had been unconsciously holding and turned from the window.

His father lay curled in a fetal position in an open long metal cylinder the soft black of a switched-off video display. Tubes and wires ran from his body to the capsule's lid, which rested on its hinges beside him. Yukio saw the device as a fusion of his father's passion for ancient religion and modern tech, a burial barrel as re-imagined by a circuit designer. His father hated hospitals and had not wished to die in one. He wanted to die in one of the two centers of his world, his office or Oshima Island. When the stroke hit him, the office was closer.

Yukio's mother sat beside the cylinder. She was doubled over, her head in her hands. Yukio thought she was crying and looked away in respect. Dr. Jippensha, the family's long-time physician, leaned over his father. Yukio heard the murmurs of Jippensha's mumbling but understood only "Hisato," his father's name.

Jippensha straightened, turned off the monitor, and bowed deeply. "I am sorry. He is dead."

Yukio suppressed an irrational urge to run to the cylinder, check the reading himself, and find a setting the doctor had missed. Instead, he bent his head slightly in acknowledgment. "The capsule?"

"Yes, it's working. His blood still flows; his brain still gets the oxygen it needs." Jippensha paused. "But I think—"

Yukio was not going to change his mind now. "Thank you, Doctor. I understand and appreciate your feelings. Please close the capsule; then you may go."

Jippensha started to speak once more but caught Yukio's gaze and remained silent.

Yukio's mother looked up. "Yukio—"

Yukio winced at the use of his familiar name in front of Jippensha. "Mother."

He meant it more as a reprimand than a response, but she ignored his tone. "Doctor Jippensha is right. Let your father be. His memories aren't what you need. You need—"

"Mother." He stretched out the word, embarrassed even more.

She walked to him. "Hisato's memories will teach you nothing you cannot learn in other ways." She leaned closer and lowered her voice. "Yukio, you can't bring him back, so let him go. Let his spirit proceed on the forty-day journey. There is no need to desecrate his body—"

"Akako!"

She stopped instantly; he had never before used her first name. He had no desire to hurt her, but he was determined to get the knowledge that in life his father had never had time to impart. He stared at his mother, willing her to understand, then noticed the doctor was still there. "Jippensha."

The doctor bowed once more and left.

Yukio's mother turned to leave also, but he touched her shoulder and she hesitated.

"We will finish the first stage of the process in a day, at most two," he said. "When that's done, I will have him cremated, and I'll take his ashes to the temple myself. Will that make you feel better?" It was more than he had wanted to offer; he had no desire to go to Matsushima ever again.

She stared at him for a moment, nodded, and left.

When Yukio heard the door shut, he walked to the desk and sat in the chair that was now his. At thirty, he was the youngest chairman ever of Fujiura Corp. But for the circumstances, perhaps, finally, he would have made his father proud. His father. Yukio rubbed his eyes, slid the keyboard and control panel from beneath the desktop, and turned off the projector and sound system.

Matsushima vanished. The room fell silent. Neon ads and multi-story video displays scorched the walls with the reds, pinks, oranges, and blazing whites of nighttime Tokyo. Yukio piped in the audio feed from outside and held down the volume control. The buzz of street life slammed into the room, bathed him in sounds he understood: cars and people and advertisements surging in a jangled torrent of life that surrounded him, affirmed his living status, and pushed back the death that filled the room. He walked to the window and stretched out his arms, willing the city's life to flow over him, around him, into him. He craved its vitality, wanted that energy to carry him through this next step.

He wiped away a tear, disgusted at his lack of control, sure that even in death his father would be embarrassed by the display. He returned to the desk, shut off the speakers, and muted the window display. His assistant, Masataro, as calm and alert as always, appeared on the desk's screen the moment he opened the intercom.

"Yes, sir."

"Tell the lab team it's time."

"They are waiting outside your office."

Yukio was not sure whether he wanted to punish Masataro for his ghoulishness or praise him for his efficiency.

"Sir, I am sorry. Should I send them in?"

"Thank you, and yes." Yukio did not know what else to say. The only thing to do was to move forward.

Four men quietly entered his office and began wheeling out his father's body. The only one he recognized, Doctor Ishiwa, the project's head, paused at the door.

"Yes," Yukio said.

"I must tell you again," Ishiwa said, "that we do not know how well this procedure will work, or even if it will work at all. We've never fully succeeded in any of the simpler tests, and this is an entire . . . memory set."

Yukio stood for emphasis. "I understand, but we have no other options. You make it work, or we lose my . . . the chairman's memories."

Ishiwa bowed and left.

Yukio examined the list of pending items on his desk's display. The moment called for mourning, but business had to continue. His father would have done the same, would have demanded he keep working. Yukio opened the one item that glowed red. "Masataro, get me Kensu."

"He, too, is waiting," his assistant replied.

Yukio rubbed the bridge of his nose. He had to hand it to Kensu; after losing the company's top job to Yukio, the man had not slowed at all. "Send him in."

As Kensu entered, he bowed deeply, then waited for Yukio to speak.

"I must focus on the Board and our investors, as well as on the new RAM technology, and, of course, the memory project," Yukio said. "You must keep pushing on the Vladivostok deal." Yukio watched closely to see if Kensu would react; the man had fought for months against this deal, and Yukio's win of Board approval for it had cost Kensu his shot at the job Yukio now held. Kensu showed nothing, so Yukio continued. "TIOKO needs cash. Make sure they get it from us." Acquiring the Vladivostok-based TIOKO, the Tikho-okeanskoye Morye shipping and services conglomerate, would give Fujiura control of its trade paths east and west, enlarge its service offerings, and ultimately attract new large customers in both the Americas and eastern Europe.

Yukio turned away from Kensu as the man bowed and left the room, closing the door quietly behind him.

Continuing to run the business was necessary, but it did not make Yukio happy. He swiveled his chair to face the window and pushed the volume control upward until the amplified sounds of the streets below filled the room, until he was bathing in the rush of life, and then he leaned back and closed his eyes.

Late the next afternoon, Masataro led Ishiwa into Yukio's office.

"We have done all we can," Ishiwa said. "The scan and download are complete, so we have captured all the . . . raw data we know how to capture."

"So I may now access his memories?" Yukio asked.

Ishiwa stared at the floor before responding, "Not exactly." He looked up at Yukio. "As I warned, we have never completely succeeded, even in partial scans."

"Your past efforts do not matter now," Yukio said. "What is the state of his memories?"

"We have downloaded from his brain all the information we know how to find. We believe we missed nothing, but we have no way to be sure. The bigger problem is assembling the mass of raw data into memories you can access. Our latest software is working on it, but progress is slow and unpredictable."

"Do you have any complete memories?"

"We may," Ishiwa said, "but we cannot be sure. Our assembly programs have yielded several files that pass the few filters we've been able to construct. Per your instructions, however, the files are in the private storage area we set up. Because no one but you is allowed to access them, we have no way of knowing for sure what the programs have produced." Ishiwa cleared his throat and looked again at the floor. "Perhaps when it is convenient, you could—"

"Of course," Yukio said. "Leave me. I'll check now and let you know."

Yukio pulled out of his bottom right desk drawer the special laptop Ishiwa's team had prepared. A thick fiber cable snaked from its back into a network connection buried under the desk. A second, slightly thinner cable led to a thick pair of VR goggles that sat on the laptop. Yukio opened the laptop and let the retinal scanner verify his identity. He put on the goggles, which for the moment were clear and silent, and opened the first of the three memory files in the directory before him.

The goggles flashed into action, and sound poured from the integrated headphones. He was in his office, the Matsushima display playing on the window. Two men sat across from him: Yukio himself, but younger, and Kensu. Yukio felt strange, outside himself, as if he had split in two. He glanced at the keyboard beneath his—no, his father's—fingers, heard the gentle click of the keys, and then looked at the center of the office window, where a chart of sales projections replaced Matsushima. The chart sloped gently downward in the enterprise services sector, the department Yukio was then running. Yukio flushed with the same shame he had felt at that time, at having to report that a department of his had lost money. His stomach knotted at the memory of the shame, and at the anger he had felt from his father. As his gaze—his father's gaze—shifted to the younger Yukio in front of him, he realized how clearly his younger self had showed those same emotions, and he was even more embarrassed for himself. He shook his head: He could only imagine the shame and anger his father had felt.

Yukio stopped the memory playback. The goggles cleared. He closed his eyes and breathed slowly, calming himself. That meeting had convinced him both that he hated his job and that those feelings were irrelevant, because he could not let his father down.

After a few minutes, he tried each of the other two memories available to him. They were useless, jumbles of flashing colors and discordant sounds.

He called Ishiwa. "The first in the list is real. The others are not; delete them."

"Yes, sir," Ishiwa said. "Should we continue to run the assembly programs?"

"Of course," Yukio said. "We will hope they will yield more memories the company can use." He broke the connection before Ishiwa could speak again.

When Kensu arrived, Yukio was studying the manufacturing plan for the new RAM module, whose flexed nano-tubes delivered the largest single-module memory capacity ever available—enough capacity, Yukio mused, that one module could hold the entire raw download of his father's mind. The module and the new technology it embodied should vault Fujiura into the lead in that crucial market segment.

Kensu interrupted Yukio's contemplation. "TIOKO refused our offer." The man almost smiled as he told Yukio the news.

"How much did you offer?"

"I started low, of course," Kensu said, "with the share price as of close of business yesterday."

For a second Yukio wanted to hit Kensu, but he forced himself to lean back in his chair and reply calmly, "I thought we agreed on offering a premium."

"Yes," Kensu said, "and we will, but I saw no reason not to try a lower price first and perhaps save us a considerable amount."

Yukio stared across his desk at Kensu until the man looked slightly downward. "The reason, as I believe we discussed, is that we are not the only ones pursuing them, and now we have risked offending their Board. Kensu," he paused until the man looked at him, "though I appreciate your reservations about this deal, I am sure you also appreciate that I have committed to our Board that we will make it happen. If you would rather not work on it . . ."

"I will contact them again," Kensu said, "and make our apologies, as well as a new offer."

"Thank you." Yukio stood and bowed to Kensu, remembering his father's advice to always be most polite after a victory.

Kensu returned the bow and left.

Yukio's phone flashed; his mother. He accepted the call and winced as he saw her slight smile; she had heard the news. Her information sources within the company had always amazed him.

"I'm sorry the procedure did not work," she said, continuing to appear to be anything but sorry.

"On the contrary, mother, it did. I have already reviewed the beginning of one memory, and I am confident our software will assemble more."

"Perhaps I misunderstood," she said, "but—"

Yukio cut her off. "Some of the assembled memory files have proven to be worthless, but we are far from done." He fought to stay quiet, but her happiness at the failed memories was more than he could take. "Aren't you at all sorry about those memories we may lose? They are father's memories, and now they may be gone."

"No," she said. "They were gone when he died, as they should be. His spirit must move on, and so must ours. We have *our* memories of him; that is enough."

Maybe for you, thought Yukio, *but not for me. You knew him for decades, even before Fujiura and Matsushima became his life. I never knew him, not really.*

"So you insist on continuing?" she said.

Her question angered him further. "Yes. The software is running non-stop across the largest grid we can spare. I'm sure we'll be able to restore more memories, maybe many, many more. Memories that will be very useful to the company."

"To you, you mean."

Yukio refused to rise to the bait. "Yes, to me, as the head of the company."

His mother sighed and leaned forward until her face completely filled the display. "Let him go, Yukio. I know he gave you less than you wanted, but he's gone, and whatever you have of him now is all you can ever have. I wish you two had been closer, but he was always so busy, so dedicated, so—" she smiled. "—so like you."

I am not like him, Yukio thought. *Not at all. I would never have a child I did not want and could not find the time to raise. This job is my duty; it was his love.* Yukio shook his head. *Not at all like him.*

"You will keep your promise?" she asked.

He had almost forgotten she was there. "Yes," he said. "I'll pick up his ashes in the morning and take them to the temple."

"Good. There are only thirty-eight days before the temple ceremony; let his spirit spend those days on Matsushima."

Yukio reached to turn off the phone. "I will, Mother, I will."

Yukio had considered driving to the red moon-crossing bridge that linked Oshima Island to the mainland and then walking to the island, but that felt wrong. His father would have taken the boat from Hon-Shiogama across Matsushima Bay, and he was carrying his father's ashes, so in the end Yukio took the boat, too. The sky glowed a clear blue a shade lighter than the water. He kept the boat's engine on full, anxious to be done with it. The hull bounced on the small waves of the bay and jarred his spine. The wind mussed his hair and made his eyes water. His skin was sticky from the salt in the air.

When he reached the small dock at the foot of the temple path, Yukio tied up the boat and removed the urn from the cabin safe. He followed the path that led from the water into the pines.

He reached the first torii gate in less than five minutes. Its cedar cross-piece was rough, worn and pocked by time. He considered going on to the temple himself, but he was in mourning and tradition forbade it. Besides, why risk angering the kami? Though he did not actually believe in those spirits, he also knew there was no point in taking such a risk. He would see the temple at the burial; no need to go there sooner. He put the urn at the gate's base, clapped his hands three times to get the attention of the priests, and bowed deeply twice. Then he sat to wait.

The sun on his face was strong but not hot, its light filling the pines with a soft glow that scattered many shades of a single golden hue. The view provided a strange contrast to the arcing lines of color that filled the Tokyo nights; he was more comfortable in the neon. At first the island seemed silent, but as he sat longer he could hear the cries of gulls on the water and the sounds of other birds he did not recognize in the trees above him. The bushes and pine trees on either side of the path occasionally rustled in the wind. Despite himself he began to relax, the ancient rhythm of the place working its way into him. For a moment he almost touched the peace he had seen his father experience on their trips here, and in that moment he glimpsed why his father had fought for this place, why he had lavished so much time and love upon it. But did a man have room in his heart for only one love? Obviously not: His father clearly loved the company and, in his own way, his wife, too. Would one more love have been so hard? Yukio stared at the urn and wondered what he would say if the ashes became his father, magically reconstituted by the kami for a moment of temptation on his death journey. But the words would not come.

He looked up and saw the priest. He had not heard the man coming. Yukio stood and bowed deeply; the priest returned the bow. Yukio picked up the urn and handed it to the priest, who bowed once more and without a word turned and headed back up the path.

The mail icon flashing on his desk's console was the only light in his office late that night. The room, which was huge by Tokyo standards, easily larger than the homes of many small families, now only hemmed him in, squeezed him, trapped him. The island wasn't what he wanted, but he missed the sense of infinite possibility that beckoned from the hazy lines where horizon blurred into water and treetops faded into air. He had hoped to regain that sense by darkening the office and erasing its boundaries; instead, the faint light from the console made the space seem even smaller.

His father would never have wasted so much time. Yukio punched up the lights and turned to the display.

His mother's request to know if he had delivered the urn sat atop the inbox. He sent her a simple typed message, unwilling to face her.

Masataro had forwarded him a note from the head of their Chinese manufacturing plant; Yukio would soon receive a prototype of the new RAM module.

Kensu wanted to discuss the latest developments in the TIOKO deal. Yukio called him at home and was pleased to see a ripple of surprise play over the man's face as he realized Yukio was still at work. "What has happened that you would not e-mail me?" he said.

"The TIOKO Board is now open to our offer," Kensu said, "but they have some requirements."

"Of course."

"Most are ones we anticipated, but the price remains a problem." Kensu hesitated before continuing. "They want a ten percent premium over today's closing price, which of course was already up on the rumor of their sale. Meeting that price in cash would leave our reserves below acceptable levels, and they are not interested in a share-swap deal. I do not see how we can continue."

Yukio knew Fujiura Corp., understood the company better than he would ever understand the trees and plants of Oshima. Fujiura was an electronic and physical organism that he, like his father, nurtured and managed. TIOKO was a necessary addition to the chain that carried the material blood of Fujiura to the far-flung parts of its corporate body, as natural as the roots of the pines that spread through the soil at Oshima. He had spent months convincing the Board, including his father, of the importance of the acquisition for Fujiura's long-term health. He was prepared in ways he had reviewed only with his father, whose final approval of the deal signaled one of the few times Yukio felt he had impressed the man.

"Our American services subsidiary has a high valuation and

a shelf registration we can use for a quick offering to raise the cash. Get our brokers there to place the stock, and set a price with TIOKO now so we have a fixed target."

Kensu bowed his head slightly. "I should have thought of that. I apologize for not doing so." He looked intently at Yukio. "If you would prefer someone else finish this . . ."

You would have thought of it, Yukio wanted to say, if you had focused on completing the deal and not on avoiding it. Instead, he said, "I am confident you would have found this solution. I would have no one else complete the acquisition." Kensu was a good man, Yukio thought, a man who genuinely loved the company and who probably should be running it—who would actually enjoy running it.

Kensu bowed again, deeper this time. "Thank you. I will not let you down."

Yukio bowed, said, "Good night," and hung up.

Most of the remaining messages were routine, except for the last, which was from Ishiwa. The memory-retrieval processing was proceeding, and the software had assembled three more files. From their sizes none of the memories were long, but all, to the best of the software's very limited abilities to judge, were sufficiently complete to be worth saving. Yukio responded to the messages Masataro had not already handled, then locked his office.

He put on the goggles and started the first new memory in the directory.

He was again sitting in the office, but in an earlier version of it, a large PC filling the front right corner of the desk. An old, audio-only phone sat on his left. He watched his hands, his father's hands, come to his eyes and rub gently. He called home and heard his mother's voice, heard her initially happy greeting and then the subsequent resignation in her voice as he explained he would not be there for many hours, that he was in a pitched battle on the London exchange for a Yugoslavian manufacturing plant that would be a key element in his penetration of the rapidly growing Eastern European market.

He turned back to the screen, where columns of changing figures danced as madly as the lights in the darkening street below. The figures blurred. He walked to the office's private bathroom and stared at himself, his father, in the mirror. His face sagged with fatigue, the whites of both eyes streaked with red. He splashed water on his face—Yukio flinching as the water came at him, for a moment lost and not realizing the water wasn't there.

He looked again at himself in the mirror and slowly shook his head. "Akako, Yukio, I am so sorry," his father said to the reflection. He dried his face and muttered, "No time to be tired." He returned to the desk and stared at the display.

The goggles cleared, and Yukio was back in his office—his office, not his father's. Yukio took off the goggles and leaned his head on the desk. The fatigue of the memory should have vanished, but he was still tired. He supposed he should have realized his father would have felt bad about working late and would get tired, that anyone would, but it had never occurred to him. He wondered why his father did not simply quit for the day and leave, but he realized instantly that in this job he, too, would never have left at such a crucial time.

He tried the other two memories, but both were worthless, incoherent jumbles of light and sound. When he finished checking them, his mail light was once again flashing. Yukio yielded to its summons.

For the next three weeks, the programs worked steadily but with little success. They emitted a few fragments daily, each of which Yukio tested in the evenings. All but two were the now commonplace failures.

One of the two real memories was a fleeting glimpse of the inside of one of the company's planes, interior lights dim, his father staring at the ceiling and then closing his eyes. The other was a fifteen-second view of a menu in a second-rate Bangkok restaurant. Monkey brains were the special.

Late Friday night, Yukio sat in his office, as usual both desperate to go home and completely unwilling to do so. On Wednesday, Fujiura had begun sample production of the new RAM modules. Three night-black prototypes, Yukio's showpieces for the board meeting earlier that day, sat still and empty in front of him, their darkness a pleasing contrast to the lighter cedar of his desk. By Monday, manufacturing would have yielded at least a few thousand modules, enough to seed the major Fujiura sites worldwide. Yukio was deciding how to allot the precious modules until more were ready. He played for a while with a simulation, watching stacks grow and shrink on his corporate map as he tried different distributions. Finally, he found one that gave the right mix to the shrinking but still vital American market and the constantly growing Chinese one. He mailed the simulation to Masataro with a brief explanatory note.

Kensu, still at work, called and asked to meet with him. Yukio agreed.

Kensu was flushed and obviously excited when he entered the office. "TIOKO has signed the deal, and we've privately placed the entire American shelf offering. It's done. The more I met with the TIOKO people, the more I understood the fit. This is going to be a great deal for us." He bowed deeply. "Thank you for making this happen, and for letting me finish it."

"Thank you for the effort," Yukio said. He had once seen the TIOKO deal and integration as his newest triumph, a sure way to finally impress his father. Now, the thought of working on the integration, as vital to Fujiura as it was, only wearied him. He looked carefully at Kensu, took in the man's obvious joy in the deal, and thought yet again how much better suited for Yukio's job Kensu was. "I was hoping," he continued, "that you would be willing to add to your duties the task of leading the integration team. I can think of no one better to entrust with such a vital project."

Kensu sat back, caught off guard for a moment, then recovered and bowed. "It would be my privilege. Thank you."

"We'll discuss it further on Monday," Yukio said.

"I'll be prepared," Kensu said, as he left.

Yukio checked the log of the day's memory reconstruction. Four new ones awaited him, but all proved to be failures. No new memory of consequence had appeared in several days. The only memory of any length was the first, the unpleasant one he had started but never finished. It was time to check the rest of it, to be done with it. He put on the goggles, an image flashed into place, and sound played through the headphones.

He was in his office, the Matsushima display on the window. Kensu and his younger self sat across from him. Seeing himself was a bit easier this time, though still unsettling. He glanced at the keyboard beneath his fingers, heard the click of the keys, and looked at the center of the office window, where a chart of sales projections replaced Matsushima. The chart sloped downward in the enterprise services sector, Yukio's department. Yukio again relived the shame he had felt at that time, the feeling growing as his gaze—his father's gaze—shifted to the younger Yukio in front of him and his younger self showed the same emotion.

He heard his father's voice, which he now realized was oddly distorted through the man's head, as his father had heard it himself. He had always found his father's voice powerful, but the version the man himself heard was lighter, higher. "This trend must not continue. You—" Yukio noticed a hesitation he had not caught at the time—"we must do better. Your department is losing money; you must fix it."

Yukio watched himself look briefly downward and nod. "Yes, sir." He wanted to rip off the goggles, to wipe out the memory—and the past with it—but as the memory played on he forced himself to stay with it.

The window cleared, Matsushima reappeared, and his father continued, "That is all; you may go." He watched as his younger self and Kensu stood, bowed, and left.

He was his father, alone. He looked at the window. Matsushima Bay sparkled in the sunlight. He heard his father's breathing, slow and deep, the same sounds Yukio made when he fought for control. He opened a drawer and stared at the framed picture lying inside: Akako and Yukio, both smiling, stood together on Yukio's university graduation day.

His father's fingers gently touched the photo, and his voice again filled the headphones. "I am so sorry, Yukio. With all your talents, all your gifts, I have never understood why you stayed here. As long as you are here, though, I cannot show you any favoritism, or you will be ruined. I know you will succeed, but I hate making you pay the price for that success. I wish you could find happiness."

As he put the photo back in the drawer, the memory ended.

Yukio opened the drawer where the photo had been, then remembered Masataro clearing and packing his father's possessions. He closed the drawer, leaned back, and shut his eyes.

He had always assumed his father's roughness came naturally, easily. He had not expected the awkwardness, the pain at hurting his son. Yukio could not fault his father for his behavior; he would have done the same thing to the head of a troubled department, had done similar things many times before.

He walked to the window and touched the image of the Bay.

It was the same image his father had watched. He wished his father could have talked to him as he talked to the photo, but his father never had, and now he never would.

His father had found comfort in the preservation of Matsushima and in the company. Yukio had tried to find comfort in the company, in preserving what his father had built, but he had failed. In that moment he had no clear idea of what he needed, but he knew that whatever it was, it would not come from his father. He would have to keep what good he could remember of the man, and find the rest in himself.

He looked first at the memory directory and then at the module on his desk. He sent Ishiwa a message to meet with him first thing Monday morning, then headed home.

On the fortieth day after his father's death, Yukio and his mother knelt behind a priest at the temple on Oshima Island. Matsushima Bay lay clear and placid at the edge of their view. Clouds dotted the sky, and light breezes played through the pines, the air rich with the tang of salt and pine. His father's urn rested on the floor in front of the curtain that blocked the sacred view. The priest recited softly, his words barely intelligible.

Yukio turned his head slightly. The tall, slender grave marker, its polished teak reflecting the sun brightly, sat in the cemetery behind him and to his right. Running down its length was the Buddhist burial name his father had chosen: "He who is beyond the ten thousand things."

The priest finished and motioned for Yukio to take the urn. Yukio picked up the case that sat at his feet and stepped to the urn. He opened the case and withdrew the memory module that held the only copy of his father's download. He carefully snapped the gleaming black module in half, then dropped the pieces into the urn with his father's ashes. He lightly sounded the gong beside the curtain, bowed deeply, picked up the urn, and backed slowly away.

Once out of the temple, he walked to the grave marker and set the urn at its base. The priest would bury the urn later.

Yukio returned to his mother. His father had moved beyond the ten thousand things, beyond the details and tangles of life, the commitments and losses, the pains and joys. Yukio was not yet beyond the ten thousand things that bound him to his father, but he was now making his own path. The Board had agreed to his plan to transition his job to Kensu; in six months he would leave Fujiura. He had no plan beyond that, but he was more at peace than he had been in years.

His father's spirit was free to take the next step in its journey. So, too, was Yukio.

A Better Sense of Direction

Mike Wood

We ran out of tinned spaghetti-in-tomato-sauce less than seven years into the voyage. For my daughter, Stella, it was a crisis. Stella had always hated space rations, but she was okay with tinned spaghetti. It was the only thing she ever seemed to eat. Stella was six years old, and anyone who has ever spent time with a six-year-old will know how fussy they can be with food. Stella's relationship with tinned spaghetti was more a fixation. She didn't just eat the stuff; she didn't just *play* with it; she *communed* with it.

The spaghetti crisis wasn't the first trauma to follow Stella's unplanned arrival on the crew list, but for Jodie and me, it was probably the most unsettling. Accommodation on a starship is cramped, and privacy is a scarce commodity, so a tantrum under these conditions, let me tell you, is a tantrum on steroids.

Stella was the first true child-of-the-stars. She was conceived on the starship and she was born on the starship. Children had always been part of the mission plan, hence the low average age of the crew (Babes in Space, they called us). But it had never been part of the plan to have the first birth take place only nine months out of Earth orbit.

To be fair, a young crew is an impetuous crew, and Jodie and I, being scientists (of a sort), were drawn to experimentation. Our ship, Castor, had been suspended at L2 for the three days that were set aside for crew embarkation and provisioning. Jodie and I were amongst the first to board. We had just three days of weightlessness before the photon engines were due to fire-up, hitting us with the point-two gee of thrust that would be our constant companion for the next twenty-odd years; ten years accelerating then ten more years to wind it back down.

"Jodie," I said, "have you ever wondered what it might be like in zero gravity?"

"I don't need to wonder. *This* is zero gravity. It sucks. I've been puking for four hours."

"No, Jodie, you misunderstand. I'm talking about what *it* might be like. You know . . ." I winked. I worked my eyebrows up and down my face in a choreography of suggestiveness.

"Ah."

She got my drift.

"Did you misunderstand what *I* just said, Luke . . . about the puking?"

"Space-sickness is in the mind. All you need is something that will take your mind off it."

"And you reckon . . ."

"Undoubtedly."

"Well, okay then."

So we had three days—three days in which to explore the boundaries of science. Well, let me assure you, zero-gee-nooky is not up to much. It's tricky, it's horribly messy, and it is *not* a cure for space-sickness. Also, it is rife with unexpected dangers. I managed torn ligaments as well as a four-day concussion, while Jodie brought the whole, sorry experience to a close by dislocating her thumb. Then the engines powered-up. With the return of gravity the space-sickness sufferers perked up . . . but not Jodie. *Her* space-sickness metamorphosed, seamlessly, into morning sickness.

Captain Bligh (her real name's Catherine Blair) was furious when we told her the results of our adventure. She even threatened to turn the ship around and send us home, but the accountants, God bless them, saved us on that call. What the captain *did* insist on, though, was that we share a cabin and assume joint responsibility for the baby's upbringing. This was fine by me; I'd had a thing for Jodie ever since college. Jodie wasn't quite so pleased, though, and she sulked about the arrangement for many months afterwards. I put this down to hormonal changes. I knew she would come round eventually, and I was right. She gave up throwing stuff at me a couple of years ago, and we moved to a mutually stress-free and congenial silence. Our relationship did not blossom into what you'd call love, but at least she stopped trying to trick me into the air-lock.

I first noticed Jodie at college. It was her walk. She had the action. Jodie's walk could stop traffic, usually in a way that involved broken glass, rolling hubcaps and seeping pools of oil and antifreeze. She didn't seem to realize the effect that she was having on her immediate environment. She would glide through town with those hips all swaying and pulsing to a Caribbean beat, and the traffic accidents would simply pile up around her. And then I noticed the T shirts, with slogans printed across her boobs: "Beam me up Scotty," ". . . to boldly go," "Make it so." *She was a Trekky.*

I tracked down the local branch and joined. I went to all the meetings, the screenings . . . I bought the Spock ears. I learned enough Klingon to get by, and I moved in on her inner circle.

But we never spoke. I was one of her entourage; the drooling, pathetic onlookers; the pimply male adolescent no-hopers. I seemed destined to be, forever, a voyeur by day and a fantasist by night.

Then I overheard a conversation. She and a small group of her inner circle friends had signed up for Castor and Pollux. Jodie was hard-core Trekky, and she was heading for the stars. The very next day I signed up myself. I went through the interviews and the pre-selection training and the medicals . . . I hung in there. The numbers were pared down. Each evening the TV audiences voted, and more of us fell by the wayside until, at last, the United States of Europe had their four viewer-selected reps: Me, Jodie, Jorge and Chantel. Jodie and Jorge drew Castor, and I drew Pollux, with Chantel. I was supposed to be ecstatic, but I was devastated. The two ships were to fly, side-by-side, for twenty-odd years, and there could be no physical contact between the crews. I never really wanted to even make the trip, I mean, twenty years! I'd faked the psychs; I had motivation but it wasn't space that drove me on.

I wrote the email. I was bailing, and my finger was actually hovering over the send button when the news broke; Jorge had concealed a genetic disorder that came about from his tight-fisted father using a back-street baby-designer during his conception, and he was bumped. The reserve, Henri, was French, like Chantel, so they shunted Jodie over to Castor with me. Two Brits, two French. There were also four Asians—the rest, thirty-two on each ship, were American.

Jodie and I became a team, sort of. And, well, you know the rest.

So, the spaghetti crop failed, and Stella went *on* one for a couple of weeks. Things were so desperate I even tried replicating spaghetti by extruding homemade pasta through a spare photon diffuser, then mixing in some tomato paste and boiling the lot to hell and back. Everyone, the whole crew, loved it . . . except Stella. It wasn't the same as tinned. It got me posted in the galley, though. I was happier there. My specialty was drive systems, but I'd faked the exams. It made me a bit jumpy when I was poking around in there with my greasy rag when there're so many lives hanging on my imaginary expertise. The engines were sparky-clean, but I knew jack about fixing them if they ever stopped firing. Brad, the cook, on the other hand was a choux-chef, and very frustrated in a culinary world of concentrates, *and* he knew more about photon drive systems than I did. So we swapped, and we were both happier for it.

Stella sleeps through these days, and so, therefore, do Jodie and I. So, when I was dragged from sleep by the alarm after only four hours of zzs, I felt particularly cheated. I'd only recently reacquainted myself with the luxury of eight straight hours. But it wasn't Stella, this time; it was Captain Bligh, calling the full crew to the galley, the only room where we could all assemble. Last time we were here was when the weird stuff started happening with the marker stars, a few years ago.

"Thanks for coming down," she said, as if we had any choice. "We have a problem."

"It's the thrust isn't it?" Jodie said. There were a number of nodding heads. Quite a few had noticed.

"Pollux has been pulling away from us for a couple of days. Nothing serious to begin with, but in the last few hours it's become more noticeable."

"I've got greens right across the board," said Brad. "Can't be the engines."

"Unless we're venting, for'ard, it can't be much else," said Bligh. "Brad, I want you and Luke to get your heads together and run a full set of diagnostics on the drive. I'll come and help. Anyone else got any ideas?"

There were blank looks.

"Okay, so we need an end-to-end integrity-check . . . everyone. The instruments aren't showing any anomalies, but *they* could be faulty. It's hands-on, I'm afraid. I want every inch of the hull examined."

The gathering broke up amid a sotto-voce chorus of grumbles and curses. An end-to-end was a miserable task, involving hours of crawling and wriggling into the most claustrophobic, cold and inhospitable corners of the ship. I was relieved to have drawn the cerebral option.

It took Captain Bligh five hours to find the cause. She called us all back to the galley. I saw what she had found, and suddenly I developed an overwhelming urge to go end-to-ending; to find one of those cold, cramped corners and hide there.

"Here, in my hand, I have a photon diffuser," she announced. "There are carbon deposits. The resulting hot-spots have damaged the machining." And now she raised her voice to an accusatory level. "I was puzzled about the carbon. How could carbon deposits form in this way? The components were installed in ionised white-room conditions."

She scratched some of the black carbon off and rubbed it between her fingers.

"Ladies and gentlemen," she said, "this is pasta."

And she looked straight at me.

Everybody looked straight at me. They looked at their chapped and blistered fingers, the result of five hours of arctic end-to-ending, then they looked, again, at me.

There are times when one longs for a duvet under which to crawl.

The captain wasn't finished.

"What is more," she said, "this is the spare. The one in the engine—the one currently holding us back to just point eight gee, is in better shape."

She looked straight at me again, then looked at each of the thirty-five worried faces.

"Questions?"

"What's the bottom line?" This was Anjana, the pilot.

"The bottom line is, at our current loss of acceleration, status quo maintained, we've added about four years to our journey time. On the other hand, my gut feeling is that the diffuser will continue to degrade, then . . . who knows?"

"Don't we have more than one spare?"

"There's triple redundancy on all the stressed parts. The diffuser isn't stressed. We have one spare to cover the minimal risk of build flaws. The planners are at fault, they didn't anticipate the additional stresses imposed by cookery."

"How about Pollux? Can we use their spare?" said Jodie.

The captain shook her head. "The unstressed parts, the minimal redundancy items, are shared inventory. We carry some of the spares, Pollox carries others. This is the one spare diffuser for Castor *and* Pollux. I called Captain Schiffer, just to be sure, and he confirmed—this is the only one."

"Can't we repair it?" I asked. My voice was tiny and unwelcome.

The captain looked at me for a long, silent moment, then said, "No."

"Daddy, why don't people like you any more?" It had only taken Stella a couple of days to pick up the bad vibes.

"What makes you think nobody likes me?" I didn't have a comfortable answer, so I was stalling for time.

"They call you names."

"They're just a bit upset, that's all."

"Why?"

"It's going to take us all a bit longer to get to New World, that's all."

"Why?"

"Your daddy made a mistake with the engines, honey. It's nothing more. They're all over-reacting." Jodie had leapt to my defense. This was unprecedented. I began to think that she was, well, starting to warm towards me a little. Then I realized that she was deflecting our daughter away from an associated matter. I had made the pasta to try and appease Stella's long and apocalyptic temper tantrums. Stella had wanted spaghetti.

"If everyone's so upset about us taking longer, Daddy, then why don't we just go straight there?"

"No, honey, we're going slower, that's all. It will take us a few more years because we're not gaining speed quite so quickly," said Jodie.

"So why don't we just go the short way?"

I took over trying to explain. "If I want to go from the front of the ship to the back of the ship it will take longer if I walk slower, see?"

Stella exploded in a frustrated storm of tears.

"I *know* that. You *said*. But if you want to get there quicker . . . Why . . . ! Not . . . ! Go . . . ! The *short* way!" She screamed the words. She threw her beaker of juice across the room. It bounced off the holo' and sticky, fluorescent orange liquid exploded onto the front screen and dripped down onto the carpet. Jodie and I looked at each other. We'd seen this sort of thing coming before. We knew the signs.

"I'm not sure what you mean, honey. Explain to me." I tried to sound patient.

Stella's bottom lip was quivering with frustration or rage or something, but she gathered some control, then, with a straight arm, she pointed out to her left.

"New World is there," she said. Then she pointed straight up above her head, towards the front of the ship.

"We're going *that* way. We're just going down the *spaghetti!*" she shouted the last word.

I looked over at Jodie and shrugged. I was worried that my daughter was having some kind of a mental crisis. Maybe living in space all her life . . .

Jodie came over and put her hand lightly on my arm.

"Wait," she said. She didn't want me saying any more. Her eyes held a strange, almost wondrous expression. "Explain again, darling, for Mummy."

"We keep going all over the place. Like we're going down the spaghetti. It's stupid. Why can't we just go straight there?"

"What do you mean, honey, down the spaghetti."

Stella explained. It sounded ridiculous. I smiled to humor her. Jodie smiled, too. But her smile was different. It was almost as if she was taking this nonsense seriously.

We settled Stella down for bed, eventually, and Jodie wanted to talk. We pulled out the sofa-bed and relaxed onto it with a glass of wine each. This was great. I'd never felt so close to her, even when we were doing the "science" thing back at L2. I wanted this moment to last. I forced myself to listen; not to rubbish what she was saying to me.

"I think I know what she's trying to tell us, Luke. I think she might know something. I think there *is* a quicker way."

"Jodie, come on. You used to get lost around college when . . ." I bit my lip. I shouldn't have said it. I'd gone and put my foot in it again. She'd go off on a hissy fit now and storm out.

But she didn't.

Jodie nodded. "Yes. Back home. I admit. I never knew where I was. I could never find my way round town, even. But out *here*, for the last . . . three . . . four years, it's been different. I've felt that I've *known* where I am. But . . . it's felt wrong. *We've* felt wrong. I've had this idea that we've . . . *that we've been going the wrong way!*"

She was so intense. Her eyes were burning. She held my forearm in a talon-like grip. I was loving this, even though I had no idea what she was talking about; even though the two women in my life appeared to be going off their heads.

"I think we should speak to Catherine. I think *Stella* should explain this to Catherine."

"Tell Captain Bligh? She'll lock us up."

"I don't think so."

"Captain Blair, do you mind if I ask, how was your sense of direction back on Earth?"

It was a strange opening. I cringed. Jodie had unusual ideas about how to break into a topic gently. We were sitting around the captain's wardroom table, Jodie, myself and Stella.

The captain gave a half laugh. "It's an odd question, but I suppose it won't harm to say, I was pretty hopeless. I was terrible with a map. Why do you ask?"

Jodie smiled. "I have a theory. Stella has something to tell us. It's a little weird but I think *you'll* understand.

"Stella, tell the captain what you told me and Daddy."

Stella began to unfold her bizarre theory again. She was hesitant at first—a little scared of the captain—but she soon got into her stride. She started with the spaghetti. She explained how we were at one end of a piece of spaghetti and New World was at the other end. New World shone down the spaghetti and we could see it shining from the ship, so we followed the light. She said how every star was at the end of a different piece of spaghetti, and how it was silly to follow the light round all the curves and loops and knots, when it would be much quicker and shorter to travel in a straight line and go to New World directly.

Then Jodie took over the narrative.

"Is it possible that some of us can see the shape of space; but that on Earth, where gravity gives everything a top and a bottom, we get confused? Even out here we are confused because, after spending our lives living on Earth we're conditioned to straight lines and up and down."

"Go on." The captain wasn't laughing, or shouting, or sneering. In fact she had that same eureka spark in her eye that I had seen in Jodie the previous evening.

"I know this is a dodgy bit of gender stereotyping, but isn't it widely viewed that women have a poor sense of direction, even though everyone's scared to say it out loud? But could it be that women have the better sense of direction, that they can see the curves of space-time, but on Earth we are confused because the Earth's surface makes us think two-and-a-bit-dimensionally?"

"Two-and-a-bit?" The captain and I spoke in unison.

"Yeah. We could move around on the surface of the planet. It's hard to go up; it's even harder to go down. If you want to take the quickest way to the shops you don't usually pick up a shovel."

The captain nodded, in a spooky, knowing way. I simply held up my hands in an Oh-my-God-they're-all-nutters kind of expression.

"Stella isn't conditioned," Jodie continued. "She's a child of the stars. She sees what is plain to see and she believes we are all stupid not to see the obvious."

"But there's gravity on the ship," I said. I had to say something to show that at least *I* wasn't a couple of bricks short of a wall.

But the captain waved an impatient hand at me. "That's thrust," she said. "Nothing to do with gravity."

She leaned over the table and pulled a rolled-up platter screen from a drawer. She tapped her fingers on the desk to activate her implants, then, with rapid finger movements, called up a star map on the screen. It showed Earth, and New World connected by a straight dotted line. A small pulsating red dot indicated the depressingly short distance along the line that Castor and Pollux had traveled in just under seven years. The captain began to explain the map to Stella, but before she had uttered more than a couple of sentences Stella was up on her knees, on the stool and pointing at the chart.

"You see!" She shouted. "It's wong! *You all keep getting it wong*! It's the wong shape. It's all straightened out."

Captain Blair reached up into a locker above her head. She brought down an ancient globe of the stars and set it on the table.

"Is this better?" she asked.

Stella stared at it for a long moment. Then she shook her head.

"No. Worse," she said. "There's no inning or outing. There's no . . . through . . . or around. It doesn't even *look* like outside."

Captain Blair clasped her hands together and pressed her index fingers to her lips. She spoke in a quiet voice.

"She's talking about multi-dimensions, isn't she. She's six-years old and she can visualize the universe in multiple dimensions. In one short sentence she has explained the weirdness."

Blair was right. We stared at the globe. It looked just like the sky seen from Earth, albeit inside out. But a few years ago, a year or so into the voyage, the weirdness had started. The stars had begun to shift out of position. The markers—the pulsars—had moved. We lost track of the galactic equator, completely. We'd all met in the galley and worked the problem. We decided that we were seeing some kind of relativistic effect—an optical illusion—but back then we weren't doing relativistic speeds . . . not really. We'd dismissed it. New World was still straight ahead. We could follow our noses. We'd be fine so long as we didn't have to make the return trip. A couple of the crew had decided to do a study of it, but they'd got nowhere. Now, here was a six-year-old girl telling us why. As we'd moved through space our visual perspective had changed. We had moved into a different part of the spaghetti bowl and everything looked wrong to us.

"Stella?" the captain leaned across the table and gently grasped both of Stella's hands. She peered into Stella's eyes, and in a quiet but firm voice she asked the question.

"Stella, would you be able to show us the way to New World? Could you show us which way to turn?"

The captain's tough, but when she announced that she'd been told, by a six-year-old girl, that New World would be much closer if we made an eighty-degree course correction; that it would be the first of many such adjustments; that she couldn't be precise about it, because ever since the weirdness had started we didn't even know the direction in which the galactic equator lay; so we would now be guided by the six-year-old, who was to show us the way by pointing... When she announced this, there was mayhem. She then added that she would ask all the women in the crew for validation of the directions; but only those women who, on Earth, had displayed a serious lack of spatial awareness. Only those who could not read a map would be consulted.

Mutiny was considered, by the men. But Captain Bligh is one scary person, and mutiny did not happen.

She also explained the plan to Captain Schiffer on Pollux. He is a man. His specialty is astral navigation. We only got to hear of his response through gossip and rumor. There was talk of a pirated audio file that started doing the rounds, but it was intercepted and destroyed, so we only have canteen-talk as to the range of colorful adjectives that were used. Pollux would not be joining our ship of fools.

Over the following weeks the crew formed into four distinct groups. Those who could read maps back on Earth—most of the men—became known as the mappies. They sulked. The idea that this strange new way of looking at the universe might have some credibility was an affront to them. They were offended by it. There were some women who were also a little mappy, but they tended to keep quiet about it; they felt a little left out. There were a handful of non-mappy males who probably knew what was going on but stayed out of it, finding the whole thing to be a challenge to their manhood.

Then there were the non-mappy females. The Stella camp. I tended to hang out with this group, for, although I was one hundred percent mappy, I believed them. Stella was my daughter. I believed her and I was proud of her.

For the Stella camp, a new era had dawned. They were excited and moved by the realization that *they* had been the true possessors of an innate, accurate sense of direction all along. The scientists among them wanted to explain things, and there developed a small sub-sect called the Stella Theory Cosmology Group. Catherine Blair, the captain, was a leading light amongst them. It took them a little over three weeks to come up with a credible theory that explained the new universe.

"Dark Matter is the key," Catherine explained at one of their lectures. "The shape of the universe that we see: star clusters, galaxies, expansion . . . these are how the universe *used* to be, or *should have* been. We see it this way because we see light as straight lines, whether it *is* straight or not. But then Dark matter got in between and wrinkled everything up. The real universe is being contracted; packed into an ever smaller can of spaghetti by the gravitational pull of dark matter, even though the individual strands, along which we can see, are getting longer, giving the illusion (to the mappies) that we are in an expanding universe."

I put my hand up. I'd been attending STCG lectures right from the start, even though this alienated me from most of the other men on the crew.

"I have a question. If there is all this heavy dark matter between the strands, what's to prevent us plunging into a black hole, or something, as soon as we turn off the star track?"

Blair nodded. "That's a fair point. I think the key is to always head for a star—any star. So long as we can see a star in front of us we are on *a* star track and we can free-wheel along between the dark matter. We just have to avoid heading towards the parts of the sky that are empty."

"So, we have to skip from strand to strand, where the spaghetti meets, and we stay out of the sauce." Stella grabbed my hand and gave it a squeeze. I smiled down at her. I was getting the hang of this non-mappy stuff.

When we made the turn the sky went wild. It was like Guy Fawkes night. There were blue-shifts and red-shifts, and stars stretched, smeared and splattered all over the sky. The mappies huddled in dark corners of the ship and moaned. Some of them turned to drink, others went to their databases and rediscovered religion.

The women had a party. Five of the non-mappy men came out of the closet and went along. They had a great time. I was with Jodie and Stella, so I had to behave.

It took seven years. We actually did our first fly-by of New World after only eighteen months, but we arrived at a fair clip, and had a lot of speed to lose. Stella's good, but she hadn't thought of the dynamics of losing relativistic velocities, so we had to wander around our new star system for a while, decelerating like crazy by sitting on our weakened engines. Once we'd lost enough of our velocity we did a few close passes by some of the system's gas giants, using first their gravity, then later, when we felt we wouldn't be ripped apart, we used their atmospheres for a bit of pants-on-fire aero-braking.

New World's a fine place to call home. A warm, orange sun; oceans, mountains, trees and plenty of indigenous wildlife that we cannot eat and that does not want to eat us—the genetic and protein differences are too great—so we are safe from one another.

We sent a message to Pollux. Captain Blair told them that we'd put the kettle on for them. They'll get the message in about eight years, but it won't help them, they will have started the deceleration phase of their voyage by now, so short-cuts won't work. They should be with us in about twenty years. They'll be much younger than us of course.

I'll tell you what I like about New World the most, though. I know my way around. I've drawn a few maps, and it's become a bit of a hobby. They're no use to the women, though. The women haven't a clue . . . forever getting themselves lost, especially Stella. But nobody says anything about this to them, not to their faces, anyway.

Tweak

Jack McDevitt

Civilizations, if they survive their nuclear age, seem always to follow the same path. "*It is inevitable*," said the ship.

Sikkur adjusted the picture with one mandible while supporting his snout with the other. Kayla nodded. "It's good to know," she said, "that everything has a happy ending."

On-screen, thousands of the creatures labored on the Morgan Monument.

Kayla brought up the BBC, where one of the anchors was going on endlessly about Mr. Morgan, the prime minister, how his thirty-two years in office had been a period of endless prosperity. A guest commented on his popularity. "*Never had a leader like this.*"

"What are you thinking?" Sikkur asked.

"I liked it better when it was called *Trafalgar* Square. It had a better ring."

"I agree," Sikkur said. "But Trafalgar is probably dead."

She glanced through the viewport at the clouds. They were moving out over the ocean again, headed west. "It is incredible," she added.

"You do not mean the monument?"

"No. Not the monument." She gazed at him with deep-set eyes, dark and intelligent, intended for use under a different sun. "I mean the consistency of it all."

He switched to another feed. This one from a satellite over Canada. Men and women worked contentedly on the Gulf of St. Lawrence Canal Project. And then to demonstrations on the streets of Toronto. People marched around a government building, bearing signs, MILLWORKERS FOR MYERS and MYERS IS THE MAN.

Kayla's chair squeaked as she changed position. "Whether we look at places like Bakyubah on the far side of the Galaxy, or the civilizations of the Parah Cloud, or Greater Wahkni near the Hole, wherever we go, it is always the same: If they survive the atom, soon after they begin tweaking their genes."

Below, in the western Atlantic, a few rain clouds drifted through the late afternoon.

Sikkur fished a snack out of the ready box. A red gufer. It squirmed as he popped it onto his tongue and sucked it down. "It must be an intriguing period for everyone," he said, "when they arrive at the stage where they can control evolution." He listened to Kayla's breathing. "Yes, I'd like to have been there when they first realized how to do some of these things. Increase intelligence by tweaking a gene. Grant musical genius. Provide a handsome brow." He took a deep breath. "A godlike business."

"Which gene was it, dear?" She combined a smile with a flick of her eyes. Whenever she did it, the bridge brightened.

"Which are you talking about, love?"

"The brow. The brow. I've always been impressed by a stately brow."

He snorted. She *did* like to kid around. "As if *I'd* know," he said. The sea sparkled in the sunlight.

Kayla was a glorious creature, the exquisite curve of her fangs, the way her eyes lit up when sudden movement caught her attention. Of course, she lived in a society where everyone was physically appealing. When everybody was beautiful, were they all just average? Was the cumulative effect no greater than it had ever been? It was a question for philosophers. However that might be, Kayla's charms ensured there were no long evenings on the *Stardust*.

The scientists had virtually stopped the ageing process. Had granted Sikkur and Kayla endless courage. And, of course, they had social skills *par excellence*.

"*It is where the manipulation should have stopped.*" Baranka had said that. Had said it again and again. A few others had taken up the cry. But they were old. Many hadn't had the benefit of the various enhancements, and never understood that the point of being alive was to be happy. "*Unlimited happiness will make us slaves.*" Foolish notion. Was Sikkur a slave? Was Kayla?

Fortunately, like the humans, the home race had had excellent leaders. Each one better than the last. It would be a joy to go back and report that, from one end of the Galaxy to the other, wherever one found an advanced species, good times reigned.

The *Stardust* was approaching the United States. Sikkur picked up images of workers in the capital city taking down an obelisk which was, according to Global News, going to be replaced by a temple dedicated to the current president, Mark Ramsay Howard.

The satellite zeroed in on the project. It was apparently dinner time, a warm, pleasant day. A crowd of women was moving into the work area, carrying thermos containers and bags of food. Somewhere a band played, and people sang the praises of the president.

"No question about it," said Kayla. "They've found their happiness gene."

He tapped his scaled breast. "Gives me a warm feeling right here."

"*It is indeed exhilarating,*" said the ship.

She treated herself to one of the gufers and stared contentedly at the screen. "I envy them. Why don't we go down and help? Tote that barge? Maybe make some points with their boss? It would do us good to haul a little masonry around."

"Kayla," he said, "you know we're not supposed to do that. As much as I'd like to."

She did that thing again where she lit up the bridge. "I can't see any harm in it."

Squish

S.E. Ward

I was at the commercial end of the spaceport, clearing Orion Roaches, when they opened the cargo bay doors on the *Paul Bunyan* and the Ant tumbled out. It sat there a moment—stunned, probably; I couldn't quite remember where I'd seen a blue Ant species before—and ran back into the ship before anyone could step on it.

Crap, I thought. There went my long weekend with Günther.

See, once upon a time, I was an entomologist. Sarah Smith-Schmidt, Ph.D., lover of insects across the span of the explored galaxy. Fangs? Beautiful. eyes? The more the merrier. Multi-segmented bodies for which I had to create brand-new nomenclature? Be still my heart.

And then, on a Martian layover (with Günther, our second honeymoon), one of the little buggers bit me. Rodmov's Weevil. Green with tiger stripes. Cute as the dickens. Stowed away on a shipment of hydroponic cellulose. (Well, we *thought* it was hydroponic.) Toxin that corrodes steel.

I woke up two weeks later with a robotic leg, a case of arthritis that made solar flares worse than tax time, and an altered opinion of Rodmov's Weevil. I was grounded. Earth. The next time I saw a weevil, I squished it. With the robotic leg.

It felt *good*.

For a moment, I glared at the cargo ramp. If no one else had been watching, I might get through at least one sweaty, Ant-free night with my husband before anyone set the quarantine. But Mike, the bay supervisor, lifted his eyebrows in that "what are you standing there for?" look he always gives me when I've got things I'd rather be doing.

I held up my hands. "Mike, Günther's coming in from the Ceres Research Station tonight, okay? I haven't seen him in three months. Just quarantine the ship. I'll get to it on Monday."

"And what do I tell Fred Gold when he comes in on Monday to pick up his electronics shipment? 'Sorry, Fred, you've got Ants. Sarah? Oh, sorry, she couldn't stick around. She had to go and—'"

The screech of the ship's quarantine doors drowned his voice. I saw his lips moving. Didn't help.

The doors closed. "—So I guess you'll have to call her in bed on my *videophone!*"

I stared. Mike stared back. The little vein on his temple started to throb. I could get rid of the Ants, or I could find myself locked in a cargo bay until Monday.

I sighed. "Let me call Günther."

Mike let me use his videophone. It rang four times, and the screen blipped to life. I cringed at the tanks and tanks of insects lining the wall behind Günther's desk; if they were on the transport ship, their residents would be staying with us until he went back to Ceres.

"*Ja*, Günther Schmidt. What is it?" I couldn't see Günther, but I heard him banging around under the desk; one of his specimens had probably gotten loose. He clicked his tongue like he always did when he was concentrating. (I'd grown *very* familiar with the sound on our honeymoon, and it always left me in a good mood.)

"Hi, teddy bear," I said.

Günther shot up so fast his glasses fell off. I winced at the crack of his skull on his chair.

"*Gummibärchen!*" He clambered into his chair, a capture jar in hand. He wiggled his eyebrows. "You are after a little preview of the weekend, *ja?*"

"No, sweetie. Sorry. I've gotta work."

Günther swore—in German—and I just stopped myself from doing the same.

"Mike is a *scheisshund*," Günther said. He rubbed his head so his streaky grey hair went everywhere. "It can't wait? I packed the 'Shorts.'"

Every nerve ending in my body went *poink*. The Shorts. The ones from the German-Martian engineering colony. The ones Günther had replaced *three times* after I tore them. Off. And then some.

"'Schnitzel inside?'" My mouth went dry when Günther nodded and a sly smile crept across his face.

Mike was a dead man.

But I shook my head. I didn't want to have to face both Mike *and* Fred Gold. Fred was five feet even, ninety pounds sopping wet, and the first person in history to make an AI shut itself down from sheer mortification.

"Sorry, teddy bear. Not even for schnitzel."

Günther's smile fell. "What's more important than schnitzel?"

"We got Ants."

And I cringed inside when Günther jumped and smacked his head on the back of his chair again.

"*Welche spezies?*" he roared. "*Gott in himmel—*"

"Whoa, whoa, whoa, teddy bear, settle down!" I held out my hands to the videophone camera, but Günther kept bouncing in his chair like a five-year-old on candy. "English! English!"

Günther bounced again, but stiffened. He straightened his shoulders, pushed his glasses up his nose, and did the little tapping dance with his feet that meant he was only pretending to be a sane, rational adult. The steady *click-click-click* of his shoes made my eye twitch. I sighed.

"Which species?" he said. He turned as red as the Shorts.

"Blue ones."

Günther sat up. A creeping feeling ran up and down my spine, and I tried to remember *where* I'd seen the species before.

"How large?" said Günther. "Worker? Soldier?" He twitched in joy, and said, "*Queen?*"

I measured against my forearm. "Fifteen centimeters? Six inches? Worker. Ran straight back inside."

And in Günther's overjoyed scream, I remembered which species it was: *Caerulus kalii*. Discovered by Günther himself. Named during his Hindu mythology kick because they had six arms, were blue, and could clean a rabbit to the bone in fifteen seconds flat. I covered my face with both hands and wished I had never called him in the first place.

"Is there a colony?" he said. "Do you have a queen? How many did you see?"

"I don't know, Günther. I only saw the one. I've got to go in there tonight and see if there are any more."

Günther clasped his hands together. "*Liebling*, I will be your eternal servant if you could bring me live samples. I've never found a queen."

Oh, brother. "Günther, there's not that much schnitzel in the *world*."

"There could be! For you!"

I stamped my robotic foot against the floor. "Günther, hear that?" I rapped my leg with my knuckles. "Hear the ringing? I'm not an entomologist anymore. I'm an exterminator. I don't study them. I squish them."

He gave me his puppy eyes. "Please?" He bent down and rustled in something for a moment, then came up holding the Shorts. "There's schnitzel inside."

"Günther . . ."

If he weren't stuck on Ceres eleven months a year, it wouldn't be so bad. But until he decided he liked bees with non-necrotizing stingers and butterflies that ate nectar rather than blood, long weekends it was. I put up my hands.

"Fine, I'll see what I can do. First mandible that gets near me, though, and I'm turning the place into an abattoir."

Günther kissed the videophone camera. When he drew back, his lip print clung to the lens, and he grinned like he'd just been pithed.

"*Ich liebe dich*," he said. I forced a smile to hide the fact that I'd gone all gooey inside. (It's the German. And the schnitzel. And, well, Günther.)

"I'll see you when I finish the job, teddy bear," I said. "At least long enough to ruin another pair of Shorts."

Günther wiggled his eyebrows. As soon as we hung up, I rolled back my sleeves.

I was gonna find me some Ants.

✧   ✧   ✧

The problem with Ants is twofold.

Y'see, while Earth ants are prone to milking aphids and starting wars, and are commonly possessed of a venom that makes you itch like the end of the world, they're pretty easy to deal with. I step, they squish.

Ants, on the other hand, always with a capital *A*, are intelligent little buggers. They tend to develop things like language or technology. It might not be high technology, but they'll at least build a machine to milk the aphids. This means that they're subject to quarantine. Ever since that mess between the Cetacean Republic, the animal rights loons, and Norway, the last thing we need on this planet is another intelligent species.

Since they *are* intelligent, though, that means that the quicker they die, the less likely anyone is to pass a law to keep the damn things alive.

So I put on my body armor. It's a carbon-bonded suit, kinda like a wetsuit. Günther thinks it's sexy as hell. I think it needs another two inches in the bustline.

Armored up, and armed with a respirator, a canister of hydrogen cyanide, and an up-to-date will, I hit the cargo bay. Mike saluted. I gave him the finger and entered my passcode for the quarantine door.

Inside, I turned on my headlight. All around sat crate upon crate of electronics, courtesy of LunaCorp. (As a kid, I always liked to watch the giant glowing logo wax and wane across the moon's face.) No Ants. However, a few of the crates had been opened. I crept closer, gripping the nozzle of my cyanide sprayer.

All I found was an empty cardboard box. "NEW!" it read. "TRANSLATRON 3000! BABIES! FOREIGN DELEGATES! FUN WITH YOUR DOG!"

"Hell, Fred, what are you up to now?" LunaCorp had come out with at least three universal translators in the previous fifteen years, all banned on Earth. One of them was almost entirely responsible for the mess with the whales, the loons, and Norway. Fred probably got the new model on discount for that very reason.

For the same reason, I didn't much like the idea of the Ants getting hold of them. Fred was bad enough, and all he cared about was the value of his alleged shareholders. But Ants? Intelligent Ants?

I charged the sprayer hose with fresh cyanide and put my finger on the trigger. My robotic leg tensed for the first squish.

The steel shipping crates felt cold through my armor as I crept through the dark. Every time I put my foot down, I braced for a crunch that never came. A crackle came from above. Mechanical. An amplifier. I tensed.

And yelped when something dropped from the ceiling onto my head.

I fired a burst of cyanide powder at the ceiling. The Ant—a worker—skittered down the side of my head and sat on my boobs. It clicked its tiny jaws. I aimed the cyanide nozzle at it.

"*Kore, tsuiteru?*" a mechanical voice said.

Now, I've eaten in enough sushi bars to know what Japanese sounds like, but don't ask me to understand more than "Two beers and another dragon roll, please." The Ant on my chest cocked its head, then looked back over its shoulder and clicked. Another whine. A bunch of languages I didn't understand. I raised an eyebrow and lowered the nozzle a couple of inches.

And then, "*Prüfung, eine, zwei, drei.*"

Testing. One, two, three.

I was gonna *kill* Fred.

I gripped my forehead just above my goggles. Under my breath, I said, "Great. You can get your own damn samples, Günther Schmidt."

A rapid crackle. The Ant on my boobs tensed. The mechanical voice said, "It knows the four-armed queen!"

"The *what*?" I picked up the Ant by the thorax. It wriggled. The amplifier screamed.

"Put me down! The four-armed queen who speaks the sacred tongue! She'll smite you!"

I started to ask what the hell the sacred tongue was. A hundred tiny clicks rose on every side, and the amplifier whispered before it got swallowed in feedback.

Günther. Clicking. Damn it.

Just to be sure, I clicked my tongue, once. The sounds all around me stopped. Going hot in the face, I did my impression of Günther on our honeymoon.

The cargo bay echoed with triumph.

"The four-armed queen's delegate has spoken!" the amplifier said. "We are home!"

Home? I lifted my cyanide nozzle. No animal rights loons were going to show up on my watch, especially over a herd of bloodthirsty

Ants. I knocked the Ant off my boobs and pinned it on its back with the cyanide nozzle. A hush fell through the cargo bay. If I didn't know any better, I'd think the Ant was cowering.

"Have we angered the four-armed queen?" said the amplifier. Somehow, though, the voice was louder. Deeper. Like getting in trouble in front of your whole kindergarten. I hesitated. And looked up.

Two Ants were watching me. One was a foot long. The other was a foot long plus a bulbous, rippling, pale blue abdomen. A queen. Both wore clay crowns.

The queen had feathers on her head. Grey feathers. Streaky. And glasses made of twigs.

I sagged. The Ant beneath my cyanide nozzle wriggled free. Günther was never going to let me live this down.

I took a step back. A squeal of the amp made me lift my robotic foot just in time to see an Ant cowering from my boot. I nudged the Ant away, and a swarm of its fellow workers rushed to calm it down. They looked a bit thin, really. For Ants. I had the strangest thought that they were refugees.

"What's going on here?" I said, and the translator's amplifier spat forth a series of clicks and clacks.

"We come to find the four-armed queen!" said the queen Ant. A steady stream of workers took the eggs she laid even as she spoke. "Our nest is gone! She will gather us in her mandibles and carry us to—"

The translator whined. I'm pretty sure it meant "Paradise." Somehow, I didn't think these guys had Günther's tanks on Ceres in mind.

"Look." I crouched to look the Ant queen and king more or less in their dozen eyes. "You've really got Günther—"

"Hail the queen!" said the Ants.

I sighed. "You've got him all wrong. He's not a god. He's not even a *queen*."

The queen stiffened. "The four-armed queen is a king? Where is his queen?"

I hesitated. "Yeah, about that. You're talking to her."

I heard the silence that swept through the cargo bay. Next thing I knew, a hundred Ants swarmed up my body. I screamed. They pushed me on my butt. A huge soldier crawled up between my legs.

"Hey, hey, hey, buddy!" I shoved her away. "Keep off the queen!"

The soldier only clicked like a schoolmarm and crawled straight back up me. Ants. Everywhere. Swarming up and down and left and right. I felt the cyanide nozzle slip from my hand. No way to fight. No way to get them off me. So I did the only thing I could.

I lifted my robotic foot and brought it down on the first thing that moved.

In the stunned silence after the crunch, I realized exactly how stupid an idea that was.

A dozen clicks echoed from all sides. I looked down my body to see every soldier in the colony standing with mandibles ready to take a bite. My suit was tough, but an entire colony of half-starved, carnivorous Ants? Yeah. I held my breath—it was that or hyperventilate—and felt the workers ease my leg aside.

A single worker lay in a blue-and-green smear. It lifted its head, clicked once, and slumped to the cargo bay floor. A few workers eased it free and carried it to the queen, who took it in two of her arms and rocked it. I had never seen either an ant or an Ant do anything like it. And, believe me, I've seen my share of Ants.

The queen clicked. The amp said, "That's that, then. Not even the four-armed king wants us."

You know, I used to think insects were cute. Stupid, but cute. Maybe it was the queen's Günther suit, and maybe it was the rocking. Maybe it was the dozen sets of half-inch-long mandibles poised to tear my flesh and my total lack of defense. But, damn it, for a second there, I almost felt sorry for the crunchy little things.

Okay, so I did feel sorry for them. It happens.

I lifted my head. The soldiers tensed, but I sat up in a series of slow movements and held up my hands.

"Sorry. It was an accident."

A few clicks. The amp said, "Yeah, right."

"Will this ship be leaving the planet again?" said the queen. She held herself tall, but she wouldn't look at me. She almost seemed to be putting on a brave face for the others.

"Yeah. A few days." I folded my arms and rested them on my knees. My robotic leg twitched—it does that when I get upset—and

I pressed the reset button at my hip to steady myself. I looked at the Ants. The workers slunk into the shadows of Fred's crates. At an order from the king, the soldiers backed away, too.

Damn it.

Some weekend it had turned out to be. And, to make things worse, Günther would be back to Ceres on Monday. No matter how much we loved each other, he needed more than just me to keep him on Earth.

I stopped.

No, it was a stupid idea.

But . . .

Mike just about screamed me deaf when he found out I'd sent Günther into the *Paul Bunyan*. (Günther had just about screamed me deaf, too, but in German and between kissing me until my lips were numb.) Mike's problem had to do with words like "insurance," "liability," "termination." Big words. Legal words. I'm an entomologist, not a lawyer; I pretended not to understand him.

Fred, too, had issues. He screamed words like "shareholders," "profit margin," "livelihood," and "lawsuit." He didn't listen to me—Fred's good at that—but he listened to Günther, whose counter-argument mentioned "species," as well as "endangered," "legal status," and the killer, "contraband technology."

Yeah. Fred got *real* quiet after that.

Finally, Fred stormed out—he muttered something about his lawyer—and Mike followed. (Mike said something about my continuing paycheck. Again, I pretended not to understand him.) Günther took another look inside the cargo bay. He came out grinning.

"So, *ja*," he said. "A good research project? I like the queen's self-decoration."

I rolled my eyes. "You would. Look, is the Ceres Station going to let you bring an entirely unknown species into the labs? You know how mad they got when you lost the Heliotrope Jumping Spider."

Günther shrugged. "I found it."

"Yeah, by following the holes it had dissolved through the walls to the life-support unit. Günther, look." I ran a hand through my hair. "There's only one planet in the entire solar system that's got enough animal rights loons to let you keep these guys."

Günther bared his teeth. "*Gummibärchen*—Sarah—You saw what happened to Norway—"

"Well, we're not in Norway. We're in America. Hell, what about Germany? You're always saying you can't get a decent home-cooked meal off-world."

"Mars isn't too bad." But Günther shuffled his feet and looked between me and the *Paul Bunyan*.

"But it's not the same," I said.

"But the permits. *Gummibärchen*, they'll have to stay in quarantine for months. We'll have to stay with them—"

"Please?" I said. My robotic leg creaked as I came close enough to put my arms around his neck (and my boobs against his chest). "I'll help you, teddy bear. I might even give up exterminating if you're there to stop me."

Günther opened his mouth. Closed it. Looked down at my boobs and gulped.

"What about Mike?" he said.

"Mike who?" I said, and I kissed him.

After a few moments, Günther drew his head back and sighed. "I suppose I can videocommute."

I chuckled. Stupid Ants. They *were* kind of cute.

But enough about Ants. And Ceres. And Mike. And Fred.

It was time to get me some schnitzel.

Touching the Dead

J. Kathleen Cheney

The colonel, Shironne decided, must be one of those clever people, the kind who liked to fix things. She could sense him waiting for them there in his office, his curiosity held at bay, but only just.

Her mother took her hand and laid it on the tall back of a chair. Shironne ran her gloved fingers along the wood, straightened her skirts and sat down. She pulled her braid over her shoulder, well aware that she presented a ragged picture—the blind girl in a child's dress. More than two years old now, it was too short in the skirt and sleeve. Even so, she'd grown accustomed to the feel of it against her over-sensitive skin, and that made the old blue woolen tolerable.

"Madam Anjir, Miss Anjir," the colonel said in a deep, sincere voice. "I'm honored to have you here."

Shironne smiled in response, returning his goodwill without thinking. He stood and approached them, his boots crossing a hard floor, only a few steps. She guessed he must be quite tall.

"I'm sorry to trouble you, Colonel . . ." her mother began, sounding official, as a politician's wife should.

"Cerradine," he supplied.

". . . Colonel Cerradine. This is the Investigations Office, isn't it?

We've come to inquire about the death of an army gentleman, a Sergeant Merha. The hospital sent us here to talk to you."

"And why would you be making inquiries into this man's death, Madam?"

He didn't walk away, but Shironne thought she heard the movement of his clothes, as if he'd sat down, perhaps on the edge of his desk. She could smell him from there: wool and leather and the oily black smell of a gun. She caught a faint whiff of cologne or soap, something exotic and manly. She didn't recognize it, but liked it much better than the cloying musk her father favored.

"It's me, not her," Shironne told him.

The colonel's attention turned on her then. His interest didn't fall all over her like an exuberant puppy but sat back and observed her like a cat, distant and willing to wait for its prize. "And why would you do that, Miss Anjir?"

"Because I promised my maid Benia I would find out what happened to him," she admitted, knowing it sounded like a childish whim. "I . . . um, she was upset and she kept asking why someone would kill him, and I promised without thinking, sir."

"It's never a good idea to make rash promises, Miss Anjir," he said with laughter in his tone.

Harder than he knew. With Benia's distress falling all about her like an enveloping wave of water, she'd been carried away. The woman's emotions had overridden her own, stealing her judgment. "I do realize that, sir."

"Hmmm," he said. "Unfortunately, I can't give you that answer yet, ladies. We've only begun to investigate his death. I will, however, send word around to your residence as soon as I do have information." His feet moved away toward the other side of the room.

He felt regretful, Shironne decided, because he couldn't help them. "You misunderstand me, sir. I thought I could help you. Figure out who killed him, I mean."

He didn't dismiss her idea immediately. Instead, the emotions in his mind locked away as calculation took over. A moment passed in silence. "Madam Anjir," he asked then, "do you intend to permit this if I agree?"

Her mother radiated surprise, but quickly tamped it down. She'd expected the colonel to refuse. "I gave my promise, sir," she said, "but I must ask that this be handled with the utmost discretion. My husband wouldn't wish it known we came here."

"No, I expect not," he said.

Shironne sensed animosity in the colonel's thoughts and wondered if he already knew her father.

"My people will be perfectly discreet, Madam," he said. "Now how did you think to help me, Miss Anjir?"

"I wondered if I might touch the body, sir."

The colonel walked with her across the level lawn of the Army Square. Her mother had described the square to her when they alighted from their carriage, but Shironne hadn't been able to fix anything in her mind save the location of the army's administration building on one side of the green and the hospital on the other.

She'd heard men calling out in the distance, a drill or a parade. Their voices drew forth a childhood memory of seeing military men in their sharp blue and brown uniforms, parading along the streets of Noikinos with their long rifles on their shoulders. It was an old memory, and she couldn't remember if their trousers were blue with a brown stripe down the side, or the other way around. Perhaps they didn't have a stripe at all. The men were gone now, their drill finished, and only the normal sounds of horses and carriages came from the square.

The colonel led her through the entry doors of the hospital. Shironne knew the scents well, having spent more time in the company of doctors in the last few years than she cared to. They traversed a flight of stairs leading down to the army's morgue.

She tried not to smell the un-circulated air, pressing a gloved finger under her nostrils. The cool room stank of ripeness and chemicals, of bowels emptied and strong soaps, one scent layering over another. *Someone should throw open a few windows and let the wind sweep through*, she thought, and then wondered if the place had any windows to open. Shironne tightened her other hand on the colonel's sleeve, queasiness welling in her stomach.

Male voices protested her presence, and the colonel went to speak with the men, leaving her standing alone. An older-sounding man argued the appropriateness of a young girl seeing such things, which made Shironne want to laugh. The colonel prevailed in the end, and Shironne felt the men's protests, both mental and vocal, fading into the distance, past closing doors.

"There are people who specialize in investigating these things, Miss Anjir," the colonel said from several feet away. "If you want to back out now, I can send for one of them."

"No, sir. I promised." She sensed his concern. He felt curious, but worried for her sake as well. "I . . . um, don't know where the body is."

"Directly ahead of you, a foot or so."

She heard cloth sliding over an unmoving surface. A sudden surge of unpleasant scents accompanied the sound. It was the smell of old blood, like meat gone stale in the summer heat, coppery and—to her confused mind—green.

The colonel stepped away, carefully folding up his worry and training his mind back to observation.

Shironne removed one of her gloves and tucked it into her waistband. With the other hand, she reached out and located the edge of the table. Wood, she thought. Her cotton gloves never completely blocked her impressions. She touched a bare finger to the table, sensing things that had crossed it in the last few days, the fluids a body made. There were tiny bits of skin from many people ground into the table's surface, and harsh chemicals. She recognized carbolic acid, long since faded past usefulness. Other things she didn't recognize, or recognized but didn't have names for.

She gritted her teeth and stretched out a hand. It contacted something cool—skin chilled to the temperature of the room. The body remained calm, unmoving despite the seething life that went on inside the dead shell. Shironne grimaced.

The colonel's hands touched her sleeves then, drawing her away.

"No," she insisted, and his hands relented. His worry wrapped around her like a fog and just as quickly fled, hidden back in some corner of his mind.

Shironne laid her palm where her finger had touched—an arm, the muscles exhausted as if the man had recently fought. She ran her fingertips along it, feeling for the hand at its end.

"His hands have been cleaned," she said, sensing soap on the man's skin.

"The mortuary service would have washed the body."

She felt the fingers, finding faint traces of ink, of food, of other things, under the film of the soap. "If he had a gun, sir, I don't think he fired it."

"Why not?" The colonel's mind didn't reflect doubt, only curiosity.

"There's no . . . um, evidence of the gun being fired. There's something left when someone does that, but I don't know what to call it, though." She'd only ever touched a gun once before, and had no names for those things beyond *gun* and *bullet*.

The colonel's fascination grew. "We haven't found his pistol, I believe."

Shironne ran her fingers back up the arm and touched the dead man's chest. She found the edge of a wound and forced her senses deeper. A knife, tearing through the skin and into the heart, ruining its rhythm—a knife killed him. She could almost picture the blade in her mind. "Do you have the knife?"

"No, the killer took it. We hope he still has it."

"It should be long and narrow. If you find it, I can tell you if it's the one, I think."

"By touching it?"

"Yes, sir. It would have his blood on it, and I would recognize his blood now, sir." She had no words to explain that either.

"If I'd stabbed someone, I'd clean the knife," he pointed out.

"But it's hard to get everything off, sir. There might be little bits of blood left, maybe so small you can't see them, but *I* would be able to feel them."

Shironne touched her hand to the sergeant's cold, unshaven jaw, sensing the first stages of bruising there. She'd felt it on her mother's skin before, when a bruise hadn't yet had a chance to swell, the blood vessels all broken and angry under the skin. She suspected the colonel had seen the mark on the man's face.

She took a deep breath and forced herself to feel past the flesh. Memories lingered in the dead man's mind, not fluttering about crying for attention as a living person's would but lying about like leaves scattered in the fall. They were rotting, gone skeletal. She remembered holding a moldered leaf as a little girl and gazing at its delicate framework, back in the days before her eyes had gone sightless.

She dug into the sergeant's tattered memories. His mind held on to brief images: childhood recollections, scattered smells. There

were faint snatches of her maid, Benia, in that chaos, different
from what Shironne knew of the woman: the smell of her skin,
the turn of her ankle, the curve of her back as her hair fell black
against it.

Startled by the strange perspective, Shironne shook her head,
trying to clear it. She lifted her hand from the body's chilly brow,
keeping it well away from her clothes. "I don't think I'll find out
anything else, sir. Is there someplace I can wash?"

The colonel turned her about, hands on her shoulders. "Straight
ahead about ten feet there's a sink. Can you find that?"

She put her gloved hand out in front of her and stepped off
the distance. She found the edge of the sink and ran her fingers
around it. Then she stripped off her second glove, located a lump
of lye soap and turned on the tap. The soap's slick feel made her
want to grind her teeth, but she bore it. Once convinced her hands
were sufficiently clean, she worked her gloves back on.

The colonel thought curiosity at her. "How long have you been
blind?"

Shironne turned toward the sound of his voice. "About a year
and a half, sir. Since I was thirteen."

"I've never known anyone blind before," the colonel said. "You
seem quite self-sufficient."

"My mother is very insistent." Her father would want her out
of the house the moment she came of age at seventeen. Legally,
her mother had no means to forestall her expulsion.

"You also seem quite determined to carry on with this investigation, Miss Anjir, despite your mother's . . . lack of enthusiasm."

Lack of enthusiasm didn't begin to describe her mother's senti-
ments. Mama had been brought up very properly, taught that a
girl should learn to manage her husband's household, bear his
children, and follow his commands in all things. Shironne, on
the other hand, knew she wouldn't catch a husband—not now—so
none of those imperatives mattered for her any more. "She's
very reserved, Colonel," Shironne said, "but Mama says that I'm,
um . . . the interfering sort."

She sensed his amusement. He let her feel it, as if he held it
out on a platter for her mind to see. "You're very good at controlling your emotions, sir."

"I was well trained," the colonel answered. "You must be very
sensitive."

"Yes, sir, far more so than my mother." At first, her skin had felt so raw that every breath, every touch, every morsel of food had all been agony in the overwhelming flood of sensation sweeping through her. Her father's very presence had been a torment, his ever-present anger rousing in her a screaming fury of her own. He still made her teeth hurt, even now.

"So your mother's a sensitive as well," the colonel said. "I should have expected that."

Shironne frowned. She'd revealed a secret her mother wouldn't want exposed. "She . . . no one . . ."

"I know who your mother is, Miss Anjir. I would never say or do anything to harm her."

He meant his words sincerely. Shironne sensed it.

"Why don't I take you back to the office now?" He put a hand under her elbow, guiding her toward the stairs.

"What do you mean, you know who my mother is?" She tried to judge his mind through the muted contact of his hand on her sleeve.

"Hmm. An alderman's wife," he stated correctly.

But his original words had nothing to do with her father, she could tell. "No, you meant something else."

His mind turned quickly, making inferences from her words, tying them back to what he'd seen in the morgue. His hand slipped away from her elbow, taking with it her tie to his thoughts, leaving her access to his emotions alone.

"Amazing," the colonel said, with no hint of offense. "You don't actually have to be touching my skin."

Shironne wondered what he used for reference. "Should I?"

"Do you not know what you are?" Wonder floated through his emotions, not hidden this time.

"A freak," she whispered. "Witch-blood." They told stories of people like her kept caged in a foreign palace—a menagerie, only not filled with beasts. She had read such stories with appalling relish as a little girl, never suspecting then she might someday belong in one of those cages herself.

The colonel laughed. "Ah, no. Come with me, Miss Anjir. Your mother and I need to have a discussion."

He returned his hand to her elbow, guiding her up the last steps and out of the hospital. The cool fall breeze felt clean after the fetid air of the morgue, even if it did brush her cheeks with a touch of factory smoke.

Her mother waited in the colonel's office, anxiety spinning about her in a tight skein. "Are you all right, sweetheart?" she asked as they came through the door.

Shironne wished she could put her arms around her and be held for a moment, but Mama was a politician's wife and had to keep up her cultured image. "I'm fine, Mama. It was . . . unpleasant, but I'm fine."

Her mother tucked away her fretfulness. "Did you find out what you needed?"

"No. I . . ." Shironne turned in the colonel's direction, a sudden inspiration electrifying her. "Can you take me to where he lived?"

"Sweetheart," her mother protested, "I'm certain the colonel has other . . ."

"I promised, Mama. I told Benia I would find out why."

"Madam Anjir," the colonel said in a grave voice, "I'm willing to take her there. I am curious."

Her mother flinched at his last word. Shironne felt it both through Mama's tight grasp on her hand and in her sudden air of anger. "My daughter is not a circus freak, Colonel Cerradine. She didn't come here to entertain you."

"No, Madam, she came to fulfill a promise, and I intend to help her do so." The colonel radiated honesty, so clearly that Shironne wondered if he practiced at home.

"Colonel, my husband doesn't want her seen . . ."

"Is he the one who first used the word 'freak,' Madam?" the colonel asked in an irritated voice. "The proper term is touch-sensitive."

Silence reigned for a moment.

Shironne felt fear tumbling through her mother's heart. The emotion reflected through her own body, sending goose bumps shivering along her arms. A trickle of perspiration ran down her back. Shironne fought the response, trying to keep it from taking over her own thoughts. "What do you mean, Colonel?"

"If I'm not mistaken, Miss Anjir, you are a rare form of sensitive, much more acute than most. The talent does run in certain families."

The colonel waited for her mother to admit something. When he got no response, he continued. "I was raised at the Fortress, Madam, as were many of my staff. We don't view such things as most people do. We're a little more open-minded."

The Fortress housed the king and his family, long whispered

to possess unusual "talents." They wouldn't consider her talent a disturbing taint then, or proof of impure blood as Father constantly insisted.

Her mother didn't respond to the colonel's statement.

"The prince is one of my closest friends," he tried again. "I would never harm a member of his family."

Shironne decided he'd approached the topic so obliquely because he feared Mama had never admitted it to her. He didn't wish to expose her secret.

"I . . . um," her mother faltered, ". . . my husband . . ."

"Doesn't want anyone to know," the colonel finished. "I understand. I can see he asks you to keep many secrets." A distinct flash of anger accompanied his words.

Clearly, the cosmetics Mama used to hide the new bruise hadn't fooled him. Shironne sensed her mother's fleeting humiliation.

She knew the expression Mama would be wearing now. She'd seen it often as a little girl. Savelle Anjir was tall, beautiful and elegant, always cloaked in the mantle of the serene politician's wife. Only after her odd sensitivity developed had Shironne begun to understand that her mother's cool tranquility was a façade.

"He is my husband, Colonel," Mama insisted with a quaver in her voice. "He may ask what he wills."

"Why not go to your brothers for protection?"

Officially, her mother had no brothers. "That is not your concern, Colonel," she said more firmly.

Shironne sensed his frustration, but her mother would never give in to his gentle and well-intentioned suggestions. It would cause a scandal. Shironne spoke into the stretching silence. "Colonel, do you think I might go to his apartments?"

"I will accompany you there shortly," the colonel answered, "if your mother permits."

"Her father . . ."

"Would not want her seen. I recall, Madam. Let me go talk to Lieutenant Kassannan. I'll see if she can't come up with something and accompany us there." He walked out of the room, leaving the two of them alone.

Being exposed as the old king's bastard had always been Mama's greatest fear. While the king and the prince might be her half-brothers, she had never met them even though she sometimes half-wished for it.

"He won't say anything, Mama. I can tell," Shironne assured her.

Her mother sighed. "We need to get home, sweetheart. We don't have the time to go visit this man's rooms."

The butler always snitched to Father if Mama left the house for too long. Father paid him well. "You could go back, Mama."

"And leave you here alone?" Her voice sounded incredulous.

"I'll be safe with the colonel. I can tell. If you go back, the butler probably won't even notice I didn't come in. He never notices me. I'll come back as soon as I'm done and I'll make certain he doesn't see me. Cook won't say anything." Her mother still didn't like the idea—Shironne could sense her worry. "I gave my word, Mama. I must."

Her mother understood duty all too well. She sighed again and finally agreed to the plan, unhappily so.

The colonel returned then, seeming pleased with himself. His step even sounded lighter. "Why don't you put this on, Miss Anjir?"

He handed her something. Shironne turned it about in her gloved hands, determining she held a woman's hat. She righted it and placed it on her head.

"There's a veil." He folded it down over her face.

Judging by her mother's smothered laughter, she must look ridiculous. The hat tilted, dipping down over her face. Its headband came into contact with her forehead, hinting at the woman who'd worn it before, an aged deposit of oils, dirt, and skin.

"It's a little large," the colonel observed.

Her mother tucked away her amusement, deciding to be firm again. "Colonel, I will let you take her, but I must return to my house. Could you possibly send her back there—with a suitable escort, of course?"

"Of course, Madam Anjir."

"Are you really in the Army?" Shironne asked the woman who led her down the steps of the administration building—Lieutenant Kassannan. Realizing she'd been rude, she put her hand over her mouth only to tangle her fingers in the veil of the over-large hat.

"Yes, miss," the lieutenant said, not sounding the least offended. "The Investigations Office does take on female workers."

Shironne wondered if she heard that question often. She'd known there were women who served in the Army, but had never thought to meet one. Clearly, the colonel considered women competent to do something other than run a household. "Do you enjoy it?" she asked.

"Yes, miss," the lieutenant said. "It's my calling, I think. I am good at what I do."

The colonel joined them, his boots ringing on the steps. Shironne heard a carriage driving up, the horses' hooves closer than she'd expected. Lieutenant Kassannan helped her up and then sat next to her, her mind as politely disciplined as the colonel's.

"I knew about my mother's birth," Shironne told the colonel after they started on their way, "but she doesn't like to talk about it."

"I suspect your mother's friends would be shocked if they learned of it," he said.

The carriage had a smooth ride, far better than the aging one her family owned. "My mother doesn't really have any friends," Shironne said. "Father doesn't like for her to meet people."

That made the colonel angry. The lieutenant's mind reflected suspicion as well.

"I mean, she meets people at political things," Shironne amended, "just not on her own." Father preferred to keep his beautiful and purportedly well-born wife close.

"Hmm," the colonel said.

The carriage began slowing. They'd traveled only a short distance, so she knew they'd stayed in the same district of the city. The colonel straightened her hat's veil. "Are you ready?"

"Do I look as ridiculous as my mother thought?"

"Yes," the colonel answered. The lieutenant laughed and agreed as they rolled to a stop.

The colonel handed her down from the carriage onto a cobbled street. Other traffic passed by, but not much. The factories smelled nearer than before. Trees rustled in the faint breeze. The veil confused her, brushing into her face, startling her skin with the feel of silk lace and dye.

She heard the lieutenant jump down from the carriage, her booted feet striking the cobbles. From the sounds she made, Shironne deduced that Lieutenant Kassannan must wear trousers just as the colonel did.

"Why don't we go in?" the colonel asked. He took Shironne's gloved hand and laid it on his sleeve, leading her up a few steps and into the entryway of a house.

Home-smells surrounded Shironne, and the taste of dirt. The owner didn't keep it as clean as her house. "Is this his house?"

"It's a boarding house," the colonel explained. "He had a flat here. I sent a message ahead, to let the landlady know we were coming back."

"Oh." She should have realized that. A sergeant wouldn't have the money to own a house. In fact, Benia claimed that as the reason they hadn't married yet.

Voices echoed along hallways, distracting her. Late morning, and most of the residents should be at their work, Shironne guessed. Not all, it seemed. Two women argued somewhere above them, one angry, another pleading, their words indistinct at this distance.

"Upstairs, sir," the lieutenant said.

The colonel drew Shironne toward the sounds of the voices and they mounted the stairs. Someone passed close by as they came out onto the second floor landing, causing the colonel to halt abruptly. She hummed a lullaby under her breath, a fog of vague despondency surrounding her.

"I beg your pardon, Madam," the colonel said, even though she'd been the one to walk into him.

The woman's attention focused on him, her sudden interest pronounced enough to make Shironne wonder for the first time if the colonel was a handsome man. Then the woman's attention drifted away like smoke caught on the wind. She continued on up the stairs without even responding.

The landlady, identifiable by the keys jangling at her waist, met them when they stopped at a doorway. She fawned over the officers in a subservient fashion and unlocked the door for them, curious and uneasy thoughts making a messy cloud around her in Shironne's mind. The colonel thanked her and informed her they would send for her if they needed further assistance—a polite way of asking her to go away. She left them, taking her worry and noisy keys with her.

Shironne laid a gloved hand on the doorframe and stepped through onto a wood floor. "How is the room laid out?"

The colonel entered behind her, giving her a brief description. The sitting room possessed only a low table, two chairs and a tea service near the hearth.

"Could you take me to a chair?" Shironne asked.

He took her hand, curiosity in his mind again, and placed it on the back of a chair. She sat and removed her left boot. "Is there anything on the floor?"

"A braided rug in front of the hearth."

Shironne stood and started away from the chair, feeling about with her bared foot. She couldn't sense much from the wood itself, but wood kept things. She felt dirt trapped in the grain, bits of skin and hair, food and saliva, all ground together into dust, only faintly identifiable. The pine floors had recently been scrubbed with lye and water.

Shironne reached a spot near the middle of the room and stopped, her foot poised barely touching the floor. Blood had flowed there. "Did he die right here?"

"That was where they found the body this morning," the lieutenant confirmed from just inside the doorway.

"There's a lot of blood."

"I don't see anything," the colonel said. "The landlady must have scrubbed it after they took the body."

"But she didn't get it all. You never get anything really clean, sir. I can feel the blood in the cracks between the boards, and in the grain of the wood."

"Hmmm. Are your feet as sensitive as your hands?"

"No, sir, but more than . . . um, say, my elbow."

"Interesting."

Shironne moved her foot about, taping spots on the bare wood. The blood had spread wide, which made her suspect the body laid there for some time. "How long before anyone found him, sir?"

"We don't know for certain. They found the body early this morning and carried it to the morgue at about seven."

She began making a wider circle, trying to determine what else the floor could tell her. "Someone barefoot was here, someone with small, dirty feet. They got some of the blood on them and probably left footprints."

"Gone now. A child or a woman?"

"Female, but definitely not my maid. Benia never goes barefoot. Once I told her what was really on the floor," Shironne almost laughed, remembering the woman's unseen horror, "and now she can't do it anymore."

She continued feeling her way outward. She crossed a spot where many shod feet had passed, leaving dirt from the street outside. She came to a halt and pointed in the direction of the traffic. "What's that way, sir?"

"Bedroom," he said.

She followed the track the feet had walked.

"There's a closed door about three feet in front of you," the colonel warned her.

Shironne reached out a hand and located the door. She slid off one of her gloves and touched the porcelain doorknob. "The landlady cleaned this, too."

"She'll want to let these rooms again quickly."

"That doesn't help me much."

"I don't think she had you in mind."

Shironne turned the knob and pulled the door open. The bedroom smelled stale, as if air didn't pass through it. "Is there no window?"

"No," the colonel replied from close behind her. "It's a tiny room, only the bed and an armoire. Hardly space to turn around."

She stepped into the room, unexpectedly cracking her shin on a metal bed frame on her first step. She hissed, tears starting in her useless eyes.

"I'm sorry," he said. "I should have warned you."

"Not your fault, sir," she said, regaining her equilibrium. She hated doing things like that—things people expected a blind girl to do.

She leaned down and touched the bedclothes, feeling wool, worn and coated with years of human use. They'd been washed recently, but soap never got rid of everything. "The landlady must have re-made the bed."

Frustrated, she reached out her gloved hand and tugged back the blanket, exposing the sheets. She pulled back the upper one, hoping not to dislodge the lower sheet at the same time.

"I don't believe your mother would approve of this," the colonel said, his mind abruptly focused on her actions.

"She's not here," Shironne reminded him. She ran her bare hand lightly across the sheet, starting at the head of the bed. "The landlady may have made the bed," she told the colonel, "but she didn't change the sheets."

The colonel radiated disgust.

"The sheets—they feel of him, the same man who bled on the floor."

"How can you tell?"

"I . . . um, don't know how, sir. I just know. Different people just feel different to me. I don't have any words for it. I recognized his blood because I'd touched his body. I recognize the sheets for the same reason, but I can't explain how."

"The sheets?"

"Um . . . what's on the sheets, sir. People leave bits of themselves behind; hair, skin, spit . . . other things." She slid her hand farther down the sheets and stopped. "I can feel him here," she said, "and . . . um, also my maid, Benia."

"I think perhaps we've seen enough."

Shironne almost laughed at his sudden squeamishness. "Colonel, I've touched this sort of thing before. I've known for some time my maid had a lover. Perhaps you shouldn't mention it to my mother, though."

He packed away his worry and sighed. "You are a most unusual young lady."

"Thank you, sir. It's just . . . I mean, how can I miss that sort of thing?" The world never stopped for her too-sensitive skin. "The odd thing is, another woman had been in this bed. The barefoot one, I think, although I'm not certain. I didn't really get much of a feel of her from the floor."

"Ah. I'm sorry for your maid, then," the colonel said with a hint of sympathy followed by a quick flare of suspicion.

"Benia wouldn't do this, sir. She loved him."

"People sometimes do irrational things when wounded."

"But she couldn't have lied to me about it, sir. People can't fool me if I'm touching them."

That revelation sparked another fit of cogitation on his part, so Shironne returned her attention to the sheets. "Sir, I don't think the barefoot woman was his lover, or at least . . . um, not since these sheets were washed."

"Hmm." He worried again.

"I mean, I can feel a lot of him on the sheets, and a lot of Benia, but only hints of the other woman. I mean, if she was his lover too, there would be more . . ." She stopped, not certain how to explain it.

"There would be more," he said firmly, sparing her.

"Yes, sir."

"So another woman was here," he said. "There could have been a fight over her."

"And perhaps her husband killed the sergeant?"

"It would make sense," the colonel said. "At least now we have a possible motive to follow up on."

"I really don't think he would have brought another woman here, sir. He loved Benia."

"No, you know she loved him. Can you be certain he felt the same?"

Shironne dug back through her own memories, trying to recall everything Benia had ever said of her sergeant. "I just can't believe it, sir."

The colonel thought cynical thoughts. "You're very young. You want to believe the best of others."

"I'm fifteen," she told him, wondering if he could possibly know the evil in others' minds the way she did. "Is there anything else here I could feel, sir?"

She heard him move past her into the small room. He opened the armoire and then shut it. "The landlady has removed everything already. Lieutenant?" he called back to the main room.

"Yes, sir," the woman replied promptly.

"Find out what the landlady did with the sergeant's personal property." The lieutenant agreed and left, her quiet presence fading away with her footsteps. "I think we know now why she looked nervous."

Shironne followed her own trail back to the chair she'd sat in and felt around to retrieve her shoe. She finally located it and pulled on her sock. She was tying her shoe when the colonel came to tower over her.

"I believe we're at a dead end for now," the colonel said. He touched a hand to her shoulder. "I should get you back to your house before your father misses you."

Anger flared through his thoughts again.

"He doesn't watch me as close as Mama."

He took his hand away. "Still, I suspect he might blame her if he knew you were missing, wouldn't he?"

"Yes, sir." She'd already chanced her father's ire by being gone this long.

"Why don't I take you back then?" he said. His tone didn't indicate a question.

Shironne sighed and rose. "I need to know, though, when you find out who did it."

"I'll get you word. I promise."

✧   ✧   ✧

The butler believed Mama's fabrication about locking Shironne in her room for the entire afternoon. When he found Shironne below stairs chatting with Cook in the kitchens, he roundly upbraided the woman for abetting her delinquency. The butler would prefer she be locked away permanently, Shironne knew. He feared her "oddness" might be catching.

She put a tearful Benia off with the assurance that the colonel would keep them informed, feeling horribly guilty the whole time.

"I hope he finds out who did it," Shironne said that night while her mother brushed out her hair. Her father hadn't returned home for some reason, the best possible end to any day. "Benia seems like she'll never be happy again."

"I know. I sense it too. Did he say he would let us know what he found?"

Trepidation accompanied her mother's question, coupled with a hint of anticipation. Mama apparently had mixed feelings about the colonel and his inquisitive nature. "He said he would. I asked him to contact Cook, though, by way of the servant's entrance."

Her mother's relief spread about her like a cool fog. "That should pass. Your father doesn't like for us to have visitors."

"I think the colonel understands, Mama, about Father, I mean."

Mama sighed wistfully. "Good," she said after a moment. "Do you suppose he'll be able to find the person who killed the sergeant?"

Shironne bit her lip as the brush caught a snarl in her curly hair. "I don't know, Mama. Something we looked at is just wrong."

Her two younger sisters came into the bedroom to have their hair brushed, and their conversation came to an end.

Shironne played with her cup of chocolate in the morning, still unable to place what she'd missed at the sergeant's flat. It seemed to come close, only to slip away like a fish in a pond. The landlady had cleaned everything and told the lieutenant she'd donated his clothes and blankets to the poor, which left the colonel with very little to investigate.

The second housemaid slipped into her room to take her breakfast tray. "Miss," she whispered conspiratorially, "there's someone in the kitchen to see you."

Shironne located her sturdy boots, put them on, and then hurried down the back stairs, avoiding the other servants on the way. She halted on the landing though, her mouth hanging open, when the missing idea came swimming within reach.

She found Lieutenant Kassannan waiting for her under Cook's stern eye. "The colonel would like to speak with you again," the lieutenant said when Shironne approached the servants' table. "He has an idea."

"I think I do, as well."

Curiosity surged in the woman's mind, quickly hidden away. "The colonel told me to get your mother's permission first, miss. I left the carriage waiting on the next street over, and I've brought your hat."

Shironne grinned. She *owned* the silly hat now. Her mother came down the servants' stair a moment later, evidently fetched by the second housemaid as well.

"The colonel would like to borrow your daughter again, Madam," the lieutenant told her. "If you're willing."

Shironne sensed her mother's worry. "I'd like to go. I've figured something out, and I need to tell him. I'll be careful, Mama. No one will see me."

"Sweetheart, let the colonel take care of this. You've done what you promised."

"Mama, please, I want to do this. I can be helpful."

"The colonel said we should offer her a job," the lieutenant added.

"Was he serious?" Shironne asked, her own curiosity echoed by her mother's.

"Half-way to, miss. You're young, but he would certainly be willing to take you on when you come of age."

Awfully far away, Shironne thought. "Mama, do you think I could?"

Her mother sighed, her mind turning quickly. "I suppose you must, but I want you to promise me . . ."

In the end, there were about ten things she had to pledge. In addition to not being seen, heard, or injured, she promised to stay with the lieutenant or the colonel at all times. Shironne doubted she could stick to it. She had a talent for falling into trouble.

"Miss Anjir," the colonel said as she entered his office, "I spoke to our surgeon last night. We may have proceeded under a false assumption."

"We assumed a man killed him."

"Very good," he said.

Shironne pictured in her mind the way the knife must have gone in and come out, angled sharply. She could only think of one way it had happened. "She used both hands to stab him, raised like this, above her head and then coming down, sir."

"And what could you deduce from that?"

"Well, I don't know how tall he was, sir."

The colonel came nearer. "About six inches shorter than me," he said. He held out a hand and raised her gloved fingers to it. "So the wound would have come about this high off the ground."

She felt his hand, trying to fix the height in her mind. It was too high for her to stab at herself, not with any strength behind it. If she stood on her toes, it might make the difference. "A little taller than me, then?"

"Short of average," the colonel agreed.

"Everyone thinks I'm a little girl because I'm short," Shironne lamented.

"You've disabused us of that notion," the colonel told her. "I was, however, severely castigated by the surgeon for involving you in this."

"You didn't involve me, sir. I involved myself." She drew herself up, trying to look taller. "Well, I didn't catch it yesterday, but I wonder if maybe the woman lives in the boarding house."

"Excuse me?" the colonel said.

"She was barefoot and she walked straight out the door. No one goes out a door and then stops to put their shoes on—it would be remarked. I don't think she ever went outside. She must live in the same building."

"Might it be the landlady?" the lieutenant asked.

"I think she likely sold off his property," the colonel answered, "enough to feel guilty about. She's too tall anyway."

"If I could go to there again, I might be able to find her," Shironne said.

"How?"

"I think I might recognize her if I ran into her."

"We don't have any better lead, sir," the lieutenant said. The colonel reluctantly agreed.

Once they reached the boarding house again, he helped Shironne down from the carriage, silly hat wobbling on her head. They made their way back up to the sergeant's rooms.

Shironne stopped inside the doorway. She knelt, removing one glove to feel the threshold. Dozens of people had crossed through, boots dropping street dust and horse dung in tiny bits all about. Near the edge of the doorway, she found a trace remembrance of the woman's bare, bloodstained foot. She told the colonel.

"Would you recognize her if you touched her?"

"I might, sir." Shironne laid her hand over the print, trying to get a feel for the woman. Her feet had been dirty, with that taste of blood on them, but Shironne separated out her sense of the skin and sweat from all the distractions. She rose awkwardly, the lieutenant's hand coming under her elbow to help her rise. "Maybe I could touch all the doorknobs."

The colonel thought amusement at her. "The landlady will think we're insane. Lieutenant Kassannan, why don't you go inform the woman we're going to search the premises."

The lieutenant hurried away.

"Can you do that, sir?" Shironne asked.

"On your say-so? Certainly. So, how do we proceed?"

"Perhaps if I feel each of the doorknobs, I might know if she touched one."

"Well, then, let's take one floor at a time." He led her down the hallway, grasped her gloved hand and laid it against a doorframe.

She felt for the handle with her other hand and cringed. "Ew. He should wash before he eats."

"I hope you realize the vast majority of people won't wash enough to satisfy your tastes."

Shironne laughed. "I suppose not, sir."

They tried every door on that hallway. She found a great deal of filth, but nothing relevant to the murder.

The landlady returned with the lieutenant in time to witness Shironne's confrontation with the last door. "Witch," she hissed and scurried away in fear.

"It's a good thing I'm wearing a veil."

"Some people are superstitious. Don't let it concern you." He led her to the next floor, and she proceeded to touch all the doors, finding nothing.

The stairwell to the fourth floor narrowed, forcing the colonel to walk behind her. The pine railing under her bare fingers bore the taste of only a few different hands, oil and dirt and sweat worn into the wood. "She's been here," Shironne told the colonel.

His patience turned to anticipation. Shironne sensed the lieutenant tensing as well. She located the last step and stopped on the landing. "Is the ceiling low?" she asked.

"Yes," the colonel answered.

Shironne suspected he must be stooping, given the pinched sound of his voice. "How far to the door?"

"The first is three feet ahead and two feet to your right."

She followed his directions. The knob felt only of a man. "Not this one, sir."

"Ten feet down the hallway," he said.

She walked ahead, trailing her gloved hand against the wall. She felt at the knob once she'd located the door. "Um, she has touched this one, sir."

"Kassannan, go ahead." The colonel's hand settled on Shironne's shoulder, drawing her back behind him.

The lieutenant passed her in the cramped hallway. She rapped on the door. "Army Investigations. Open up."

Shironne heard no response.

"How certain are you about this?" the colonel asked.

"I know she touched the doorknob. That doesn't mean she lives here, sir."

"We're at the end of a hall. Nowhere else to go."

The lieutenant knocked again.

Shironne heard the sound of feet on the floor inside then. "I heard something, sir."

"So did I," he said. "Let me, Kassannan."

The colonel pulled away from her. Shironne heard something strike the door and realized he must have kicked it. The sound came again. She heard a crash as the door gave, banging into the wall behind it.

"Army," he called as he stepped into the room, away from the hallway. The lieutenant followed, leaving Shironne standing alone there.

Fear prickled through the hallway. Shironne fought it, uncertain whether it was her own. She did fear abandonment in unknown places.

She laid her gloved hand on the wall and felt along it, seeking the door again. Following would be better than being alone. She found the doorframe and stepped into the room. A garret apartment, she decided. The colonel must have had to bend down to get in through the low door.

The room smelled dirty, faint hints of soured milk and urine making her wrinkle her nose. She heard the colonel speaking to the lieutenant, their muffled voices indicating they'd passed into a different room.

Shironne took a step in that direction, but stopped when her foot touched something unexpected on the floor. She tried tapping about and discovered there were objects all about her, small things that would surely trip her should she try to run. Something large huddled on the floor to her left, fabric like a jacket or blanket. Fear welled again, causing her breath to go short.

"Not in the closet, sir," the lieutenant called from far away.

"I found an access to the next apartment. Go back and get the girl."

Shironne stood frozen, very aware of the unidentified things on the floor. Dread beat through her senses. A board creaked behind her, and she heard the whisper of bare feet. A hand tangled into her braid, yanking her close against a wiry body. Her oversized hat tumbled away.

"Sir," the lieutenant called. "She's in here."

The woman held Shironne, trembling limbs pinning her. She wasn't terribly large but she had the strength of desperation.

Her fear roiled through Shironne's senses. Shironne fought to control her mind, counting silently to restore calm. She tried to breathe slowly. Something cool and metallic pressed against her cheek, shaking in the woman's hand.

"Let her go, ma'am," the lieutenant said.

The woman shifted her grip on Shironne's braid, the back of her hand coming into contact with Shironne's neck.

"Madam," the colonel said in a reasonable tone. "The girl is not your enemy. Let her go."

The woman shook Shironne by her braid. Her dirty hand brushed Shironne's neck again.

Shironne forced herself to touch the woman's mind. Her thoughts were strangely insistent and repetitive, impossibly chaotic and loud. They protested over and over that she didn't know what she'd done wrong.

"Whatever did the sergeant do to you? Why did you kill him?" Shironne asked, hoping to direct the woman's attention where she wanted it to go. Her questions sparked only uncomprehending fear.

The colonel continued to talk soothingly, as if to a child. The woman jerked Shironne farther away. Something small on the floor shifted under Shironne's foot and only the woman's painful grip on her hair kept her standing.

She focused on the circle pressed to her cheek, recognizing it for what it was. She extended her senses through the metal, feeling the touch of the sergeant's hands on it. Metal was always easy.

"The gun . . ." Shironne began.

A shot sounded, deafening in the garret room. Blood, hot and personal, sprayed across Shironne's face. The woman jerked away from her, dragging her down to the floor. Shironne yelped at a sudden flare of pain.

She felt the colonel's hands on her shoulders then, steadying her. He wiped at her face with a piece of starched linen, smoothing away most of the blood splattered across her cheek. She could feel his worry crowding around her. "I'm so sorry, Miss Anjir," he said. "I didn't realize she had a way to get back around behind us."

Shironne calmed her breathing, easier now the woman's beating panic had faded. "She's insane, Colonel."

"Was," the lieutenant said flatly. "She's dead."

"Damn," the colonel said.

Shironne took a deep breath. The colonel gave her the handkerchief and she began to scrub at her hand with it. "Um, the gun wasn't loaded."

Clicking metallic sounds followed. "She's right, sir," the lieutenant said.

"Well, the fact that she's in possession of it indicates she had some involvement in the sergeant's death." The colonel sighed, irritation surrounding him. "What a mess. Now we'll never know what happened."

"Sir, I had to take the shot," the lieutenant said.

"You're not at fault, Kassannan. I should never have brought Miss Anjir up here in the first place."

Shironne sensed his frustration. "Sir, I could find out what . . . I mean, why . . . if we don't wait too long."

His mind turned, weighing consequences and curiosity. "Are you willing to try?"

She nodded, suddenly aware that her scalp hurt. She touched her gloved hand to the sore spot.

"I'm afraid she ripped out a bit of your hair."

The realization brought tears to her eyes, the pain sharpening. Her mother would be upset and would never let her work for the colonel again. "Is it bad enough my mother will notice?" she asked, blinking away the tears.

"I will tell her myself," the colonel said sternly.

Pain washed through the room, sobbing accompanying it. "You killed her," a voice cried—the landlady.

"Sit down on the floor, ma'am," the lieutenant ordered. "We have questions for you."

"You killed her," the woman repeated.

"Yes," the lieutenant said. "Now sit down before I do the same to you. You've abetted a crime."

The landlady's pain turned to anguish. She began sobbing noisily. "I tried. I tried. I tried so hard."

"Come with me," the colonel said to Shironne, ignoring the woman. He replaced Shironne's hat, helped her stand, and walked her carefully through the room.

"What's all over the floor?" she asked.

"Toys and wooden blocks. A baby blanket, I think."

Shironne could smell the blood, strong and metallic, almost tasting it with her too-sensitive tongue. She reached out with her foot and contacted the body. Kneeling next to the dead woman, she felt for the woman's face with her bare hand. The colonel put his hand on her sleeve and directed her away from the ruined part of the woman's face.

"Witch," the landlady cried, "don't touch her."

The colonel's anger flared, but he said nothing.

"Quiet," the lieutenant snapped.

Shironne pressed her hand to the dead woman's skin. Warm and soft still, the blood no longer moved under the surface. Everything had halted, stopped in its path.

She reached deeper, searching for the scattered leaves of memory in the woman's mind. They'd had no time to decay yet, each preserved clearly for her to see. Shironne touched one and then another, confirming what she'd suspected when the woman had still been alive. She wasn't sane. She'd lost her child and then her mind.

Shironne found a distinct memory of Sergeant Merha speaking with the woman in the foyer of the boarding house. He'd been polite and kind. That simple act alone triggered her obsession with him. He was meant to give her another child, she'd believed, only he hadn't wanted her. She waited in his bed, but he didn't want to lie with her. In her desperation, she struck him.

"I really don't think she realized what she'd done, sir," Shironne said, drawing away. "She knew she'd done something wrong, because her sister ordered her up here and wouldn't let her come down again, but I don't think she understood she actually killed him. Yesterday when you ran into her downstairs, she was waiting by his door for him to come back."

"I won't send her to a madhouse," the landlady sobbed. "I'll keep her safe. I promised."

They found the sergeant's army-issued knife in the landlady's kitchen. Even under the film of soap, Shironne could still feel his blood on the blade. Together with the gun, the colonel claimed, they had evidence enough, and the landlady confessed it all.

Her mother was furious—quietly, tearfully so, but furious.

The colonel had taken her back to the Army Square where she'd been able to clean her hands and face to her own satisfaction. Lieutenant Kassannan sponged the stains from her worn brown dress, and Shironne re-braided her hair, hoping the sticky and painful patch would heal quickly. The colonel was correct in believing she'd not be able to hide it.

Sitting at the servants' table in their kitchen, he confessed everything. "Madam, I wouldn't lie to you," he finished.

"Because you know very well I would sense it if you did," her mother said in a trembling voice. Her hand stroked Shironne's hair, easing over the painful spot. "I shouldn't have agreed to this."

"Madam, I could sorely use someone with her talents. I would like her to work for me from time to time, if . . ."

"Colonel, I let her have her way this time because she gave her word. Not again."

"Madam," the colonel said in a serious tone. "Your child has a very rare talent. Is it not her *duty* to use it for the good of others?"

Shironne wondered how he knew what effect that word would have on her mother. "Mama, I think I could be really good at this."

"I will," her mother said after a moment, "consider it."

"That, Madam Anjir," the colonel said softly, "is enough for today." Shironne heard the rattle of paper. "I would like for you to memorize this. It's my address."

Her mother radiated a strange mixture of guilt and hope. "I can't . . ."

"Any hour of the day or night, Madam, you or your daughters may go there. Should you need a safe haven, I mean. My servants will know your names." He'd made sure Shironne memorized it in the carriage on the way back to the house. "After all, I did warn you that I'm one of the prince's closest friends. That makes me almost family, Madam."

Shironne heard him rise and move toward the servant's door.

"You shouldn't interfere, Colonel," her mother said without any heat behind her words. "In any way."

"Hmm. I'm just . . . the interfering sort, I suppose," he said, and then was gone.

The Spiral Road

Louise Marley

Alhasa

Gray smoke curled from the beaten copper censer and rippled gently up to the high ceiling, filling the sanctuary with the spicy smell of pursil smoke. It made Romas's nose tingle.

Angkar Rinposh, the blind lama, sat crosslegged beside the censer. He bent over the glowing coals to breathe the smoke, and his dark face shone with reflected light. Novices knelt around him, crimson cowls thrown back, shaven heads bent, topknots pointed at heaven. They hummed in perfect unison. Romas supposed each singer must occasionally stop to breathe, but he heard no interruption. Sound flowed around him, deep and monotonal, resonating against the stone walls and vibrating in his bones.

Romas fingered his own long braid, and shifted his feet. He felt overlarge and out of place, but a little giddy with pursil smoke. Pursil was Alhasa's treasure and its pride. It grew only on their high plateau, with its cool salt air and unobstructed light. Suspensions of pursil leaf healed wounds, defeated infections, eased pain. And to Angkar Rinposh, its smoke brought visions.

Romas straightened, tossing his braid back over his shoulder.

He must not be tempted by the chant, nor besotted by the smoke. The crimson cowl was not for him. Romas had devoted his life to Alhasa as a courier. He wore a brown dolman over black leggings, thick-soled sandals laced to the knee. He carried no dagger. It was the pride and the sacrifice of couriers that they went unarmed, so that no one would question their purpose. They carried messages, letters, sometimes goods. To be a courier meant to be both strong and patient and swift. Romas folded his arms, and dropped his chin. Patience, of course, was the hardest of all.

At last Angkar Rinposh lifted his head, and rubbed his sightless eyes as if he were waking from sleep. When he raised one bony dark hand the humming faded and ceased, one voice at a time. When there was silence, the lama dropped his hand, and then extended it, palm up. One of the novices hurried to help him to his feet.

Angkar Rinposh, leaning on the arm of the young monk, hobbled across the sanctuary to stand before Romas. He was bent and frail, and could weigh not half as much as Romas, but his blind gaze was commanding.

Romas pressed his hands together before his chest, and bent his head. "Holiness," he said quietly. "Do you have a message for the Chamber?"

"I do." Angkar's voice was as thin and high as the wind over the cliffs. "But I sorrow to say it." He gestured to the door of the sanctuary, and began to hobble toward it. The novice walked with him, but Angkar Rinposh led the way as surely as any seeing man. Romas followed down the long aisle and out, coming to stand beside Angkar on the steps of the sanctuary, to look down over the terraced city.

The pastel houses of Alhasa nestled in layers on the steep slopes of the plateau. Narrow lanes twisted between them like the elaborate braids of young girls. Slender streams of smoke rose from kitchen stoves to disperse before the sharp morning breeze. Tiny figures moved among the vineyards and gardens, and below everything was the sheer drop to the sea. The water was almost always shrouded by a layer of cloud below the great cliff. On rare occasions, the clouds would part to allow the Alhasi a brief and dizzying view of distant green water.

In the days of the flyers, people had sailed above the oceans, but those days were lost. The Alhasi had learned to be content with their hilltop city, their terraced farms. Pursil grew on the heights, and snow grapes, and gisko berries, and a dozen other herbs to soothe, to heal, to nourish. The herbs of Alhasa were prized by the lowland people, who traded grain and tools and cloth for them.

But now, it seemed the Callistans were no longer content with the system of barter. Threats had been made, speeches and rallies had been stated. Alhasa's Chamber had sent Romas to the blind lama to discover what he could see.

Angkar Rinposh pulled up his scarlet cowl to block the bite of the wind from his bare head. "Courier," he said.

"Yes, Holiness."

"It is not good news."

"What shall I tell the Chamber, Holiness?"

"Tell them they are coming. The Callistans are coming, with their *shou dan* and their spears. They are going to block the Spiral Road."

Callis City

Irlen braced her hands on the pitted iron balustrade and leaned forward to see past the gray-tiled rooftops. The dry wind stung the tip of her nose and chilled the rusting rail under her fingers. Fronds of hair whipped across her face, and she lifted one hand to hold them out of her eyes. "Do you see that, Old Man?" she said. "It grows smaller every year."

Her shadowy companion nodded. "Like a stale cake being eaten by rats," he said. "Crumbling away."

The skeleton shapes of the ever-diminishing spaceport loomed just beyond the city, its collapsed platforms and broken passenger tubes jutting into the twilit sky like the limbs of a massive dead tree. For years scavengers had been carting off bits of it, raiding the carcass to make cart tongues out of tower struts, chimney pots out of storage cartons, water pipes out of conduits. Irlen had never seen the Callis Spaceport before its terminals had been gutted, its observation decks toppled, but there was a vintage picture at Li Paul House, an actual photograph, from the days when such things were possible.

"What are you thinking, daughter?" her companion said.

"That we remember our history, yet fail to learn from it."

"Not so many remember, now."

"I suppose not. They're too busy surviving."

"That is human nature, my daughter."

"Does it never change, then, Old Man?"

His gesture was so familiar, the graceful lifted hands, the elegant tilted head, that a spasm of loneliness twisted in her breast. He said, with a laugh, "Perhaps when the ships come back."

She could not bring an answering smile to her lips. "That's such a stupid saying."

"The General says it all the time."

Irlen rolled her eyes, and he gave her a sympathetic look.

"You should go home, daughter. You're no good to your patients if you're exhausted."

"But it is exhausting," she said tiredly. "The wounded come back from the Spiral Road every day now, and we are stretched to the breaking point. There are few enough physicians in Callis City. I'm the only one these children have, and I'm about to lose a patient."

"Doctors lose patients. I taught you that much, surely."

"This one is so young—and we don't even know her name."

"You're doing all you can, daughter. I know that."

She gave him a sideways look. "You know everything now, I suppose."

His smile twisted a little, rueful and wise. "Not always a blessing."

Her throat tightened. She had not been able to shake a pervasive sense of isolation, ever since his death. "I wish you were here, Old Man."

He shrugged, and his image wavered before her weary eyes. "Here I am," he whispered. "Here I am."

In the ward behind her, a child began to wail. Irlen turned to leave the narrow balcony, her black vestment whipping around her legs until she closed the balcony doors.

The matron met her, rubbing her hands on her long apron. "Doctor Li Paul," she said. "The girl is worse—she's so hot."

"Did you rub her with grain alcohol?"

The matron nodded, her eyes weary, her face lined with worry.

"Did you ask the apothecary for pursil leaf?"

"I asked. He says he needs what little he has for the wounded from the war."

Irlen pressed the heels of her hands to her forehead in a helpless gesture. "War," she said bitterly. "Young men wounded, maimed, killed—and for what?"

The matron pursed her lips, and looked disapproving. "Doctor," she said, "we had no choice. Those Alhasi, they're barbarians. They practice all sorts of abominations. Do you know what they do with babies they don't want? They throw them over that cliff into the sea!"

Irlen dropped her hands and fixed the matron with a hard gaze. "How do you know any of that, Matron?"

The other woman shrugged. "Everyone knows it. The General told us."

Irlen went to the sink and began to wash her hands. "I would be happy if half what the General says is true," she muttered, but fortunately the matron didn't hear.

Irlen took a fresh cloth and the bottle of grain alcohol, and crossed to the child's bedside.

There were a dozen beds in the children's ward, and every one was full. Murmurs and whimpers filled the darkness. Often a parent came with their child, if they could be spared from home, and the matrons were grateful for their help. But this child, the one Irlen knelt beside now, had come alone, carried in the strong arms of one of the General's Guards. He had found her lying in the doorway of a bakery. Irlen had been grateful to him for bringing the girl to the hospital. Many another man would have left the child to die where she was.

They called it crystal fever, and a urine sample soon confirmed that the nameless child had it. Tiny crystals shone in the beaker, showing that the girl's kidneys had already failed, that septicemia had set in. The little one appeared to be about four years of age, and she was the classic example of a crystal fever victim, poor, young, undernourished, and abandoned.

Irlen reached in the pocket of her vestment for her ancient stethoscope, the one that had been her father's, and his father's before him, all the way back to the ships. She carefully unwound its cloth wrapping, and put its earpieces in her ears.

The silvery metal of the earpieces and the cup never degenerated, which was a blessing, since the forges of Callis were incapable of such fine work, and the necessary metals were rarely available. Irlen kept the tubing of her heirloom functional by using pond reeds. Some used finely split leather, which lasted longer, but was not as flexible.

Irlen bent her head to listen to the little girl's faltering heartbeat. Gently, she pinched the skin on the child's hand. It formed a tiny tent that collapsed only slowly, evidence of the dehydration that came with crystal fever. There was nothing to be done about it. Without a dose of pursil leaf to suppress the fever and ease the pain, the child's jaws grew tighter and tighter, until she could no longer swallow the fluids Irlen and the matron tried to trickle into her mouth.

Irlen sat back on her heels to rewrap her stethoscope, and then stayed there, watching the child try to breathe. At one time physicians could replace lost fluid in their patients, pump it directly into their veins, but Callis had lost that technique. The arid plain of Callis held sulphur and graphite, but no iron, no copper; the Callistans could make their nasty little *shou dan*, hand bombs; they couldn't make needles.

Irlen wished with all her being that she could think of something else to do.

One of the things Callis wanted from Alhasa was free access to pursil leaf, to the sweet wine made from ice grapes, to the other herbs the Alhasi cultivated, and that would not grow on the dry plains. The General could claim that the war was about the "reunion" of their peoples, that he had a moral imperative for attacking Alhasa; Irlen had no doubt he had simply decided trade was too slow, and too costly. Morality had nothing to do with it, and profit everything. There was no profit, naturally, in saving the life of a nameless child of the streets.

Irlen thrust these useless thoughts aside. She put a hand on the sick girl's tangled hair. "It won't be long now, little one," she whispered. "I'm sorry. But I'll be right here. I won't leave you, I promise."

As she waited, she let her gaze stray to the window that looked out on the balcony and the dark night. Her companion was there, a foggy form watching through the glass. Irlen nodded to him, tucked away the stethoscope he had left her, and waited for the girl to die.

The nightly caravan of wounded soldiers arrived an hour after the child drew her last breath. Irlen was called to the trauma room, and spent hours trying to mend arrow wounds, crushed bones, lacerated skin. It had been a long day and a longer night, and she was stunned to exhaustion by the weight of the work and the weeping of young men in pain. The last of the pursil leaf was gone before the Guards stopped carrying in stretchers. Irlen had to send away her blood-stained vestment before the night was out, and work on in a long apron like the one Matron wore.

As she trudged back up the stairs to the children's ward, her companion returned, a faintly gray figure in the dimness of the stairwell. She grimaced at him. "It troubles me, Old Man. They go off to war expecting glory, and they come back shocked at how much glory hurts."

"There is no good war," he said. "And no bad peace."

"You're quoting again," Irlen sighed. "As usual, I remember the quote but not the author. From the time of the ships?"

He gave her a ghostly smile. "The quote is much older than that. Benjamin Franklin, some pre-Industrial philosopher."

"Ah. Well, he was right."

"Every physician knows that," her companion said lightly. "It is politicians who don't believe it."

"All I know," Irlen said wearily, reaching for the handle of the door to the ward, "is that without pursil leaf, and the other herbs we can get from Alhasa, this will be a primitive kind of medicine. We'll be cauterizing wounds with hot irons next."

She went through the door, leaving him behind in the dark stairwell. She saw that the vacated bed had already been filled. Against the far wall of the ward, two parents stood with sick children in their arms.

Irlen gritted her teeth against the wave of despair that swept her. If only . . . just a basket of pursil leaves, and a day in which to make the medicine . . . but the General had seen to it that wasn't possible.

Alhasa

"Romas," his mother called. "There's a message for you."

Romas turned away from contemplating the ruin of the stone arches that had protected the Spiral Road for years. It made his heart ache, that ruin. Early in the days when the Alhasi had parted

from the Callistans, when they had determined to live in harmony
with their new world, rather than yearn for their lost technology,
they had carved the Spiral Road out of the living rock of the cliff,
a great ribbon of road that wound up and around the immense
plateau. To protect travelers on the middle reaches of the Road
from the high winds blowing from the sea, and from toppling
over into the abyss, the carvers had made tall, broad arches out
of the rock, at the cost of thousands of hours of labor and not
a few lives. And now the arches had been destroyed. It felt to
Romas, and to all the Alhasi, like a betrayal of their ancestors.

The city was quiet now, but throughout the night the sounds
of war had shattered the darkness.

"Romas!" his mother called again.

"Coming, *Ama la.*"

He trailed his fingers across the pursil vines that grew over the
door as he went in. His mother, her profusion of braids tucked
neatly beneath her round linen cap, held out a small scroll marked
with the seal of the sanctuary. "It's from him," she said, her eyes
as round as her cap. "From Angkar Rinposh."

Romas took the scroll, wondering at it. Why would the blind
lama send a message to his home?

"Open it!" his mother urged, her voice tight with anxiety. All
the Alhasi were anxious these days, since the first Callistan assault
on the Spiral Road had sent sparks and explosions high into
the night sky, and collapsed the ancient arches. Bits of rock had
gone crashing over the great cliff, bringing the Alhasi out of their
homes to stare fearfully downward into the night. The Chamber
had positioned archers to protect the city, but they could not
stop the destruction of the arches. They shot their arrows at the
Callistan soldiers, and the Callistans answered with spears and
hand bombs. The screams of the injured carried up the twisting
road to the city, and the Alhasi braced for a siege. A demand
had been sent to the Chamber, some nonsense about setting the
Alhasi "free"—a euphemism, every Alhasi knew, for taking control
of their resources, the herbs and grapes that wouldn't grow on
the plains. And the labor to harvest them!

Romas unrolled the scroll. "The lama wants to see me, *Ama la.*"

"Go quickly, my son."

Romas kissed her, and then dashed out into the steep street.
He ran, hurrying toward the top of the city, where the sanctuary

crowned the plateau. His sandals thumped on the hard ground, and his braid bounced over his shoulder. One or two people lifted their eyebrows at his swift passage, but most were in their houses, their doors and windows shut tight, preparing for the siege.

Callis City

By the time Irlen left the children's ward, she was staggering with fatigue. Two more children had died, their mothers wailing over them as their ragged breathing ceased. Matron, and several other parents who had come to help, had struggled to comfort them, had wrapped the small bodies, tried to calm the other patients.

The sun had risen on this chaos, red and dry. At least, for the moment, the flow of wounded soldiers had ceased, and the ones who had died were carried away. Irlen crept down the stairs to find a rickshaw, and almost fell asleep as it carried her to Li Paul House. She refused food, wanting only to collapse upon her own bed for the first time in thirty-six hours.

Her companion was not there. He usually followed her home, to haunt the old halls and the library where he had spent so many hours. They were empty now. No one lived in Li Paul House but Irlen and her housekeeper.

Irlen was too tired to notice his absence. She fell immediately into a heavy, hot sleep.

When her housekeeper woke her, it was almost dark again. She ate a hasty meal, and set out again for the hospital, grateful for the coolness of the night air. In the distance, the abandoned spaceport hulked beneath the stars. Oil lamps glimmered here and there in the city.

Irlen climbed wearily out of the rickshaw, feeling as if she had hardly rested at all. She moved slowly up the stairs, reluctant to face the renewed tragedies, the ceaseless need.

Not until she pushed open the door, and reached for her vestment, did she remember that she had not seen her companion since the night before. She stopped, the vestment in her hands, and looked back at the stairwell. "Where are you, Old Man?" she murmured. "You wouldn't abandon me now, surely?"

There was no answer.

Alhasa

This time, when Romas came into the presence of the blind lama, the two of them were alone. The novice who escorted him into the sanctuary pressed his hands together before his chest, bowed, and was gone. Romas walked alone down the aisle to the center of the sanctuary, where the censer smoked beneath the dome. Angkar Rinposh sat there alone, crosslegged, his blind eyes following the sounds of Romas's footsteps.

Romas knelt before him. "You sent for me," he said, a little hoarsely. The pursil smoke hung heavily in the air, a cloud of gray tinged with brown.

"I had a vision in the night," the lama said. He squinted at Romas as if he could see him through the smoke.

Romas fidgeted. It was said the lama saw more than any sighted person. It was said that he could see into your soul. His eyes, milky blue and ghostly, made Romas feel small and transparent. "Yo—your Holiness," he stammered.

"Yes, a vision," Rinposh said again. His blank gaze wandered away from Romas and up to the dome above the sanctuary. "I saw a tunnel—little more than a fissure, really—running through the ruin of the arches. And I saw you there. With a woman."

Romas felt his cheeks flame. "Your Holiness," he said, his voice quavering a little. "I am a courier. I would never take a woman—not to the arches—there's a war, Holiness."

Rinposh showed his teeth, white in the mass of brown wrinkles that was his face. "I know there's a war, Romas," he said lightly. "I can see it perfectly well."

Romas opened his mouth, and closed it again.

"And I can hear it, of course," the old lama went on. "Such a waste." He waved one hand in a gesture of irritation. "Still. Men make war until they learn its futility. There is nothing I can do about that." He took a deep breath, pursil smoke filling his nostrils. He breathed it out again, whiter and lighter than when he had drawn it in. "This vision came to me by way of a visitor. It's not a vision of something that has happened. It is an invitation to make something happen."

"Vi—visitor?"

The old man's eyes returned to him. "Do you have a speech impediment, Courier?"

Romas set his jaw, trying to regain his composure. "No, Holiness," he said firmly. "But I am nervous in your presence."

Rinposh showed his teeth again. "Of course," he said amiably. "And so you should be."

He chuckled, and then linked his hands in his lap, and lowered his head as if to stare into the rising smoke. "I have had such visitors before," he said after a time. "But this is the first from Callis."

Romas almost stammered "Ca—callis?" but caught himself.

"He is a ghost," Rinposh said, as calmly as if he were ordering tea. "A Callistan ghost."

Callis City

Irlen went for days without sleeping more than four hours at a time. Some patients she lost, both in the trauma room and in the children's ward. Some of the soldiers she could patch, though she did her work while they screamed in pain.

The children didn't scream. As they got sicker and sicker, they grew more and more quiet. Once or twice, they died without anyone noticing, slipping away in silence, small heartbeats slowing, shallow breaths growing less and less frequent until they ceased altogether.

Irlen lost track of time. She couldn't remember when her companion had last been at her side. On one clear, starry night, she left the trauma room and trudged slowly up the stairs to the children's ward. Evely was sitting between two cots, murmuring comforts to the children there. Two mothers hovered over their children, whispering, sponging them with cloths. Irlen went to the sink to wash her hands again, though she had done it before leaving the trauma room. She looked around at the ward, quiet for the moment, and then went out onto the balcony to breathe clean air for a few moments.

She turned her gaze, as she so often did, to the skeleton of the spaceport. A ruin, like the beautiful and ancient arches spanning the Spiral Road had been ruined, blown to bits by the General's explosives. "Everything is falling apart," she murmured into the night. "Nothing lasts."

"We do," came a soft voice at her shoulder.

Irlen turned her head. "There you are, Old Man," she said tiredly. "Where have you been?"

"I'm always with you, daughter."

"Are you? I feel like I'm always alone." Irlen heard the bitterness in her voice, and shook her head sharply. "It's just that I'm so tired, Old Man. And it all seems pointless. The crystal fever, and then this damned war—pointless."

His image wavered beside her, glimmering in the starlight. "Trying to save the children isn't pointless."

"Except I can't do it," she said. "I have nothing to work with."

"Because you have no medicines?"

"Yes. The General cut us off from our medicines with his stupid war."

She saw the familiar, gentle smile on her companion's face. "Why not go and ask for what you need?"

"Ask whom, Old Man? I have asked the apothecary, I have pleaded with the General—it does no good."

"Those people don't have what you need. You must ask those who have the medicines."

She gave a sour laugh. "That would be the Alhasi. Our enemies. I hardly think they will be feeling generous toward us."

"Perhaps not with all Callistans. Certainly not with the General. But a physician, struggling to save innocents . . ."

Irlen put one hand to her temple, as if the thought had struck her with some physical force. "Go myself," she murmured. "And ask."

"They can only say no."

"But would I . . . could I find someone to ask?"

Her companion gave the old, elegant shrug. "You will never know unless you try."

She stood there, on the balcony, her vestment whipping about her ankles, for a long time, thinking. Pondering. She stared at the ruin of the spaceport, and then turned to stare up at the distant silhouette of Alhasa's plateau. She had never been there, but the traders who brought the Alhasi medicines down the Spiral Road had told her of the beauty of the city, the colorful houses jumbled together on steep streets, the dizzying cliff falling away to the sea, the ancient and glorious stone arches, carved by hand out of the living rock.

It was the spaceport that caused the Callistans to build their city here, on the dry plain. The Alhasi had alienated Callis with their belief that the ships would never return, after one of their visionary monks had pronounced it. The Alhasi had moved all of their people to the high plateau, where the sun and the sea mists made gardens and fields richly productive. The Callistans had refused to adapt, but were happy to use the treasures the Alhasi found on their plateau. Pursil leaf in particular was prized for its opioid effect.

Irlen wondered if the Alhasi thought of the Callistans as barbarians. She wondered if the Alhasi threw unwanted babies into the sea. A fire rose in her mind, a flame that burned away her restraint.

She made a noise in her throat, one of acceptance. She whirled about, and left the balcony, leaving her companion hovering in the starlight.

Alhasa

Romas moved down the Spiral Road at dusk the next evening. Over his shoulder he carried a woven bag, carefully sewn shut by his *ama*, whose faith in Rinposh's visions brought immediate obedience to anything he might say. As Romas stepped carefully along the steep, twisting way, he wished his own faith were as strong.

To his right, and far below the precipitous road he followed, he heard the distant crash of the sea. Ahead, and almost as far below, the flashes and explosions went on, a barrage of noise and violence. The pile of rock that had once been Alhasa's pride had become its protection, and its prison gate. He heard faint cries from the archers, and from the soldiers on the other side. It was a sound as monotonous as the tides of the sea, the noise of men making war.

The descent took two hours in the growing darkness, Romas placing his feet with care on the narrow, twisting path. He had made the full descent often, passing beneath the great arches and on, all the way to the foot of the plateau. He had once carried a message all the way to Callis City, a journey of a full day's run each way. In the days of peace, Callistan traders had moved easily back and forth, unloading their carts at the bottom of the Spiral Road. The Alhasi would descend with their bags of herbs and grapes, make the exchange, then hoist the cargo of grain and tools and cloth, Callistan goods, on their backs. It had seemed an adequate arrangement to the Alhasi. Angkar Rinposh said the Callistans lacked patience.

As Romas drew close to the toppled arches, the noises grew louder. Alhasi archers had found perches in crannies and splits in the cliff. They waited, bows at the ready, for any Callistan who dared climb to the top of the ruin. The Callistans hurled spears and *shao dan* over the ruin, and the Alhasi archers did their best to dodge them. Rock and rubble crashed down on both sides.

The problem, Romas knew, was that the Callistans could hold their position indefinitely. There were many, many more of them. This war could last a long time. The Alhasi would have to do without grain, and the Callistans would have no pursil, or gisko, or ice grapes. What both sides would have, in abundance, was spilled blood.

Romas tightened the bit of scarlet ribbon around his arm that was Rinposh's token, a sign to all Alhasi that he was on the sanctuary's business. He adjusted the sack over his shoulder, and rounded a corner.

The ugliness of the battle scene shocked him to a standstill.

He was no more than a spear's throw away from the crumbled first arch. As he stumbled to a halt, a flash and a blast of sound erupted a little way to his right, throwing him off balance so that he almost fell. He saw the Alhasi archers dive for cover behind smashed blocks of stone, saw some on the ground dashing up the road toward him. As gravel and dust fell across the scene, Romas saw that one archer, a gray-haired man he recognized from Chamber gatherings, lay still, his face covered in stone dust, one leg at a nasty angle. As the dust settled, and the rocks stopped rolling, two of his fellows hurried to him, lifting him between them and carrying him past Romas and to the left, in what he saw now was a bivouac snuggled close against the cliff wall. Off to his right, unprotected now that the arches had been destroyed, the precipice fell away in the darkness. The unobstructed wind blew hard, tugging at his hair and his leggings, making him lean inward, away from the drop. Ahead of him, the noises of battle continued, the archers scrambling back to their posts, loosing their arrows, the Callistans on the other side shouting, hurling spears almost at random over the pile of stone.

Anger darkened every face he could see, and fury sounded in the voices from the other side of the tumbled stone. Peril vibrated in the air, threatened with every flying rock, every spear, every hand bomb. And Rinposh wanted him to walk through all of this as if it didn't exist.

The blind lama's scarlet token seemed almost to burn his arm.

He forced himself to take a step forward, and then another. Some of the Alhasi caught sight of him, and turned to call out. He saw their faces when they saw the token, watched them catch back their words, then turn away to hide their sympathy. There were many who could not understand the commands of the lama. No one disobeyed them.

Romas pressed on, putting one foot in front of the other. He winced as another blast shook the ground beneath his feet, and a flare of sparks shot past his head, but he had set his goal, now, and he kept moving. A spear flew above him, and he ducked, but it rattled uselessly against a chunk of rock. One of the archers shouted, and stood up to loose an arrow. Romas watched in horror as an answering spear nearly caught the archer, just missing his head as he ducked. It sailed past him into the darkness, over the precipice.

Romas forced his eyes forward, and kept moving.

Rinposh had described his vision, a channel through the chaos, a corridor created by the tumbled stone. Romas scanned the ruin ahead of him as he drew closer, but it looked impassible, a jagged mass of rock, huge tumbled blocks of stone footed in rubble of every size. Romas tried to suppress his fear that Rinposh's vision was more pursil smoke than prognostication. It didn't seem possible that there was a passage through the ruin, that a slender, wide-eyed woman would be waiting for him there.

The Spiral Road

Irlen was given a tent with the camp followers, the only other women in the encampment at the foot of the Spiral Road, but she spent no time there. The moment she stepped off the caravan, she was swept into the hospital tent, where she labored for hours with the medics. It was unbearably hot, with the great plateau blocking the wind from the sea. When she stepped outside as evening approached, a tantalizing whiff of salt carried on the still air, and made her long to be on the other side, where the road wound up the cliff above the water.

All the wounded had been either treated and sent back to their barracks, or shipped back in the caravan to Callis City. And now, as darkness approached, Irlen saw that the fighting would begin again. She knew it was dangerous, she had seen the damage done to the Callistan soldiers. But compulsion drove her. What she needed for the children in her ward was on the other side of that pile of blasted rock, and that was still an hour's walk away. The fighters were already on their way, marching up the twisting road, disappearing around the curve as they climbed.

Her companion hovered beside her in the dusk as she hesitated. "You've come this far," he said. "You won't give up now."

"I was crazy to come," she muttered. "But the General couldn't accept my offer fast enough."

"No, of course not," he smiled. "A real doctor, a volunteer . . . a patriot."

She snorted, the sound lost in the clatter of boots on rock, of orders being called, of conversations around campfires and in the cooktents. "I'll probably get myself killed."

"Oh, no," he said. "You'll find a way through."

His was the very voice of her compulsion. "Well." She straightened her long jacket, dusted her palms together. "Now that I'm here, I'm going to try."

The last of the soldiers had already rounded the curve in the steep road above her head. She set out after them with a determined step. She had nothing with her, deliberately. Her plan—inasmuch as she had one—was simply to arrive with empty hands, to find someone to ask for what she needed, to beg for help for the children in her care. Her head buzzed with the odd drive that had brought her here. It was not like her to act on impulse, and she had never done so before. But now . . . she put one foot in front of another, and climbed.

One of the medics spotted her before she had gone far, and came running after her, his boots clacking against the stone. She turned to face him.

"Doctor," he cried breathlessly. "Don't go up there! Those barbarians—they shoot arrows and throw huge stones—you've seen the damage!"

"And what do we throw at them?" Irlen asked.

His look of concern transformed instantly into a scowl of disapproval. "They are Alhasi," he said, sternly, as if she were a child. "Godless. Immoral. They are our enemies."

Irlen spun away from him, her long coat flaring. "Enemies," she muttered to herself as she resumed her climb.

"The way to destroy our enemies is to befriend them," her companion said, at her shoulder.

"Ah, I remember your saying that, Old Man. Quoting again. Lin Chu, I believe."

"You remembered this time, daughter! Good for you."

She didn't answer. The climb took all her breath.

The opening was slender and irregular, a corridor of stone formed by two great chunks that had fallen at angles to each other, frighteningly close to the precipice. Romas found that once he had inched along the base of the ruin, he was beneath the trajectory of the Callistan spears, but the explosives were still a danger. Something fell near him, and rolled across the rubble. Instinctively, he turned his face to the rock and covered his head with his arms. The hand bomb, blessedly small, blew up with a popping sound, and bits of gravel stung his back and bounced off the walls. He held still, more afraid of the drop than the bomb.

An archer above him cried, "*Khu bo*! They'll kill you!"

Romas looked up at him. He gave a slight shrug, and held up his arm.

The man nodded understanding, and touched his own arm, acknowledging the lama's token. Romas turned around, his back to the rock, and sidestepped toward the opening. When the next bomb fell, he simply closed his eyes. His fate was no longer in his hands.

Irlen, after climbing for half an hour, rounded a sharp turn. To her left, the cliff fell away into utter blackness. Ahead, the battle was in full spate. Callistan soldiers stood in lines, braving the arrows of the Alhasi, and threw spears and *shou dan* with all their might over the ruin of stone. There were already wounded, lying on stretchers in the road. Piles of the nasty-looking hand bombs lay in wagons, and bundles of spears with barbed tips waited in racks. The men shouted orders and questions at each other over the noise of the detonations on the other side. The explosions lit up the night, and Irlen could see how beautiful the arches must once have been, crenellated edges and scrolled lintels now decorating jagged fragments. As she approached, one of the captains caught sight of her.

"What's a woman doing here?" he demanded.

Someone else glanced around, and said something to the captain Irlen couldn't hear. The captain whirled, and stamped toward her through the noise and confusion.

She stopped where she was, but it was hard. The impulse that pushed her on burned in her mind. Her companion wavered, frowning, looking ahead. He lifted one arm, only faintly visible in the starlight, and pointed at the jumble of broken stone ahead. She tried to see what he was pointing at, but at that moment the captain reached her.

He stopped abruptly, his hard boots spitting bits of rock at her ankles. "What do you think you're doing?" he said harshly.

The burning in her mind became an inferno. She could hardly think how to answer the man. "I—" she faltered. "I—I'm a doctor," she said, not knowing how else to persuade him.

He gave her a hard look. "There are wounded on those litters, there," he said, pointing back the way she had come.

"I know," she said. Her eyes strayed past him, raking the ruin for a way through. Her feet inched forward of their own volition. "I know, but—"

And there it was. She knew, distantly, that the captain shouted something at her, but the compulsion in her mind allowed nothing but the awareness that her goal was just ahead, perhaps thirty yards away. She strode forward. The captain's hand grasped at the back of her coat, but she was already gone. He shouted, but her mind would not permit her to hear it. She started to run toward the cliff's edge, where she saw the break in the pile of rock. She ran directly into the path of the arrows and stones from the Alhasi side of the barrier.

"Stop!" came a shout above Romas's head.

It was the archer, but Romas knew he was not shouting at him. He was ordering the others, the fighters, to stop their barrage.

And a moment later, the hail of spears and *shou dan* from the other side stopped, too. A strange, tense silence fell over the blasted arches. Romas drew one surprised breath, and then dashed for the opening into the ruin.

Irlen was only faintly aware that the arrows had stopped falling before she reached the breach she had spotted in the tumbled rock. It was little more than a darker rectangle in the dark face of the ruin, but it was there. She stood for a heartbeat in the opening, her eyes adjusting to the dimness. The space was irregular, and close, but big enough for her to wriggle through. She slipped off her coat, to show that she carried no weapon, and dropped it on the ground. A gust of wind caught it, and it sailed out into the abyss like a great bird, its panels flapping like wings. In a heartbeat, it had disappeared into the night. Irlen cried out, shocked by a sudden dizziness, and clung to the nearest chunk of rock with both hands. When she had calmed a bit, she let go of the rock, and sidled into the break in the ruin. She began to creep forward into cold, cramped darkness.

When the torch flared, she exclaimed, and shielded her eyes with her hand. Her voice sounded dead in the narrow space.

"It's all right," came another voice, a deep one. A real one. "*Nu mo*, don't be afraid. Everything's all right."

Cautiously, Irlen opened her eyes, and let them adapt to the dancing light of a small oil torch. Her companion had left her alone with a tall, dark Alhasa. He wore a thick black braid hanging over one shoulder, and a piece of red ribbon twined around his bicep. Her heart pounded in her ears, but the compulsion that had drawn her all the way from Callis City released its hold, and she could think clearly for the first time in two days. The situation was bizarre, but she could think of only one thing to do.

She took a step forward, and held out her hand. "*Ni hao*," she said. "I am Irlen Li Paul."

Her new companion smiled, showing very white teeth. It was hard to see him well in the flickering torchlight, but he was tall and well-made, with muscled shoulders and clear eyes. His hand was hard and strong against hers. "Romas Battu," he said. "I am ashamed, now, that I did not believe Angkar Rinposh."

She dropped his hand, and stood back. "Who is Rinposh?"

"He is our lama."

"Oh—you mean the blind monk? I have heard of him. Did he tell you I would be here?"

"He had a vision, he said. Brought to him by a ghost—a Callistan ghost."

Irlen released a trembling breath. "It may be the same ghost who brought me. I can't think why else—I hardly know why I am here, Romas Battu."

"His Holiness seemed to know." The tall man smiled again, and swung a bag from behind his shoulder. "He wanted me to carry something to you." He held the bag out to her, a handsewn burlap sack, tightly filled.

She took it in her hands, surprised to find that it weighed almost nothing. She put her nose to the burlap, and sniffed. "Pursil leaves," she breathed. "And so much!"

"It was all my *ama*—my mother—had in her garden."

"But—how did you know? Why did you come here, and why . . ." Irlen hugged the fragrant sack to her, shaking her head, mystified, moved.

He pressed his two hands together before his chest, and bowed. "Angkar Rinposh sees truly," he said gravely. "I doubted him, but he was right."

Involuntarily, Irlen glanced back over her shoulder. Was he there, the Old Man, laughing? She lifted her eyes again to Romas Battu. "A vision," she said wonderingly. "You would come here—bring me this gift—because of a vision."

"Why did you come, *nu mo*? Did you have a vision? It was perhaps even more dangerous, and a further journey, for you than for me."

Irlen laughed a little. "I had no vision," she said. "But I had a compulsion. There are sick children in Callis City . . ."

"Rinposh knew this."

Irlen searched Romas Battu's eyes, trying to comprehend what had happened. She pushed away her awareness of the closeness of the stone corridor, of the peril that awaited them outside. Her skin tingled with the nearness of him, dark and tall and strong, smelling faintly of smoke and sweat and fragrant salt air.

When she found her voice, she spoke softly, her eyes stinging with emotion. "Children will live because of you, Romas Battu. I thank you. And I thank your lama, and your mother."

"They will try to take the pursil from you for their soldiers."

She lifted her chin. "They will not succeed," she said. "I will threaten to throw it over the cliff if they threaten me."

"They will try to come through this corridor."

"Block it, Romas Battu."

He nodded. "We will. Go now, while I light your way."

Irlen hesitated. It was difficult to take her eyes from his face. It was hard to return to the loneliness of Callis City, where she had only a ghost for company. But she had something, now, that she could do to help the children.

She wriggled around, holding the sack closely in her arms. He raised his torch, and its light glimmered on the constricting walls of stone.

She looked back over her shoulder, once. "Romas Battu . . ." she said hesitantly. "What do you—the Alhasi—what do you do with unwanted babies?"

He frowned. "We do not have unwanted babies here," he said. "Someone always wants a baby."

Irlen smiled, and hugged the sack closer. "If this ever ends, this stupid war . . ." she began, but her voice trailed off, weak and wistful. She looked ahead, to her side of the corridor, to the war waiting outside.

"They will tire of it," he said, behind her. "It will end. Someday."

"When peace comes, then."

"Yes, Irlen Li Paul. When peace comes."

Irlen didn't look back again. She worked her way forward, through the cramped space, finding her way back to her own side, and out into the night.

The silence lay across the ruins of the arches like a blanket. As Romas emerged, he saw that the archers still waited on the heights, their bows at the ready, but their arrows unstrung. Nothing moved. No spear fell, and no hand bomb flew into their midst.

Romas turned his head up to the nearest archer. "We must block this corridor," he said. "Now they know it's here."

"What happened to your sack?" the man asked.

"It's gone." Romas smiled. "Rinposh has given a gift to the children of Callis," he said. He paced away from the ruined arches, up the Spiral Road toward Alhasa. The silence behind him lasted long minutes before another *shou dan* exploded in the darkness.

Sir Hereward and Mister Fitz
Go to War Again

Garth Nix

"Do you ever wonder about the nature of the world, Mister Fitz?" asked the foremost of the two riders, raising the three-barred visor of his helmet so that his words might more clearly cross the several feet of space that separated him from his companion, who rode not quite at his side.

"I take it much as it presents itself, for good or ill, Sir Hereward," replied Mister Fitz. He had no need to raise a visor, for he wore a tall lacquered hat rather than a helmet. It had once been taller and had come to a peak, before encountering something sharp in the last battle but two the pair had found themselves engaged in. This did not particularly bother Mister Fitz, for he was not human. He was a wooden puppet given the semblance of life by an ancient sorcery. By dint of propinquity, over many centuries a considerable essence of humanity had been absorbed into his fine-grained body, but attention to his own appearance or indeed vanity of any sort was still not part of his persona.

Sir Hereward, for the other part, had a good measure of vanity and in fact the raising of the three-barred visor of his helmet almost certainly had more to do with an approaching apple seller

of comely appearance than it did with a desire for clear communication to Mister Fitz.

The duo were riding south on a road that had once been paved
and gloried in the name of the Southwest Toll Extension of the
Lesser Trunk. But its heyday was long ago, the road being even
older than Mister Fitz. Few paved stretches remained, but the
tightly compacted understructure still provided a better surface
than the rough soil of the fields to either side.

The political identification of these fallow pastures and the
occasional once-coppiced wood they passed was not clear to either
Sir Hereward or Mister Fitz, despite several attempts to ascertain
said identification from the few travelers they had encountered
since leaving the city of Rhool several days before. To all intents
and purposes, the land appeared to be both uninhabited and
untroubled by soldiery or tax collectors and was thus a void
in the sociopolitical map that Hereward held uneasily, and Fitz
exactly, in their respective heads.

A quick exchange with the apple seller provided only a little
further information, and also lessened Hereward's hope of some
minor flirtation, for her physical beauty was sullied by a surly and
depressive manner. In a voice as sullen as a three-day drizzle, the
woman told them she was taking the apples to a large house that
lay out of sight beyond the nearer overgrown wood. She had come
from a town called Lettique or Letiki that was located beyond the
lumpy ridge of blackish shale that they could see a mile or so to
the south. The apples in question had come from farther south still,
and were not in keeping with their carrier, being particularly fine
examples of a variety Mister Fitz correctly identified as emerald
brights. There was no call for local apples, the young woman reluctantly explained. The fruit and vegetables from the distant oasis of
Shûme were always preferred, if they could be obtained. Which, for
the right price, they nearly always could be, regardless of season.

Hereward and Fitz rode in silence for a few minutes after part-
ing company with the apple seller, the young knight looking back
not once but twice as if he could not believe that such a vision
of loveliness could house such an unfriendly soul. Finding that
the young woman did not bother to look back at all, Hereward
cleared his throat and, without raising his visor, spoke.

"It appears we are on the right road, though she spoke of
Shumey and not Shome."

Fitz looked up at the sky, where the sun was beginning to lose its distinct shape and ooze red into the shabby grey clouds that covered the horizon.

"A minor variation in pronunciation," he said. "Should we stop in Lettique for the night, or ride on?"

"Stop," said Hereward. "My rear is not polished sandalwood, and it needs soaking in a very hot bath enhanced with several soothing essences... ah... that was one of your leading questions, wasn't it?"

"The newspaper in Rhool spoke of an alliance against Shûme," said Mister Fitz carefully, in a manner that confirmed Hereward's suspicion that didactic discourse had already begun. "It is likely that Lettique will be one of the towns arrayed against Shûme. Should the townsfolk discover we ride to Shûme in hope of employment, we might find ourselves wishing for the quiet of the fields in the night, the lack of mattresses, ale and roasted capons there notwithstanding."

"Bah!" exclaimed Hereward, whose youth and temperament made him tend toward careless optimism. "Why should they suspect us of seeking to sign on with the burghers of Shûme?"

Mister Fitz's pumpkin-sized papier-mâché head rotated on his spindly neck, and the blobs of blue paint that marked the pupils of his eyes looked up and down, taking in Sir Hereward from toe to head: from his gilt-spurred boots to his gold-chased helmet. In between boots and helm were Hereward's second-best buff coat, the sleeves still embroidered with the complicated silver tracery that proclaimed him as the Master Artillerist of the city of Jeminero. Not that said city was any longer in existence, as for the past three years it had been no more than a mass grave sealed with the rubble of its once-famous walls. Around the coat was a frayed but still quite golden sash, over that a rare and expensive Carnithian leather baldric and belt with two beautifully ornamented (but no less functional for that) wheel-lock pistols thrust through said belt. Hereward's longer-barreled and only slightly less ornamented cavalry pistols were holstered on either side of his saddle horn, his saber with its sharkskin grip and gleaming hilt of gilt brass hung in its scabbard from the rear left quarter of his saddle, and his sighting telescope was secured inside its leather case on the right rear quarter.

Mister Fitz's mount, of course, carried all the more mundane items required by their travels. All three feet six and a half inches of him (four-foot-three with the hat) was perched upon a yoke across his mount's back that secured the two large panniers that were needed to transport tent and bedding, washing and shaving gear and a large assortment of outdoor kitchen utensils. Not to mention the small but surprisingly expandable sewing desk that contained the tools and devices of Mister Fitz's own peculiar art.

"Shûme is a city, and rich," said Fitz patiently. "The surrounding settlements are mere towns, both smaller and poorer, who are reportedly planning to go to war against their wealthy neighbor. You are obviously a soldier for hire, and a self-evidently expensive one at that. Therefore, you must be en route to Shûme."

Hereward did not answer immediately, as was his way, while he worked at overcoming his resentment at being told what to do. He worked at it because Mister Fitz had been telling him what to do since he was four years old and also because he knew that, as usual, Fitz was right. It would be foolish to stop in Lettique.

"I suppose that they might even attempt to hire us," he said, as they topped the low ridge, shale crunching under their mounts' talons.

Hereward looked down at a wasted valley of underperforming pastures filled either with sickly-looking crops or passive groups of too-thin cattle. A town—presumably Lettique—lay at the other end of the valley. It was not an impressive ville, being a collection of perhaps three or four hundred mostly timber and painted-plaster houses within the bounds of a broken-down wall to the west and a dry ravine, that might have once held a river, to the east. An imposing, dozen-spired temple in the middle of the town was the only indication that at some time Lettique had seen more provident days.

"Do you wish to take employment in a poor town?" asked Mister Fitz. One of his responsibilities was to advise and positively influence Hereward, but he did not make decisions for him.

"No, I don't think so," replied the knight slowly. "Though it does make me recall my thought . . . the one that was with me before we were interrupted by that dismal apple seller."

"You asked if I ever wondered at the nature of the world," prompted Fitz.

"I think what I actually intended to say," said Hereward. "Is 'do you ever wonder why we become involved in events that are rather more than less of importance to rather more than less people?' as in the various significant battles, sieges, and so forth in which we have played no small part. I fully comprehend that in some cases the events have stemmed from the peculiar responsibilities we shoulder, but not in all cases. And that being so, and given my desire for a period of quiet, perhaps I should consider taking service with some poor town."

"Do you really desire a period of quiet?" asked Mister Fitz.

"Sometimes I think so. I should certainly like a time where I might reflect upon what it is I do want. It would also be rather pleasant to meet women who are not witch-agents, fellow officers or enemies—or who have been pressed into service as powder monkeys or are soaked in blood from tending the wounded."

"Perhaps Shûme will offer some relative calm," said Mister Fitz. "By all accounts it is a fine city, and even if war is in the offing, it could be soon finished if Shûme's opponents are of a standard that I can see in Lettique."

"You observe troops?" asked Hereward. He drew his telescope, and carefully leaning on his mount's neck to avoid discomfort from the bony ridges (which even though regularly filed-down and fitted with leather stocks were not to be ignored), looked through it at the town. "Ah, I see. Sixty pike and two dozen musketeers in the square by the temple, of no uniform equipment or harness. Under the instruction of a portly individual in a wine-dark tunic who appears as uncertain as his troops as to the drill."

"I doubt that Shûme has much to fear," said Mister Fitz. "It is odd, however, that a town like Lettique would dare to strike against such a powerful neighbor. I wonder . . ."

"What?" asked Hereward as he replaced his telescope.

"I wonder if it is a matter of necessity. The river is dry. The wheat is very thin, too thin this close to harvest. The cattle show very little flesh on their ribs. I see no sign of any other economic activity. Fear and desperation may be driving this mooted war, not greed or rivalry. Also . . ."

Mister Fitz's long, pale blue tongue darted out to taste the air, the ruby stud in the middle of what had once been a length of stippled leather catching the pallid sunlight.

"Their godlet is either asleep or . . . mmm . . . comatose in this dimension. Very strange."

"Their god is dead?"

"Not dead," said Mister Fitz. "When an other-dimensional entity dies, another always moves in quickly enough. No . . . definitely present, but quiescent."

"Do you wish to make a closer inquiry?"

Hereward had not missed the puppet's hand tapping the pannier that contained his sewing desk, an instinctive movement Mister Fitz made when contemplating sorcerous action.

"Not for the present," said Mister Fitz, lifting his hand to grasp once again his mount's steering chains.

"Then we will skirt the town and continue," announced Hereward. "We'll leave the road near those three dead trees."

"There are many trees that might be fairly described as dead or dying," remarked Fitz. "And several in clumps of three. Do you mean the somewhat orange-barked trio over yonder?"

"I do," said Hereward.

They left the road at the clump of trees and rode in silence through the dry fields, most of which were not even under attempted cultivation. There were also several derelict farmhouses, barns, and cattle yards, the level of decay suggesting that the land had been abandoned only in recent years.

Halfway along the valley, where the land rose to a slight hill that might have its origin in a vast and ancient burial mound, Hereward reined in his mount and looked back at the town through his telescope.

"Still drilling," he remarked. "I had half thought that they might dispatch some cavalry to bicker with us. But I see no mounts."

"I doubt they can afford the meat for battlemounts," said Mister Fitz. "Or grain for horses, for that matter."

"There is an air gate in the northeastern temple spire," said Hereward, rebalancing his telescope to get a steadier view. "There might be a moonshade roost behind it."

"If their god is absent, none of the ancient weapons will serve them," said Mister Fitz. "But it would be best to be careful, come nightfall. Lettique is reportedly not the only town arrayed against Shûme. The others may be in a more vigorous condition, with wakeful gods."

Hereward replaced his telescope and turned his mount to the north, Mister Fitz following his lead. They did not speak further, but rode on, mostly at the steady pace that Hereward's Zowithian riding instructor had called "the lope," occasionally urging their mounts to the faster "jag." In this fashion, several miles passed quickly. As the sun's last third began to slip beneath the horizon, they got back on the old road again, to climb out of the wasted valley of Lettique and across yet another of the shale ridges that erupted out of the land like powder-pitted keloid scars, all grey and humped.

The valley that lay beyond the second ridge was entirely different from the faded fields behind the two travelers. In the warm twilight, they saw a checkerboard of green and gold, full fields of wheat interspersed with meadows heavily stocked with fat cattle. A broad river wound through from the east, spilling its banks in several places into fecund wetlands that were rich with waterfowl. Several small hillocks in the valley were covered in apple trees, dark foliage heavily flecked with the bright green of vast quantities of emerald fruit. There were citrus groves too, stone-walled clumps of smaller trees laden with lemons or limes, and only a hundred yards away, a group of six trees bearing the rare and exquisite blue-skinned fruit known as *serqa* which was normally only found in drier climes.

"A most pleasant vista," said Hereward. A small smile curled his lip and touched his eyes, the expression of a man who sees something that he likes.

Shûme itself was a mile away, built on a rise in the ground in the northwestern corner of the valley, where the river spread into a broad lake that lapped the city's western walls. From the number of deep-laden boats that were even now rowing home to the jetties that thronged the shore, the lake was as well stocked with fish as the valley was with livestock and produce.

Most of the city's buildings were built of an attractively pale yellow stone, with far fewer timber constructions than was usual for a place that Hereward reckoned must hold at least five thousand citizens.

Shûme was also walled in the same pale stone, but of greater interest to Hereward were the more recent earthworks that had been thrown up in front of the old wall. A zigzag line of revetments encircled the city, with respectably large bastions at each end on the lakeshore. A cursory telescopic examination showed several bronze demicannon on the bastions and various lesser pieces of ordnance clustered in groups at various strong points along the earthworks. Both bastions had small groups of soldiery in attendance on the cannon, and there were pairs of sentries every twenty or thirty yards along the earthen ramparts and a score or more walked the stone walls behind.

"There is certainly a professional in charge here," observed Hereward. "I expect . . . yes . . . a cavalry piquet issues from yonder orchard. Twelve horse troopers under the notional command of a whey-faced cornet."

"Not commonplace troopers," added Mister Fitz. "Dercian keplars."

"Ah," said Hereward. He replaced his telescope, leaned back a little and across and, using his left hand, loosened his saber so that an inch of blade projected from the scabbard. "They are in employment, so they should give us the benefit of truce."

"They should," conceded Mister Fitz, but he reached inside his robe to grasp some small item concealed under the cloth. With his other hand he touched the brim of his hat, releasing a finely woven veil that covered his face. To casual inspection he now looked like a shrouded child, wearing peculiar papery gloves. Self-motivated puppets were not great objects of fear in most quarters of the world. They had once been numerous, and some few score still walked the earth, almost all of them entertainers, some of them long remembered in song and story.

Mister Fitz was not one of those entertainers.

"If it comes to it, spare the cornet," said Hereward, who remembered well what it was like to be a very junior officer, whey-faced or not.

Mister Fitz did not answer. Hereward knew as well as he that if it came to fighting, and the arts the puppet employed, there would be no choosing who among those who opposed them lived or died.

The troop rode toward the duo at a canter, slowing to a walk as they drew nearer and their horses began to balk as they scented the battlemounts. Hereward raised his hand in greeting and the cornet shouted a command, the column extending to a line, then halting within an easy pistol shot. Hereward watched the troop sergeant, who rode forward beyond the line for a better look, then wheeled back at speed toward the cornet. If the Dercians were to break their oath, the sergeant would fell her officer first.

But the sergeant halted without drawing a weapon and spoke to the cornet quietly. Hereward felt a slight easing of his own breath, though he showed no outward sign of it and did not relax. Nor did Mister Fitz withdraw his hand from under his robes. Hereward knew that his companion's molded papier-mâché fingers held an esoteric needle, a sliver of some arcane stuff that no human hand could grasp with impunity.

The cornet listened and spoke quite sharply to the sergeant, turning his horse around so that he could make his point forcefully to the troopers as well. Hereward only caught some of the words, but it seemed that despite his youth, the officer was rather more commanding than he had expected, reminding the Dercians that their oaths of employment overrode any private or societal vendettas they might wish to undertake.

When he had finished, the cornet shouted, "Dismount! Sergeant, walk the horses!"

The officer remained mounted, wheeling back to approach Hereward. He saluted as he reined in a cautious distance from the battlemounts, evidently not trusting either the creatures' blinkers and mouth-cages or his own horse's fears.

"Welcome to Shûme!" he called. "I am Cornet Misolu. May I ask your names and direction, if you please?"

"I am Sir Hereward of the High Pale, artillerist for hire."

"And I am Fitz, also of the High Pale, aide de camp to Sir Hereward."

"Welcome . . . uh . . . sirs," said Misolu. "Be warned that war has been declared upon Shûme, and all who pass through must declare their allegiances and enter certain . . . um . . ."

"I believe the usual term is 'undertakings,' " said Mister Fitz.

"Undertakings," echoed Misolu. He was very young. Two bright spots of embarrassment burned high on his cheekbones, just visible under the four bars of his lobster-tailed helmet, which was a little too large for him, even with the extra padding, some of which had come a little undone around the brow.

"We are free lances, and seek hire in Shûme, Cornet Misolu," said Hereward. "We will give the common undertakings if your city chooses to contract us. For the moment, we swear to hold our peace, reserving the right to defend ourselves should we be attacked."

"Your word is accepted, Sir Hereward, and . . . um . . ."

"Mister Fitz," said Hereward, as the puppet said merely, "Fitz."

"Mister Fitz."

The cornet chivvied his horse diagonally closer to Hereward, and added, "You may rest assured that my Dercians will remain true to *their* word, though Sergeant Xikoliz spoke of some feud their... er... entire people have with you."

The curiosity in the cornet's voice could not be easily denied, and spoke as much of the remoteness of Shûme as it did of the young officer's naïveté.

"It is a matter arising from a campaign several years past," said Hereward. "Mister Fitz and I were serving the Heriat of Jhaqa, who sought to redirect the Dercian spring migration elsewhere than through her own prime farmlands. In the last battle of that campaign, a small force penetrated to the Dercians' rolling temple and... ah... blew it up with a specially made petard. Their godlet, thus discommoded, withdrew to its winter housing in the Dercian steppe, wreaking great destruction among its chosen people as it went."

"I perceive you commanded that force, sir?"

Hereward shook his head.

"No, I am an artillerist. Captain Kasvik commanded. He was slain as we retreated—another few minutes and he would have won clear. However, I did make the petard, and... Mister Fitz assisted our entry to the temple and our escape. Hence the Dercians' feud."

Hereward looked sternly at Mister Fitz as he spoke, hoping to make it clear that this was not a time for the puppet to exhibit his tendency for exactitude and truthfulness. Captain Kasvik had in fact been killed before they even reached the rolling temple, but it had served his widow and family better for Kasvik to be a hero, so Hereward had made him one. Only Mister Fitz and one other survivor of the raid knew otherwise.

Not that Hereward and Fitz considered the rolling temple action a victory, as their intent had been to force the Dercian godlet to withdraw a distance unimaginably more vast than the mere five hundred leagues to its winter temple.

The ride to the city was uneventful, though Hereward could not help but notice that Cornet Misolu ordered his troop to remain in place and keep watch, while he alone escorted the visitors, indicating that the young officer was not absolutely certain the Dercians would hold to their vows.

There was a zigzag entry through the earthwork ramparts,

where they were held up for several minutes in the business of passwords and responses (all told aside in quiet voices, Hereward noted with approval), their names being recorded in an enormous ledger and passes written out and sealed allowing them to enter the city proper.

These same passes were inspected closely under lanternlight, only twenty yards farther on by the guards outside the city gate—which was closed, as the sun had finally set. However, they were admitted through a sally port and here Misolu took his leave, after giving directions to an inn that met Hereward's requirements: suitable stabling and food for the battlemounts; that it not be the favorite of the Dercians or any other of the mercenary troops who had signed on in preparation for Shûme's impending war; and fine food and wine, not just small beer and ale. The cornet also gave directions to the citadel, not that this was really necessary as its four towers were clearly visible, and advised Hereward and Fitz that there was no point going there until the morning, for the governing council was in session and so no one in authority could hire him until at least the third bell after sunrise.

The streets of Shûme were paved and drained, and Hereward smiled again at the absence of the fetid stench so common to places where large numbers of people dwelt together. He was looking forward to a bath, a proper meal and a fine feather bed, with the prospect of well-paid and not too onerous employment commencing on the morrow.

"There is the inn," remarked Mister Fitz, pointing down one of the narrower side streets, though it was still broad enough for the two battlemounts to stride abreast. "The sign of the golden barley-corn. Appropriate enough for a city with such fine farmland."

They rode into the inn's yard, which was clean and wide and did indeed boast several of the large iron-barred cages used to stable battlemounts complete with meat canisters and feeding chutes rigged in place above the cages. One of the four ostlers present ran ahead to open two cages and lower the chutes, and the other three assisted Hereward to unload the panniers. Mister Fitz took his sewing desk and stood aside, the small rosewood-and-silver box under his arm provoking neither recognition nor alarm. The ostlers were similarly incurious about Fitz himself, almost certainly evidence that self-motivated puppets still came to entertain the townsfolk from time to time.

Hereward led the way into the inn, but halted just before he entered as one of the battlemounts snorted at some annoyance. Glancing back, he saw that it was of no concern, and the gates were closed, but in halting he had kept hold of the door as someone else tried to open it from the other side. Hereward pushed to help and the door flung open, knocking the person on the inside back several paces against a table, knocking over an empty bottle that smashed upon the floor.

"Unfortunate," muttered Mister Fitz, as he saw that the person so inconvenienced was not only a soldier, but wore the red sash of a junior officer, and was a woman.

"I do apolog—" Hereward began to say. He stopped, not only because the woman was talking, but because he had looked at her. She was as tall as he was, with ash-blond hair tied in a queue at the back, her hat in her left hand. She was also very beautiful, at least to Hereward, who had grown up with women who ritually cut their flesh. To others, her attractiveness might be considered marred by the scar that ran from the corner of her left eye out toward the ear and then cut back again toward the lower part of her nose.

"You are clumsy, sir!"

Hereward stared at her for just one second too long before attempting to speak again.

"I am most—"

"You see something you do not like, I think?" interrupted the woman. "Perhaps you have not served with females? Or is it my face you do not care for?"

"You are very beautiful," said Hereward, even as he realized it was entirely the wrong thing to say, either to a woman he had just met or an officer he had just run into.

"You mock me!" swore the woman. Her blue eyes shone more fiercely, but her face paled, and the scar grew more livid. She clapped her broad-brimmed hat on her head and straightened to her full height, with the hat standing perhaps an inch over Hereward. "You shall answer for that!"

"I do not mock you," said Hereward quietly. "I have served with men, women . . . and eunuchs, for that matter. Furthermore, tomorrow morning I shall be signing on as at least colonel of artillery, and a colonel may not fight a duel with a lieutenant. I am most happy to apologize, but I cannot meet you."

"Cannot or will not?" sneered the woman. "You are not yet a colonel in Shûme's service, I believe, but just a mercenary braggart."

Hereward sighed and looked around the common room. Misolu had spoken truly that the inn was not a mercenary favorite. But there were several officers of Shûme's regular service or militia, all of them looking on with great attention.

"Very well," he snapped. "It is foolishness, for I intended no offence. When and where?"

"Immediately," said the woman. "There is a garden a little way behind this inn. It is lit by lanterns in the trees, and has a lawn."

"How pleasant," said Hereward. "What is your name, madam?"

"I am Lieutenant Jessaye of the Temple Guard of Shûme. And you are?"

"I am Sir Hereward of the High Pale."

"And your friends, Sir Hereward?"

"I have only this moment arrived in Shûme, Lieutenant, and so cannot yet name any friends. Perhaps someone in this room will stand by me, should you wish a second. My companion, whom I introduce to you now, is known as Mister Fitz. He is a surgeon— among other things—and I expect he will accompany us."

"I am pleased to meet you, Lieutenant," said Mister Fitz. He doffed his hat and veil, sending a momentary frisson of small twitches among all in the room save Hereward.

Jessaye nodded back but did not answer Fitz. Instead she spoke to Hereward.

"I need no second. Should you wish to employ sabers, I must send for mine."

"I have a sword in my gear," said Hereward. "If you will allow me a few minutes to fetch it?"

"The garden lies behind the stables," said Jessaye. "I will await you there. Pray do not be too long."

Inclining her head but not doffing her hat, she stalked past and out the door.

"An inauspicious beginning," said Fitz.

"Very," said Hereward gloomily. "On several counts. Where is the innkeeper? I must change and fetch my sword."

The garden was very pretty. Railed in iron, it was not gated, and so accessible to all the citizens of Shûme. A wandering path led through a grove of lantern-hung trees to the specified lawn, which was oval and easily fifty yards from end to end, making the center rather a long way from the lanternlight, and hence quite shadowed. A small crowd of persons who had previously been in the inn were gathered on one side of the lawn. Lieutenant Jessaye stood in the middle, naked blade in hand.

"Do be careful, Hereward," said Fitz quietly, observing the woman flex her knees and practice a stamping attack ending in a lunge. "She looks to be very quick."

"She is an officer of their temple guard," said Hereward in a hoarse whisper. "Has their god imbued her with any particular vitality or puissance?"

"No, the godlet does not seem to be a martial entity," said Fitz. "I shall have to undertake some investigations presently, as to exactly what it is—"

"Sir Hereward! Here at last."

Hereward grimaced as Jessaye called out. He had changed as quickly as he could, into a very fine suit of split-sleeved white showing the yellow shirt beneath, with gold ribbons at the cuffs, shoulders and front lacing, with similarly cut bloomers of yellow showing white breeches, with silver ribbons at the knees, artfully displayed through the side-notches of his second-best boots.

Jessaye, in contrast, had merely removed her uniform coat and stood in her shirt, blue waistcoat, leather breeches and unadorned black thigh boots folded over below the knee. Had the circumstances been otherwise, Hereward would have paused to admire the sight she presented and perhaps offer a compliment.

Instead he suppressed a sigh, strode forward, drew his sword and threw the scabbard aside.

"I am here, Lieutenant, and I am ready. Incidentally, is this small matter to be concluded by one or perhaps both of us dying?"

"The city forbids duels to the death, Sir Hereward," replied Jessaye. "Though accidents do occur."

"What, then, is to be the sign for us to cease our remonstrance?"

"Blood," said Jessaye. She flicked her sword towards the onlookers. "Visible to those watching."

Hereward nodded slowly. In this light, there would need to be a lot of blood before the onlookers could see it. He bowed his head but did not lower his eyes, then raised his sword to the guard position.

Jessaye was fast. She immediately thrust at his neck, and though Hereward parried, he had to step back. She carried through to lunge in a different line, forcing him back again with a more awkward parry, removing all opportunity for Hereward to riposte or counter. For a minute they danced, their swords darting up, down and across, clashing together only to move again almost before the sound reached the audience.

In that minute, Hereward took stock of Jessaye's style and action. She was very fast, but so was he, much faster than anyone would expect from his size and build, and, as always, he had not shown just how truly quick he could be. Jessaye's wrist was strong and supple, and she could change both attacking and defensive lines with great ease. But her style was rigid, a variant of an old school Hereward had studied in his youth.

On her next lunge—which came exactly where he anticipated—Hereward didn't parry but stepped aside and past the blade. He felt her sword whisper by his ribs as he angled his own blade over it and with the leading edge of the point, he cut Jessaye above the right elbow to make a long, very shallow slice that he intended should bleed copiously without inflicting any serious harm.

Jessaye stepped back but did not lower her guard. Hereward quickly called out, "Blood!"

Jessaye took a step forward and Hereward stood ready for another attack. Then the lieutenant bit her lip and stopped, holding her arm toward the lanternlight so she could more clearly see the wound. Blood was already soaking through the linen shirt, a dark and spreading stain upon the cloth.

"You have bested me," she said, and thrust her sword point first into the grass before striding forward to offer her gloved hand to Hereward. He too grounded his blade, and took her hand as they bowed to each other.

A slight stinging low on his side caused Hereward to look down. There was a two-inch cut in his shirt, and small beads of blood were blossoming there. He did not let go Jessaye's fingers, but pointed at his ribs with his left hand.

"I believe we are evenly matched. I hope we may have no cause to bicker further?"

"I trust not," said Jessaye quietly. "I regret the incident. Were it not for the presence of some of my fellows, I should not have

caviled at your apology, sir. But you understand . . . a reputation
is not easily won, nor kept . . ."

"I do understand," said Hereward. "Come, let Mister Fitz attend
your cut. Perhaps you will then join me for small repast?"

Jessaye shook her head.

"I go on duty soon. A stitch or two and a bandage is all I have
time for. Perhaps we shall meet again."

"It is my earnest hope that we do," said Hereward. Reluctantly,
he opened his grasp. Jessaye's hand lingered in his palm for several moments before she slowly raised it, stepped back and doffed
her hat to offer a full bow. Hereward returned it, straightening
up as Mister Fitz hurried over, carrying a large leather case as
if it were almost too heavy for him, one of his standard acts of
misdirection, for the puppet was at least as strong as Hereward,
if not stronger.

"Attend to Lieutenant Jessaye, if you please, Mister Fitz," said
Hereward. "I am going back to the inn to have a cup . . . or
two . . . of wine."

"Your own wound needs no attention?" asked Fitz as he set
his bag down and indicated to Jessaye to sit by him.

"A scratch," said Hereward. He bowed to Jessaye again and
walked away, ignoring the polite applause of the onlookers, who
were drifting forward either to talk to Jessaye or gawp at the
blood on her sleeve.

"I may take a stroll," called out Mister Fitz after Hereward.
"But I shan't be longer than an hour."

Mister Fitz was true to his word, returning a few minutes
after the citadel bell had sounded the third hour of the evening.
Hereward had bespoken a private chamber and was dining alone
there, accompanied only by his thoughts.

"The god of Shûme," said Fitz, without preamble. "Have you
heard anyone mention its name?"

Hereward shook his head and poured another measure from
the silver jug with the swan's beak spout. Like many things he
had found in Shûme, the knight liked the inn's silverware.

"They call their godlet Tanesh," said Fitz. "But its true name
is Pralqornrah-Tanish-Kvaxixob."

"As difficult to say or spell, I wager," said Hereward. "I com-
mend the short form, it shows common sense. What of it?"

"It is on the list," said Fitz.

Hereward bit the edge of pewter cup and put it down too hard, slopping wine upon the table.

"You're certain? There can be no question?"

Fitz shook his head. "After I had doctored the young woman, I went down to the lake and took a slide of the god's essence—it was quite concentrated in the water, easily enough to yield a sample. You may compare it with the record, if you wish."

He proffered a finger-long inch-wide strip of glass that was striated in many different bands of color. Hereward accepted it reluctantly, and with it a fat, square book that Fitz slid across the table. The book was open at a hand-tinted color plate, the illustration showing a sequence of color bands.

"It is the same," agreed the knight, his voice heavy with regret. "I suppose it is fortunate we have not yet signed on, though I doubt they will see what we do as being purely a matter of defense."

"They do not know what they harbor here," said Fitz.

"It is a pleasant city." said Hereward, taking up his cup again to take a large gulp of the slightly sweet wine. "In a pretty valley. I had thought I could grow more than accustomed to Shûme—and its people."

"The bounty of Shûme, all its burgeoning crops, its healthy stock and people, is an unintended result of their godlet's predation upon the surrounding lands," said Fitz. "Pralqornrah is one of the class of cross-dimensional parasites that is most dangerous. Unchecked, in time it will suck the vital essence out of all the land beyond its immediate demesne. The deserts of Balkash are the work of a similar being, over six millennia. This one has only been embedded here for two hundred years—you have seen the results beyond this valley."

"Six millennia is a long time," said Hereward, taking yet another gulp. The wine was strong as well as sweet, and he felt the need of it. "A desert might arise in that time without the interference of the gods."

"It is not just the fields and the river that Pralqornrah feeds upon," said Fitz. "The people outside this valley suffer too. Babes unborn, strong men and women declining before their prime . . . this godlet slowly sucks the essence from all life."

"They could leave," said Hereward. The wine was making him feel both sleepy and mulish. "I expect many have already left to seek better lands. The rest could be resettled, the lands left uninhabited to feed the godlet. Shûme could continue as an oasis. What if another desert grows around it? They occur in nature, do they not?"

"I do not think you fully comprehend the matter," said Fitz. "Pralqornrah is a most comprehensive feeder. Its energistic threads will spread farther and faster the longer it exists here, and it in turn will grow more powerful and much more difficult to remove. A few millennia hence, it might be too strong to combat."

"I am only talking," said Hereward, not without some bitterness. "You need not waste your words to bend my reason. I do not even need to understand anything beyond the salient fact: this godlet is on the list."

"Yes," said Mister Fitz. "It is on the list."

Hereward bent his head for a long, silent moment. Then he pushed his chair back and reached across for his saber. Drawing it, he placed the blade across his knees. Mister Fitz handed him a whetstone and a small flask of light, golden oil. The knight oiled the stone and began to hone the saber's blade. A repetitive rasp was the only sound in the room for many minutes, till he finally put the stone aside and wiped the blade clean with a soft piece of deerskin.

"When?"

"Fourteen minutes past the midnight hour is optimum," replied Mister Fitz. "Presuming I have calculated its intrusion density correctly."

"It is manifest in the temple?"

Fitz nodded.

"Where is the temple, for that matter? Only the citadel stands out above the roofs of the city."

"It is largely underground," said Mister Fitz. "I have found a side entrance, which should not prove difficult. At some point beyond that there is some form of arcane barrier—I have not been able to ascertain its exact nature, but I hope to unpick it without trouble."

"Is the side entrance guarded? And the interior?"

"Both," said Fitz. Something about his tone made Hereward fix the puppet with a inquiring look.

"The side door has two guards," continued Fitz. "The interior watch is of ten or eleven . . . led by the Lieutenant Jessaye you met earlier."

Hereward stood up, the saber loose in his hand, and turned away from Fitz.

"Perhaps we shall not need to fight her . . . or her fellows."

Fitz did not answer, which was answer enough.

The side door to the temple was unmarked and appeared no different than the other simple wooden doors that lined the empty street, most of them adorned with signs marking them as the shops of various tradesmen, with smoke-grimed night lamps burning dimly above the sign. The door Fitz indicated was painted a pale violet and had neither sign nor lamp.

"Time to don the brassards and make the declaration," said the puppet. He looked up and down the street, making sure that all was quiet, before handing Hereward a broad silk armband five fingers wide. It was embroidered with sorcerous thread that shed only a little less light than the smoke-grimed lantern above the neighboring shop door. The symbol the threads wove was one that had once been familiar the world over but was now unlikely to be recognized by anyone save an historian . . . or a god.

Hereward slipped the brassard over his left glove and up his thick coat sleeve, spreading it out above the elbow. The suit of white and yellow was once again packed, and for this expedition the knight had chosen to augment his helmet and buff coat with a dented but still eminently serviceable back- and breastplate, the steel blackened by tannic acid to a dark grey. He had already primed, loaded and spanned his two wheel-lock pistols, which were thrust through his belt; his saber was sheathed at his side; and a lozenge-sectioned, armor-punching bodkin was in his left boot.

Mister Fitz wore his sewing desk upon his back, like a wooden backpack. He had already been through its numerous small drawers and containers and selected particular items that were now tucked into the inside pockets of his coat, ready for immediate use.

"I wonder why we bother with this mummery," grumbled Hereward. But he stood at attention as Fitz put on his own brassard, and the knight carefully repeated the short phrase uttered by his companion. Though both had recited it many times, and it was clear as bright type in their minds, they spoke carefully and with great concentration, in sharp contrast to Hereward's remark about mummery.

"In the name of the Council of the Treaty for the Safety of the World, acting under the authority granted by the Three Empires, the Seven Kingdoms, the Palatine Regency, the Jessar Republic and the Forty Lesser Realms, we declare ourselves agents of the Council. We identify the godlet manifested in this city of Shûme as Pralqornrah-Tanish-Kvaxixob, a listed entity under the Treaty. Consequently, the said godlet and all those who assist it are deemed to be enemies of the World and the Council authorizes us to pursue any and all actions necessary to banish, repel or exterminate the said godlet."

Neither felt it necessary to change this ancient text to reflect the fact that only one of the three empires was still extant in any fashion; that the seven kingdoms were now twenty or more small states; the Palatine Regency was a political fiction, its once broad lands under two fathoms of water; the Jessar Republic was now neither Jessar in ethnicity nor a republic; and perhaps only a handful of the Forty Lesser Realms resembled their antecedent polities in any respect. But for all that the states that had made it were vanished or diminished, the Treaty for the Safety of the World was still held to be in operation, if only by the Council that administered and enforced it.

"Are you ready?" asked Fitz.

Hereward drew his saber and moved into position to the left of the door. Mister Fitz reached into his coat and drew out an esoteric needle. Hereward knew better than to try to look at the needle directly, but in the reflection of his blade, he could see a four-inch line of something intensely violet writhe in Fitz's hand. Even the reflection made him feel as if he might at any moment be unstitched from the world, so he angled the blade away.

At that moment, Fitz touched the door with the needle and made three short plucking motions. On the last motion, without any noise or fuss, the door wasn't there anymore. There was only a wood-paneled corridor leading down into the ground and two very surprised temple guards, who were still leaning on their halberds.

Before Hereward could even begin to move, Fitz's hand twitched across and up several times. The lanterns on their brass stands every six feet along the corridor flickered and flared violet for a fraction of a second. Hereward blinked, and the guards were gone, as were the closest three lanterns and their stands.

Only a single drop of molten brass, no bigger than a tear, remained. It sizzled on the floor for a second, then all was quiet.

The puppet stalked forward, cupping his left hand over the needle in his right, obscuring its troublesome sight behind his fingers. Hereward followed close behind, alert for any enemy that might be resistant to Fitz's sorcery.

The corridor was a hundred yards long by Hereward's estimation, and slanted sharply down, making him think about having to fight back up it, which would be no easy task, made more difficult as the floor and walls were damp, drops of water oozing out between the floorboards and dripping from the seams of the wall paneling. There was cold, wet stone behind the timber, Hereward knew. He could feel the cold air rippling off it, a chill that no amount of fine timber could cloak.

The corridor ended at what appeared from a distance to be a solid wall, but closer to was merely the dark back of a heavy tapestry. Fitz edged silently around it, had a look, and returned to beckon Hereward in.

There was a large antechamber or waiting room beyond, sparsely furnished with a slim desk and several well-upholstered armchairs. The desk and chairs each had six legs, the extra limbs arranged closely at the back, a fashion Hereward supposed was some homage to the godlet's physical manifestation. The walls were hung with several tapestries depicting the city at various stages in its history.

Given the depth underground and the proximity of the lake, great efforts must have been made to waterproof and beautify the walls, floor and ceiling, but there was still an army of little dots of mold advancing from every corner, blackening the white plaster and tarnishing the gilded cornices and decorations.

Apart from the tapestry-covered exit, there were three doors. Two were of a usual size, though they were elaborately carved with obscure symbols and had brass, or perhaps even gold, handles. The one on the wall opposite the tapestry corridor was entirely different: it was a single ten-foot-by-six-foot slab of ancient marble veined with red lead, and it would have been better situated sitting on top of a significant memorial or some potentate's coffin.

Mister Fitz went to each of the carved doors, his blue tongue flickering in and out, sampling the air.

"No one close," he reported, before approaching the marble slab.

He actually licked the gap between the stone and the floor, then sat for a few moments to think about what he had tasted.

Hereward kept clear, checking the other doors to see if they could be locked. Disappointed in that aim as they had neither bar nor keyhole, he sheathed his saber and carefully and quietly picked up a desk to push against the left door and several chairs to pile against the right. They wouldn't hold, but they would give some warning of attempted ingress.

Fitz chuckled as Hereward finished his work, an unexpected noise that made the knight shiver, drop his hand to the hilt of his saber, and quickly look around to see what had made the puppet laugh. Fitz was not easily amused, and often not by anything Hereward would consider funny.

"There is a sorcerous barrier," said Fitz. "It is immensely strong but has not perhaps been as well thought-out as it might have been. Fortuitously, I do not even need to unpick it."

The puppet reached up with his left hand and pushed the marble slab. It slid back silently, revealing another corridor, this one of more honest bare, weeping stone, rapidly turning into rough-hewn steps only a little way along.

"I'm afraid you cannot follow, Hereward," said Fitz. "The barrier is conditional, and you do not meet its requirements. It would forcibly—and perhaps harmfully—repel you if you tried to step over the lintel of this door. But I would ask you to stay here in any case, to secure our line of retreat. I should only be a short time if all goes well. You will, of course, know if all does not go well, and must save yourself as best you can. I have impressed the ostlers to rise at your command and load our gear, as I have impressed instructions into the dull minds of the battlemounts—"

"Enough, Fitz! I shall not leave without you."

"Hereward, you know that in the event of my—"

"Fitz. The quicker it were done—"

"Indeed. Be careful, child."

"Fitz!"

But the puppet had gone almost before that exasperated single word was out of Hereward's mouth.

It quickly grew cold with the passage below open. Chill, wet gusts of wind blew up and followed the knight around the room, no matter where he stood. After a few minutes trying to find a spot where he could avoid the cold breeze, Hereward took to pacing by the doors as quietly as he could. Every dozen steps or so he stopped to listen, either for Fitz's return or the sound of approaching guards.

In the event, he was midpace when he heard something. The sharp beat of hobnailed boots in step, approaching the left-hand door.

Hereward drew his two pistols and moved closer to the door. The handle rattled, the door began to move and encountered the desk he had pushed there. There was an exclamation and several voices spoke all at once. A heavier shove came immediately, toppling the desk as the door came partially open.

Hereward took a pace to the left and fired through the gap. The wheel locks whirred, sparks flew, then there were two deep, simultaneous booms, the resultant echoes flattening down the screams and shouts in the corridor beyond the door, just as the conjoining clouds of blue-white smoke obscured Hereward from the guards, who were already clambering over their wounded or slain companions.

The knight thrust his pistols back through his belt and drew his saber, to make an immediate sweeping cut at the neck of a guard who charged blindly through the smoke, his halberd thrust out in front like a blind man's cane. Man and halberd clattered to the floor. Hereward ducked under a halberd swing and slashed the next guard behind the knees, at the same time picking up one edge of the desk and flipping it upright in the path of the next two guards. They tripped over it, and Hereward stabbed them both in the back of the neck as their helmets fell forward, left-right, three inches of saber point in and out in an instant.

A blade skidded off Hereward's cuirass and would have scored his thigh but for a quick twist away. He parried the next thrust, rolled his wrist and slashed his attacker across the stomach, following it up with a kick as the guard reeled back, sword slack in his hand.

No attack—or any movement save for dulled writhing on the ground—followed. Hereward stepped back and surveyed the situation. Two guards were dead or dying just beyond the door. One was still to his left. Three lay around the desk. Another was hunched over by the wall, his hands pressed uselessly against the gaping wound in his gut, as he moaned the god's name over and over.

None of the guards was Jessaye, but the sound of the pistol shots at the least would undoubtedly bring more defenders of the temple.

"Seven," said Hereward. "Of a possible twelve."

He laid his saber across a chair and reloaded his pistols, taking powder cartridges and shot from the pocket of his coat and a ramrod from under the barrel of one gun. Loaded, he wound their wheel-lock mechanisms with a small spanner that hung from a braided-leather loop on his left wrist.

Just as he replaced the pistols in his belt, the ground trembled beneath his feet, and an even colder wind came howling out of the sunken corridor, accompanied by a cloying but not unpleasant odor of exotic spices that also briefly made Hereward see strange bands of color move through the air, the visions fading as the scent also passed.

Tremors, scent and strange visions were all signs that Fitz had joined battle with Pralqornrah-Tanish-Kvaxixob below. There could well be other portents to come, stranger and more unpleasant to experience.

"Be quick, Fitz," muttered Hereward, his attention momentarily focused on the downwards passage.

Even so, he caught the soft footfall of someone sneaking in, boots left behind in the passage. He turned, pistols in hand, as Jessaye stepped around the half-open door. Two guards came behind her, their own pistols raised.

Before they could aim, Hereward fired and, as the smoke and noise filled the room, threw the empty pistols at the trio, took up his saber and jumped aside.

Jessaye's sword leapt into the space where he'd been. Hereward landed, turned and parried several frenzied stabs at his face, the swift movement of their blades sending the gun smoke eddying in wild roils and coils. Jessaye pushed him back almost to the other door. There, Hereward picked up a chair and used it to fend off several blows, at the same time beginning to make small, fast cuts at Jessaye's sword arm.

Jessaye's frenzied assault slackened as Hereward cut her badly on the shoulder near her neck, then immediately after that on the upper arm, across the wound he'd given her in the duel. She cried out in pain and rage and stepped back, her right arm useless, her sword point trailing on the floor.

Instead of pressing his attack, the knight took a moment to take stock of his situation.

The two pistol-bearing guards were dead or as good as, making the tally nine. That meant there should only be two more, in addition to Jessaye, and those two were not immediately in evidence.

"You may withdraw, if you wish," said Hereward, his voice strangely loud and dull at the same time, a consequence of shooting in enclosed spaces. "I do not wish to kill you, and you cannot hold your sword."

Jessaye transferred her sword to her left hand and took a shuddering breath.

"I fight equally well with my left hand," she said, assuming the guard position as best she could, though her right arm hung at her side, and blood dripped from her fingers to the floor.

She thrust immediately, perhaps hoping for surprise. Hereward ferociously beat her blade down, then stamped on it, forcing it from her grasp. He then raised the point of his saber to her throat.

"No you don't," he said. "Very few people do. Go, while you still live."

"I cannot," whispered Jessaye. She shut her eyes. "I have failed in my duty. I shall die with my comrades. Strike quickly."

Hereward raised his elbow and prepared to push the blade through the so-giving flesh, as he had done so many times before. But he did not, instead he lowered his saber and backed away around the wall.

"Quickly, I beg you," said Jessaye. She was shivering, the blood flowing faster down her arm.

"I cannot," muttered Hereward. "Or rather I do not wish to. I have killed enough today."

Jessaye opened her eyes and slowly turned to him, her face paper white, the scar no brighter than the petal of a pink rose. For the first time, she saw that the stone door was open, and she gasped and looked wildly around at the bodies that littered the floor.

"The priestess came forth? You have slain her?"

"No," said Hereward. He continued to watch Jessaye and listen for others, as he bent and picked up his pistols. They were a present from his mother, and he had not lost them yet. "My companion has gone within."

"But that . . . that is not possible! The barrier—"

"Mister Fitz knew of the barrier," said Hereward wearily. He was beginning to feel the aftereffects of violent combat, and strongly desired to be away from the visible signs of it littered around him. "He crossed it without difficulty."

"But only the priestess can pass," said Jessaye wildly. She was shaking more than just shivering now, as shock set in, though she still stood upright. "A woman with child! No one and nothing else! It cannot be . . ."

Her eyes rolled back in her head, she twisted sideways and fell to the floor. Hereward watched her lie there for a few seconds while he attempted to regain the cold temper in which he fought, but it would not return. He hesitated, then wiped his saber clean, sheathed it, then despite all better judgment, bent over Jessaye.

She whispered something and again, and he caught the god's name, "Tanesh" and with it a sudden onslaught of cinnamon and cloves and ginger on his nose. He blinked, and in that blink, she turned and struck at him with a small dagger that had been concealed in her sleeve. Hereward had expected something, but not the god's assistance, for the dagger was in her right hand, which he'd thought useless. He grabbed her wrist but could only slow rather than stop the blow. Jessaye struck true, the dagger entering the armhole of the cuirass, to bite deep into his chest.

Hereward left the dagger there and merely pushed Jessaye back. The smell of spices faded, and her arm was limp once more. She did not resist, but lay there quite still, only her eyes moving as she watched Hereward sit down next to her. He sighed heavily, a few flecks of blood already spraying out with his breath, evidence that her dagger was lodged in his lung though he already knew that from the pain that impaled him with every breath.

"There is no treasure below," said Jessaye quietly. "Only the godlet, and his priestess."

"We did not come for treasure," said Hereward. He spat blood on the floor. "Indeed, I had thought we would winter here, in good employment. But your god is proscribed, and so . . ."

"Proscribed? I don't . . . who . . ."

"By the Council of the Treaty for the Safety of the World," said Hereward. "Not that anyone remembers that name. If we are remembered it is from the stories that tell of . . . god-slayers."

"I know the stories," whispered Jessaye. "And not just stories . . . we were taught to beware the god-slayers. But they are always women, barren women, with witch-scars on their faces. Not a man and a puppet. That is why the barrier . . . the barrier stops all but gravid women . . ."

Hereward paused to wipe a froth of blood from his mouth before he could answer.

"Fitz has been my companion since I was three years old. He was called Mistress Fitz then, as my nurse-bodyguard. When I turned ten, I wanted a male companion, and so I began to call him Mister Fitz. But whether called Mistress or Master, I believe Fitz is nurturing an offshoot of his spiritual essence in some form of pouch upon his person. In time he will make a body for it to inhabit. The process takes several hundred years."

"But you . . ."

Jessaye's whisper was almost too quiet to hear.

"I am a mistake . . . the witches of Har are not barren, that is just a useful tale. But they do only bear daughters . . . save the once. I am the only son of a witch born these thousand years. My mother is one of the Mysterious Three who rule the witches, last remnant of the Council. Fitz was made by that Council, long ago, as a weapon made to fight malignant gods. The more recent unwanted child became a weapon too, puppet and boy flung out to do our duty in the world. A duty that has carried me here . . . to my great regret."

No answer came to this bubbling, blood-infused speech. Hereward looked across at Jessaye and saw that her chest no longer rose and fell, and that there was a dark puddle beneath her that was still spreading, a tide of blood advancing toward him.

He touched the hilt of the dagger in his side, and coughed, and the pain of both things was almost too much to bear; but he only screamed a little, and made it worse by standing up and staggering to the wall to place his back against it. There were still two guards somewhere, and Fitz was surprisingly vulnerable if he was surprised. Or he might be wounded too, from the struggle with the god.

Minutes or perhaps a longer time passed, and Hereward's mind wandered and, in wandering, left his body too long. It slid down the wall to the ground and his blood began to mingle with that of Jessaye, and the others who lay on the floor of a god's ante-chamber turned slaughterhouse.

Then there was pain again, and Hereward's mind jolted back

into his body, in time to make his mouth whimper and his eyes blink at a light that was a color he didn't know, and there was Mister Fitz leaning over him and the dagger wasn't in his side anymore and there was no bloody froth upon his lips. There was still pain. Constant, piercing pain, coming in waves and never subsiding. It stayed with him, uppermost in his thoughts, even as he became dimly aware that he was upright and walking, his legs moving under a direction not his own.

Except that very soon he was lying down again, and Fitz was cross.

"You have to get back up, Hereward."

"I'm tired, Fitzie . . . can't I rest for a little longer?"

"No. Get up."

"Are we going home?"

"No, Hereward. You know we can't go home. We must go onward."

"Onward? Where?"

"Never mind now. Keep walking. Do you see our mounts?"

"Yes . . . but we will never . . . never make it out the gate . . ."

"We will, Hereward . . . leave it to me. Here, I will help you up. Are you steady enough?"

"I will . . . stay on. Fitz . . ."

"Yes, Hereward."

"Don't . . . don't kill them all."

If Fitz answered, Hereward didn't hear, as he faded out of the world for a few seconds. When the world nauseatingly shivered back into sight and hearing, the puppet was nowhere in sight and the two battlemounts were already loping toward the gate, though the leading steed had no rider.

They did not pause at the wall. Though it was past midnight, the gate was open, and the guards who might have barred the way were nowhere to be seen, though there were strange splashes of color upon the earth where they might have stood. There were no guards beyond the gate, on the earthwork bastion either, the only sign of their prior existence a half-melted belt buckle still red with heat.

To Hereward's dim eyes, the city's defenses might as well be deserted, and nothing prevented the battlemounts continuing to lope, out into the warm autumn night.

The leading battlemount finally slowed and stopped a mile

beyond the town, at the corner of a lemon grove, its hundreds of trees so laden with yellow fruit they scented the air with a sharp, clean tang that helped bring Hereward closer to full consciousness. Even so, he lacked the strength to shorten the chain of his own mount, but it stopped by its companion without urging.

Fitz swung down from the outlying branch of a lemon tree, onto his saddle, without spilling any of the fruit piled high in his upturned hat.

"We will ride on in a moment. But when we can, I shall make a lemon salve and a soothing drink."

Hereward nodded, finding himself unable to speak. Despite Fitz's repairing sorceries, the wound in his side was still very painful, and he was weak from loss of blood, but neither thing choked his voice. He was made quiet by a cold melancholy that held him tight, coupled with a feeling of terrible loss, the loss of some future, never-to-be happiness that had gone forever.

"I suppose we must head for Fort Yarz," mused Fitz. "It is the closest likely place for employment. There is always some trouble there, though I believe the Gebrak tribes have been largely quiet this past year."

Hereward tried to speak again, and at last found a croak that had some resemblance to a voice.

"No. I am tired of war. Find us somewhere peaceful, where I can rest."

Fitz hopped across to perch on the neck of Hereward's mount and faced the knight, his blue eyes brighter than the moonlight.

"I will try, Hereward. But as you ruminated earlier, the world is as it is, and we are what we were made to be. Even should we find somewhere that seems at peace, I suspect it will not stay so, should we remain. Remember Jeminero."

"Aye." Hereward sighed. He straightened up just a little and took up the chains, as Fitz jumped to his own saddle. "I remember."

"Fort Yarz?" asked Fitz.

Hereward nodded, and slapped the chain, urging his battle-mount forward. As it stretched into its stride, the lemons began to fall from the trees in the orchard, playing the soft drumbeat of a funerary march, the first sign of the passing from the world of the god of Shûme.

Creation: The Launch!

Laura Resnick

Don't call me Ishmael.

Yes, technically, it's my name. Believe me, sweetie, I know. And I assure you, I have not suffered in silence. It is so not ME.

Then again, is "Ishmael" a name that's right for anyone? I mean, okay, maybe for a metro-sexual pop star with fabulous lashes and no last name. Or possibly someone in the whaling industry (and don't look at me like that, I didn't even want whales in Creation). But, honey, for a creative consultant, it is a tough name to adapt to.

(Oh, can I say "adapt" here? I hear there's been some controversy about adaptation since we launched Creation.)

But, all right, sure, I know—it could have been worse. At least I didn't get stuck with a name like Laban, Esau, Hagar, Methuselah, Nehemiah, or Walter. Those poor schmucks. (And people wonder why we added therapists to Creation after we saw what God had wrought.)

In fact, this whole naming thing was high on my list of hot targets for a major revamp. Such an obvious flaw in the grand plan. But then we got so close to the launch, and what with one thing and another, I barely had time to put the finishing touches on the Big Bang before the Lord God was all, like, "Hey, I'm separating the darkness from the light, and I'm doing it NOW." I'm telling you, He has the patience of a two-year-old child—and, yep, they were indeed made in His image, right down to the temperament.

Well, maybe you know how insane a launch is! I mean, gaga-smack-a-rooney-cuckoo with lunacy on top, honey. So a lot gets overlooked in the heat of the moment—not to mention the heat of cosmic matter spinning madly through space in all different directions at a gazillion miles per second. Plus, to be totally up-fro, bro, the Big Guy is not that easy to work with. I don't think I'm letting the feline out of the bag when I say he can be unbelievably touchy. (You've read Genesis, right?) In fact, when our first effort at Creation totally flopped while we were still out of town and on the road with our early material... Well, for a while, I honestly feared the Master of the Universe would commit suicide by swallowing hot primordial ooze.

Which was a total overreaction, of course. (Deities. Always so high-strung.) As I kept telling Yahweh, it was only natural that He would need a few dry runs before we had a success on our hands. No one had done Creation before, we were trying for something completely new and original! You can't expect to pull off the most ambitious launch in Eternity without first learning from a few failures.

For one thing, the Lord God hates loud noises, so we tried a Big Sigh, a Big Hum, a Soft Bang, and even a Small Bang before I finally convinced Him that we had to go full throttle, no holding back. "God, sweetie, pumpkin," I said, "Creation needs to commence with a big bang! With the Big Bang! With the biggest cosmic explosion of light and matter that ever was, or ever will be!" This is the kind of input where I really earn my salary. Clients are so held back by their own limitations.

Well, once God agreed to go with the Big Bang, He got a little more confidence in my guidance. So, fortunately, it didn't take me long to nix the whole "polka-dotted universe" plan, along with some of His other less-inspired ideas. (Frankly, it's thanks to me that you're not reading this with your belly button and eating your own hair for sustenance.) And by the time we got down to the fine details of planetary-planning, I could tell we were onto something really special. I loved the idea of a place that had land, sea, rivers, people, plants, animals, plumbing, and ethnic food! And the whole idea of a planet tilting on its axis to create seasons—I mean, isn't that just darling?

"God," I said, "this time, we're really going to launch. And this is going to be your best work ever! Your chef d'oeuvre. Your pièce de résistance."

And the Lord God said, "I like those nasal-sounding phrases you're using, Ishmael. We should come up with a language that sounds just like that."

"God, please don't call me Ishmael."

"But it's your name. The name that I gave you."

"We've talked about this before, Lord. I'd rather You call me Rafe. Or perhaps Thad. Something that won't sound so out of place on the Upper West Side."

"You mean the Upper North Side," God corrected.

"I don't think we should call it that," I said. "Trust me on this."

Well, now that we obviously had a solid Creation strategy and some exciting concepts to work with, God got very competitive. He started worrying that some other omnipotent being might beat us to the punch, so He was very eager to launch right away. I really should have put the brakes on, we weren't at all ready yet. But you try saying "no" to the Lord God Almighty and see what happens. (I'll tell you what happens. Supernovas happen.)

So, naturally, once we launched, it was just one problem after another. We spent eons running around putting out the fires.

For example, there was that whole problem with the firmament, which we discovered too late can look exactly like New Jersey when viewed in the wrong light. In fact, certain parts of the firmament are New Jersey. No one saw this coming; if we had, naturally, we'd have postponed the launch.

And since seven is such an asymmetrical number of continents, I begged Yahweh to wait until we could design a better look for them. I mean, that whole Asia thing is so over the top. It's simply massive. We needed to transfer some of it to Europe to create a sense of balance. And Japan just hangs out there, as if we'd left a fifth leg on a mammal! Plus, sweetie, how many deserts does the world really need, for goodness sake? And Mexico across the Gulf from Florida? Totally lopsided! No sense of proportion at all.

"Let's organize this," I said to the Lord God, "let's make a statement with our continents. Let's not just have random land-masses flopping all over the planet."

But no. What do I know? I am only the creative consultant on the biggest project in the history of the Universe. So we launched Creation right away. With the Middle East still plopped haphazardly between three continents like an uninvited guest, and Antarctica stuck down at the South Pole like planetary genitalia. (I know, I know. Believe me, I tried to make Him see reason. But I am just a servant of God Almighty—and you know what clients are like.)

So we wound up having to relocate a ton of creatures after they saw the landscape that God intended to give to them, i.e. New Jersey. It made the exodus from Egypt look like a cakewalk by comparison, let me tell you. For a few millennia there, I was afraid the launch would collapse completely, and we'd have to start all over. Since then, of course, the shifting of tectonic plates and subsequent earthquakes have continued proving my point (we so needed a better layout for the landmasses) but you don't say "I told you so" to Jehovah. You just don't.

So, anyhow, we barely got past the firmament crisis, and God started naming things. He was off and running! "This is an arma-dillo, that's a slug, this is an avocado, over there is a ficus." He really had no gift at all for it. I'd realized ever since He named me Ishmael, shortly after creating me to help launch His grand plan, that we needed a better system. But then, suddenly, it was too late, we'd launched, and there was the Creator, naming every-thing in sight: "We'll call this part a penis, and that a vagina, and I think we should call this characteristic 'perspicacity.'" It was a disaster.

I was meanwhile up to my supernovas in PR problems after someone on my staff leaked the bit about Eve being taken from Adam's rib. I blame myself. It was Yahweh's idea—I mean, hon-estly, most of Creation was His idea, I just guided the packaging, He really deserves a lot of credit for the Universe—but I should have seen the inevitable problems before we were blindsided by them: If Man was created in the image of Yahweh, but Woman was created from Man's rib, well, you're obviously going to have considerable problems perpetuating the species. Or even holding a decent conversation.

The critics simply shredded us for this. The Lord God was

devastated by some of those early reviews. And while I didn't disagree in principle with the comments, I thought their tone was way harsh.

Look, it was an honest mistake. Also an isolated one. We didn't have this problem with any other species. But with His favorite creation (i.e. the one based on himself, thankyouverymuch), Yahweh got a little carried away. (He called it lyrical. I call it showing off.) Ergo the whole "I made your mate from your rib" stunt. Which was, even He has admitted since then, rather childish. And certainly shortsighted. Picture this: "Hello, I'm Adam. And this is my wife, Eve, who happens to be approximately seven inches long and has no orifices."

This is why prelaunch planning is so important. Mistakes like this could have been avoided, thus sparing a certain deity the need to work so much overtime, under considerable pressure from the media, to completely redo one of Creation's most high-profile species.

So, okay, God saw His mistake, and He went back and re-created Adam and Eve equally—thus leading to some confusing rewrites in Genesis that have still not been straightened out. (But don't even get me started on that.)

Then the next thing you know, the Lord of Hosts said to me, "I don't like their design, Ishmael."

"Don't call me Ishmael."

"It's clumsy and inelegant. And have you noticed that they're not very bright? Especially Adam."

"Nor is Adam's character all that one might desire," added Lucifer, joining us without warning.

God's thoughtful frown became suddenly thunderous. "I told you to go away!"

Lucifer smirked as he mimicked Adam: "'The apple? What apple?'"

I advised, "Leave it alone, Lu," while God smoldered.

But Lucifer never knew when to quit. Still mimicking Adam, he whined, "'The woman tempted me.'"

"I thought snakes were a bad idea from the start," I muttered, remembering who had tempted Eve. "I hate snakes."

"They're not so bad," Lucifer said, "But I really don't care for the name. Who thought up that one, I wonder?"

And God cast Lucifer out of heaven. Just like that. "Hah!

Maybe now," the Lord God said, "he'll stop getting into so much trouble."

(Oh, yes, that certainly made the next few millennia trouble-free. Gooooood thinking.)

"So, you were saying, Lord?" I prodded. "Something about Adam and Eve?"

"I can hardly tell them apart from the apes," God complained.

"But that was the plan," I reminded him. "And I think we wound up with a nice continuity to the whole primate look, right across the board."

"I'm not satisfied," God said.

Clients, I thought.

"Why not, Lord?"

"Adam and Eve seem somehow like eight-track tapes or the first Star Trek movie," God mused, "like we just haven't quite found our feet yet."

"Feet were an excellent idea, Lord," I said encouragingly. "I'm so glad You added them right before the launch. I mean, imagine if everything in Creation had been like snakes. No feet." I shuddered. "Ugh!"

And, to be clear, feet were totally the Big Guy's idea. What can I say? I work only with the best.

"Mankind just seems like . . ." God shrugged restlessly. "I don't know. I just feel that they'll always be dismissed as My early work, you know? I should have done better."

"But we—"

"In fact," God said, still pondering His Creation, "many of these creatures don't look quite right to me. Perhaps . . ."

"Yes, Lord?"

"Perhaps you were right, Ishmael."

"I'd prefer 'Rafe,' Lord. Or 'Thad.'"

"Perhaps we launched Creation before it was really ready."

"Oh. Gee. Y'think?" I said.

"What is that tone in your voice?" God demanded.

"It's something I just invented."

"Hmm. Interesting. Shall we call it 'granola'?" God suggested.

"I was thinking 'sarcasm,'" I said.

"'Sarcasm'? Really?" God looked dubious. "Well, since you invented it, I grant you the privilege of naming it. But are you sure that's what you want to call it?"

"If I may return to the point, Lord, I cannot deny that we launched Creation a trifle too soon, but—"

"So I wonder if we should go back to the drawing board?" Yahweh mused. "Try for something better."

"You mean . . . scrap Creation and start all over again?" I felt rather faint. We'd used up everything in the Big Bang. "I'm not sure we have enough cosmic matter left over to do that."

"Couldn't we just reuse all the same matter and energy over again?"

"Revert the entire cosmos to its original inchoate form?" I said in horror.

"Would that be a problem?" the Lord God asked.

I thought of the eons of hard work and detailed planning that I had put into the Big Bang, and I knew I couldn't possibly do it all over again. At least, not without first taking a very long vacation in the sort of luxury resort that we'd neglected to Create yet. God just had no idea what that project had taken out of me. I'd rather give up my feet than destroy Creation and redo the whole job from scratch. Even if, as I was forced to agree, the cosmos would probably benefit from better planning on the next go-round.

So I did the only thing that a being in my position could do: I soothed my client. "Yahweh, sweetie," I said. "These are natural second thoughts that any omnipotent Creator is bound to have after launching such a demanding and ambitious project. Okay, so there are a few design flaws we need to work out. But, come on, Big Guy, that was to be expected! How many absolutely perfect Universes can You name, after all?"

"Well . . ."

"God, I promise You, we can make the little fixes without reorganizing the whole cosmos—again."

God bit His mighty lower lip. "So you . . . you think Creation is pretty good? I mean, you really like My work?"

"Yahweh! Babydoll! I think Creation is brilliant!"

"You're not just saying that?"

The creative ego is so fragile.

"God, I think Creation is going to run forever."

"Yeah?"

"Yeah," I said warmly. "So, buck up, Lord! No more nonsense about smooshing everything back into a handful of protoreactive microcosmic antimatter. Let's not throw out the baby with the bathwater!"

The Lord Almighty frowned. "What's bathwater?"

"It's something we should definitely Create before the planet gets any more crowded."

"Ah!" God said. "One of those little fixes you mentioned."

"Exactly," I said, relieved I'd got Him past the whole let's-scrap-Creation-and-start-all-over crisis.

"But how are we going to fix Mankind?" God asked. "And some of these other creatures? And I'm not so crazy about some of the plants, either."

"What in particular—?"

"Hey, I know!" God said. "Maybe we could make Mankind look more like ferns, and ferns look more like pachyderms, and pachyderms look more like rocks."

I could see that the Maker of All Things was just running on fumes now and about to make some bad decisions on impulse. That kind of snap-judgment Creating had given us cockroaches and quicksand. When would He learn the value of planning?

So, heading off trouble before it could get really cosmic again, I said, "Let's not do anything hasty, Lord. We've got all Eternity, after all."

"Yes, but I . . . I . . ." God got distracted and peered off into the distance.

"Is something wrong, Lord?"

"Hmmm. What are Adam and Eve doing? How odd!"

"Are they gathering food? Food was, by the way, a truly inspired notion, God. A first-rate improvisation!" Okay, so He's no planner, but I never said He didn't have talent by the boatload.

"No, they're not gathering food . . ."

"Building a shelter?" I stood on tiptoe, trying to see.

"No . . ."

I saw some movement in the distance, squinted, and recognized Adam and Eve. "Why, Lord, I think they're . . ."

"They're . . . Yes, Ishmael, you're right. They're procreating."

"Interesting," I said. "Although, perhaps . . . Do you think it looks a little . . ."

"Ungainly?" God said. "Uncomfortable?"

"Is that how they're supposed to look?" I asked.

"Well, it's in accordance with the design."

"Hmmm."

"But it's a bit . . . It doesn't really . . . There's no . . ."

"Yes, God, I see Your point."

"And Eve looks positively bored," the Lord God noted.

"Which can't bode well for procreation as a going concern."

"We need to work on this," God said decisively.

"Agreed, Lord," I said. "But, please, I beg You, let's do it intelligently. No going off half-cocked without a good design plan in place."

"Oh, don't be such a wet blanket, Ishmael. Er, Rafe. Thad."

I blinked away a sudden tear, touched by God's backing down on the name thing. "Oh, I guess You're right, Lord God Almighty. It's Your Creation, after all. If You want to play around with it, have a little fun, where's the harm?"

"Just a few experiments," God assured me with a benevolent smile. "Some trial runs on a few modifications I have in mind."

"As You wish, Lord," I said, giving in.

I can't deny anything to my biggest client.

That was many eons ago, and the Big Guy is still tinkering, always expanding and improving on His original material. And it's still the one, the only, the original Creation! The Lord God's work is always maturing and evolving, He doesn't rest on His laurels.

(Oh, can I say "evolving" here? I hear there's been some controversy about evolution since we launched Creation.)

Midnight at the Quantum Cafe

K.D. Wentworth

The torrid summer air tasted of industrial sludge as I stood ankle-deep in the rubble at the edge of the street and gazed into the darkness. A car rolled by, its occupants skittish and silent, then I caught the acrid stench of smoke. Somewhere, not too far away, Chicago was burning again.

My heart lifted. When this reality was at its nastiest, I always felt there was a slight edge in my favor. Foolish, I know. With each roll of the universe's proverbial dice, the probability of any particular outcome remains the same, but a man grasps at whatever straw glimmers before him, and I thought if I went to the cafe often enough, I might find another Marissa, one just different enough from the one who left to still love me.

I hurried down into the nearest station, took the next train, its gang-marks worked in fanciful chartreuse, and got off two stops to the south where the air tasted of ketones and shimmered like a veil even a few feet away. I stepped out of the car, eyes stinging, shoved my hands in my pockets to create the illusion I was carrying, and waded through discarded paper wrappers and beer bottles up the stairs to the street.

No use hurrying, I tried to persuade myself as I turned my face east. Either it would be there, or it wouldn't. No variable I could introduce would make any difference.

I rounded the corner and squinted down the block as I had so many times before. The haze refracted the glow of each street lamp into a nimbus of light so that I seemed to be standing inside a nebula and could make nothing out from more than ten feet away. Drops condensed on my cheeks. Tiny bursts of electricity tingled against my skin. The air trembled as though afraid.

Transition, I thought. The cafe was either coming or going.

From behind, a pair of brutish *Otts* shouldered me into the bricks as they passed. Their hide gleamed blue in the uncertain light; their eyes were black pits. Crimson jewels had been implanted into their elongated skulls, more scintillating than any mere ruby. They snarled as they passed, baring jagged yellow fangs, but did not strike. I had not been so fortunate on other nights. I rubbed a scar on my ribs through my shirt and slowed to let them get well ahead.

Otts hail from some other unimaginable Earth where evolution evidently took a hellish turn, or perhaps alien invasion repopulated the planet at some point. Either way, they disdain humans, whatever the variety. I could only hope enough of them hadn't gotten through to crowd the rest of us out tonight.

It always seems to be midnight at the cafe. Why it doesn't manifest anywhere during the day has been the subject of much discussion amongst the regular patrons, but Jaeko, the bartender, never volunteers any answers. Dressed in a worn leather jacket, he stumps back and forth behind the bar, reminiscent of a marmot crossed with an ape. His black eyes, bright with an old wisdom, blink in that hairy face of his and he serves another round of drinks, never what you ordered, but always some concoction that does what you need.

Electric pink gleamed through the haze, then I caught a green so bright, it seared an afterimage into the retina, neon lights spelling out letters in some language I've never been able to decipher. The cafe was within reach, at least for the moment. One can never be sure until it is observed. The act of conscious attention somehow opens a passageway when conditions are right. In hundreds of other locations on alternate Earths, the cafe also existed tonight because someone like me had looked up and seen it.

The double doors swung open at my approach and two women, eight feet or more tall, swept through. Their spiky hair was the gaudy pink of roses, their cheeks pierced with glittering brass symbols of rank. They walked arm in sinewy arm with long sleek weapons slung across their broad shoulders.

Rammats from a savage world of violent warrior cultures. I stepped aside and bowed my head and they let me live, one more time.

The air drifting out the double doors had a subtle spice I'd smelled before, familiar, though I couldn't place it. I remembered how bewildered I'd been on my first encounter, the strangeness of the speech and dress, the bizarre foods, the predominance of nonhuman life-forms. I'd left my apartment earlier that evening, feeling restless and lonely, then caught sight of a woman who looked like my lost love, Marissa, and followed her down street after dark street, until we both turned a corner and suddenly the cafe was there, garish against the black night sky.

There was no sign of Marissa, if that was really who I'd been following, so thinking she'd gone in, I entered myself, then slunk into a shadowy corner and stared until Jaeko brought me a seething blue drink and patiently fit my trembling fingers around the glass. It had been hot, not cold, and tasted like sugared formaldehyde, but after a few sips I could string thoughts together again.

"Firs nigh?" Jaeko leaned on my table, propping one hairy arm over the other. His vocal apparatus, though capable of speech, has difficulty shaping final phonemes.

I nodded, still shaking, then let another sip burn down my throat.

"Jus keep you head down," he said with a wink of his surprisingly humanlike eye. "No one ever bother a firs nighter unless he get out of line." He raised a slim black rifle from its hiding place below the counter, then slid it back out of sight again. "Nex time, though, you got you own bac."

With that sage advice, I watched the bewildering parade of customers in silks, leathers, naked blue hide, and armor, even a few who could have been from my own Earth, who glanced at me with indifferent eyes, then looked away.

I stayed for hours, but no Marissa appeared, not even someone who resembled her slightly. When I finally summoned the courage to try to leave, I'd feared I was trapped there forever, but then walked right back into the shabby, vandalized remnants of my own gang-ruled Chicago.

The next night I came back and found only a burned-out

building that had once held a pharmacy. Broken glass crunched beneath my shoes as I walked up and down, looking for some sign the cafe had ever been here.

I stayed away for a month after that, convinced I'd hallucinated the whole episode, but then, on a glacial December evening, when ice crystals stung my face and the brutal wind sledgehammered out of the north across the lake, I walked that way again and saw the pink and green letters gleaming through the darkness like an overpriced strumpet on the stroll.

That was the night I first encountered Alont. I was sitting at the long curving black bar, staring down at the reflection of my face in a spill, when the noise died. I turned and a woman stood framed in the double arch of the doorway, taller than most men, straight in a way models only dreamed of being, her hair and eyes both an intense orange. I'd never seen anyone more different from my sweet wife, Marissa.

A raw, half-healed scar snaked down her temple and cheek. She wore silver-gray leather harness on her upper body that concealed nothing, along with a worn belt and knife sheath at her waist. Those audacious orange eyes flicked over me and moved on.

Jaeko nodded as she passed, drawing stares in her wake as a magnet draws iron. "Alont," he said. "Big trouble. My advice: Fin a rock and bash you head in instea. Less painful."

Hell, most of what walked in that door looked like trouble. I picked up my drink, something pungent and lukewarm, reminiscent of spoiled lemonade laced with antifreeze. A body slid onto the stool next to me and naked skin pressed against my trousered thigh. Heat pooled between us like a lava flow. I shivered.

"Hey there, Rafe," she said, somehow knowing my name. "How's it hanging?"

I looked up, startled. Orange eyes gleamed at me like twin suns. My mouth gaped as I tried to think of something to say, then a hand seized my coat from behind and jerked me off onto the tile floor. I hit my head and sprawled there, blinking up at the ceiling, while a *kunj* soldier in dull-brown combat gear stepped over me and sat in my place with the clank of metal.

"Hullo, Alont," he said, his voice the deep subsonic rumble of a bull elephant. Black smudges gleamed beneath blue eyes.

"Shag off," she said in what sounded vaguely like an Australian accent. "I got no time for hair-faces."

"What about that?" He turned around and kicked me in the stomach. I gagged and belatedly crawled out of reach.

"That there's fresh meat," she said as I fought to breathe. "You, you're just last week's kill."

"Not too dead for you," he said, "as I recall." He ran a hand over that creamy expanse of naked thigh.

She drew a rippled blade and sliced two of his fingers off with no more fuss than if she were swatting an insect. They dropped close to my face on the floor, curled like question marks. "I said, *shag off.*"

Blood fountained as, with a cry, he staggered away, staring at the stumps. She turned back to the bar and shoved three small black triangles at Jaeko.

He nodded and hobbled back to the rows of bottles to concoct something. Alont reached down with one hand and plucked me off the floor by my shirt. "I been to your world," she said, settling me back on the stool as though I weighed nothing. "Couple a times."

Something clicked in my left ear. Out of the corner of my eye, I saw a snub-nosed gun aimed at Alont and jerked back.

She twitched, then her knife bloomed in the soldier's right eye like a steel flower. He fell backwards and lay spread-eagled on the tile. Red pooled around his head like some hellish crimson lake and the coppery stink of blood filled the air. His mouth gaped open as though he wanted to ask something.

The hairy bartender was now wielding the slim black rifle he'd shown me on the my first night. I got a better look this time. It seemed to be made of ceramic. Two bright red jewels pulsed at its business end as though about to fire. "Tha wil be doubl, for the mess," he said levelly.

"Don't get your knickers in a twist," Alont said and dumped a handful of black triangles on the bar. "Rules say I'm allowed to finish what someone else starts. Won't go no further, boyo." She turned back to me. "You ever slip into 'nother world?" I noticed a bruise on her jaw and livid finger tracks on her throat.

"Uh, no," I managed around the pain in my gut. "I didn't know it was even possible."

"Is," she said. "All them other worlds is out there too, every time you leave, but you have to learn the trick of seeing them, 'stead of your own."

"It's hard enough just to get *here*," I said.

She wiped the bloody knife on my shirt, then slid it back into the sheath at her waist with an air of abstraction as though, like breathing, it required no attention. "I can show you."

"Thanks, but I'll pass," I said as two salivating *Otts* dragged the carcass behind us away. What they were going to do with it, I didn't want to know, any more than I wanted to see the brutish worlds my fellow customers hailed from.

Grinning, Alont seized the back of my coat and hustled me outside. The double doors swung closed behind us and I stood shivering in the bitter wind, tethered in her grip like an errant poodle. The night sky glittered above us, an river of dark-blue ice.

"You was beginning to look a bit soft around the edges," she said. The biting wind whipped her orange hair across the scar on her cheek. "Means 'nother you is close. Not good to hang out in there too long. Lots of you scattered through all them worlds. Spend too much time in that damned cafe, one comes along and—bam! The two of you might overlap like old Jaeko."

I subtly tried to free myself without success. "He didn't always look like that?"

She looked around, as though searching. "Used to be downright pretty. I danced him in the back room couple of times before he forgot to go home one night and got himself thoroughly spliced."

Had Jaeko once been human, then? The nape of my neck prickled with dread.

"Now, you, you're not pretty," she said, "but I'd hate to see you spliced all the same." She turned, looking over my head, her orange eyes intent. "There!"

I followed her gaze and saw a glimmer of white headlights in the murky air. "What?"

"'Nother world," she said. "Not mine. We don't have them sort of groundcars. They'd get smashed inside a day, tops."

As we watched, an elongated, glimmering green car swept toward us through the shadows. Judging by its sleek lines, it was not from my world either. Two passengers sat inside, but neither seemed to be driving. Their faces were illuminated pale blue by the interior lights. Absorbed in conversation, they didn't seem to notice us.

"I recognize the clothes," Alont said. "Soft sort of place. Been there a few times. They talk nice enough, but got no bottom."

"What's your world like?" Crystallized breath hung around us like a fog. Shivering overtook me and I fought to keep my teeth from chattering. Was it this cold on all the worlds tonight?

"Tough," she said, then grinned so that the scar on her face stood out. "No one on my world takes guff off no one." She stared up at the sky. "No one lives too long either. You just do what you want while you can."

I tucked my rapidly numbing hands under my arms. "So why do you come here?"

"Why do you?" Her eyes mirrored the frosty stars above. "I always ask you that. Figure one of you might actually be able to tell me some night."

"Don't be ridiculous," I said. "We've never met before."

"Not this you and me," she said.

Two *Otts* burst through the door and stared at us. Alont threw back her head and snarled, brandishing me like a weapon in her left hand, her knife in her right. Hanging there, I did my best to look fierce as well.

They hesitated, then dropped their eyes and moved on. She followed them with her savage gaze, bare breasts heaving. Her teeth gleamed pink and green in the light from the cafe's neon. "Too bad," she said as the pair disappeared into the darkness. "A tussle would've cleared my head right nice."

"Yeah," I said and this time did manage to extract my arm from her grip. My heart pounded as I backed away. "What fun."

She stepped into the hazy night and was gone, as though between one step and the next, a light had been extinguished. I followed, but found myself instead in the smoldering rubble of my own Chicago.

Tonight, almost two years later, I didn't see Alont when I pushed through the doors. After the suffocating summer heat of my world, it was cool inside, as though the depths of winter were just a few feet away. Jaeko's hairy form was behind the bar, looking more human than usual.

"She's not here," he said, mopping at an invisible spill on the bar's gleaming black surface. His words were much clearer too, in keeping with his improved appearance.

"I'm not looking for her, or anyone else, for that matter," I said and slipped onto my usual bar stool. "I just want a drink."

"Sure," he said. His eyes, bright with some emotion, perhaps disbelief, flicked to the door, then back.

Did other versions of me come here sometimes, I wondered, looking for Alont, or fighting with *Otts*? Did I leave my blood as a scarlet offering on the floor some nights? Maybe in other worlds I was tougher or smarter. Maybe in other lives, I had something important to do and someone still to love.

Jaeko brought me a hot, bitter concoction, which reeked of sage like Thanksgiving dressing. I let a sip burn down my throat.

Then it seemed suddenly, as though I remembered another life, one without hostile, disinterested students and gangs and rubble, one in which a stainless-steel-and-glass Chicago gleamed under the sun and impeccably dressed people hurried to work. I was one of those people, confident and assured. I carried a briefcase, talked with an elegant woman who walked along on my arm, had friends . . . associations . . . prospects . . .

I blinked and shuddered, mired in someone else's life. Where had that come from?

Jaeko seized the glass out of my hand. "Time to go," he said briskly. "Pay up and hit the road."

"But I'm not finished!" I said as he dumped the steaming contents of my glass down the sink.

Three *Rammats* strode past, their long dirty hair clicking with beads, the last one bleeding from the shoulder. Her blood was curiously dark, almost purple, but perhaps that was only the cafe's lights. Over in the corner, someone, or some*thing*, sat down at an unfamiliar instrument, a bit like an oversized vacuum cleaner, and played music born of no tonal scale ever favored by humans. The raw notes battled with one another and scraped my already bruised nerves.

"Go!" Jaeko said and motioned an ungainly waiter with the face of a toad over to a side table with a tray of spoiled-looking food.

"I'm not ready," I said and dug a few wrinkled bills out of my pocket. "Look, I haven't been here for weeks. You can't be tired of my company already."

In the back, someone was smoking a substance that smelled like burning plastic. My eyes began to sting as the red smoke feathered along the ceiling.

"Terrible night," Jaeko said without meeting my gaze. "Trouble all round. Come back some other time."

"If I leave, I may not get back for months," I said. "You know that."

"Not exactly the worst that could happen." His hairy ears twitched.

The black doors quivered, then Alont walked in, but she was different, her orange hair cropped short, her face unscarred. She wore long robes of flowing red, a hood pushed back on her shoulders. A *kunj* soldier took one look at her, then edged away as she flung herself into a chair at one of the tables and stared down at clenched hands.

"New look," I said and slipped into the chair next to her.

"Shag off," she said and her hand darted to the sheath on her belt.

"Whatever you say." My chair scraped across the tile as I stood and retreated out of reach. The memory of severed fingers danced behind my eyes. "Have you been in one of those other worlds you were telling me about?"

She looked at me sharply. "You and me've talked before?"

"A bit."

"Some of me do that sometimes," she said, "talk to fricking strangers. Don't know why."

"Just friendly, I guess." An *Ott* with blood on its face peeked out of the back room, grinned at me savagely, then withdrew.

"I shouldn't waste time on hair-faces," she said. "Got too much to do."

I studied her weary face, the bloodshot orange eyes that gleamed in the dimness, maps of someplace I wouldn't want to venture. "Like what?"

"You're real nosey," she said and drew her knife. At least it was the same, the metal rippled and evil looking.

"Sorry," I said and found a small round table set back in the shadows. Maybe Jaeko was right and I should leave. Tonight wasn't looking promising. Only the thought of my boring, cramped, empty apartment kept me from heading back.

Two Lobos burst through the doors, their faces painted gray and black to mimic wolves, their eyes as feral as anything that ever bayed at the moon. I looked away. In the way of the cafe, if I didn't see them, then maybe they weren't really here.

Feet shuffled, then a hand seized my shoulder and artificial claws bit through my shirt. I jerked to my feet, warm blood trickling down my ribs.

"Howl much, brother?" a voice rasped in my ear.

"Sure," I said, rigid with pain, "every night, just like clockwork."

The claws tightened and agony shimmered through my brain like sheet lightning, white and fierce. I tried to twist free, but the claws only tightened in my torn flesh.

"I don't think so," another voice said, higher, female, probably. "He don't look to have the knack."

Something cold sniffed the nape of my unprotected neck. My skin crawled. "L-look," I said, "I don't want trouble. Just tell me what you want!"

"A good hunt." The female's breath was hot and moist against my bare skin. "But you don't look like the one as could give it to us."

"Oh, that there fellow's soft as mallow," Alont said. "That all you're up to?"

"You got something else in mind then?" The male cast me against the hard edge of a table, where I sank to the floor, winded and trembling.

Above, Alont's rippled knife gleamed in the cafe's dim lights. "Come ahead and find out!"

The three of them stared into one another's eyes, hackles raised, noses twitching. The Lobos weren't just painted fools, I suddenly realized. There was more of the true animal in them than I had ever credited. Obviously, I never looked closely enough all those times I'd encountered one here. I gathered my knees to my chest and shivered.

The Lobos glanced aside, then backed up in tandem until they reached the doors.

Alont crinkled her eyes and laughed until the pair turned and fled. "They always do that," she said, reaching down to pull me to my feet. "Got no bottom, if you just stand up to them."

"I guess I n-need to come armed, then," I said, my teeth chattering with reaction. Cold sweat glued my shirt to my back. "I'll do better next time."

"What you need, bucko, is to stay out of here, if you can't take care of yourself," she said. "This here's no playpen."

Jaeko emerged from behind the bar long enough to shove a glass of something cold and blue into my hand. I threw back my head and downed half in a single gulp. Molten ice seeped into my shattered nerves and eased my shaking, chasing the pain of my clawed shoulder before it.

"Your world's too soft," she said. "Hell, *you're* too soft. This place is not for the likes of you."

"Then I'll have to toughen up," I said and sat down heavily at the bar, staring at my hands around the glass. Jaeko snorted and turned away to stock bottles out of surprisingly mundane-looking cardboard boxes on the floor. "I bet you didn't have it so easy the first few times you found your way to the cafe either."

"This? This here's nothing," she said and resheathed her knife. "Fact is folk from my world come here to relax."

"Oh, yeah, I forgot," I said. "Your world is so terrible, much worse than this." I tipped the last of my icy blue drink down my throat.

"You want to see bad?" she said and seized my arm.

"Hey!" I tried to pry her hand off.

"Come on, then. I'll show you!" She dragged me backwards off the stool and out the double doors.

Outside, the black night sky shimmered red and gold, like some mad aurora borealis. I struggled to free myself, but Alont just laughed, her coarse orange hair flying in the wind, and marched me onward as though disciplining an errant child.

"It changes, you know," she said, "every time one of you lot comes through the door. *You* bring the Lobos and the *Otts*, and even me, when you decide to see us. We don't just come here on our own."

My shoulder ached as I dug my heels in and managed to slow her down. "I do not!"

"It's the nature of this fricking place." She released my shirt and stood back, hands on her solid hips. "Everyone who walks in changes it."

I looked around. The ruined buildings I'd expected to see were gone. The dark horizon was flat and remote, unimpeded by construction of any kind. Overhead, a black shape swept through the sky like a bird, but far too large. I shivered even though it was hot. We weren't in my Chicago. Just a few steps beyond the cafe's doors, she'd forced me into unknown country. How did she keep doing that? Overhead, rose and green streamers intertwined like snakes and danced across the sky. "Where are we?"

"In the place I made." She blinked up at the unseen stars. "I didn't mean to, anymore than you meant to make yours, but I didn't know any better back when I started out."

The black shape banked and turned toward us. Alont drew her knife and stared upwards with a fierce joy. "Nasty creatures about—got to be careful here."

The air was cleaner than my world's, filled with unfamiliar woody scents. My heart was racing as the eerie lights overhead reflected from her knife. "How do I get back?"

"Open your eyes and decide to see it," she said, her own gaze fixed on the dark flyer. The wind picked up and swirled her tattered red robes around those long, bare legs.

"See what?"

"Whatever you want." With a sharp screel, whatever-it-was angled its wings and plummeted toward us like a stone.

I swore and fell to my knees, arms over my head. "Get us the hell out of here!"

"Do it yourself," she said. "Me, I fancy a good fight!"

The cafe still lay behind me, I realized. I lurched back onto my feet and fled toward its familiar face. Inside, a trio of *Otts* were quarreling over a bloodied body that looked a bit like Jaeko, but he was still unpacking bottles behind the bar.

He nodded his hairy head, his eyes gone red this time, where before they'd been black. His human aspect had faded. "Troubl, tha one," he lisped. "Didn I tel you?"

I slid onto the stool and tucked my hands under my arms, unable to stop shaking. Jaeko was right. I really had to stop coming to this place. With a sudden strong pang, I wanted to go home, but feared what might lie beyond those swinging doors.

"Go hom, Raf," Jaeko said. "Haven you had enough fo one nigh?"

The doors opened again and a man stood framed in the blackness of the night outside. He was of middle stature and clearly human with wavy brown hair tousled by the wind, puzzled hazel eyes, a deeply wrinkled brow. A battered briefcase was clasped under one arm. He turned to scan the room and I could see someone had scratched a gang sign into the black leather with the careless tip of a knife. I remembered that day, the briefcase lying on my desk, my back turned for just a second as I wrote on the board, then the burst of laughter that filled the classroom.

"Too lat." Jaeko shook his head and reached for a damp cloth. "Shoul hav lef when I said." He raised his voice and called out to the man, "She's no here tonigh! Go hom!"

"Alont?" The stranger raised his briefcase with both hands before him like a shield. He took another step into the room and I *felt* him, as though he were trying to climb into my skin. Our eyes met and something leaped between us. For a second, we were one, he, standing in my shoes, I, in his. Our minds fused and I saw that he was still married to Marissa, while in my world she had left me over two years go.

Whatever was between us flared, so hot and bright, I could taste his essence, then we both fell back on our rumps. When I could see again, he was gone and I sat on the floor, while a newly arrived crowd of half-naked blue humanoids stepped around me.

Jaeko peered over the bar at me and shook his hairy head. "You would thin two of th same person woul neve com here at the sam tim, but it always happen. The more simila they are, the more likely to overlap."

But all I could think of was that there *were* still worlds where Marissa still loved me. The knowledge soothed my mind like a sweet balm. Worlds where she still stretched out beside me at night, her skin warm and moist from the shower, fragrant with her favorite soap, worlds where she could still look at me with love.

Other Rafes. Other Marissas. The desire to live in one of those places twisted like a white hot poker in my gut. I pulled myself back onto my feet using the bar stool, trembling.

"Oh, sit dow," Jaeko said and took me by the arm. His eyes stood out in his animal face.

"But I've got to go to her!" I passed a hand over my hair, finding it wild and disordered. "She's out there, in his world. If I hurry, maybe the way is still open."

"Idiot, you knocked him loose." Enunciating with exaggerated care, Jaeko deposited me on the stool as though I weighed nothing, then shuffled back behind the bar, his motion rocking apelike side to side. "He won't be going home, but it could have easily been you. Think about that."

"She's there." The possibilities whirled through my mind. He'd had my briefcase, even down to the defaced side. He must have had my same job, many of the same details of my life. If I could just find my way into his world instead of my own—

Then I thought of what Jaeko had said and looked up as he placed a simmering orange concoction before me in a tall glass. "What did you mean—I 'knocked him loose?'"

"When two similar bodies meet here, sometimes they overlap,

like me, and you get the sum of their parts, and sometimes they collide and go their separate ways, with at least one of them knocked loose from his own world, sometimes both."

We could have been merged then, like Jaeko, but instead we had repelled each other. "So where is he?" I said. "Did I somehow fling him back into his own world, with her?"

"You're still here, so he must be the one who's lost," Jaeko said. "The poor bastard's unstuck from everything he's ever known, wandering."

I took a drink of the orange liquid. It tasted like battery acid. I shuddered. "I didn't mean to hurt him."

"Yeah, righ," Jaeko said, lapsing back into his lisp. "Forget it. No one ever listen anyway." He ran the tips of his fingers over his muzzle. "I didn."

"If he's lost," I whispered, "then she'll be alone. She'll need me."

"It won be *your* she," Jaeko said wearily, as though he'd given this warning many times. "And you're no *her* man."

"But I could be!"

Alont sauntered through the door, looked around the room, settled her gaze on me. Her hair was black with green highlights tonight, not orange, her face unscarred. Another Alont, just like there had been another me. So many worlds.

"You." She headed in my direction.

I slid off the stool. I wanted Marissa, not this hulking amazon. "Got to go, Jaeko," I said and shoved a handful of paper bills across the counter.

He nodded, then curled his fingers around the money and waved me off.

"I got a message for you." Alont blocked my path.

"Some other night," I said and ducked my head.

"No, now!" She seized a handful of my hair and nearly jerked me off my feet.

I wrenched free, leaving behind a sizable quantity of hair. My head stung and I was suddenly angry. "I don't want to talk," I said, "or dance, or fight, or any of the other things you think you do so well! I just want to—"

"Go to her!" she finished, her black eyes scornful. "Right?"

"Right!" I swung at her face.

She slipped aside easily, then struck me to the floor. "Well, the message is she don't want to see you."

My head reeled. I put the back of a knuckle to my split lip. "You don't know that," I said. "In fact, you have no idea who we're even talking about."

"I know," she said, a thin crooked smile on her lips. "Marissa."

I stared, at a loss for words.

"Now you done your part, she don't want to see you no more. This here was her place first."

"She's been here before?"

"Every night, bucko, 'til you started showing up. Now, she slips out the back door when you come in."

"But I found this cafe on my own," I said. All around us, creatures and humans and things that might have been human a long time ago were watching us, listening, more than a few with smirks on their insufferable faces. Bastards. I'd been here often enough to know how they loved a scandal.

"According to Marissa, you couldn't find your arse with both hands and illuminated arrows," she said. "How do you think a screwup like you could ever find your way across freaking worlds? She brought you here that first time, had to practically lead you by the blooming balls, by all accounts!"

"My Marissa?"

"Not yours, fathead, *his.*"

"The—other Rafe, the one in the doorway?"

"She wanted to be rid of him, just like your Marissa wanted to be rid of you, only he wouldn't take no for an answer, so she went looking for another, a close match to the original, so that the two of you would either repel or overlap one another. Either way, she'd be free."

She'd set me up to knock him loose. I sank back onto the stool in stunned silence.

"So now you can get the hell out," said a velvet voice behind me. "You're not wanted here anymore."

I looked up to see her, Marissa, both like and unlike the woman who had walked out on me two years ago. Small and dark, with shimmering black hair, she had a tiny mole on her cheek I'd never seen before, and her hair parted on the right, not the left. But it was her, down to the way her gray eyes glittered in the dimness and that unforgettable sinuous sway in her hips.

Alont reached out and put an arm around her, drawing Marissa's pliant body close.

"He was so damned possessive," Marissa said, "swore we were made for each other, that he'd never let me go."

"I thought of saying that," I said, "but I didn't think you—she'd—go for it."

"Smart boy," Marissa said, "smarter than you know. You were a good puppy. Your Marissa was never forced to get rid of you."

"So now," I said, "what happens? You two go off into the sunset and that poor schmook just wanders forever looking for his way home?"

"Maybe," she said, gazing up at Alont. "Maybe not. It's not my problem anymore."

"You used me!" I could feel the heat rise in my face. "If it weren't for me, the other Rafe would still be okay!"

"Oh, don't give yourself too much credit," Marissa said as Alont stepped between us, rippled knife already gleaming in her hand. "It took a helluva lot of work to use you. You really are incredibly dense, you know."

"Go hom," Jaeko said. "Show's ove. What's done is done. No goin back now."

Someone laughed in the back of the room. The band took up its demented music again. A bottle fell off a nearby table and rolled across the floor until it fetched up at my foot, its bright label fanciful and utterly foreign. I felt impotent and useless, like chaff blown before the leading edge of a storm.

"He's gon," Jaeko said, too weary evidently to speak clearly. "Tha can't be change."

"Because encountering me severed his tie to his own world." I couldn't bear to look at Marissa, and yet couldn't look away.

"Righ," Jaeko said. "Nothin to be don."

"But we can cross over into other worlds," I said. "Alont showed me."

"Takes stamina," Alont said with a feral grin. "Takes hair on your chest and grit in your gizzard. I don't see the likes of you stalking from world to world anytime soon now."

"He's out there somewhere," I said, trying to get a picture of it clear in my mind, "waiting for someone to see him so he knows where he is, just like the cafe."

"Can't be you," Jaeko said. "Next tim you two mee, if you eve do, coul be you'll overla, like all those othe me, or perhaps you'll both be knock loose, so then there's two wanderin foreve lost, instea of jus one. Of all those who coul go and look, it can't neve be you."

My mind whirled. There had been a moment when we were close enough to sense one another, but not repel. If I could find him and come just that close and no further . . .

"Yes, *pobrecito*, go!" Marissa's laugh was low and throaty, achingly familiar. "Then, if you look hard enough, beg long enough, maybe someone will see you too and you'll both finally know where you are."

For a second, her gray eyes shimmered green, then hazel, and I glimpsed countless Marissas crowded in behind them. She had come here often, almost "every night," Alont had said, so she must have met herself many times. My Marissa was probably in there, along with so many others that counting them would be like trying to number the recursive images of one mirror reflecting in another.

"Was it worth it?" I asked, my face burning. "Just to be rid of me?"

"Don't flatter yourself," she said. "You were the least of my worries."

"Gives her strength," Alont said with a broken-toothed grin. "With each new self, she absorbs what they know, picks up their resolve."

"But you can never go home again," I said. "Not like that."

"Idiot, like this, I'm at home wherever I go." Marissa turned to Alont and gazed up at the taller woman.

"And the next time you meet one of your selves, she might knock you loose," I said. "Then you'll all be wandering lost."

"Never happen." She smiled ferally. "Never met one I couldn't absorb."

The cafe's mellow light played along the bridge of her nose, the black curls of her hair. She was like a spider, spinning her web here every night, preying on herself over and over. Even worse, she *liked* what she was doing, perhaps even needed it in some sick way, and she would go on, night after night, either absorbing her other selves like waves or repelling them into the darkness to wander across all the possible worlds, forever lost.

I turned to Jaeko. "And what about you? Are you just waiting for another Jaeko to show up and undo what you've already done to yourself?"

His nose wrinkled. "Already happen a couple dozen time, then one comes in and overlap me and we star all ove again."

"Why do you do this to yourself?"

He lowered his eyes and rubbed industriously on a smudge on the bar's gleaming black surface. "Keep life from gettin dull."

It was his own personal version of roulette, I thought numbly, the Russian variety.

A bevy of creatures came in, small and spindly with ridges along their backbones. They flocked across the floor like birds, their scales gleaming silver in the low light, swarmed over the back tables and settled there gazing about with quick, nervous blinks.

Jaeko sighed and emerged from behind the bar to get their order.

I turned back to Alont and Marissa. "You can't do this anymore."

"And who's going to make us stop, bucko?" Alont's hand crept to her knife sheath.

"Besides, they like it," Marissa said, "if it's any of your business, which it's not."

Her face was tilted up to the light so that deep red highlights glinted in her black hair, highlights I'd never suspected were there. I couldn't see any hint of the woman I'd once known. "Did you ever love me at all?"

"*She* did, once," she said, "before she met the rest of me. They don't love you a bit."

"Go home," Alont said.

My fingernails dug into the palms of my hands. Yes, go home, I told myself, teach bored and hostile children things they don't want to know and live with the knowledge of Marissa and the cafe and what she was doing to countless other Marissas, ones who maybe still loved someone at the moment, but who wouldn't after she was done with them.

"I can't do that," I said.

"I'm bored," Marissa said to Alont. She stretched, arching her back like a leopardess. "Kill him and then we'll go."

Alont drew her gleaming knife as Jaeko hobbled past with the newcomers' order. The hairy bartender looked at the knife with disdain. "Not in here," he said severely, "unless you goin to clean up the mess you self."

She seized the back of my shirt and dragged me flailing through the doors out into the dull black night. My heart was hammering as I struggled to free myself. "How many Alonts are in you?" I asked. "How many of yourself have you murdered?"

"None," she said with a savage grin. "Seems Alonts don't mix well. Whenever I meet another, we both just go spinning off. Sometimes I have a helluva tough trek finding my way back, but I always do. And, those times when I stay lost, it don't matter. Marissa here hooks up as well with one Alont as another. It seems we're all of a like mind."

I twisted in her grip. "And that doesn't bother you, when some other Alont takes your place?"

"Hell, no!" she said. "They's all me, more or less. This way I can be lots of places at the same time, have lots of adventures, never be bored or tied down."

I slumped. It was all too alien, too far outside what I'd been led to expect from the universe. "You don't have to kill me," I said. "Just let me go. I won't come back to the cafe again. There's nothing here for me."

"But I *want* to," she said, tightening her grip. The knife gleamed green and pink in the cafe's neon glare.

"Let him go, Alont!" The male voice rang out of the darkness beyond the front walk.

Alont peered into the night. "Who says you have any say in what happens here?"

"This gun says." A hand waggled and the sign's garish lights reflected off metal.

It wasn't yet another version of me. The voice was too low, underlain by an almost familiar gravelly bass.

Her fingers loosened marginally and I wrenched myself free.

"Now," said the unseen figure. "Do what you said: Go home and don't come back."

"All right," I said, "just as soon as I can find my way out. I can't see my Chicago from here."

"You aren't knocked loose, are you?" A man stepped out of the darkness so that the neon played green and pink over his hair and he and Alont's knife seemed made of the same stuff. He had shaggy brown hair dusted with silver and eyes almost lost in shadow and looked reassuringly human.

"I don't think so," I said.

"Hell, I'll knock you loose—permanently!" Alont lunged at me, knife extended like an offering. "Then you won't never need to go home again!"

The man raised his arm and fired one shot from a pistol he'd been holding down at his side. Alont screamed and fell short so that the knife only drew a liquid line of white-hot fire along my ribs. She collapsed against my legs, trapping my feet with her weight.

"I always hate killing her," my rescuer said. "But she's rather apt to insist."

One hand clasped my bleeding side. The breath sobbed in and out of my lungs. My throat had constricted to the size of a toothpick. I stared down at the fallen woman. What was I doing here? How had I let this sick game get so far along?

Alont's hand twitched, then she was still. "Marissa will be angry," I said inanely and lurched backwards to free my feet.

"Her?" the man said, then tucked the pistol inside his waistband. He was wearing dark fatigues in mottled blues that looked vaguely like a uniform and a beret that drooped over one ear. "She won't care. There are plenty of other Alonts. It just thins the herd when you pick one off."

He moved closer so that I could see his eyes, dark brown, full of compassion and mysteries, ancient almost . . .

"Jaeko!" I said.

"Yeah," he said. "One of them anyway." He looked up at the flat blackness overhead, devoid of stars, familiar or unfamiliar. "I'll go around to the back so that you can concentrate and bring up the path to your world."

I glanced at the cafe. "Aren't you going in?"

His mouth twisted in a mirthless smile. "What for?"

"To knock the other Jaekos loose," I said. "So they can go home."

"Don't you get it?" he said. "This is what the cafe is all about. They *are* home, just like Marissa and the Otts and the rest of the demented puppies in there, like you too, if you don't turn your back on all this."

"Did you?" I said.

He shrugged. "I've been away so long, I don't remember where home is anymore, or what it was like."

"But you're not going in?"

"Not—tonight." His brow creased and I could see the hint of other Jaekos lurking within. "Some other night, I'll be too bored, so I'll roll the dice, go in and see what happens, overlap or blast myself out into the farthest reaches. Tonight, I just dropped by to have a peek."

Someone laughed inside, shrill and nasty. It wasn't Marissa, maybe even wasn't human, but it cut through me. "You know what Marissa does," I said, "and Alont."

"They're not the only ones," he said. "Don't let it get under your skin. Go home, while you've still got one."

The breeze surged, then I felt the electric tingle against my face. Hot, fetid air, humid as some distant jungle, filled my lungs. *Transition.* Someone, or something, was coming up the walk. The air danced, once again alive with possibilities. I could almost see other universes crowding in, waiting for someone to notice and bring one of them into being.

Blueness flashed, then Jaeko moved aside as a trio of women approached. Their cheeks were shaded a deep violet, their foreheads inset with fire opals. Chains of tiny silver bells chimed on their bare ankles and they carried the scent of some heady perfume with them, a bit like rum laced with cinnamon. They glanced at me with knowing eyes, as though we had met before, then swept past.

Relief swept over me. At least none of them were Marissa. "What she's doing is wrong," I said, turning back to Jaeko as the doors swung closed. "I just can't get past that."

"You think that's the only nasty party game going on in there?" He shook his head, a thin smile on his face. "Hers is quite tame by some standards and none of it's got anything to do with you."

I turned to him. "Then what's it got to do with you?"

He grinned. "Nothing."

I felt as though something slimy had just crawled across my neck. "And yet here you stand, night after night?"

"Not every night," he said, rocking on his heels like a young man about to go out on his first date. "Sometimes I go in and enjoy the show."

Jaeko inside knew what was going on here, just like this one outside knew. Everyone who came here knew, it seemed, except me. A fury that had been on low boil suddenly exploded through me, igniting each atom in my body until I was aglow with white-hot, incandescent anger.

I kicked the gun he was still holding loosely in his left hand, so that it went spinning off into the night, then jumped him as he scrambled after it.

"Hey, what you do want?" he said, then grunted as I kneed the small of his back. His arm flailed back at me, but missed. "What's your problem?"

"I want it all to stop!" I shouted in his ear. "I want the universe— the universes—to be a better place than this! I want it all to mean something and not be just some crummy crapshoot where anyone can do anything to anyone else and it doesn't goddamn matter!"

"Oh, man," he said, "you are so stupid!"

I seized a handful of his hair and jerked his head back, then was shocked to find him laughing.

"You wouldn't get it," he said, "would you, if you came here every night for a thousand years!"

I horsed him onto his feet. "Shut up!"

"You're pathetic!" He slumped against me, hot and sweaty, laughing so hard he could barely breathe. "I've never seen anything like it! Thank God I stayed outside. This is so much better than anything I'd see in there!"

"Shut up!" I backhanded him across the face and felt the skin on my knuckles split. "You don't have the faintest idea what you're talking about!"

He kept laughing though, and my hand ached, and the lurid green and pink of the sign kept flashing on/off, on/off. I didn't know what to do. A strain of music began inside. Someone broke into an off-tune song, then I seized his collar and marched him through the doors.

Jaeko-at-the-bar looked up, his animal face creased in what was probably surprise. And Marissa looked up from where she sat in a stout blue figure's lap, face-to-face, her shirt torn open to the waist. And no less than three Alonts, of varying coloration, looked up, all of them skulking around the periphery of the room.

Marissa smiled a lazy cat-smile and stretched. "My," she said and winked at me. "Unsuspected depths here, I see."

There was another blue flash, so bright, I could taste it on the back of my throat. The Jaeko-in-my-hands throbbed with light, the pulsations coming faster and faster. Jaeko-at-the-bar shimmered as well, his frequency approaching, then matching the other's so that they were momentarily in phase.

And then my hands closed, suddenly empty. The two Jaekos were somewhere *else*, both quite lost for the moment. I staggered as air rushed in from all sides to fill the vacuum where the two had been.

"Pity," said Marissa. She trailed red nails down the column of her throat. "But one of him will be back. He always is. Maybe the next time it will be the good-looking one instead of the hairy little bugger."

With an incoherent cry, one of the three Alonts suddenly rushed another and both flared out with a flash equal to Jaeko's. Someone screamed as I glanced around the dining room, but no one else even looked up. What I could see of their eyes was blank and disinterested.

They all knew what I was just beginning to understand. Those who were knocked "loose" would either be back, or they wouldn't, and either way it didn't matter. There were always plenty more Alonts, just as there were plenty more Jaekos, Rafes, and Marissas. We were none of us unique, but strangely in abundance across all of creation, infinitely varied and yet distressingly the same at heart. Strike down one, and two or four or eight would spring back up. In this playground, nothing was ever lost and certainly nothing ever gained. Conservation of energy after all. How—comforting.

I threaded through the tables, noting the odor of spilled drinks, the cloying oversweetness of one balanced by the astringency of the next. Conversation resumed its constant low buzz as I picked up Jaeko's cloth and edged behind the bar. The colored rows of half-filled bottles fanned out across the glass shelves, the condiments, both familiar and alien. And on the other side, another shelf below the bar itself, hidden from customers' eyes, weapons of every sort imaginable, most of which I had no idea how to operate. But with time, I thought, with time, I would figure it all out. At least I recognized Jaeko's familiar black ceramic rifle. I picked it up and it felt warm to my fingers, ready to go.

Someone leaned over the bar and ordered. Without conscious thought, my hands went to work. Perhaps other versions of myself had worked at this craft from time to time, or perhaps in some other universe I had always done this.

"Enjoy yourself, sweetums, while you can," Marissa said over her shoulder as she left arm in arm with a burly green-haired soldier. "There's always tomorrow when Jaeko or one of your own twins will come back and, before you know it, you'll be the one out wandering in some godawful backwater or seeing life from three levels down inside your own skin."

I picked up a fluted glass and polished it with the soft white towel as the doors swung shut behind her, watching the *Otts* in the other room, the nameless soldiers, the deformed children, all the restless shifty eyes. Hides gleamed, bright with alien texture, skulls nodded and dipped, teeth of varying sizes flashed. Someone shouted and threw an opponent across the room. Glassware shattered over by the wall as three *rammats* faced off. A pair of eyeless patrons swept in and threw me a condescending sneer.

Marissa was wrong. The cafe has never seen a "tomorrow," and it never will. Even I have come to understand that much. It's always the cusp of midnight in this out-of-the-way pocketverse, that pregnant instant when night flashes over into day and reality eats its own tail yet again, when everything and everyone is on the knife-edge of *becoming*.

That first night, I thought I came here to find my lost love, but now I know better. I came here, as do we all, to find myself, only to learn there is no one true Marissa, Alont, or Rafe, just as there is no tomorrow or yesterday, only endless branching possibilities and *now*, that enduring moment before what might be is forcibly shaped by someone's conscious attention.

Voices rise. Arguments twine through one another like vines fighting for purchase on a sheer glass wall rising up forever. A *rammat* snarls. A *kunj* soldier breaks a table over his mate's head and splinters bounce like freed electrons off the walls and corners. It's midnight again, or still, or always, and we all drink up as we wait for someone to come through those doors and observe us into existence yet one more time.

Swing Time

Carrie Vaughn

He emerged suddenly from behind a potted shrub. Taking Madeline's hand, he shouldered her bewildered former partner out of the way and turned her toward the hall where couples gathered for the next figure.

"Ned, fancy meeting you here." Madeline deftly shifted so that her voluminous skirts were not trod upon.

"Fancy? You're pleased to see me then?" he said, smiling his insufferably ironic smile.

"Amused is more accurate. You always amuse me."

"How long has it been? Two, three hundred years? That volta in Florence, wasn't it?"

"Si, signor. But only two weeks subjective."

"Ah yes." He leaned close, to converse without being overheard. "I've been meaning to ask you: have you noticed anything strange on your last few expeditions?"

"Strange?"

"Any doorways you expected to be there not opening? Anyone following you and the like?"

"Just you, Ned."

He chuckled flatly.

The orchestra's strings played the opening strains of a Mozart piece. She curtseyed—low enough to allure, but not so low as to unnecessarily expose décolletage. Give a hint, not the secret. Lower the gaze for a demure moment only. Smile, tempt. Ned bowed, a gesture as practiced as hers. Clothed in white silk stockings and velvet breeches, one leg straightened as the other leg stepped back. He made a precise turn of his hand and never broke eye contact.

They raised their arms—their hands never quite touched—and began to dance. Elegant steps made graceful turns, a leisurely pace allowed her to study him. He wore dark green velvet trimmed with white and gold, sea spray of lace at the cuffs and collar. He wore a young man's short wig powdered to perfection.

"I know why you're here," he said, when they stepped close enough for conversation. "You're after Lady Petulant's diamond brooch."

"That would be telling."

"I'll bet you I take it first."

"I'll counter that bet."

"And whoever wins—"

Opening her fan with a jerk of her wrist, she looked over her shoulder. "Gets the diamond brooch."

The figure of the dance wheeled her away and gave her to another partner, an old man whose wig was slipping over one ear. She curtseyed, kept one eye on Lady Petulant, holding court over a tray of bonbons and a ratlike lap dog, and the other on Ned.

With a few measures of dancing, a charge of power crept into Madeline's bones, enough energy to take her anywhere: London 1590. New York 1950. There was power in dancing.

The song drew to a close. Madeline begged off the next, fanning herself and complaining of the heat. Drifting off in a rustle of satin, she moved to the empty chair near Lady Petulant.

"Is this seat taken?"

"Not at all," the lady said. The diamond, large as a walnut, glittered against the peach-colored satin of her bodice.

"Lovely evening, isn't it?"

"Quite."

For the next fifteen minutes, Madeline engaged in harmless conversation, insinuating herself into Lady Petulant's good graces. The lady was a widow, rich but no longer young. White powder caked the wrinkles of her face. Her fortune was entailed, bestowed upon her heirs and not a second husband, so no suitors paid her court. She was starved for attention.

So when Madeline stopped to chat with her, she was cheerful. When Ned appeared and gave greeting, she was ecstatic.

"I do believe I've found the ideal treat for your little dear," he said, kneeling before her and offering a bite-sized pastry to the dog.

"Why, how thoughtful! Isn't he a thoughtful gentleman, Frufru darling? Say thank you." She lifted the creature's paw and shook it at Ned. "You are too kind!"

Madeline glared at Ned, who winked back.

A servant passed with a silver tray of sweets. When he bowed to offer her one, she took the whole tray. "Marzipan, Lady Petulant?" she said, presenting the tray.

"No thank you, dear. Sticks to my teeth dreadfully."

"Sherry, Lady Petulant?" Ned put forward a crystal glass which he'd got from God knew where.

"Thank you, that would be lovely." Lady Petulant took the glass and sipped.

"I'm very sorry, Miss Madeline, but I don't seem to have an extra glass to offer you."

"That's quite all right, sir. I've always found sherry to be rather too sweet. Unpalatable, really."

"Is that so?"

"Hm." She fanned.

And so it went, until the orchestra roused them with another chord. Lady Petulant gestured a gloved hand toward the open floor.

"You young people should dance. You make such a fine couple."

"Pardon me?" Ned said.

Madeline fanned faster. "I couldn't, really."

"Nonsense. You two obviously know each other quite well. It would please me to watch you dance."

Madeline's gaze met Ned's. She stared in silence, her wit failing her. She didn't need another dance this evening, and she most certainly did not want to dance with him again.

Giving a little smile that supplanted the stricken look in his eyes, he stood and offered his hand. "I'm game. My lady?"

He'd thought of a plan, obviously. And if he drew her away from Lady Petulant—she would not give up that ground.

The tray of marzipan sat at the very edge of the table between their chairs. As she prepared to stand, she lifted her hand from the arm of her chair, gave her fan a downward flick—and the tray flipped. Miniature daisies and roses shaped in marzipan flew around them. Madeline shrieked, Lady Petulant gasped, the dog barked. Ned took a step back.

A ruckus of servants descended on them. As Madeline turned to avoid them, the dog jumped from Lady Petulant's lap—for a brief moment, its neck seemed to grow to a foot long—and bit Madeline's wrist. A spot of red welled through her white glove.

"Ow!" This shriek was genuine.

"Frufru!" Lady Petulant collected the creature and hugged it to her breast. "How very naughty of you, Frufru darling. My dear, are you all right?"

She rubbed her wrist. The blood stain didn't grow any larger. It was just a scratch. It didn't even hurt. "I'm—I—" Then again, if she played this right . . .

"I—oh my, I do believe I feel faint." She put her hand to her neck and willed her face to blush. "Oh!"

She fell on Lady Petulant. With any luck, she crushed Frufru beneath her petticoats. Servants convulsed in a single panicked unit, onlookers gasped, even Ned was there, murmuring and patting her cheek with a cool hand.

Lady Petulant wailed that the poor girl was about to die on top of her. Pressed up against the good lady, Madeline took the opportunity to reach for the brooch. She could slip it off and no one would notice—

The brooch was already gone.

She did not have to feign a stunned limpness when a pair of gallant gentlemen lifted her and carried her to a chaise near a window. Ned was nowhere to be seen. Vials of smelling salts were thrust at her, lavender water sprinkled at her. Someone was wrapping her wrist—still gloved—in a bandage, and someone who looked like a doctor—good God, was the man wielding a razor?—approached.

She shoved away her devoted caretakers and tore off the bandage. "Please, give me air! I've recovered my senses. No, really, I have. If-you-please, sir!"

As if nothing had happened, she stood, straightened her bodice over her corset, smoothed her skirts, and opened her fan with a snap.

"I thank you for your attention, but I am quite recovered. Good-bye."

She marched off in search of Ned.

He was waiting for her toward the back of the hall, a fox's sly grin on his face. Before she came too close, he turned his cupped hand, showing her a walnut-sized diamond that flashed against the green velvet of his coat.

Turning, he stepped sideways behind the same potted fern where he had ambushed her.

He disappeared utterly.

"Damn him!" Her skirts rustled when she stamped her foot.

Ignoring concerned onlookers and Lady Petulant's cries after her welfare, she cut across the hall to the glass doors opening to the courtyard behind the hall and across the courtyard to a hideously baroque statue of Cupid trailing roses off its limbs. She stopped and took a breath, trying to regain her composure. No good brooding now. It was over and done. There would be other times and places to get back at him. Stepping through required calm.

A handful of doorways collected here in this hidden corner of the garden. One led to an alley in Prague 1600; tilting her head one way, she could just make out a dirty cobbled street and the bricks of a Renaissance façade. Another led to a space under a pier in Key West 1931. Yet another led home.

She danced for this moment; this moment existed because she danced.

Behind the statue Madeline turned her head, narrowed her eyes a certain practiced way, and the world shifted. Just a bit. She put out her hand to touch the crack that formed a line in the air. Confirming its existence, she stepped sideways and through the doorway, back to her room.

Her room: sealed in the back of a warehouse, it had no windows or doors. In it, she stored the plunder taken from a thousand years of history—what plunder she could carry, at least: Austrian crystal, Chinese porcelain, Aztec gold, and a walk-in closet filled with costumes spanning a millennia.

She dropped her fan, pulled the pins out of her wig, unfastened her dress and unhooked her corset. Now that she could breathe, she paced and fumed at Ned properly.

She really ought to go someplace with a beach next time. Hawaii 1980, perhaps. Definitely someplace without corsets. Someplace like—

✧　　✧　　✧

The band played Glenn Miller from a gymnasium stage with a USO banner draped overhead. There must have been a couple of hundred G.I.s drinking punch, crowding along the walls, or dancing with a couple of hundred local girls wearing bright dresses and big grins. Madeline only had to wait a moment before a G.I. in dress greens swept her up and spun her into the mob.

Of all periods of history, of all forms of dance, this was her favorite. Such exuberance, such abandon in a generation that saw the world change before its eyes. No ultra-precise curtseys and bows here.

Her soldier lifted her, she kicked her feet to the air and he brought her down, swung her to one side, to the other, and set her on the floor at last to Lindy hop and catch her breath. Her red skirt caught around her knees, and sweat matted her hair to her forehead.

Her partner was a good-looking kid, probably nineteen or twenty, clean faced and bright eyed. Stuck in time, stuck with his fate—a ditch in France, most likely. Like a lamb to slaughter. It was like dancing a minuet in Paris in 1789, staring at a young nobleman's neck and thinking, you poor chump.

She could try to warn him, but it wouldn't change anything.

The kid swung her out, released her and she spun. The world went by in a haze and miraculously she didn't collide with anyone.

When a hand grabbed hers, she stopped and found herself pulled into an embrace. Arm in arm, body to body, with Ned. Wearing green again. Arrogant as ever, he'd put captain bars on his uniform. He held her close, his hand pressed against the small of her back, and two-stepped her in place, hemmed in by the crowd. She couldn't break away.

"Dance with me, honey. I ship out tomorrow and may be dead next week."

"Not likely, Ned. Are you following me?"

"Now how would I manage that? I don't even know when you live. So, what are you here for, the war bonds cash box?"

"Maybe I just like the music."

As they fell into a rhythm, she relaxed in his grip. A dance was a dance after all, and if nothing else he was a good dancer.

"I didn't thank you for helping me with Lady Petulant. Great distraction. We should be a team. We both have to dance to do what we do—it's a perfect match."

"I work alone."

"You might think about it."

"No. I tried working with someone once. His catalyst for stepping through was fighting. He liked to loot battlefields. All our times dancing ended in brawls."

"What happened to him?"

"Somme 1916. He stayed a bit too long at that one."

"Ah. I met a woman once whose catalyst was biting the heads off rats."

"You're joking! How on earth did she figure that out?"

"One shudders to think."

The song ended, a slow one began, and a hundred couples locked together.

"So, how did you find me?" she asked.

"I know where you like to go."

She frowned and looked aside, across his shoulder to a young couple clinging desperately to one another as they swayed in place.

"Tell me, Ned, what were you before you learned to step through? Were you always a thief?"

"Yes. A highwayman and a rogue from the start. You?"

"I was a good girl."

"So what changed?"

"The cops can't catch me when I step through."

"That doesn't answer my question. If you were a good girl, why do you use stepping through to rob widows, and not to do good? Don't tell me you've never tried changing anything. Find a door to the Ford Theater and take John Wilkes Booth's gun."

"It never works. You know that."

"But history doesn't notice when an old woman's diamond disappears. So—what do you use the money you steal for? Do you give it to the war effort? The Red Cross? The Catholic Church? Do you have a poor family stashed away somewhere that you play fairy godmother to?"

She tried to pull away, but the beat of the music and the steps of the dance carried her on.

The song changed to something relentless and manic. She tried to break out of his grasp, to spin and hop like everyone else was doing, but he tightened his grip and kept her cheek to cheek.

"You don't do any of those things," she said.

"How do you know?"

He was right, of course. She only had his word for it when he said he was a rogue.

"What are you trying to say?"

He brought his lips close to her ear and purred. "You were never a good girl, Madeline."

She slapped him, a nice crack across the cheek. He seemed genuinely stunned—he stopped cold in the middle of the dance and touched his face. A few bystanders laughed. Madeline turned, shoving her way off the dance floor, dodging feet and elbows.

She went all the way to the front doors before looking back. Ned wasn't following her. She couldn't see him at all, through the mob.

In the women's room she found her doorway to Madrid 1880 where she'd stashed a gown and danced flamenco, then to a taverna in Havana 1902, and from there to her room. He wouldn't possibly be able to follow that path.

Unbelievable, how out of a few thousand years of history available to them and countless millions of locations around the world, they kept running into each other.

Ned wore black. He had to, really, because they were at the dawn of the age of the tuxedo, and all the men wore black suits: black pressed trousers, jackets with tails, waistcoats, white cravats. Madeline rather liked the trend, because the women, in a hundred shades of rippling silk and shining jewels, glittered against the monotone backdrop.

Gowns here didn't require the elaborate architecture they had during the previous three centuries. She wore a corset, but her skirt was not so wide as to prevent walking through doorways. The fabric, pleated and gathered in back, draped around her in slimming lines. She glided tall and elegant, like a Greek statue.

He hadn't seen her yet. For once, she had the advantage. She watched behind the shelter of a neoclassical pillar. He moved like he'd been born to this dance. Perhaps he had. Every step made with confidence, he and his partner might have been the same unit as they turned, stepped, turned, not looking where they were going yet never missing a step. It always amazed her how a hundred couples could circle a crowded ballroom like this and never collide.

He was smiling, his gaze locked on his partner's the whole

time. For a moment, Madeline wished she were dancing with him. Passing time had cooled her temper.

She'd already got what she came for, a few bits of original Tiffany jewelry. After a dance or two, she could open a door and leave. In a room this large, she could dance a turn and Ned would never have to know she'd been here.

But she waited until his steps brought him close to her. She moved into view, caught his gaze and smiled. He stumbled on the parquet.

He managed to recover without falling and without losing too much of his natural grace. "Madeline! I didn't see you."

"I know."

He abandoned his partner—turned his back on her and went straight to Madeline. The woman glared after him with a mortally offended expression that Ned didn't seem to notice.

"Been a while, eh?"

"Only a month, subjective."

"So—what brings you here?"

"That's my secret. I've learned my lesson about telling you anything. You?"

He looked around, surveying the ballroom, the orchestra on the stage, the swirl of couples dancing a pattern like an eddy in a stream. Each couple was independent, but all of them together moved as one entity, as if choreographed.

"Strauss," he said at last. "Will you dance with me, Miss Madeline?"

He offered his hand, and she placed hers in it. They joined the pattern.

"Have you forgiven me for that comment from last time?"

"No," Madeline said with a smile. "I'm waiting for the chance to return the favor."

Step two three turn two three—

"Do you believe in fate?" Ned said.

"Fate? I suppose I have to, considering some of the things I've seen. Why do you ask?"

"It's a wonderful thing, really. You see, we never should have met. I should have died before you were born—or vice versa, since I still don't know when you're from. But here we are."

"That's fate? I thought you were following me."

"Ah yes."

Madeline tilted her head back. Crystal chandeliers sparkled overhead, turning, turning. Ned didn't take his eyes off her.

"Have you thought of why I might follow you?" he said.

"To reap the benefits of my hard work. I do the research and case the site, and you arrive to take the prize. It's all very neat and I'd like you to stop."

"I can't do that, Madeline."

"Why not? Isn't there enough history for you to find your own hunting grounds without taking mine?"

"Because that isn't the reason I'm following you. At least not anymore." He paused. He wasn't smiling, he wasn't joking. "I think I'm in love with you."

Her feet kept doing what they were supposed to do. The music kept them moving, which was good because her mind froze. "No," she murmured.

"Will you give me a chance? A chance to show you?"

It was a trick. A new way to make a fool of her, and it was cruel. But she had never seen him so serious. His brow took on furrows.

She stopped dancing, and he had to stop with her, but he wouldn't let go. There, stalled in the middle of the ballroom floor, the dance turned to chaos around them.

"No. I can't love you back, Ned. We're too much alike."

For a long moment, a gentle strain of music, he studied her. His expression turned drawn and sad.

"Be careful, Madeline. Watch your back." He kissed her hand, a gentle press of lips against her curled fingers, then let it go and walked off the dance floor, shouldering around couples as they passed.

He left her alone, lost, in the middle of the floor. She touched her hand where he had kissed it.

"Ned!" she called, the sound barely audible over the orchestra. "Ned!"

He didn't turn around.

The song ended.

She left the floor, hitched up her skirt and ran everywhere, looking behind every door and every potted fern. But he was gone.

If Ned followed her, it stood to reason others could as well.

Her room had been trashed. The mirror over the vanity was shattered, chairs smashed, a dresser toppled. Powdered cosmetics dusted the wreckage. The wardrobe was thrown open, gowns and fabric torn and strewn like streamers over the furniture.

She didn't have windows or doors precisely to keep this sort of thing from happening. There was only one way into the room—through a sideways door, and only if one knew just the right way to look through it. So how—

Someone grabbed her in a bear hug. Another figure appeared from behind her and pointed a bizarre vice-grip and hairbrush looking tool at her in the unmistakable stance of holding a weapon. A third moved into view.

She squirmed in the grasp of the first, but he was at least a foot taller than she and he quickly worked to secure bindings around her arms and hands that left her immobile. All wore black militaristic suits with goggles and metallic breathing masks hiding their features.

The third spoke, a male voice echoing mechanically through the mask. "Under Temporal Transit Authority Code forty-four A dash nine, I hereby take you into custody and charge you—

"The what?" Madeline said with a gasp. Her captor wrenched her shoulders back. Any struggle she made now was merely out of principle. "Temporal Transit Authority? I've never heard of such a thing!"

"You've never stepped through to the twenty-second century, then."

"No." Traveling to one's own future was tough—there was no record to study, no way to know what to expect. She'd had enough trouble with her past, she never expected the future to come back to haunt her.

"I hereby take you into custody and charge you with unregulated transportation along the recognized timeline, grand theft along the recognized timeline, historic fraud—"

"You can't be serious—"

He held up a device, something like an electric razor with a glowing wand at one end and flashing lights at the other. He pressed a button and drew a line in the air. The line glowed, hanging in midair. He pressed another button, the line widened into a plane, a doorway through which a dim scene showed: pale tiled walls and steel tables.

He opened a door, he stepped through, and all he needed to do was push a button.

In that stunned moment, the two flunkies picked her up and carried her through.

They entered a hospital room and unloaded her onto a gurney. More figures appeared, doctors hiding behind medical scrubs, cloth masks, and clinical gazes. With practiced ease they strapped her facedown, wrists and legs bound with padded restraints. When she tried to struggle, a half-dozen hands pressed her into the thin mattress. Her ice-blue skirt was hitched up around her knees, wrinkling horribly.

"Don't I get a lawyer? A phone call? Something?" She didn't even know where or when she was. Who would she call?

A doctor spoke to the thug in charge. "Her catalyst?"

"Dancing."

"I know just the thing. Nurse, prep a local anesthetic."

Madeline tensed against her bindings. "What are you doing? What are you doing to me?"

"Don't worry, we can reverse the procedure. If you're found innocent at the trial."

She lost track of how many people were in the room. A couple of the thugs, a couple of people in white who must have been nurses or orderlies. A couple who looked like doctors. Someone unbuttoned her shoes. Her silk stockings ripped.

Needle-pricks stabbed each foot, then pins of sleep traveled up her legs. She screamed. It was the only thing she could do. A hand pushed her face into the mattress. Her legs went numb up to her knees. She managed to turn her face, and through the awkward, fore-shortened perspective she saw them make incisions above her heels, reach a thin scalpel into the wounds, and cut the Achilles' tendons. There was no pain, but she felt the tissues snap inside her calves.

She screamed until her lungs hurt, until she passed out.

She awoke in a whitewashed cell, lying on a cot that was the room's only furnishing. There was a door without a handle. She was no longer tied up, but both her ankles were neatly bandaged, and she couldn't move her legs.

Gingerly sitting up, she unfastened the bodice of her gown, then released the first few hooks of her corset. She took a deep breath, arching her back. Her ribs and breasts were bruised from sleeping in the thing. Not to mention the manhandling she'd received.

She didn't want to think about her legs.

Curling up on her side, she hugged her knees and cried.

She fell asleep, arms curled around her head. The light, a pale florescent filtering through a ceiling tile, stayed on. Her growling stomach told her that time passed. Once, the door opened and an orderly brought in a tray of food, leaving it on the floor by the bed. She didn't eat. Another time, a female orderly brought in a contraption, a toilet seat and bedpan on wheels, and offered to help her use it. She screamed, batted and clawed at the woman until she left.

She pulled apart her elegant, piled coif—tangled now—and threw hairpins across the room.

When the door opened again, she had a few pins left to hurl at whomever entered. But it wasn't an orderly, a doctor, or a thug.

It was Ned, still in his tails and cravat.

He closed the door to the thinnest crack and waited a moment, listening. Madeline clamped her hand over her mouth to keep from crying out to him.

Apparently satisfied, Ned came to the bed, knelt on the floor, and gathered her in an embrace.

"You look dreadful," he said gently, holding her tightly.

She sobbed on his shoulder. "They cut my tendons, Ned. They cut my legs."

"They're bastards, Madeline," he muttered, between meaningless noises of comfort.

Clutching the fabric of his jacket, she pushed him away suddenly. "Did they get you too? What did they do to you?" She looked him over, touched his face—nothing seemed wrong. "How did you get here?"

He gave her a lopsided smile. "I used to be one of the bastards."

She edged away, pushing herself as far to the wall as she could. Ned, with his uncanny ability to follow her where and whenever she went. He didn't move, didn't try to stop her or grapple with her. She half expected him to.

"Used to be." she said. "Not still?"

"No. It began as a research project, to study what people like me—like us—can do, and what that meant about the nature of space and time. But there were other interests at work. They developed artificial methods of finding doorways and stepping through. They don't need us anymore and hate competition. The Temporal Transit Authority was set up to establish a monopoly over the whole business."

"And you—just left? Or did you lead them to me?"

"Please, Madeline. I'm searching for a bit of redemption here.

I followed you. I couldn't stop following you. I knew they were looking for you. I found your place right after they did. I wish—I should have told you. Warned you a little better than I did."

"Why didn't you?" she said, her voice thin and desperate.

"I didn't think you'd believe me. You've never trusted me. I'm sorry."

No, she thought, remembering that last waltz, the music and his sad face and the way he disappeared. *I'm sorry*.

"You were following me all along. We didn't meet by chance."

"Oh no. It was chance. Fate. I didn't know about you, wasn't looking for you. But when I met you, I knew the Authority would find you sooner or later. I didn't want them to find you."

"But they did."

"Once again I apologize for that. Now, we're getting out of here."

He started to pick her up, moving one arm to her legs and the other to her shoulders. She leaned away, pressing herself against the wall in an effort to put more distance between them.

"Please trust me," he said.

Why should she believe anything he said? She didn't know anything about him. Except that he was a marvelous dancer. And she needed to dance.

She put her arms around his neck and let him lift her.

"Come on, then." He picked her up, cradling her in his arms. She clung to him. "Get the door, would you?"

She pulled the door open. He looked out. The corridor was empty. Softly, he made his way down the hall.

Then Ned froze. Voices echoed ahead of them, moving closer. Without a word, he turned and walked the other direction. If he had been able to run, he would have rounded the next corner before the owners of the voices saw him. But he held her, and he couldn't do more than walk carefully.

Footsteps sounded behind him. She looked over his shoulder and saw a doctor flanked by a couple of orderlies enter the corridor.

"Hey! Stop there!" The doctor pointed and started running.

"All these bloody doors lock on the outside," Ned muttered. "Here, open that one."

She stared. The door had no handle, no visible hinges or latches. Ned hissed a breath of frustration and bumped a red light panel on the wall with his elbow. The door popped in with a little gasp of hydraulics.

He pushed through into what turned out to be a supply closet, about ten foot square, filled with shelves and boxes, and barely enough room to turn around. He set her on the floor and began pushing plastic tubs at the door. He soon had enough of a blockade to stop their pursuers from shoving through right away. He kept piling, though, while the people outside pounded on the door and shouted.

Madeline cowered on the floor, her legs stuck out awkwardly. "You can't dance for both of us, and I'm too big for you to carry me through."

"Yes."

"You shouldn't have come. Now you're caught too."

"But I'm with you," he said, turning to her with the brightest, most sincere smile she had ever seen. "It makes all the difference." He went back to throwing boxes on the stack.

She caught her breath and wondered what she'd have to do to see that smile again.

"Help me stand." She hooked her fingers on a shelving post as far above her as she could reach and pulled. Grunting, she shifted her weight to try and get her feet under her.

"Madeline, good God what are you doing?"

"Standing. Help me."

He went to her and pulled her arm over his shoulders, reaching his own arm around her waist. Slowly, he raised her. She straightened her legs, and her feet stayed where she put them.

There. She was standing. She clenched her jaw. Her calves were exploding with pain.

"Do you think there's a door in here?" she said, her voice tight.

"There're doors everywhere. But you can't—"

"We have to."

"But—"

"I can. Help me."

He sighed, adjusting his grip so he supported her more firmly. "Right. What should we dance?"

She took a breath, cleared her mind so she could think of a song. She couldn't even tap her toe to keep a beat. She began humming. The song sounded out of tune and hopeless in her ears.

"Ravel. 'Pavane for a Dead Princess,'" Ned said. "Come on, dear, you're not done yet. One and two and—"

She held her breath and moved her right leg. It did move, the foot dragging, and she leaned heavily on Ned because she didn't dare put any weight on it. Then the left foot. She whimpered a little. Ned was right behind her, stepping with her.

The pavane had the simplest steps she could think of. At its most basic, it was little more than walking very slowly—perfect for a crippled dancer. It was also one of the most graceful, stately, elegant dances ever invented. Not this time. She couldn't trust her legs. She dragged them forward and hoped they went where they needed to be. Ned wasn't so much dancing with her as lurching, ensuring she stayed upright.

There was a kind of power, even in this: bodies moving in desperation.

She tried to keep humming, but her voice jerked, pain-filled, at every step. They hummed together, his voice steadying her as his body did.

Then came a turn. She attempted it—a dance was a dance, after all. Put the left foot a little to the side, step out—

Her leg collapsed. She cried out, cutting the sound off mid-breath. Ned caught her around the waist and leaned her against the shelving. This gave her something to sit on, a little support.

Without missing a beat, he took her hand and stepped a half-circle around her. He held her hand lightly, elevated somewhat, and tucked his other hand behind his back. Perfect form.

"This just doesn't feel right if I'm not wearing a ruff," he said, donning a pompous, aristocratic accent.

Hiccupping around stifled tears, she giggled. "But I like being able to see your neck. It's a handsome neck."

"Right, onto the age of disco then."

The banging on the door was loud, insistent, like they'd started using a battering ram, and provided something of a beat. The barricade began to tumble.

"And so we finish." He bowed deeply.

She started to dip into a curtsey—just the tiniest of curtsies—but Ned caught her and lifted her.

"I think we're ready."

She narrowed her eyes and looked a little bit sideways.

Space and time made patterns, the architecture of the universe, and the lines crossed everywhere, cutting through the very air. Sometimes, someone had a talent that let them see the lines and use them.

"There," Ned said. "That one. A couple of disheveled Edwardians won't look so out of place there. Do you see it?"

"Yes," she said, relieved. A glowing line cut before them, and if they stepped a little bit sideways—

She put out her hand and opened the door so they could step through together.

Lady Petulant's diamond paid for reconstructive surgery at the best unregistered clinic in Tokyo 2028. Madeline walked out the door and into the alley, where Ned was waiting for her. Laughing, she jumped at him and swung him around in a couple of steps of a haphazard polka.

"Glad to see you're feeling better," he said. And there was that smile again.

"Polycarbon filament tissue replacement. I have the strongest tendons in the world now."

They walked out to the street—searching the crowd of pedestrians, always looking over their shoulders.

"Where would you like to go?" he said.

"I don't know. It's not so easy to pick, now that we're fugitives. Those guys could be anywhere."

"But we have lots of places to hide. We just have to keep moving."

They walked for a time along a chaotic street, nothing like a ballroom, the noises nothing like music. The Transit Authority people knew they had to dance; if they were really going to hide, it would be in places like this, where dancing was next to impossible.

But they couldn't do that, could they?

Finally, Ned said, "We could go watch Rome burn. And fiddle."

"Hm. I'd like to find a door to the Glen Island Casino. 1939."

"Glenn Miller played there, didn't he?"

"Yes."

"We could find one, I think."

"If we have to keep moving anyway, we'll hit on it eventually."

He took her hand, pulled her close and pressed his other hand against the small of her back. Ignoring the tuneless crowd, he danced with her.

"Lead on, my dear."

The Lord-Protector's Daughter

L.E. Modesitt, Jr.

I

The sound of Mykella's boots echoed dully as she descended the stone staircase to the lowest level of the Lord-Protector's palace. When she reached the small foyer at the bottom, she paused and glanced around. The ancient light-torch in its bronze wall bracket illuminated the precisely cut stones of the wall and floor with the same tired amber light as it always had—so far as she could remember.

Why was she down in the seldom-visited depths? Had it just been a dream? Had she actually seen the gauzy-winged and shimmering figure no larger than a child—though full-figured—who had appeared at the foot of her bed. The soarer had touched her. A tingle had run through her body, and then the soarer had "spoken" to her . . . and vanished, but those few words echoed in Mykella's thoughts.

If you would save your land and your world, go to the Table and find your talent.

Could that figure have really been a soarer—one of the Ancients?

She'd heard tales of people seeing soarers, but whenever the Southern Guard or the city patrollers tried to track down someone who had been rumored to have seen them, the reports turned out to be groundless.

Mykella sniffed. Rumors and tales, tales and rumors. Golds were far more reliable in predicting what folk did and did not do. That, she had learned in her informal oversight of the Finance Ministry for her father. Still, she thought she had seen and heard a soarer, and family lore had held that the legendary Mykel, the first Lord-Protector, had been directed to Tempre by a soarer after the Great Cataclysm. Almost for that reason alone, Mykella had thrown on tunic, trousers, and boots and slipped out of her chamber. The guards patrolling the corridor outside the family quarters had only nodded, whatever they might have thought.

She looked through the archway separating the staircase foyer from the long, subterranean hallway that extended the entire length of the palace. The dimly lit passageway was empty, as it should have been. While the ground-level door to the staircase she had just descended was always locked and guarded, as the Lord-Protector's daughter, she had the keys to all the locks, and no guard would dare refuse her entry to any chamber in the palace itself. She'd never quite figured out the reason for the boxlike design of the Lord-Protector's palace, with all the rooms set along the corridors that formed an interior rectangle on each level. The upper level remained reserved for the family and the official studies of the highest ministers of Lanachrona; but there was only one main staircase, of graystone, and certainly undeserving of the appellation "grand staircase," only one modest great dining chamber, and but a single long and narrow ballroom, not that she cared for dancing. More intriguing were the facts that the stones of the outer walls looked as if they had been cut and quarried but a few years earlier and that there were no chambers truly befitting the ruler of Lanachrona.

Mykella walked briskly down the underground corridor toward the door set in the middle of the wall closest to the outside foundation. Once there, she stopped and studied it, as if for the first time. The door itself was of ancient oak, with an antique lever handle. Yet that lever, old as it had to be, seemed newer than the hinges. The stones of the door casement were also of a shade just slightly darker than the stones of the corridor wall. Several of the stones bordering the casement were also darker, almost as if they and the casement had been partly replaced in the past.

After a moment, Mykella tossed her head impatiently, hardly disarranging short-cut black locks, then reached out and depressed the lever. The hinges creaked slightly as she pushed the door open, and she made a mental note to tell the steward. Doors in the Lord-Protector's palace should not squeak. That was unacceptable.

At first glance, the Table chamber looked as it always had, a windowless stone-walled space some five yards by seven, without furnishings except for a single black wooden chest and the Table itself—a block of blackish stone set into the floor, whose flat and mirrored surface was level with her waist—or perhaps slightly higher, she had to admit, if only to herself. She was the shortest of the Lord-Protector's offspring, even if she did happen to be the eldest. But she was a daughter and not a son, a daughter most likely to be married off to some heir or another, most probably the Landarch-heir of Deforya, a cold and dark land, she'd heard, scoured by chill winds sweeping down from the Aerlal Plateau. She only seen the Plateau once, from more than thirty vingts away while accompanying her father on an inspection trip of the upper reaches of the River Vedra. Yet even from that distance, the Plateau's sheer stone sides had towered into the clouds that enshrouded its seldom-glimpsed top.

Her thoughts of the Plateau and Deforya dropped away as she realized that there was another source of illumination in the chamber besides the dim glow of the ancient light-torches. From the Table itself oozed a faint purplish hue. Or did it?

Mykella blinked.

The massive stone block returned to the lifeless darkness she'd always seen before on the infrequent occasions when she had accompanied her father or her brother Jeraxylt to see the Table.

"Because it is part of our heritage," had invariably been what her father had said when she had asked the purpose of beholding a block of stone that had done nothing but squat in the dimness for generations.

Jeraxylt had been more forthright. "I'm going to be the one who masters the Table. That's what you have to do if you want to be a real Lord-Protector." Needless to say, Jeraxylt hadn't said those

words anywhere near their father, not when no Lord-Protector
in generations had been able to fathom the Table.

Mykella doubted that anyone had done so since the Cataclysm,
even the great Mykel, but she wasn't about to say so. Before
the Cataclysm, the Alectors and even the great Mykel had been
reputed to be able to travel from Table to Table. Another folktale
and fanciful fable, thought Mykella. Or wishful thinking. No one
could travel instantly from one place to another.

Yet . . . once more, the Table glowed purple, and she stared at
it. But when she did, the glow vanished. She looked away, and
then back. There was no glow . . . or was there?

She studied the Table once again, but her eyes saw only dark
stone. Yet she could feel or sense purple. Abruptly, she realized that
the purplish light was strangely like the soarer's words, perceived
inside her head in some fashion rather than through her eyes.

What did it mean? How could sensing a purple light that wasn't
there save her land? How could that be a talent? If the soarer had
not been a dream, if she had appeared, why had she appeared to
Mykella and not to her father or to Jeraxylt?

Slowly, she walked around the Table, looking at it intently, yet
also trying to feel or sense what might be there, all too conscious
that she was in the lowest level of the palace in the middle of
the night—and alone.

At the western end of the Table, she could feel something,
but it was as though what she sensed lay within the stone of the
Table. She stopped, turned, and extended her fingers, too short and
stubby for a Lord-Protector's daughter, to touch the stone. Was it
warmer? She walked to the wall and touched it, then nodded.

After a moment, she moved back to the Table, where she peered
at the mirrorlike black surface, trying to feel or sense more of
what might lie beneath. For a moment, all she saw in the dimness was her own image—black hair, broad forehead, green eyes,
straight nose, shoulders too broad for a woman her size. At least,
she had fair clear skin.

Even as she watched, her reflection faded, and the silvery
black gave way to swirling silvery-white mists. Then, an image
appeared in the center of the mists—that of a man, except no
man she had ever seen. He had skin as white as the infrequent
snows that fell on Tempre, eyes of brilliant and piercing violet,
and short-cut jet-black hair.

He looked up from the Table at Mykella as though she were the lowest of the palace drudges. He spoke, if words in her mind could be called speech. She understood not a single word or phrase, yet she felt that she should, as though he were speaking words she knew in an unfamiliar cadence and with an accent she did not recognize. He paused, and a cruel smile crossed his narrow lips. She did understand the last words he uttered before the swirling mists replaced his image.

". . . useless except as cattle to build lifeforce."

Cattle? He was calling her a cow? Mykella seethed, and the Table mists swirled more violently.

The Table could allow people to talk across distances? Why had no one mentioned that? There was nothing of that in the archives. And where was he? Certainly not within the sunken ruins of Elcien. Could he be in far Alustre, so far to the east that even with the eternal ancient roads of Corus few traders made that journey, and fewer still returned?

Alustre? What was Alustre like?

The swirling mists subsided into a moving border around a circular image—that of a city of white buildings, viewed from a height. Mykella swallowed, and the scene vanished. After a moment, so did the mists.

The strange man—could he have been an Alector? Hadn't they all perished in the Cataclysm? Mykella didn't know what to think. Still . . . she had thought of Alustre and something had appeared. Could she view people?

She concentrated on her father. The mirror surface turned into a swirl of mists, revealing in the center Lord Feranyt lying on the wide bed of the Lord-Protector, looking upward, his eyes open. Beside him, asleep, lay Erayna, his mistress. After the death of Mykella's mother, her father had refused to marry again, claiming that to do so would merely cause more problems.

Mykella felt strange looking at her father, clearly visible in darkness, and she turned her thoughts to Jeraxylt. Her brother was not asleep, nor was he alone. Mykella quickly thought about their summerhouse in the hills to the northeast of Tempre. The mist swirled, and then an image of white columns appeared, barely visible in the dark.

She tried calling up images of places in Tempre, and those also appeared. So did an image when she thought of Dereka, and she viewed the city squares in Vyan and Krost, but even the mists vanished when she tried to see Soupat or Lyterna. Finally, she stepped back from the Table. It still glowed with the unworldly purple sheen, but she could now distinguish between what she saw with her eyes and what she sensed.

She shivered. Telling herself that it was merely the chill from the cold stone of the lower levels, she eased back out of the Table chamber, carefully closing the door behind her.

Once she had climbed the two flights of stairs and returned to her own simple room, Mykella sat on the edge of the bed. What had really happened?

II

Mykella hadn't thought she would sleep, not with all the questions running through her head, but she had. She even overslept and had to hurry in getting washed up on Duadi morning. Dressing wasn't a problem for her, not the way it was for her two younger sisters, particularly Salyna. Mykella just wore black nightsilk trousers and tunic over the full-shouldered black nightsilk camisole and the matching underdrawers, with polished black boots. Her father insisted on those undergarments whenever they were to leave the palace, and it was simpler to wear them all the time. It seemed almost a pity that few ever saw them, and most of those who did would not have recognized them for what they were, since they cost more than a season's earnings for a crafter. Soft and smooth as they were to the touch, they could stop any blade or even a bullet, although a bullet impact would leave a widely bruised area of flesh beneath.

More than a few had tried and failed to learn the herders' secrets, but now few tried, especially since the Iron Valleys were so cold and forbidding and their militiamen were vicious fighters. What was the point of fighting and losing golds and men when the only thing of value was nightsilk that was cheaper to buy than to fight battles over?

Mykella hurried down the corridor and tried to ease into the breakfast room of the family quarters through the service pantry.

Feranyt looked up from the head of the table, polished dark oak that had endured many Lords-Protector and their families.

"Mykella . . . I had wondered when you would join us, especially when I heard you had gone prowling through the lower levels of the palace last night."

Mykella managed a rueful smile as she took her place on the left side of the table—the place that had once been her mother's. "I couldn't sleep. I knew I could walk around down there safely—and quietly." She looked directly across the table at Jeraxylt, seated to her father's right. "There were others who weren't exactly quiet or sleeping, either."

Jeraxylt smiled lazily, even white teeth standing out against his tanned face and the dark blue uniform of the Southern Guard, then shrugged. "I got a very good night's sleep."

Mykella lifted the mug of already-cooled tea. Jeraxylt wasn't about to admit anything, and her father certainly wouldn't press his son, not when they'd both been engaged in a similar fashion. She took a slow sip of the cool tea and waited to be served.

"You look good in that uniform." Salyna smiled at her older brother. "The seltyrs' daughters and the High Factors' daughters think so, too."

"How would you know, little vixen?" Jeraxylt grinned at his youngest sister.

"I'm a girl, silly brother. I know."

Rachylana raised her left eyebrow. Lifting a single eyebrow was one of the skills Rachylana had pursued, as if such unusual talents were required of a middle daughter.

Jeraxylt ignored the gesture.

"What are you doing today?" Mykella asked. "Playing Cadmian again?"

"I'm not playing. I'm going through all the training a Southern Guard gets."

"Father won't let you serve, not in a combat position, anyway." Mykella eased her head sideways to let the serving girl—Muergya on that morning—set a platter with an omelet and ham strips, along with candied prickle, before her.

"Lord-Protectors don't serve. They command."

"Didn't Mykel the Great serve?" Mykella asked innocently.

"That was different. Besides, we don't know that. He probably just had the scriveners write the history that way," replied Jeraxylt.

"Be careful how you speak of history, Jeraxylt," cautioned the Lord-Protector. "You are the heir and will be Lord-Protector because of that history. Disparage it, and your disparage your own future."

"Lord-Protector . . ." Rachylana looked to her father. "Why don't you just call yourself Landarch or prince? That's what you are, Father, aren't you?"

Feranyt offered his middle daughter a patronizing smile. "Rachylana . . . names and titles carry meaning. The words 'Lord-Protector' tell our people that our duty is to protect them. A Landarch or a prince rules first and protects second, if at all."

Mykella caught the hint of a frown that crossed Jeraxylt's brow. The fleeting expression bothered her, as did a feeling, one that was not hers, yet that she had felt. That feeling had combined pride, arrogance, and a certain disdain.

After hurriedly eating the undercooked omelet and greasy ham, and gulping down the candied prickle because she knew she needed to, Mykella stayed at the breakfast table only until her father rose. Then she departed, washing up slightly before making her way to Finance chambers on the east end of the palace—still on the upper level.

Kiedryn was already at his table desk in the outer chamber, and the door to the smaller study that belonged to Joramyl, as Finance Minister, was closed, not that Mykella expected Joramyl to appear anytime soon.

Mykella glanced at the white-haired chief clerk. If anyone would know what the soarer had meant, Kiedryn might. He'd claimed to have read every page in the archives.

"Do you know if the Mykel the Great had a special talent?" she finally asked, standing beside the smaller table that was hers. "Do the archives say anything about that?"

"He had many," replied Kiedryn. "He could kill men without touching them. He could walk on water and even on the air itself. He could disappear from sight whenever he wished. He brought an army through the steam and heat when the River Vedra boiled out of its banks during the Great Cataclysm. He was called the Dagger of the Ancients because he cut anyone or anything that stood in his way. He married Rachyla because she was the only one who could stand up to him."

"Do you believe all that?"

"Mostly," replied the chief clerk. "No one with less ability could have created Lanachrona out of the chaos that followed the Cataclysm. The western lands are still mired in chaos, with all their little lordlets and the seltyrs of Southgate playing them off against one another, and the situation with the nomads to the southeast is even worse . . . and always has been."

"But you didn't say he had a talent, one talent."

Kiedryn laughed sardonically. "You didn't ask it that way. Talent—that's what they say that the nightsheep herders have up in the Iron Valleys. Maybe Mykel had it, and maybe he didn't. The archives don't say." He shook his head, almost mournfully. "You'd have to have something like that to handle those beasts."

Mykella bit back the reply she might have made. Why couldn't anyone just answer her questions? Rather than upset Kiedryn, and to no avail, she settled at the table and began to look over the latest entries in the master ledger. When she reached the end of the third page, she frowned.

Then she stood and walked to the rows of individual account ledgers set on the dark wooden shelves built into the inner wall, picking out one and taking it back to her table desk. After studying the second ledger for a time, she turned to the chief clerk.

"Kiedryn? The barge tariffs on shipments from the upper Vedra are down for the harvest season. They're even lower than those for the spring, and spring tariffs are always the lowest."

"Mistress Mykella," replied the chief finance clerk with a shrug, "I cannot say. We did send patrollers to visit all the factors and bargemasters."

"And?"

"They all claimed that they had paid their tariffs, and most of them more than last year. Almost all still had their sealed receipts."

Mykella stiffened. "What did Lord Joramyl say?"

"He claims that some of them must be lying, or that some of the tariff-collectors had pocketed the tariffs. He told your father this last week."

What Kiedryn was not saying was that no one except the Lord-Protector was likely to contradict Joramyl, since he was not only the Finance Minister of Lanachrona, but the only brother of the Lord-Protector as well.

But why had her father said nothing?

Mykella went to the cabinet at the end of those set beyond

Kiedryn's table desk and opened it, leafing through the folders there until she found the list of factors. She carried the list back to her table and began to copy names.

III

By Quinti afternoon Mykella had studied the accounts enough to estimate that at least two thousand golds had been siphoned out of the Treasury over the past two seasons, just from the seasonal tariffs on the bargemasters and the seltyrs and High Factors... or rather that those golds had never been put into the Treasury after having been collected. But her calculations were only estimates based on past years' collections and various ratios between barge landings and other records—and she might be wrong. Nonetheless, she would have wagered almost anything that more than a few golds that should not have now rested in Joramyl's strongboxes in his westhill mansion, with its high walls and guarded gates. But there was not a shred of hard proof, and she'd been careful to be polite to Joramyl when he had come into the Finance chambers.

She'd been careful as well in not letting Kiedryn know what she had been doing, other than her normal supervision and questioning. The last thing she needed was for the clerk to mention anything to Joramyl.

How could she discover proof? Could the Table show her anything?

It was certainly worth a try.

Late that afternoon, just before the palace guards were relieved by those on evening duty, Mykella carried a stack of ledgers down from the Finance chambers to the door to the lower levels. She could feel the eyes of one of the patrolling guards on her from a good ten yards away. She maintained a resigned expression as she neared the door.

As she stopped short of the door, the guard looked at her directly, and she could sense a feeling of curiosity, a question why the Lord-Protector's daughter was lugging around ledgers by herself.

"These are the personal accounts of the Lord-Protector, but they're several years old. They aren't needed often, but they need to be kept in a safe place, and the older records are stored on the lower level," she explained. "I'll be there a bit because they have to be put in order." She tried to press the need for safety toward the guard.

Abruptly, the man nodded and stepped forward. "Do you need help, Mistress Mykella?"

"If you'd hold these while I unlock the door, I'd appreciate it. These records are only for the Lord-Protector, the Finance Minister, and the head clerk. They'd prefer to keep it that way." She offered a pleasant smile.

She could sense his feelings as she closed and locked the door behind her—too handsome for a Lord-Protector's daughter.

Handsome? That was a word for men, not women. Yet Mykella knew she didn't possess the ravishing beauty of Salyna or the exotic looks of Rachylana. She was moderately good-looking, if less than imposing in stature, but she could think . . . and liked thinking—unlike all too many of the women in her family and in Tempre, where a woman's duty was always to her husband and her sons.

It took Mykella only a few moments to add the ledgers to those in the Finance storeroom, and she was about to leave and lock the chamber when she realized that she sensed something. She whirled toward the door to the corridor, but no one had entered, and she heard nothing except the sound of her own breathing. Her eyes traversed the rows of simple wooden shelves that held the older ledgers, covered in a fine layer of dust. The shelves had been built against the stone walls, and there was nowhere to hide.

She frowned. It felt as though someone had been in the chamber, but how could she sense that? She looked at the ledgers to the left of those she had added. The dust was gone from one of the ledgers—and she realized that one volume was missing. Since the black leather binding and spine did not reveal the contents, she had to look through three others before she determined that the missing volume held, not surprisingly, the details of barge tariffs from five years previously.

A chill ran down her spine. She shook her head, then stepped back and left the chamber, locking it behind her. She crossed the corridor and walked back toward the Table chamber, where she entered cautiously, although she felt that no one was around. The chamber was empty, and the Table looked the same—dull dark stone with a mirrored surface, but she could sense more easily the purplish glow. This time, though, the purple felt almost unclean. She could also sense, somewhere beneath and below that purple, a far stronger and deeper shade, what she could only have called a blackish green.

Were the two linked? How? She tried to see or sense more, but could discern only the two separate shades—one superficial and linked to the Table and the other deeper and somehow beneath it, trailing off into the earth.

She finally stepped up to the Table and slipped a sheet of paper out from her tunic, concentrating on the first name on her list—Seltyr and High Factor Almardyn. All that the Table showed were swirling mists. The same thing happened when she tried Barsytan, only a High Factor, and then Burclytt. Had she just imagined that she had been able to see people in its mirrored surface? She concentrated on Rachylana.

The mists barely appeared and swirled before revealing Rachylana. She sat on a stone bench in the solarium on the upper southeastern corner of the palace. Beside her, with his arm around her, was Berenyt—Joramyl's only surviving offspring—for now, at least.

Mykella shook her head. Cousin or not, Berenyt would flirt with anyone, even the Lord-Protector's daughter. After what Mykella had discovered, she had to question whether Berenyt's flirtation with Rachylana was merely his nature . . . or part of something else. Yet Rachylana knew nothing about finances and cared about the workings of the Lord-Protector's government even less.

After a moment, Mykella let the image lapse. She tried the name of another factor, but the Table only showed the mists. She glanced down the list until she found a name she recognized—that of Hasenyt. This time, Table displayed an image of the sharp-featured and graying factor standing at the barge docks just north of the grand piers. Hasenyt gestured to a man in a dark gray vest—a bargemaster, from his garb.

In the end, the Table proved useless for what Mykella had in mind because it would only show what people were doing at the moment when she was looking, and it would only display images of those whom she knew. In addition, except for a handful of the oldest cities on Corus, the Table would not show her anyplace that she had not visited.

That meant she would have to find a way to visit the factors on her list, and that required help. She hated to ask anyone for assistance, but there was no other way, not in Tempre, where a woman, especially a Lord-Protector's daughter, never appeared in public unescorted.

IV

That night, Mykella lay in her bed, looking up at the unadorned ceiling, thinking. What was the darkness below and beneath the purple glow of the Table? Why hadn't she seen it earlier? Why did the purple feel almost unclean and repulsive?

Question after question swirled through her mind. Was Joramyl the one diverting tariff golds? If so, why? Just to line his pockets and pay for his extravagances? Or was he plotting more? And if he were not the one, who could it be?

It would be so much easier if she had the powers that Kiedryn had claimed for Mykel the Great—even being able to move around unseen would be helpful.

From her bed, she absently scanned the wall shelf to the right of her small dressing table, taking in the carved onyx box that had been her mother's and the pair of silver candlesticks, the base of each a miniature replica of eternal greenstone towers that flanked the grand piers. At that moment, she realized that the room was pitch-dark, with the window hangings closed and not a single lamp lit, yet she could discern the shape of every object in her chambers.

Another facet of her talents? Or had she always been able to do that?

That had to be something awakened by the soarer's touch. But why her? She had no real power in Lanachrona. She didn't even have any real influence over her father or her brother.

She shook her head, then smiled wryly in the darkness. Too bad the palace corridors weren't kept that dark.

V

Mykella was up early on Sexdi and one of the first in the family at breakfast. She had to force herself to wait to ask what she wanted to know until her father was well settled and taking a second mug of spiced tea.

"What was Lord Joramyl like when you were growing up, Father?" Mykella asked, taking a sip of the plain strong tea she preferred to the cider most women drank or the spiced tea her father liked. "He seems so proud and distant now." Arrogant, self-serving, and aloof were what she really thought, but saying so would only have angered her father.

"He's always been proud, but he was always kind to Mother and Lalyna. He'd bring them both special gifts from all the places he served in the Southern Guard. Your aunt's favorites were the perfumes he brought back from Southgate when he was your grandfather's envoy there. She even took the empty bottles when she left for Soupat." He shook his head. "I knew she'd have trouble with the heat there, but Father insisted on it."

"Did you play games together?" Mykella pursued.

Feranyt shook his head. "Joramyl was never one for games. Except for leschec. He got to be so good at it that he beat old Arms-Commander Paetryl. We didn't play it together. He was too serious about it for me."

Mykella could sense that even thinking about Joramyl and leschec bothered her father. "Did you spar with weapons?"

"Father forbid it after I broke Joramyl's wrist. I was better, but Joramyl wouldn't ever quit."

The more her father said, the more concerned Mykella became. It wasn't that his words revealed that much new, but what she had discovered about the missing tariff golds gave a new meaning to her father's childhood memories. "Do you think that he feels he'd be a better Lord-Protector than you?"

"Mykella! How could you ask that?" murmured Rachylana, leaning close to her sister.

"Father?" Mykella kept her voice soft, curious, hard as it was for her.

"I'm sure he does." Feranyt laughed. "Each of us thinks we can do a better job than anyone else, but things turn out the way they do, and usually for good reason."

Mykella couldn't believe what she sensed from her father—a total lack of concern and a dismissal of Joramyl's ambitions.

"Joramyl's passion for detail serves us well, dear, as does yours. I'd like to think that my devotion to doing what is right should be the prime goal of a Lord-Protector. If one does what is right, then one doesn't have to worry about plots and schemes nearly so much."

Feranyt smiled broadly. "Besides, you can't please everyone. Joramyl only thinks you can, that ruling is like finance and numbers, that there is but one correct way to approach it. If he were ever Lord-Protector, he'd quickly discover that's not the way it is."

"If anything happened . . . do you think he'd be a good Lord-Protector? As good as you are?" Mykella pressed.

"Probably not, but he'd be far better than anyone else in Tempre, except for Jeraxylt, of course." Feranyt inclined his head toward his son. "But enough of such morbid speculations." He rose. "I need to get ready for a meeting with an envoy from the Iron Valleys. Their council is worried about Reillie incursions from Northian lands."

"What does that have to do with us?" asked Jeraxylt.

"I'm certain I'll find out," replied the Lord-Protector. "They are claiming that the Reillies have been armed with weapons having a Borlan arms mark."

"We sell to whoever pays," Jeraxylt said. "Are they going to demand that we stop selling goods because they can't defend their own borders?"

"I doubt that they will express matters . . . quite so directly, Jeraxylt. Nor should you, outside of the family quarters." Feranyt smiled, then turned and left the breakfast room.

Rachylana quickly followed, as did Jeraxylt.

Salyna looked to Mykella. "You know Rachylana will tell Berenyt everything you said this morning?"

"I hope she has better sense than that." Despite what she said, Mykella knew that Salyna was right. She rose and offered her youngest sister a smile. "What are you doing today?"

"Watching Chatelaine Auralya supervise the kitchens. I'm learning from her. It's more interesting than adding up numbers in ledgers. For me, that is. I don't have your talents."

"We all have different talents," replied Mykella. What else could she say?

"You ride well," Salyna pointed out.

"So do you, better than I."

"I'm not bad with a blade, Jeraxylt says." There was a shyness and diffidence in Salyna's words, but pride beneath them.

"You've been using a sabre?"

"A blunted one," Salyna admitted. "It's fun. I can see why Jeraxylt likes the Guard."

Mykella couldn't imagine sparring with blades as being fun, but she just smiled as she slipped out of the breakfast room. After leaving Salyna, Mykella walked slowly toward the Finance chambers.

Kiedryn was already at work, and Mykella settled herself at her own table, where she began to check the individual current account ledgers. There were no new entries of tariff collections from the bargemasters or the other rivermen. She didn't expect any, since all the accounts were current, and the next collections were not due until after the turn of spring. So she turned her attention to the Southern Guard ledgers.

The accounts there showed a surplus. Mykella frowned. The Guard had not used what had been set aside. In fact, the expenditures were almost one part in ten lower than at the same time in the previous year, and that was with less than half of winter left to run.

At that moment, she heard a hearty voice in the corridor outside the Finance chambers—Berenyt's booming bass.

"Just heading in to see my sire—if he's there. If not, I'll harass old Kiedryn." Berenyt was two years older than Mykella, despite the fact that his father Joramyl was younger than his brother the Lord-Protector. Berenyt had taken a commission as a captain in the Southern Guard and ended up in command of First Company, one of the two charged with guarding the palace and the Lord-Protector.

Mykella couldn't make out to whom Berenyt was speaking, but she could sense that the other was male, and vaguely amused. She was not. After what she'd seen in the Table and what she'd discovered, she didn't want to see him anytime soon, much less talk to him.

"Is Father in?"

"No, ser," replied Kiedryn. "I haven't seen him yet this morning."

Mykella could easily sense what the chief clerk had not said—*I've never seen him this early.* She tried to visualize herself with the shelves of ledgers between her and Kiedryn . . . and Berenyt.

Berenyt turned in her direction, frowning, and blinking. "Oh . . . there you are, Mykella. For a moment . . ." He shook his head. "You haven't seen Father this morning?"

"We seldom see him in the morning," Mykella replied. "I've always assumed that he had other duties."

"He does indeed."

Behind the words Mykella detected a sense of more than she could possibly understand, mixed with condescension and amusement. She managed a simpering smile, although she felt like gagging, and replied, "He offers much to Lanachrona."

"As does your Father." Berenyt's words were polite enough and sounded warm enough, but the feeling behind them was cool. He turned from Mykella back to Kiedryn. "I'll find him somewhere, but if I don't, please tell him I was here."

"Yes, ser."

Mykella merely nodded, if courteously.

After Berenyt had left, she just sat at her table, not really looking at the ledger before her. For just a moment when he had first looked in her direction, she thought, Berenyt had not really seen her. Had that been her doing? Or his abstraction and interest in other matters? How could she tell?

She really wanted to work more with the Table, but she dared not go down too often because, sooner or later, the guards would reveal how often she was going there, and either Jeraxylt or her father would discover her destination. That would lead to even more questions, and those were questions she dared not answer truthfully—and she detested lying, even though she knew that sometimes it was unavoidable, especially for a woman in Tempre.

The soarer's words kept coming back to her, although she had not seen or sensed the winged Ancient except the one time. Was using the Table her talent? Just to be able to see what was happening elsewhere? And what about her growing ability to sense what others were feeling? Or the sharper sight in the darkness?

VI

That evening after dinner, Mykella sat in the family parlor, a history of Lanachrona in her lap. She'd read some of the parts about Mykel, but there was nothing there about how he had accomplished anything—except a paragraph dismissing the legend that he had been a Dagger of the Ancients. Mykel suspected that dismissal was proof that he had been, but what a Dagger of the Ancients might have been she had no idea. Kiedryn's explanation had conveyed nothing, and her own brief searches of the archives had revealed nothing she did not already know.

Rachylana had not joined them after dinner. She had eaten little at table, claiming she had not felt well. Mykella had sensed the truth of her words and the physical discomfort behind them. Jeraxylt and her father rarely joined them in the evenings, not with their other evening interests. So the youngest and eldest daughters had the parlor to themselves.

Mykella stared at the darkness beyond the window, a darkness broken only by the scattered lights of Tempre, those that could be seen from the second level of the palace and beyond the gardens that surrounded it on all sides—except the hillside to the northeast beyond the walled rear courtyard. She knew that unseen danger surrounded them all, especially her father and brother, not only from the warning of the Ancient, but from what she had begun to sense.

After each of the times she had visited the Table, Mykella felt that she had gained something in what she could feel or sense. Yet . . . how could merely sensing or feeling more than others could save her land? She thought about Berenyt's momentary reaction once more, then glanced to the green velvet settee closest to the fire in the hearth, where Salyna was sitting, working on a needle-point crest. Finally, she spoke. "Salyna . . . I need your help."

"I'd be happy to, but . . ." Her younger sister's forehead wrinkled up into a puzzled expression. " . . . how could I help you?"

"I just want you to look out the window for a little while, and then look back at me. Take your time looking out the window."

"Look out the window and back at you?"

"Please . . . just do it."

"I can do that." Salyna's words continued to express puzzlement, but she turned and stared out the window.

Mykella concentrated on trying to create an image of the arm-chair in which she sat—vacant without her in it, the lace doily just slightly disarrayed . . .

"Don't do that!" Salyna's words were low, but intense.

"What did I do?" asked Mykella, releasing the image of the empty chair.

"It . . . it was awful. You weren't there. I knew you had to be . . . but you weren't. What did you do?"

Mykella wished she hadn't tried the shield. "I hid. I did it to see if I could move so quietly that you couldn't see me. What else could I have done?" She could sense Salyna's confusion, as well as her sister's feeling that Mykella couldn't have gone any-where else.

For a long time, Salyna looked at Mykella without speaking. Finally, she asked, "What's happened to you?"

"Nothing," Mykella replied.

"Don't tell me that. You haven't been the same for the last week. You look at Jeraxylt—when he's not looking—as if he were roasting baby hares alive. You've asked Father more questions this week than in the last year. Now you're practicing hiding, and hiding from me."

"I'm worried," Mykella confessed. "I feel that something's not right, but I can't even say what that might be." That was certainly true, if not quite in the way Salyna would take it.

"Are they talking about marrying you off to that autarch-heir in Deforya?"

"Landarch-heir," Mykella replied. "Not in my hearing."

"You can't stay here, Mykella." Salyna straightened herself on the settee. "What would you do? Who would dare marry you? Father wouldn't let anyone of any status do so, because your sons would have a claim on being Lord-Protector, and he wouldn't accept anyone who didn't have position. You don't have any choice."

Mykella bit back what she might have said. "We'll have to see what happens. Has Father said anything about you?"

"He's said that one of the seltyrs in Southgate has a son."

Mykella couldn't help but wince. Southgate was far worse than Tempre for women.

"They say he's nice." Salyna's voice was level.

Mykella could sense the concern. "I do hope so."

Salyna finished a stitch, then rolled up her needlework. "I can only do this so long before my eyes cross." She yawned, then stood. "I'll see you in the morning."

"Good night." Mykella closed the history and set the volume on the side table, watching as Salyna left the parlor. She could tell her sister was disturbed.

What could she do? Except for functions like the upcoming season-turn celebration and parade and ball, or the High Factors' ball, or riding with escorts, she was effectively confined to the palace. And when she was out, she was never alone.

Could she use her "disappearing" skill when she took the inside main corridor back to her chambers? Getting past the guards at night should be easier because their post was in the main corridor, well back from the corner of the palace that held the family quarters, and they walked a post between the main staircase and the quarters rather than standing in one place in front of a single door or archway.

Mykella stood and walked to the doorway. How could she do what she had in mind? Sitting in a chair was one thing, but she needed to move. She couldn't keep creating a new image of the hallway without her in it with every step. Could she just create the feel of everything flowing around her as if she were not there?

She moistened her lips and eased the door open. Then she tried to visualize the light from the parlor flowing around her, as if the door had swung open without anyone there. Her vision seemed to dim, but she could sense the doorframe and the open door when she stepped out into the main corridor. One of the guards turned.

She had no idea if he saw her or if the light from the open door had attracted him. She closed the door, and it creaked as she shut it. After a moment, the guard turned away. She moved as quietly as she could, putting down one boot carefully, then the next, walking not toward her chambers, but toward the guards.

". . . thought I saw someone there . . . woman . . ."

The other guard turned in her direction. "There's no one here. Who would be up except for his regal heirness, strutting around in a tailored uniform that would never do in combat, panting after another pretty ass?"

Mykella stopped, hoping the guard would say more.

"He looks good in uniform . . . have to say that."

". . . jealous?"

"Wouldn't you be?"

The other guard snorted. "Just walk the post."

Mykella neared the two, but neither even looked at her, and they turned away. So did she, but by the time she stepped into her chambers, Mykella was breathing heavily. She was so lightheaded that she felt as though she had raced up and down the main staircase of the palace a score of times.

But . . . the guards had not seen her. She smiled broadly as she sat on the edge of her bed. Her smile faded as she recalled Salyna's words.

VII

The gray light of a winter Septi morning seeped around the edges of the heavy window hangings. Mykella sat up in her bed. Her chamber, while not excessively chill, was far from comfortable, which was not unexpected since it had neither stove nor hearth.

Thrap.

"Yes?"

"It's Zestela, Mistress."

Mykella wanted to tell the head dresser to go away, but that would only postpone matters. She smiled. Perhaps she could test her skills and give the presumptuous dresser a bit of a shock as well. She slipped from under the covers and took three steps so that she stood against the wall beside the large armoire that held her everyday garments. She shivered at the feel of the cold stone tiles on her bare feet. Even the flannel nightdress didn't help. Still, when Zestela stepped into the chamber, she would not be able to see Mykella at first.

Mykella then twisted the light—that was the only way she could explain it—and called, "You can come in."

"Yes, Mistress."

The door opened, and Zestela bustled in, cradling a long formal gown in her arms and glancing around, seeking Mykella. She frowned as she stepped toward the foot of the bed, then looked back toward the armoire. "Mistress?"

Mykella waited until the dresser looked back toward the door before releasing the sight-shield . . . if that was what it was. "I'm here."

Zestela jumped. "Oh! I didn't see you."

"Sometimes I feel like no one does," replied Mykella dryly.

Rachylana entered the chamber. "No one overlooks you, Mykella."

Mykella ignored her sister's words and turned to the dresser. "What is it?"

"Lady Cheleyza sent this gown. She thought you might find it suitable for the reviewing stand for the season-turn celebration."

Mykella glanced at the drab beige fabric with the pale green lace. She shook her head. "I'd look like a flour sack in that. I'll wear the blue one I wore at the last turn parade."

"But . . ." stuttered the dresser.

Rachylana frowned. "Cheleyza is only being kind, and you have worn the blue before . . . several times."

"People will have seen me in it before. Is that so bad?"

Rachylana and Zestela exchanged glances.

"You can't keep wearing the same blue dress," Rachylana finally said.

"Then," Mykella said, "have the dressmakers make me one just like the blue, except in green, brilliant green. The next time, I'll have something else to wear that looks good on me."

"Yes, Mistress." Zestela bowed and slipped out.

Rachylana stared down at her older sister. "You're being difficult. Salyna said you were in a terrible mood last night, and I can see that hasn't changed."

"Because I don't want to look drab in public? Perhaps you'd do anything for dear Berenyt and his mother, but I do draw the line in some places. I'd rather represent Father, in wearing something that looks good and doesn't cost more golds."

Rachylana just looked at Mykella, then, without a word, turned and left.

Mykella could sense the anger, and she should have managed something far less direct, and only gently cutting, but she'd never been that good at fighting with words and expressions.

The rest of Septi was more routine, and, although conversation at breakfast was more than a little cool, neither Feranyt nor Jeraxylt seemed to notice. After eating, Mykella hurried to the Finance chambers and continued her quiet efforts to check on all the receipts that had been recorded in the past few seasons.

She knew she had to visit the Table chamber again, if only to see if she could learn more about how it worked, but that would have to wait until evening, when she could plead tiredness and retreat to her chambers.

The day dragged, and when she finally reached her chambers after dinner, it felt like torture to sit and wait, but she knew Salyna or Rachylana would come by and ask how she was.

Salyna did, announcing her presence with the lightest of knocks. "Mykella?"

"Yes?"

"Are you all right?"

"I'm fine. I just need to be alone."

"You don't want company? Sometimes that helps."

"Thank you, Salyna. I appreciate it, but I need to think some things out."

"You're sure you're all right?"

"I'm sure." Mykella couldn't help smiling fondly at her sister's good-hearted concern. "I know where to find you if I need to talk."

"I'll hold you to it."

Mykella waited longer, a good glass, or so she thought, before she snuffed the wall lamp, not that she needed it much anymore at night, except to read, and moved to the door. She could not sense anyone nearby, and she drew her sight-shield around her, eased the door open, then closed it behind her. The guards didn't even look as she slipped along the side of the corridor, down the main staircase, and along the west corridor toward the rear of the palace.

The staircase guard at the rear of the main level posed another problem because he was stationed almost directly before the door she needed to unlock. She thought for a moment, then moved to one of the doors directly in his line of sight. Using one of her master keys, she unlocked the door, then depressed the lever and gave it a gentle push, moving away and hugging the side of the wide hallway. She stopped a good two yards short of the guard and flattened herself against the wall, waiting.

Several moments passed before the guard saw the open door.

"Who goes there?" He took several steps forward, peering through the dimness only faintly illuminated by the light-torches in their bronze wall brackets, not that all of them worked. It was a miracle that so many devices of the Alectors still functioned.

The corridor remained silent. Unseen behind her sight-shield, Mykella eased toward the stairwell door. Behind her, the guard advanced on the open door. Mykella slipped the key into the lock, then opened the staircase door, slipped through it, and closed it, quietly locking it behind her.

She took a long, slow breath before starting down the steps.

When she entered the Table chamber, she had the feeling that something had changed. A purplish mist seemed to rise from the mirrored surface of the Table, and the air even felt heavy and slimy. She wanted to turn and run. She didn't, but instead moved toward the Table.

Before she could even think about what she might wish to see, the swirling mists appeared, followed by the visage of the same Alector she had seen before.

You have returned. Excellent. The violet eyes fixed on her.

"Where are you? In Alustre?" She avoided looking directly at the Alector, sensing that was what he wanted.

Alustre? That would be most unlikely at present. But you are in Tempre, are you not?

"Where else would I be?" Mykella tried to feel what was happening with the Table.

You could use the Table to see all of Corus, and with my help, you could rule it all.

Mykella distrusted those words, even as the wonder of the possibility that mastery of the Table could create that kind of power washed over her.

She glanced up, only to see a pair of misty arms rising from out of the Table itself, arms and hands that began to extend themselves toward her, arms that exuded a cold and purple chill. With absolute certainty, she understood that if those arms ever touched her, she would be dead. Her body might live, but what was Mykella would be dead.

She stepped back, but the arms kept moving toward her. She created a sight-shield between her and the arms. The arms pressed against the shield, pushing it back and forcing Mykella to retreat as more purpleness flowed from the Table into those icy extensions that threatened her.

What could she do? Frantically, she tried to add another layer of sight-shields, only this time trying to make them stronger, welding them together.

She could feel herself being squeezed, pressed against the stone wall, but she could not give in. She had to hold on. Abruptly, the flailing of the arms against the barrier of her shields lessened. Then the arms themselves began to dissipate, fading and collapsing into the Table.

Were it not for the distance, steer, you would be mine.

Yet the unspoken words sounded hollow, and the purplish glow of the Table subsided, dropping until it almost vanished, as if the struggle between the distant Alector and her had exhausted it.

Mykella uttered a single sigh, almost a sob, shuddering as she stood there in the dimness of the Table chamber. She had to get out. She had to leave.

She forced herself to stand there, breathing deeply, waiting until she was no longer shaking or shuddering. Only then did she leave the chamber, making sure that the door was firmly closed behind her before she made her way to the staircase up to the main level. Once she reached the landing, she paused. The guard was back in position, standing less than a yard from the door.

As quietly as she could, she unlocked the door, then, holding the key in her hand, slowly depressed the lever and eased the door ajar, gathering her sight-shield around her. She could squeeze out, but barely, so long as the guard did not turn. Even if he did, he would not see her, but she wanted no attention paid to the lower level and the Table chamber.

She managed to get the door closed, but not locked, before the guard whirled. Mykella froze, standing unseen beside the door.

The guard stared at the closed door. "Not again."

Mykella eased a coin from her wallet and threw it down the corridor. It clinked loudly.

The guard turned, then stepped forward as he caught the glint of silver.

Mykella locked the door, then eased along the side of the hallway. She was exhausted and trembling by the time she reached her chamber, where, after sliding the seldom-used door bolt into place, she just sat dumbly on the edge of her bed.

As she sat there, still shaking, a greenish golden radiance suffused the room, and in its center hovered the Ancient, a winged and perfect version of a feminine figure, if less than the size of a six-year-old girl.

You have done well, child.

Mykella wasn't certain what to say to the Ancient . . . or if she could. She had so many questions, but she knew she could not delay. "Was that an Alector?"

Rather an Ifrit from the latest world they are bleeding of life. You must watch the Table to see that they do not try again, and you must become stronger. You will not take them by surprise again.

"I hardly know what I'm doing," Mykella protested.

You must learn to use your Talent.

"How can I learn with all the plotting and scheming going on here?"

If you learn, then the plotters can do little to you. If you do not, it matters little whether the plotters succeed or fail.

"Give me some useful advice." Not all these general platitudes.

Seek and master the darkness beneath the Table. With that, the
Ancient faded and vanished.

Mykella sank onto her bed and buried her face in her pillow,
trying to stifle the sound of her sobs and frustration.

VIII

On Decdi morning, nearly three days after her last and nearly
deadly encounter with the Alector—or Ifrit—Mykella finally made
her way back down to the Table chamber. Continuing her critical
review of the ledgers holding the Lord-Protector's accounts had
been slow, and less than encouraging, because she saw the same
patterns everywhere. There were revenues missing from almost all
the accounts, she thought; but any given amount was small, and,
again, she had no real proof, only calculations and estimates and
comparisons. That lack of real evidence was yet another reason
why she had forced herself to revisit the Table, although she was
dreading doing so. But the Ancient had been most definite, and
Mykella had the feeling that matters were not about to improve
by themselves, and greater control of the Table seemed to be the
only possible way she could help her father against what appeared
to be her uncle's machinations.

Because it was light, the only guards on the main level were
posted in the rotunda of the main entrance, although, since it was
end day, they took turns walking the halls. With her sight-shield,
however, that arrangement was much easier to avoid.

Mykella entered the Table chamber with trepidation, but the
Table itself continued to hold a diminished purplish glow, and
she released a long sigh as she approached it. Once there, she
tried to perceive more than the vague sense of what the Ancient
had called the darkness beneath. For a time, all she could feel
was the slimelike purpleness, faint as it was.

Then she gained a stronger feeling of the darkness below, deeper
and darker and far more extensive than she had sensed before yet
carrying a shade of green much like that of the soarer herself.
From somewhere, she recalled that to use some properties of the
Table, one had to stand on it. Did she dare?

She laughed softly. How could anything more happen if she stood on the block of solid stone? Still . . .

After a time, she climbed onto the Table and looked down at the mirror surface beneath her. The surface reflected everything, and she was more than glad, absently, that she was wearing her usual nightsilk trousers. From where she stood, she tried once more to feel, to connect to the dark greenish black well beneath the Table itself. She pushed away the thought that there couldn't be anything but more rock beneath the stone of the Table, immersing herself in the feeling of that darkness, a darkness that somehow seemed warmer than the purple, though both were chill.

She began to feel pathways—greenish black—extending into the distance in all directions. Was that how Mykel had traveled? She reached for the pathways, feeling herself sinking through the Table, even below it, with chill purpleness and golden greenish black all around her.

Surrounded by solid stone! Cold solid stone . . .

She had to get out. She had to! Mykella forced calm upon herself and concentrated on feeling herself rise upward until she was certain her boots were clear of the Table. Only then did she look down—to discover that her boots were a good third of a yard above the surface of the Table.

That couldn't be!

The sudden drop onto the hard mirrored surface of the Table convinced her that it could be—and had been. She tottered there for a moment, then straightened. Had that been how Mykel had walked on air and water? By reaching out to the darkness beneath the ground?

She almost wanted to scream. She kept learning things, but what she learned—except for being able to conceal herself—didn't seem to provide the sort of skills she needed.

Mykella eased herself off the Table and studied it, just trying to sense everything around it. As she did, she gradually became aware that there were unseen webs or lines everywhere. Ugly pinkish purple lines ran from the Table to the south, to the southwest, and to the northeast, but those lines did not touch the far-more-prevalent blackish green lines that were deeper and broader—stronger, in a sense. When she looked down, she was surprised to sense a greenish black line running from herself into the depths and connecting to the stronger web.

She shook her head. Somehow she was connected to the world, but everyone was, and she couldn't see how that could help—except that she might be able to travel that web, if the old tales were right. But she wasn't ready to run away. Besides, what good would that do except land her someplace else, where she'd be penniless and totally friendless? As a woman of position in Tempre, she was powerless enough, if comfortable, and anywhere else would likely be far worse . . . and far, far less hospitable. And, if she were honest with herself, she wasn't certain she wanted to feel herself sinking through and surrounded by solid cold as chill as ice.

She straightened and looked directly at the Table. At least, she ought to be able to see what Joramyl was doing.

When the swirling mists cleared, she saw Joramyl with three other men in a paneled study. The four seated around a conference table were Joramyl, Berenyt, Arms-Commander Nephryt, and Commander Demyl. Whatever they were discussing was serious enough that there were frowns on most faces. Then Joramyl said something, and both Demyl and Nephryt laughed. After the briefest moment, so did Berenyt.

Try as she might, and as long as she watched, Mykella could not discover more, and after a time, as her head began to ache, she stepped back from the Table.

She still felt like screaming in frustration, but she was too tired . . . and too worried.

IX

Duadi came and went before Mykella saw Jeraxylt again since he'd been off on "maneuvers." Just after breakfast on Tridi morning, she cornered her brother just outside the family breakfast room.

"Have some of the Guard left or been stipended off?"

"How would I know?" Jeraxylt looked past her down the corridor toward the staircase to the main level of the palace.

"You know everything about the Guard," Mykella said gently. "You've told me how many companies and battalions there are . . ."

"The numbers change every week, and every season. There might be a few less now. Some of the companies are understrength."

Jeraxylt paused. "I wouldn't know about stipends to ranker guards. I do know that Majer Querlyt petitioned for an early stipend because of deaths in his family. The Arms-Commander granted it. Commander Demyl said that there were reasons to grant it, but they only gave him a half stipend, and if he'd served two more years, it would have been full."

"Was he a good commander?"

"One of the best. He and Undercommander Areyst were the ones who turned back the Ongelyan nomads three years ago, and he hardly lost any men at all. Neither did Areyst."

"Jeraxylt? How would you like to help me?"

"Mykella . . . I am rather . . . involved in my training."

"What I have in mind will certainly not interfere with your training." She offered her most winning smile.

"Whom do you want to meet?" He grinned broadly.

"It's not that kind of help." She didn't need Jeraxylt's assistance in meeting men, not that she'd seen any in the Southern Guard or around the palace who appealed to her. "I need to follow up on some of the tariff collections, and I need an escort."

"Mykella . . ."

"Of course, I could make it known that you've been bedding Majer Allahyr's younger daughter."

"So?"

"Father wouldn't be pleased that you're taking your pleasures with the younger sister of his mistress, nor would he like it known. Besides, you'll get to ride through Tempre in that uniform, and everyone will know who you are and admire you."

"Why don't you ask Arms-Commander Nephryt?"

"My asking him might make matters . . . difficult, because, well . . . I hope you understand. Anyway, the collections don't match up. You don't want to see Father cheated, do you?"

"I don't know . . ."

"Would you like to be cheated when you become Lord-Protector?" she asked. "Would you like to see the cheating continue until you do, then have to be the one to tell everyone that they can't keep doing what they've done for years?"

Jeraxylt thought about that for a moment. "How do you know . . ." He shook his head. "You and your ledgers and figures." Then he cocked his head and smiled.

Mykella could sense what he was feeling—the mix of wanting

to show initiative, the appeal of being seen in uniform, and the idea of wanting to call in a future favor from Mykella.

"I can get some of my squad to do it tomorrow afternoon," he said after a moment. "I'll make it a squad exercise. They'll think it's all an excuse, but it's the sort of thing they'd think I'd want to do." Another smile followed. "You do realize . . ."

"That I'll owe you a favor? Yes. But it has to be the same kind—nothing that's improper."

Jeraxylt nodded. "I'll expect the same diligence from you when I'm Lord-Protector."

When he stepped away, she realized that she could sense that her brother also had one of the unseen threads that ran from him into the ground—but his thread was more of a golden brown. Did everyone have such a thread? What did it mean?

After she left the family quarters, Mykella headed toward the Finance chambers for another day of looking at figures and trying not to appear concerned.

X

Mykella was already mounted, her ledger in the saddlebag, waiting in the cold winter air of early afternoon. She was vaguely surprised at how warm the nightsilk riding jacket was, but she was most comfortable as she studied the rear courtyard of the palace.

That was when Jeraxylt rode in and reined up beside her. "The squad's in front."

"Thank you." She smiled and urged the gelding forward beside her brother's chestnut.

Neither said anything until they were at the head of the column.

"Where do you want to start?" he asked. "At the barge piers or the Grand Piers?"

"Actually, the first place is that of Seltyr Almardyn."

"You said we were visiting tariff-collectors," Jeraxylt murmured, his tone cool.

"No," replied Mykella softly, "I said we needed to check on the tariff collections, and that means visiting those bargemasters and trade factors who paid them."

"They'll just say that they paid . . ."

"They have to have receipts . . . and I'll know if they're accurate."

"You would." The words were under his breath. "Column! Forward!"

Seltyr and High Factor Almardyn's warehouse was less than a block to the south of the Grand Piers, an ancient stone structure of two stories with a series of loading docks on the west side.

Jeraxylt had the squad rein up in front of the front entrance, a simple doorway, though with an ornate marble arch above it. He accompanied Mykella to the door. "You *would* start with a seltyr."

"He's first on the list."

Clearly, the sound of a squad of guards had alerted someone, because Almardyn himself opened the doorway. His eyes widened as he looked from Jeraxylt to Mykella, and back to Jeraxylt, but he barely paused before saying, "Please come in."

Mykella noted that his lifethread was more of a deeper brown, and somehow . . . frayed.

The two followed him to the study, a small white-plastered chamber with a table desk and wooden file boxes stacked neatly to the right. There, Almardyn turned. "Both the Lord-Protector's heir and daughter at my door . . . I am indeed honored. Might I ask why?"

"It's a bit . . . unusual," Mykella said. "You might know that I oversee the accounts of the Finance Ministry for my father . . ."

"I did not know, but would that all daughters were so dutiful . . ."

Mykella could sense the doubts.

"And I discovered that some figures had been entered incorrectly. It might be that an entire column had been one set of numbers off, but since several of the payment receipts were spoiled, it seemed that the easiest thing to do was to check with those who paid the last tariffs." Mykella did her best to project absolute conviction and assurance, along with a hint of embarrassment about Lord Joramyl.

"What would you like of me?"

"Just a quick look at your receipt for your fall tariff," Mykella said. "I may not have to visit every factor, but since the lists are in alphabetical order . . ."

"I'm the fortunate one. Just a moment." Almardyn turned and lifted one box, then another, opening the third. "Should be on top here. Yes." He turned and extended a heavy oblong card, bordered in the blue of the Lord-Protector. "Here you have it. The seal is quite clear."

"I'm certain it is," Mykella replied. "The fault lies not with you or the tariff-collector." She copied the number into the new ledger she carried, one she had designed to show the discrepancies. Almardyn had paid a good ten golds more than had been entered in the collection ledger. She straightened. "Thank you very much, Seltyr and High Factor. Your diligence and cooperation are much appreciated."

"I'm certain your sire appreciates yours as well," replied Almardyn.

"We do thank you," Mykella said, inclining her head slightly before turning to depart.

Little more was said, until Mykella and Jeraxylt had left the factor's building.

"For all your fine words, he'll still think you're checking to see if he's a thief," murmured Jeraxylt as they walked out to their waiting mounts and Jeraxylt's squad.

"Not after word gets around that everyone's been visited," replied Mykella. "Besides, is anyone going to fault a Lord-Protector for checking on tariff collections once in a while during his reign?"

"It's going to cause problems," predicted her brother.

"I'm sure it will, but it will create more problems if we don't verify that it's happening and how much Father is losing."

"That's the only reason I can see for this."

Out of the twenty-three bargemasters and High Factors Mykella visited, she managed to meet eighteen. With the exception of Hasenyt—the sole factor whom the Lord-Protector and Mykella knew personally—every single one had a receipt for paying more golds than had been entered in the ledger as received, a fact Mykella revealed to no one.

She had to work hard to keep a pleasant expression as they rode back toward the palace. She had no more than reined up outside the gates to the courtyard, about to take her leave of Jeraxylt, when another officer rode toward them. He was blond, of medium height, and muscular. While his face was calm, she could sense the anger.

"Oh, frig . . ." muttered Jeraxylt. "I knew this would be trouble. That's Undercommander Areyst."

The Undercommander reined up and looked directly at Jeraxylt. His green eyes conveyed a chill that was not reflected in the tone of the words that followed. "I don't recall authorizing any sort of patrol in Tempre."

Mykella eased her gelding forward, cutting between Jeraxylt and the senior officer. She smiled politely. "Undercommander? Does the Finance Ministry serve the Lord-Protector?"

Areyst turned to her, not that he had a choice. "I beg your pardon, Mistress Mykella?"

"I asked you if the Finance Ministry served the Lord-Protector."

Areyst's thin lips turned up slightly at the corners. "How could I contest that, Mistress?"

"On behalf of the Ministry, I requested an escort to check some tariff records. Perhaps I should have contacted you directly, but was there any harm done by Jeraxylt's arranging the escort for me?" Mykella extended the ledger she carried. "I was cross-checking the entries in this ledger. Would you care to see them?"

"I think not, Mistress. Your word, as is your sire's, is more than enough."

Mykella thought she sensed a grudging admiration from the Undercommander, the third man in the chain of command for the Southern Guard, although his anger had not totally abated. "Thank you, Undercommander. I apologize if I've caused any difficulty; but, as always, I have only the best interests of the Lord-Protector and the people of Tempre at heart, as I know you do." Mykella tried to project true concern, which she felt, because she could sense the basic honesty of Areyst, whom she had only seen previously from a distance, or in passing. She added, "If there is any fault, it must be mine, for I was the one who requested the service. If you find that a fault, please tell the Lord-Protector directly, and let him know that it was my doing. Jeraxylt was only trying to accommodate me."

Areyst smiled faintly, an expression now devoid of bitterness or anger and holding barely veiled amusement. "It might be best if it were logged as a commercial verification patrol. I would request, if further such patrols are needed, Mistress Mykella, that you contact me."

"I would doubt the need anytime in the immediate future, Undercommander, but I will indeed follow your advice." And she would, because she could sense that honesty and loyalty ran all the way through him . . . and through a lifethread that held a faint green amid a golden brown.

Areyst eased his mount forward slightly and nodded to Jeraxylt. "Your squad will be doing arms practice on foot tomorrow. Riding the stones is hard on mounts."

"Yes, ser."

Only after Areyst had ridden off, eastwardly, in the direction of the Guard compound, did Jeraxylt turn to Mykella. "You owe me double for this."

"I do," she acknowledged demurely. *And you owe me far more than you realize.*

XI

After the evening meal, at which Feranyt made no mention of patrols, thankfully, Mykella retired to her chambers to study the ledgers. What she had suspected was in fact true. The total discrepancy for the fall tariffs was close to two hundred golds. If the same had been true for the other four seasons, and her estimates suggested that it had been, Joramyl—or someone—had diverted close to a thousand golds from just seventeen factors and bargemasters. Her calculations suggested that other diversions were also taking place, but she was not about to try further excursions without presenting what she had verified to her father.

Then, too, much as she still dreaded it, Mykella knew she needed to follow the soarer's advice about the darkness beneath the Table. Despite her fears, she did need to learn more. So, after it seemed quiet in the family quarters that night, she left her room once more.

This time, she merely waited until the stair guard moved before slipping behind him.

The Table remained as it had, nearly quiescent, but the darkness beneath seemed stronger and closer. Did she want to try to travel those dark webs? Given her father's lack of concern about Joramyl, she might indeed need to escape Tempre.

She stepped up and onto the Table, seeking the green blackness once more. Again, she found herself sinking through and beneath the Table and into the depths beneath. She could not move, and a chill filled her from her bones outward.

Chill? What was so cold?

She tired to reach for an even-more-distant blackness, then began to sense movement, but it was as though she remained suspended and frozen in place while the greenish darkness swept by her. The motion ended. She willed herself to rise and found herself in a different darkness—a mere absence of light—and the biting cold of a raging winter. Somewhere above her, the wind howled. She exhaled, and ice crystals fell from the steam of her instantly frozen breath.

Her entire body was so cold, so tired . . .

She shook her head. Wherever she was, if she didn't leave, she would likely freeze to death in the darkness where she stood. Trying to reach the darkness beneath her was far harder. Her eyes watered, and her tears began to freeze on her cheeks. Even sliding downward seemed to take forever. While she had thought the depths would be warmer, she remained cold, immobile, icy tears frozen in place on her cheeks in the silent depths.

Tempre! She had to reach Tempre. This time, she called up an image of the Table chamber, with her standing before the Table, its purple mist just faintly sensed.

At last, she felt movement.

Later, how much later, she could not tell, she found herself standing before the Tempre Table for a long moment before her legs collapsed, and another darkness enfolded her.

When she woke again, beside the Table, she knew it had to be close to dawn, and it took every bit of strength she had to hold the sight-shield long enough for her to return to her chambers. There, she slumped onto the bed, dragging the quilts around her in an attempt to get warm.

XII

Mykella had hoped to be in the Finance chambers before Kiedryn or Joramyl, but she'd been so tired that she'd nearly slept through breakfast. Her sleep had been anything but peaceful, with nightmares about struggling through a blinding blizzard of black snow, trying to reach . . . something.

Her stomach was roiling, and she knew she couldn't face the day and what she had to do without something to eat, and that meant Kiedryn was already at his table desk when she arrived. Fortunately, as she had expected, Joramyl was nowhere to be seen.

She gathered the ledgers she needed, then wrapped the sight-shield around them, not that Kiedryn more than glanced in her direction as she paused by the door. "I need to get something. I'll be back before long."

The chief clerk merely nodded.

She had to wait outside her father's study for nearly half a glass before Seltyr Porofyr departed, and she could make her way inside. She slid the door bolt behind her.

"We wouldn't be interrupted, anyway, daughter," offered Feranyt.

For a moment, Mykella studied her sire, with her senses, more than with her eyes. His lifethread was almost the same as Jeraxylt's—golden brown—and for the first time she noted that there was a knot of sorts in the thread, as if tiny threads from all over his body merged into that nexus that connected him to the lifethread.

"Perhaps not, ser," replied Mykella after a pause. She laid the ledgers on the corner of the Lord-Protector's desk. "Father . . . I've been worried about your accounts. Receipts have been going down, yet everyone has been saying that times are good. I couldn't track everything, but I did track the fall tariffs of the bargemasters and the High Factors . . ." She went on to explain how she had cross-checked by visiting most of those on the lists and how their sealed receipts uniformly showed greater payments than those shown as received. She used each ledger to point out the exact differences. ". . . and since we don't use tariff farmers the way they do in some places, the numbers should agree, but they don't. Someone has diverted or pocketed nearly a thousand golds this year—"

"You only know about two hundred for certain."

"I can only prove two hundred at the moment. The ledgers suggest a thousand."

"We can only go with proof, daughter."

Why couldn't her father see? Why wouldn't he?

"Mykella . . . you've been diligent and thoughtful, and I appreciate what you've let me know. Corruption is always a problem, because there aren't enough golds to sate all men's appetites." He looked at his daughter more closely. "You're exhausted. You have black circles under your eyes. You shouldn't have pushed yourself so hard."

"Father . . . I don't see how this could have happened without Lord Joramyl knowing something about it."

Feranyt laughed, ironically. "Just how often does he even come into the Finance chambers? I suspect that you and Kiedryn do most of the work, after the entry clerks take in the papers and order the entries."

Mykella was tired, if not for the reasons her father had suggested.

"Dear child . . . I am the Lord-Protector, and you'll have to trust me to handle it. It's not something that can be rushed."

"You are the Lord-Protector, Father, and I am your daughter. But please don't think I'm overstating matters."

"Mykella, I understand your concerns for me, but if I rush and handle matters wrongly, things will only be worse." He paused. "I will look into it and do what is necessary."

She could sense that, if she pressed her father, it would do no good, and he would only resist. "That's all I wanted, ser. Do you need the ledgers?"

"Not right now, but keep them safe."

"I can do that." Mykella straightened.

XIII

Mykella had struggled to stay awake the remainder of Quinti, and had slept poorly that night and awakened early on Sexdi. She was walking toward the breakfast room when she saw her father waiting outside. His face was stern, and she could sense concern . . . and sadness. He motioned to her.

"What is it?" she asked.

"I said that I would look into what you found out," Feranyt began.

Mykella waited.

"There was a great deal of validity to your findings. So much so that . . . well . . . Kiedryn is dead. He took poison last night, and left a note, saying that he'd stolen far too many golds. He said he was sorry, but he didn't want to disgrace his family. The note pleaded not to make matters public . . ."

Mykella managed not to gape. Kiedryn? He had likely been the only honest one there, besides Mykella herself.

"His family will have to accept exile, of course, but there's no reason to make it public."

"Kiedryn couldn't have . . ." Mykella protested.

Feranyt shrugged sadly. "I know you thought he was honest,

but at times appearances are deceiving. I saw the note. Joramyl showed it to me, and we even compared the writing to his. He wrote it, without a doubt."

Under what sort of duress? Mykella swallowed.

"I know this is hard for you, daughter, but that sort of hard truth comes with ruling. Those you trust most are often those who betray that trust."

"But . . . Joramyl?"

"He's been as solid as a rock. His assistant steward will take over until we find a permanent replacement for Kiedryn. I'm counting on you to help him."

"Yes, ser." Mykella felt that her voice was coming from someone else. Why couldn't her father see what was happening? Yet she could sense that trying to convince him that his own brother was behind it all was futile. Speaking against Joramyl would only result in her being unable to do anything . . . not that what she had done had gone as planned.

Feranyt patted her on the shoulder. "I'm counting on you. I need to get ready to meet with that envoy now."

After he continued toward his study, Mykella turned toward the breakfast room, only to find Jeraxylt standing there.

"Father was pleased, you know," offered Jeraxylt. "He said you handled things the way a smart woman should . . . finding out what was happening, you know, and letting him know."

A smart woman? How smart had she been? Poor honest Kiedryn had been poisoned and set up as the guilty party, when Joramyl was the one who'd been diverting the golds—and now matters were even worse because both her brother and her father believed Joramyl, and she had no proof at all who had diverted the golds . . . and no way to obtain it now that everyone was convinced of Kiedryn's guilt.

Mykella barely ate any breakfast, but she did manage a full mug of tea that helped settle her stomach.

Then, girding herself up, she made her way to the Finance chambers.

The man who rose when Mykella entered the outer chamber was barely a span taller than she was, and squat, like a human toad, she thought. He smiled, and from behind the sincere expression flooded insincerity. Even his lifethread seemed snakelike, holding a sickly yellow brown. "Maxymt, at the service of the Lord-Protector."

"I'm pleased to meet you, Maxymt. The Lord-Protector has asked me to make sure you're familiar with the ledgers and accounts."

"Once I've had a chance to become familiar with these, you really won't have to check the ledgers, Mistress. The Lord-Protector's daughter shouldn't be doing a clerk's work." Oiliness coated the insincerity of every word.

"How well do you know the accounts?" she asked. "Could you tell me which ledger holds the receipts from the smallholders?"

Maxymt smiled, showing brilliant white teeth. "I'm certain that won't be hard to determine . . . assuming that Kiedryn was not too . . . creative."

"I'm sure that you will be able to learn," Mykella replied, "but while you are, I'm certain my father would wish me to continue as I have."

"As you wish, Mistress Mykella."

She could sense a most palpable dislike behind the honeyed words. Now what could she do, except try to strengthen those talents awakened by the Ancient? "First, I'll show you the summary ledgers, then the individual account ledgers, and you can go through each one to gain some familiarity."

"Yes, Mistress Mykella."

Almost a glass later, Joramyl hurried into his Finance study, smiling at Maxymt, who was still studying the master ledger, and at Mykella for a moment. Berenyt followed his father, and he did not look at Mykella.

Mykella had to know what they were saying. The moment Maxymt turned his head, she gathered her sight-shield around her and tiptoed to the study door, where she stood, ear against the crack between door and jamb, trying to make out what the two said.

". . . talk about it here . . ."

". . . wanted you to know . . . Mykella's sharper than she looks . . . don't think she'll accept . . . knew Kiedryn too well . . ."

". . . what could she do, Berenyt? The Lord-Protector saw the confession . . . she's just a woman, barely more than a girl. If my brother weren't so sentimental, he'd have long since sent her to Dereka and gotten a pile of golds for her as well . . . what women are for . . . golds and heirs . . . At least, he doesn't listen to her the way he did to her mother. Good thing Aelya died when she did."

Mykella stiffened. There had been something more there, behind the words, and she missed the next phrases.

"... besides, Feranyt's offsprings' meddling served us well ... not have to worry about Kiedryn any longer ... now ... don't come see me here more than once a week ... Off with you."

"Yes, ser."

Mykella slipped back to her table and released the sight-shield.

Maxymt started. Then he stared at Mykella. "Where did you come from?"

"Come from? I've been here all along."

"You weren't there a moment ago."

Mykella shook her head. "I haven't left the chamber. You would have heard my boots. Everyone's always said that I walk heavier than some of the guards. I did drop my figuring paper and had to bend down to get it."

"That must be it." Maxymt shook his head.

Mykella could tell that he wasn't totally convinced, but she hadn't been able to hang on to the sight-shield any longer.

Once more, Berenyt didn't look in her direction when he hurried out of his father's study.

XIV

Over the next week, Mykella waited for something to happen, some tragedy or catastrophe, but she could see or sense nothing. Various tariff receipts continued to appear in the ledgers, but now, none showed any discrepancies. To Mykella, that was only proof of Joramyl's cunning, but, again, what could she say? Negotiations proceeded with the envoy from Southgate, and her father mentioned, obliquely, something about an envoy from Deforya.

All she could do was to practice what she had been learning. She had become adept enough with the sight-shield that she could move anywhere unseen. She'd even visited the palace gardens in the dead of night. She'd also traveled from the Table chamber to three others, avoiding the one somewhere in the icy north, but where they were, she had no idea, because all three had been walled shut from the outside. One was chill, and the air seemed thin. Could it have been in Dereka?

She also continued to observe with her life-senses, if that was what they were, and from what she could tell, only her lifethread held that strange combination of black and green, and she had the feeling that the green was becoming more brilliant. But was she just imagining that? Was she imagining everything?.

She observed Joramyl, if intermittently, through the Table. He continued to meet with the Arms-Commander and Commander Demyl, sometimes with Berenyt present, but not always. Outside of the fact that they were plotting, she could tell nothing from what she saw. Berenyt kept flirting with Rachylana, and Rachylana had become ever more distant from Mykella.

Before she knew it, Mykella was in the reviewing stand with her sisters and her father, as the companies of the Southern Guard stationed in Tempre rode past in celebration and recognition of the end of winter and the turn of spring. The small reviewing stand was set at the base of the Grand Piers, equidistant from the green towers at each end. The mounted Guard companies rode northward toward the Piers along the great eternastone highway that split farther to the south, heading west to Hafin and southwest to Southgate, due south to Hyalt and east to Krost and the wine country of Syan. Once the guards reached the reviewing stand, they turned onto the Palace Road, heading due east back to their compound.

When she'd been little, Mykella had once asked her mother why the reviewing stand wasn't before the palace, but Aelya had just smiled, and said, "It's tradition. Tradition is very important. Someday you'll understand how important."

Tradition might well be important, but the day was raw and damp, under heavy gray clouds, and a chill wind blew out of the northeast with such vigor that Mykella wouldn't have been surprised to see snow by the next morning.

Mykella stood to her father's left. Had he not been riding with the Southern Guard, Jeraxylt would have stood to his right. Instead, Lord Joramyl did. To Mykella's left was Cheleyza, Joramyl's second wife, only five years older than Mykella.

"I don't ever get tired of watching the guards," offered Cheleyza. "They ride so well."

And they're all so handsome. That thought was as clear to Mykella as though Cheleyza had shouted it.

"They do ride well," replied Mykella. "Here comes Second Company, and you can see Berenyt there, at the front."

"He rides well, too." Cheleyza paused. "What are you wearing to the ball tonight?"

"Something blue . . . I think. And you?"

"Blue and silver, with a special shimmersilk scarf from Dramur. Joramyl wants me to look my best."

"I'm certain he does." Mykella kept the sarcasm she felt out of her voice. Even so, she could sense Salyna's amusement from behind her.

"He is very particular about the way I look."

"Many husbands are, I've heard."

"You'll find out, dear."

After Second Company came First Company, and Mykella was happy to change the subject by noting, "There's Jeraxylt, leading his squad." She could also see a well-endowed redheaded girl at the end of the reviewing stand, taking a special interest in her brother.

Following First Company were the senior officers of the Southern Guard, followed in turn by the headquarters group. First came Undercommander Areyst, and Mykella sensed both respect and sadness as he bowed his head to the Lord-Protector. Behind him was Commander Demyl, but while the commander looked toward the reviewing stand and bowed his head to the Lord-Protector, Mykella could sense the contempt. Arms-Commander Nephryt merely radiated arrogance.

What could she do? She knew what others were thinking and feeling, and yet she had no proof of anything beyond what she had shown her father, and now, even that proof had been reduced to uselessness by Kiedryn's supposed suicide.

XV

The ballroom was on the southeast corner of the main level of the palace, and had been created centuries before by merging a series of chambers, so that it was long and comparatively narrow, with windows only on the eastern and southern walls. A parquet floor, now ancient, if polished and shining, had been laid over the stone floor tiles, and the wall hangings were of blue and cream. The orchestra was seated on a low platform set against the midpoint of the long inner wall of the ballroom.

Mykella stood at one side of the orchestra, beside Salyna, and only a few yards from where her father and Joramyl chatted amiably. Standing in the receiving line and smiling politely had been more than enough to boil her blood and curdle any thoughts she might have had about the milk of human kindness. Rachylana was already off dancing, and Mykella wished that she were, not that she cared that much for dancing, but the hypocrisy of Joramyl's apparent concern for his brother the Lord-Protector was making Mykella more than a little uncomfortable.

As the orchestra began to play another melody, Undercommander Areyst eased across the space before the platform toward Mykella. He bowed politely. "Might I have this dance, Mistress Mykella?"

"You might." Mykella inclined her head and smiled.

Areyst took her right hand in his left and positioned his left hand at waist level on her back, guiding her gently into the flow of dancers.

"After our last meeting, Mistress Mykella, I've discovered that you're quite good with numbers and ledgers. That is an unusual preoccupation for the daughter of the Lord-Protector."

"Not so unusual as one might think," replied Mykella. "A Lord-Protector's daughter should know her heritage, yet she cannot mingle so freely as a son. From where golds are collected, and in what amounts, and where they are spent and at what frequency can tell a great deal . . . if one knows where and how to look."

"Pray tell, what do they say to you?"

"The Southern Guard is currently understrength. It lacks as many experienced officers as it once had. Supplies such as tack for mounts are more costly than in the past, possibly because of the depredations of the Ongelyan nomads several years back—"

"That was several years ago, though." Areyst guided her past another couple.

"Tack requires leather. Calves take several years to become steers," Mykella pointed out.

"Tell me more."

"Ammunition supplies are down, most probably because gunpowder costs are up, and that is because brimstone has become more costly. I wouldn't be surprised if you or the Commander had considered ordering great care in rifle practice."

"Considered? That is an odd way of putting it."

"If you had actually done so, Jeraxylt would have let it slip. Since you have not, and since you are a prudent officer, I would wager that you have considered it but possibly did not because that might have made the seltyrs of Southgate and the plains nomads more bold. It might also have encouraged the Landarch to request a concession or two."

Areyst laughed. "Would that some of my officers understood so well."

Mykella forbore to comment on that.

"What else might you tell me from your ledgers? About something other than the Guard?"

She could tell he was interested, and not merely patronizing her. "The vineyards in Vyan had a bumper crop last year, and that reduced tariffs . . ."

"Reduced?"

"There were so many grapes that the prices went down, and tariffs are leveled on prices. Not so much as if the crop had failed, but the slight increase in tariffs on raisins showed that the cause was a surplus of grapes."

Areyst looked directly at her. "You could unsettle any man, Mistress Mykella."

"I don't usually speak so, especially to men, Undercommander, but you did ask, and you were interested, and since you were most kind to my brother, I thought you deserved an explanation of sorts."

"Your golds will tell what has occurred. Can they tell what will happen?"

"No more than good judgment and observation," she replied. "Some things are obvious. If tariff collections are lower than in the past, that will mean that expenses must be reduced, or tariffs must be raised. If times are hard, raising tariffs will create unrest and discontent. Yet, if one reduces expenditures, say, for the Southern Guard, that can create another kind of discontent." She smiled. "Would you not agree?"

"That is true if the Guard is required to do as much as before, or more," Areyst acknowledged.

"But when times are hard, there are always more challenges to the Lord-Protector and the Guard."

At the end of that dance, when Areyst escorted her back to her sisters, Mykella could tell that her comments had not so much upset Areyst as put him in a far-more-thoughtful mood than when he had asked her to dance. Strangely, she found that thoughtfulness far more attractive and appealing than a smile or pleasant and meaningless banter would have been.

"You left the Undercommander with a most-serious expression on his face," observed Salyna. "That's not what you wish to do with a man who has no wife. You want to put him at ease."

"He asked some most-serious questions," replied Mykella, "and I made the mistake of replying seriously." She doubted that it had been a mistake, but it was wisest to say so.

XVI

Three days later, at breakfast, Feranyt looked up from his tea and asked Mykella, "Have you been prowling around the lower levels of the palace again?"

"Ser?" Mykella counterfeited confusion. Besides, she hadn't been prowling. "No, Father. I haven't been prowling anywhere. I have more than enough to do teaching Maxymt about the accounts. Why?"

"There have been reports, strange things, doors opening with no one around, silvers lying on the stones, door locks clicking when no one was there . . ." He kept looking at her.

Mykella was surprised—and more than a little worried, not that there were reports, but that such reports had been brought to her father only weeks after the events had occurred. Was that just another indication of how out of touch he really was?

Feranyt chuckled. "I can see you're as surprised as I am. Good. I wouldn't want you to make a habit of nocturnal prowling."

Not like Jeraxylt, she thought, without voicing the thought.

After breakfast, she made her way to the Finance chambers, thinking about both her father's questions and Undercommander Areyst. She'd been concerned about the Undercommander ever since they had danced that single waltz at the ball because he came across as direct and honest. After what had happened to Kiedryn and what she had sensed from both Nephryt and Demyl, the thought that something might happen to Areyst was more than a little disturbing. Yet how could she even warn Areyst without putting him in danger? And what could she say—that he was the only honest senior officer left in the Southern Guard and that he was in danger because he was? Who could possibly believe that? Equally problematical was that she was unlikely to see him anytime soon, and to create any public opportunity would be noted, and jeopardize him, while any use of the sight-shield to reach him might well create questions better left unraised. Then, too, there was the problem that she found him attractive ... and, if anyone discovered that, she'd soon be on her way to Dereka—or somewhere even worse.

Once in the Finance chambers she turned to the ledgers, reviewing the entry clerks' work and Maxymt's entries. She had to admit that Maxymt had learned quickly and that he was probably sharper with figures than Kiedryn had been—and that worried her as well.

She forced herself to concentrate on the columns of figures in the ledgers before her. Slowly, slowly, the figures began to absorb her, and she was beginning to see yet another pattern ...

"Mykella!" Salyna burst through the door to the Finance study.

Mykella looked up from the ledger, biting off the words of annoyance she had almost voiced when she sensed the grief and fear radiating from her sister. "What's the trouble?"

"Jeraxylt ..." Salyna opened her mouth, then closed it. Her body shook with silent sobs.

Mykella bolted to her feet. "What about Jeraxylt?"

"He ... there was an accident ... they were practicing with blunted sabres ... and his broke. So did the other guard's, but ..."

Mykella glanced to Maxymt, then back to Salyna. Somehow, Maxymt was surprised ... yet not surprised.

"I'll be back when I can," Mykella said, moving toward Salyna.

XVII

The ceremony for Jeraxylt was private and held in the family's hillside mausoleum behind the palace. Beside the honor guard, only the family—including Joramyl, Berenyt, and Cheleyza—and the senior officers of the Southern Guard were present.

Under a clear silver-green sky, her head lowered, Mykella studied the mourners standing under the graystone arches of the open stone structure. Her father radiated sadness in a distant way, and Salyna had trouble holding in sobs. Silent tears ran from the corners of Rachylana's eyes, but Berenyt stood beside her.

To the right of Feranyt stood Joramyl, his head bowed. Within him, Mykella could detect, not so much a sense of triumph or gloating, but a feeling of acceptance and inevitability. Arms-Commander Nephryt actually seemed saddened, but Commander Demyl held within himself a sense of righteousness and duty.

The ceremony was brief, beginning with an acknowledgment by his father of Jeraxylt's death, followed by a short statement about the meaning of his life by Arms-Commander Nephryt.

After that, Undercommander Areyst stepped forward to deliver the final blessing. "In the name of the one and the wholeness that is, and always will be, in the great harmony of the world and its lifeforce, may the blessing of life, of which death is but a small portion, always remain with Jeraxylt, son of the Lord-Protector. And blessed be the lives of all those who have loved him and those he loved. Also, blessed be both the deserving and the undeserving, that all may strive to do good in the world and beyond, in celebration and recognition of what is and will be, world without end."

His words had been offered with dignity and a clear sense of sadness and mourning, for which Mykella was grateful. She didn't know if she could have concealed her rage if either Nephryt, Demyl, or Joramyl had offered the blessing.

In the moment of silence that followed, Mykella eased over to the Undercommander. "Thank you for the blessing. You offered it well, and in a spirit of honesty that reflects the past heritage of the Southern Guard."

She could sense him stiffen inside.

"I know you embody that spirit, and that made the blessing meaningful. Thank you." She inclined her head as if in respect, and murmured. "Take great care of yourself."

From his internal reaction, she could sense he had heard.

Areyst inclined his head in response, then straightened. "I could do no less in serving Tempre and the Lord-Protector."

"It was still appreciated, Undercommander." Mykella eased back toward her father.

"Mykella?" inquired Feranyt.

"I just thanked him for the blessing. He offered it well, and he meant it." She stepped back and waited for the honor guard to begin the long walk back to the palace.

XVIII

That night, unsurprisingly, Mykella knew she would not sleep, or not well. Had her actions led to Jeraxylt's death? Would the "accident" have occurred had he not accompanied her on her visits to the factors? She had the clear feeling that, although she had not intended it that way, at the very least, her inquiries had been indirectly responsible.

She had to do something, even if that something were futile, and after retiring to her chambers and waiting, she gathered the sight-shield around her and made her way down to the Table chamber, slipping past the guards with an ease born of practice.

Once inside the chamber, she wasted no time but walked to the Table itself, where she looked down and concentrated on trying to see Joramyl, but when the swirling mists cleared, she found herself looking at the image of the Ifrit. At least, she thought it was the same Ifrit.

You have returned once more. Most excellent. The violet eyes burned, and immediately, she could sense the misty purple arms rising out of the Table.

Mykella only took one step back, throwing up her shields against the arms, yet those arms did not move toward her as they swelled with purplish power and malevolence, but toward her lifethread where it passed through the solid stone toward the greenish blackness below. Instinctively she extended her shields to protect it, and the arms lunged toward her midsection and that node where the fine lines of her being joined to form her lifethread.

Mykella managed a second set of shields, but she found herself being pressed back by the expanding force of the arms. The Table itself was glowing an ever-brighter purple, so bright that she wanted to close her eyes, although she understood closing them would do nothing because the glare was in her senses, not in her eyes.

Did the arms have a node, something similar to what the Ifrit sought to attack in her? She made a probe, like a sabre, extending from her shields, angling it toward a thickness in the leftmost of the arms facing her.

Just as suddenly, one of the arms hurled something at her. Her shields held as the object shattered against them, but Mykella found herself being thrown back against the stone wall of the chamber. Her boot skidded on something, and she went to one knee. She put out a hand to steady herself, and found the stone floor wet, with fragments of ice chips.

Ice? The arms had thrown that icicle with enough force to disembowel her had it not been for her shields.

I will not be defeated by something attacking me from inside a stone Table. I will not! She forced herself erect and called on the darkness, and the greenish depths to which her lifethread was somehow attached.

A purplish firebolt sprayed against her shields, and she staggered, but moved forward, calling ... drawing on the greenish blackness of the depths, the green that recalled the Ancient.

The entire chamber flared greenish gold, and under that flood of fully sensed but unseen light, the purplish arms evaporated into mist and haze, then vanished.

The Ancients ... still there ...

There was a sudden emptiness around the Table, as it subsided to the faintest of purplish sheens. Then, that, too, vanished.

Mykella felt a smile appear on her face. Exhausted as she was, she had learned two things. Her shields were proof against weapons, some of them, at least, and she could stand up to the distant Alector. And if she could stand against an Ifrit, surely she could hold her own against Joramyl and his scheming supporters, could she not? Could she not?

XIX

On Quattri, Mykella was nearing the Finance chambers in late afternoon, after returning from carrying a summary of recent expenditures to her father in his study.

He had seemed tired, almost gray, and had taken the sheets from her with a weary expression. "Thank you, Mykella."

While he had not actually dismissed her, he might as well have, for his eyes had dropped to the papers on the table desk before him. Mykella had slipped out, once more asking herself what she could do. Sooner or later, either Joramyl or Berenyt would become Lord-Protector, and with the weariness she saw in her sire, she feared it would be sooner, and that was her fault.

With Jeraxylt's death, he had become quieter, more withdrawn, as well. Why was it that everything she tried to do had made matters worse? She tried to warn her father and only succeeded in warning Joramyl. She'd let Jeraxylt know, and that had made him a danger to Joramyl, and now her brother was dead.

Her thoughts were interrupted by the sight of an officer in a Southern Guard uniform standing outside the Finance door, waiting. It was Berenyt.

She forced a smile as she neared him. "Good afternoon."

"Good afternoon, Mykella. You're looking well."

"After all that's happened, you mean?"

"It's been a difficult time for everyone," he replied.

What bothered her immediately was that he clearly believed that. Why had times been difficult for Berenyt? He hadn't been close to Jeraxylt, and he certainly hadn't cared anything about Kiedryn.

"It has, but we'll manage. Life does go on."

"It does"—he nodded—"often for the best, although we don't always see it that way. You know, Mykel the Great lost his entire family in the Cataclysm? You have to wonder if he'd been so good a Lord-Protector without suffering that loss."

"I'm sure he wouldn't have wished that." Mykella barely kept her voice pleasant.

"You know, Mykella, it's too bad that Jeraxylt had that accident."

Mykella had doubted that Berenyt's words were ever anything but carefully chosen, and this was no exception. "It was a surprise to all of us. He was always so careful in arms practice."

"He wasn't always as careful in other matters. He could have been a great Southern Guard and Lord-Protector, if he had concentrated on arms. That was his strength."

Mykella managed to keep her expression puzzled. "Jeraxylt was always careful, and he certainly did concentrate on arms."

"He should have. He should have concentrated on those more, rather than using you as a front for his calculations."

Mykella wasn't sure from the swirl of feelings within Berenyt whether he actually believed that Jeraxylt had been the one to discover the diversions of golds and brought them to the Lord-Protector's attention or whether Berenyt was not so indirectly offering her a way to disavow what she had discovered. Although she felt frozen inside, Mykella managed to offer a sad smile. "We all have different talents."

"With all of your abilities, Mykella, it's too bad we're cousins." said Berenyt, not quite jokingly.

"I like you, too," Mykella replied politely. Always implying, never saying, that was Berenyt's style. He never really used words that committed to anything, even as he was implying the unthinkable.

"It really is," insisted Berenyt.

Even though his eyes remained fixed on her face, Mykella could sense the physical appraisal . . . and the muted lust. She barely managed not to swallow or show her disgust. "We are cousins. Nothing will change that."

"You might wish otherwise." Berenyt smiled brightly.

"What I might wish, Berenyt, has seldom changed what is."

"That's true, Mykella, but often what I've wished has." With a pleasant smile, he nodded, then turned and walked down the corridor.

Within herself, she shuddered.

Then, for a time, she stood outside the Finance door before reaching out and opening it.

XX

Early on Quinti morning, Mykella donned black, from nightsilk all the way outward to boots, tunic, and trousers, as well as a black scarf that could double as a head covering, if necessary. The events of the past week, especially Berenyt's words and her encounter with the male Ifrit the night before, had convinced her that anything she could do as a woman—anything that would be seen as acceptable for a woman, she corrected herself—would not save her or her father, or her sisters, from Joramyl and his schemes.

She needed to discover if what the Ifrit had attempted against her was something she could master—and use, if she had to. She had a sickening feeling that would be necessary.

Under cover of her sight-shield, she made her way to the small building behind the palace that served as the slaughterhouse. She waited until no one was looking, then opened the door and closed it behind her, walking as quietly as she could toward the open-roofed slaughtering courtyard in the back.

Three lambs, close to being yearlings and mutton, were confined in a pen—an overlarge wooden crate. Several fowl were in the next crate.

Melmak, the head butcher, looked to a rangy youth. "We need to get on with it. The first one."

As the youth folded down the front of the crate and lifted a blunt stunning hammer, Mykella reached out with what she could only call her Talent and grasped the lamb's lifethread, a thread that felt both thinner and yet coarser, or stronger, than her own seemed to be. But no matter how she tried, she could not break the thread.

The hammer came down, and the lifethread remained. Then the youth dragged the stunned animal over to the iron hook and chain. Only after he slit the animal's throat did the lifethread break—spraying apart at the node, as if all the tiny threads unraveled all at once.

Mykella tried to work on the second lamb, but just as she thought she had understood how to undo those threads, the assistant completed the kill.

She struggled to work more quickly on the last animal—and she succeeded. It died before the assistant even raised his bloody knife.

"It's dead."

"Never seen the like of that before," said the butcher.

"Melmak, ser, you just scared it to death."

"Off with you. You hit too hard with the hammer."

As she turned away, Mykella felt chill inside. She'd never killed anything before—except spiders and flies and the like. Still, the lamb would have died one way or the other. And Jeraxylt and Kiedryn had both been killed by Joramyl's plots.

She stiffened, then walked back across the rear courtyard toward the palace, still holding the sight-shield.

XXI

True spring had finally arrived in Tempre—or at least several days and afternoons warm enough to enjoy the private gardens to the northwest of the palace, and on Decdi Mykella slipped away from the palace to the gardens and their budding foliage to be alone. She was edgy, and still had trouble sleeping, even though the ledgers showed no more diversions, and the actual receipts matched the ledger entries.

One of her favorite places was a small fountain in the northwest corner of the extensive walled garden. There, water trickled down what resembled a section of an ancient wall, and tiny ferns circled the shallow pool below. In summer and fall, miniature redbells bloomed.

She was halfway across the garden on the side path when she heard a feminine laugh from behind one of the boxwood hedges forming the central maze. The laugh was Rachylana's, and Mykella could sense that her sister was not alone. She moved closer, drawing her sight-shield around her.

"You're much more beautiful than Mykella." That voice was Berenyt's.

"Mykella has her points."

"But so many of them are sharp . . ."

Mykella snorted. Time to put a stop to this particular scene. "Rachylana! Where are you?" As if she didn't know.

There was absolute silence from the hidden bower, but Mykella dropped the sight-shield and moved toward it, making sure her boots echoed on the stones of the curving pathway. When she came around the last corner of the boxwood hedge before the bower, Berenyt stood.

"Mistress Mykella." His words were pleasant.

Mykella could sense the unvoiced condescension and the irritation. "Good day, Berenyt," Mykella said politely. "I didn't realize you were here."

"It was a most pleasant end day, and I happened to encounter your sister, and she suggested we enjoy the garden. It has been such a long and gray winter."

"It has indeed," Mykella agreed, "some days being even grayer than others."

Berenyt bowed. "I will not intrude further. Good afternoon, ladies." His smile was clearly for Rachylana. He stepped gracefully past the sisters and made his way down the hedge-lined path that would lead him out of the maze.

Mykella waited for the outburst that was certain to follow once Berenyt was out of earshot.

"You came out here looking for us, didn't you?" accused Rachylana.

"No. I came out here to be alone, but you were giggling and making over him. He's your cousin."

"He's going to be Lord-Protector someday. Father won't wed again."

Mykella had tried to avoid thinking about that. "If Lady Cheleyza doesn't have a son, and if nothing happens to Berenyt."

"He'll still be first in line."

"He's your cousin," Mykella repeated.

"So?"

"Berenyt's just using you," Mykella said, not concealing the exasperation in her voice. "You're behaving like every other silly woman, even like a tavern trollop. You think that he cares for you. All he wants is information and power. He really doesn't even want to bed you, except to make his position as heir-apparent to his father more secure."

"That's not Berenyt."

"That's very much Berenyt. While you're thinking he's appreciating you, he keeps asking you questions, doesn't he? He flirts, but never says anything." Mykella's words were edged with honey more bitter than vinegar.

Rachylana lunged toward Mykella.

Mykella stepped aside, but also called up the unseen webs of greenish energy.

Rachylana reeled away from the unseen barrier and staggered back, nearing toppling over the stone bench. "You hit me!"

"I never touched you, but I certainly should have. You tripped over your own feet, and you'll trip over more than that if you're not careful."

"You and your pride. You seem to think that you can do anything a man can, and you can't," snapped Rachylana. "You're the one who'll trip." She straightened herself and smiled. "You seem to forget, Mykella, that you're a woman, and women need to carry themselves with care if they're to acquire what they wish."

Mykella had never forgotten that she was a woman. How could she, reminded as she was at every turn about what women couldn't do, shouldn't do, or ought not to do? She said nothing more as Rachylana turned and stalked down the garden path.

Only after Rachylana had left did Mykella walk to the far corner of the garden. How could she make people pay attention to her—truly pay attention to her? She was half a head shorter than her sisters, and she was a woman. Her voice and perhaps her posture were the only commanding aspects she possessed.

Could she use her talents . . . She paused. The Ancient had not said talents. She had said Talent—the same sort of Talent that her ancestor had possessed. Could she summon the Ancient?

Standing in the shadows of late afternoon, she concentrated on the Ancient. Nothing happened.

How could she reach the soarer? Could she find the blackness below? She wasn't all that far from the Table, not really. This time, she reached downward toward the greenish black darkness. Surprisingly, touching that underground web was far easier away from the Table. Did the Table make it harder?

The Table interferes with many things. The soarer hovered to Mykella's right, in the deeper shadows. *You have called me.* A sense of amusement radiated from the soarer. *What do you wish?*

"Some assistance with a few small things," Mykella said.

Why should I offer such?

"You wanted me to deal with the Ifrit, didn't you? I did. Now, I may need to deal with others."

Mykella gained the sense of a laugh.

You need little from me. You can already tap the lifeweb of Corus.

"Outside of the shields and the sight-shield, I don't know much," Mykella confessed.

You can kill, reminded the soarer.

Mykella winced. Did the Ancient know everything?

Only what you have done, because you have accessed most of your Talent.

"It doesn't seem that way."

That is because you do much when you are not linked to the lifeweb. If you link to the web itself, all that you do will be strengthened. The soarer vanished.

"Who were you talking to, Mykella?"

At the sound of Salyna's voice, Mykella whirled. "Salyna?"

"I thought you were talking to someone, but there wasn't . . . there isn't anyone here." Salyna frowned.

Hadn't Salyna seen the soarer? Did one have to have some vestige of Talent to see the Ancients? Was that another reason why the soarer had contacted Mykella?

"Mykella?"

"Sometimes . . . sometimes I just have to talk things out to myself," Mykella temporized.

"What's a lifeweb?"

"Oh . . . that's something I learned in the archives. Everything in the world that is living is tied together. That's what the Alectors thought." Mykella hoped that her hasty explanation would be enough. "I was trying to work out . . . about why some things happen. Sometimes, it helps to put it in words."

"I thought I was the only one who did that," offered her youngest sister, pausing, then adding, "You know . . . you really made Rachylana mad."

"I'm certain I did, but she shouldn't be sneaking off and flirting with Berenyt. They're cousins."

"He can be nice."

"He can. Of that, I'm most certain." Mykella smiled. "We might as well head back so that we won't be late for supper."

Salyna nodded, clearly glad not to say more about Rachylana and Berenyt.

Mykella knew she had much to practice in the days ahead.

XXII

By Londi night, Mykella had managed two more small skills. In addition to getting light to flow around her to render her invisible to others, in trying to use her Talent to focus a lamp into a dark corner of her chamber to help locate a broach she had dropped, she had stumbled across another skill. In the end, she managed to concentrate or focus light around her without making her less visible. The effect was to heighten her presence, as if she were outlined in light.

If she were the Lord-Protector, such a skill might be valuable, but for now, it was merely a curiosity.

She also managed to project a whisper the length of the long corridor at night. She'd almost laughed when the duty guard had jumped and whirled.

She'd had no success in trying to walk on air. She could lift herself almost a yard above the floor, but she could not figure out how to move laterally. Nor could she even imagine how one could walk on water, when the blackness she drew upon had to be so far beneath the surface.

Going to work on the ledgers had become more and more of a chore, because Maxymt and the clerks had clearly gotten the word to make sure all the entries agreed. Yet Mykella felt that if she did not keep overseeing the accounts, matters would revert to what they had been.

On Duadi, as she was checking the latest entries in the master ledger, the door to the Finance chambers slammed open, and Salyna rushed in. "It's Father! He's had a seizure. He's dying, and he wants you!"

Mykella bolted from her table desk, dashing after her sister toward the Lord-Protector's apartments.

At the door to the bedchamber stood Joramyl. His face wore a concerned look, and there was worry beneath the expression, although Mykella had the feeling that the internal worry was somehow . . . different.

"What happened?" Mykella asked.

"We were having an afternoon chat in his study, and he began to shake." Joramyl shook his head. "He tried to stand, and his legs gave out. I helped him here to his bed and summoned the healer . . ."

"Mykella . . . he needs you." Salyna pulled on Mykella's sleeve.

Mykella turned.

Treghyt, the white-haired healer Mykella had known for years, stood at the far side of the wide bed on which Feranyt lay, still in the brilliant blue working tunic of the Lord-Protector although the neck of the tunic had been opened and loosened.

Mykella moved to the nearer side of the bed and bent over the shuddering figure of her father. "I'm here. I'm here, Father." She forced the tears back from her eyes.

". . . Lord-Protector . . ." gasped Feranyt.

"You're the Lord-Protector," Mykella insisted quietly, taking her father's hand in hers, aware that his fingers were like ice. She could feel his lifethread fraying as she sensed it.

"Joramyl, and . . . after him . . . Berenyt . . . they . . . must . . ."

"Berenyt?" blurred Mykella.

". . . still of our blood, daughter." Feranyt took short shallow breaths, each one more labored than the one previous. "Promise me . . . promise me. The Lord-Protector must . . . must be of our blood."

"The ruler of Tempre must be of our blood," repeated Mykella. She could promise that.

The faintest smile crossed Feranyt's lips before a last spasm convulsed him

"He's gone," said the angular healer, looking toward Joramyl, who remained standing beside the doorway. "Lord-Protector."

Mykella wanted to protest. She did not, but straightened, looking down at the silent figure of her father. There was an ugly bluish green that suffused his form, fading slowly as his body cooled. Poison? It had to be, and she had no doubts about who had been behind it. Yet how could she prove it when the only evidence was what she could sense and that no one else could?

And if she insisted it had been poison, too many questions would arise as to how and why she knew. Besides, her father was dead. So was Jeraxylt, and Joramyl was Lord-Protector. And . . . all of it had happened because—or at least sooner—she had noted discrepancies in the ledgers and tried, as best she could, to do something about it.

XXIII

After her father's death, Mykella knew she had little time in which to act, especially after both the healer and Joramyl concluded that her father had died of a brain seizure. Over the next two days, she made several more trips to the slaughterhouse, working so that the animals died from her efforts only instants after their blood gushed out, and so that Melmak never knew what was truly happening.

She also made other arrangements . . . and forced herself to wait. Waiting was the hardest part, and that was the part of the role of a woman of Tempre that had always challenged her.

On Quattri, Joramyl requested Mykella, Rachylana, and Salyna to join him in the Lord-Protector's study immediately after breakfast.

Mykella led the way and could not have said that she was surprised to find Joramyl behind her father's table desk, at least the desk she had thought of as her father's. Nor was she particularly amazed to see Berenyt there, although he was standing.

"If all of you would be seated." Joramyl gestured to the four chairs set in a semicircle before the desk.

Mykella recalled that there were usually only three there.

After waiting until the four were seated, Joramyl went on. "Everything has been arranged for your father's funeral tomorrow. There will be a week of mourning following the ceremonies. The procession will be public, the interment and final blessing private, in keeping with tradition. Do you have any questions?"

"Who will do the blessing?" asked Salyna.

"Would you like to, since you asked?" inquired Joramyl. "I had thought that Mykella might offer the statement of his life, since she is the eldest."

Salyna nodded.

"Is that acceptable to you, Rachyla?" asked Joramyl.

"Yes."

A silence descended on the study. Mykella waited, unwilling to be the one to speak.

Joramyl cleared his throat. "Now . . . uncomfortable as it may be, we need to talk about your future." The Lord-Protector-select's words were mild.

Mykella could sense the calculation and the disdain behind the politeness. "Now? We have not even had Father's funeral."

"By the end of the week after the funeral, of course, you will all retire to your father's hill villa for a half season of mourning. By then, the envoy from Southgate should have arrived, and we can begin the negotiations for Salyna's marriage. I have renewed the negotiations with Deforya as well, Mykella."

Mykella wasn't aware that those negotiations had ever been broken off. "Salyna isn't old enough to be married to anyone," she said quietly

"She needs the protection of a strong consort, especially now," suggested Berenyt. "So do you and Rachylana."

"And whom would you suggest?"

"Cousins have married," Berenyt said.

Joramyl merely offered the slightest of smiles.

"You and Rachylana?" asked Mykella.

"If such were to occur, I would leave that decision to the two of you." Berenyt smiled.

"Perhaps you and Rachylana should discuss such matters," added Joramyl, gazing pointedly at Mykella. "Your father did wish his successors to be of his blood."

Mykella looked blankly out the window. If Berenyt married

Rachylana, no one would ever complain, not loudly, that Joramyl had succeeded her father, because both bloodlines would be united in their children. But ... it was wrong.

Yet, if she challenged Joramyl and Berenyt, she would be acting against her own sister. And what could she really do? Could what she had learned sustain her against Joramyl and the leaders of the Southern Guard?

After a moment, she inclined her head politely. "That is true. He did wish his successor to be of his blood, and his successor will be."

Berenyt relaxed ever so slightly. Joramyl did not, although he smiled broadly. "I'm sure he would have been glad to know that you intend to support his wishes."

"I am a dutiful daughter," Mykella replied, inclining her head, "and his wishes are and will be my command."

XXIV

That evening, after a cold dinner, Salyna followed Mykella back to her chamber.

"What do you want, little sister?" asked Mykella gently.

"Rachylana's worried, Mykella," Salyna said quietly.

"Why should she be worried?" replied Mykella. "Berenyt will ask for her hand, whether he loves her or not, and she'll become the wife of the future Lord-Protector of Tempre."

"She thinks you'll do something stupid, like try to poison Joramyl or something like that, and that you'll be killed, and we'll be exiled."

Mykella laughed, a low and ironic sound. "You can tell her that I never once thought of poisoning anyone, not after I saw what it did to Father."

"Father? You think he was poisoned?"

"I can't prove it to anyone. But he was healthy. He had a glass of wine, and he had a seizure. He was dead in less than half a glass. That all happened less than half a season after Jeraxylt died in a sparring accident. Most convenient, don't you think?"

"I had wondered." Salyna's face crumpled, and her eyes brightened. "But what can we do? You can't ... Either it was all the way Uncle Joramyl said it was ... or ..." She said nothing for a moment, before asking, "If you're right, who would believe it?"

Mykella nodded. "And if anyone poisoned anyone now . . . I'm most certain everyone would look at me. You're too sweet, and Rachylana has everything to lose."

"But . . . they'll send me to Southgate."

"That's possible." Mykella didn't want to let her sister know anything, for Salyna's own protection. "You'd be safer there."

"What . . . about you?"

"They're still talking about marrying me off to the Landarch-heir of Deforya. I understand it's not too bad a place, except that it's cold and dry."

"Do you know what he's like?"

"That doesn't seem to matter, does it?" replied Mykella.

"But . . . Mother loved Father . . ."

"They were fortunate, and they had met some years before," Mykella pointed out.

"What will happen, Mykella?" Salyna's voice was small.

"We'll have to see, won't we? But there's no use in worrying right this moment." Mykella wrapped her arms around Salyna, all too conscious that her younger sister was the taller.

XXV

Mykella rose early on Quinti. She prepared herself for the ordeal ahead, in all the ways that she could, including her dress, a severe dark green and high-necked gown, trimmed in black. Her head-scarf was black, but of shimmersilk—and had been her mother's—and her cloak was black. Under the long skirt of the gown, she did wear black boots, well-polished ones.

She forced herself to eat at breakfast, but kept to herself until the time for the ceremony. She said little as she joined the others before they were escorted to the small reviewing stand set up on the north side of the boulevard, directly in front of the wall enclosing the palace. More than a thousand people lined the space on the south side of the boulevard, crowding the area between the low wall that comprised the northern edge of the public gardens and the edge of the boulevard.

As the late Lord-Protector's eldest surviving child, Mykella stood on the uppermost level of the stand, under a clear green sky, with a cool breeze blowing out of the northwest. To her right was Joramyl, and beyond him, Berenyt. To her left were her sisters, and beyond them, Lady Cheleyza. Below the family were the seltyrs and High Factors of Tempre—in effect the councilors of the city and more—and their wives.

"I can see the Guard is leaving the Grand Piers now," Joramyl said conversationally.

"It won't be that long now." Berenyt concealed his impatience badly, so much so that Mykella could have read it clearly even without her Talent.

As her cousin had predicted, it was not that long before the funeral procession appeared, led by two guards riding on each side of a riderless horse whose saddle was draped in the blue of the Lord-Protector. Behind them rode Second Company, and all the officers and men wore black-edged blue mourning sashes. Behind them came the caisson carrying her father's coffin, drawn by four black horses.

Just before the caisson carrying her father's coffin, draped in the blue of the Lord-Protector, drew abreast of the reviewing stand, Mykella stepped forward. She drew upon the lifeweb darkness beneath her and Tempre and focused light around her . . . then around the coffin, not enough to be blinding, but just enough, she hoped, so that all who watched saw the faint link of light between her and the coffin of the late Lord-Protector. Then she projected respect and honor for her father the Lord-Protector, easing it out across the area, but she let that projection center on her as the caisson passed. The riders of Second Company looked back, and those of First Company, following the caisson also fixed their eyes upon the Lord-Protector's daughter. Mykella remained motionless, but she did not bother to try to control the tears that rolled down her face.

Then, once the last of the riders had passed, she stepped back

"How . . . did that happen . . ." murmured someone.

"Don't say a word," murmured Joramyl.

Mykella let tears roll down her face as she watched the caisson heading into the palace grounds and toward the mausoleum on the hillside behind the palace.

After the last horseman in the procession had entered the palace gates, as Mykella walked down the steps toward the honor guard that would escort them to the mausoleum, Salyna slipped beside her.

"What did you do?" whispered Salyna. "They all looked at you. Joramyl got that stern stone look he gets when he's displeased."

"I didn't do anything," Mykella lied, "except step forward a bit to pay my respects to Father—publicly."

"But everyone looked at you..."

Mykella certainly hoped so.

Joramyl certainly had felt both anger and worry, but he had said nothing to Mykella. Even so, she maintained a Talent-shield around herself as she let the honor guard escort them through the plaza in front of the palace, then through the rear courtyard and the rear gate to the memorial garden around the private mausoleum—well to the east and uphill from the regular palace gardens.

Once the coffin had been carried into the mausoleum, and everyone had assembled in the small outer rotunda, Joramyl began the ceremony.

"We acknowledge that the Lord-Protector of Lanachrona has died, and that he has left a legacy of love and goodness bestowed on his family and people throughout a long and prosperous life. We are here to mourn his loss and offer our last formal farewell in celebration of his life." With that, he stepped back and nodded to Mykella.

Mykella stepped forward. She waited several moments before she began to speak, letting silence fall across the mausoleum and the area beyond. Her eyes traversed the three Southern Guard officers present, but she did not look sideways at Joramyl, nor at her sisters.

"Our father was the Lord-Protector of Lanachrona, but he was more than that. He was a good man, a caring man, and a trusting man, who loved his wife, his children, his larger family, and his people. He believed most deeply that the principal goal of a Lord-Protector was to protect his people, both from those outside the borders of Lanachrona and from those within our borders, for there are enemies in both places. He spent his efforts as Lord-Protector to assure peace and prosperity for all his people, and not just a favored few. And... to the end of his days, he believed in the goodness of those around him. We will miss him, and so will Lanachrona."

While her words were brief, Mykella did not know that she could have said more, or that more needed to be said.

After another silence, Salyna delivered the blessing. "In the name of the one and the wholeness that is, and always will be . . ."

Mykella listened intently, but while Salyna almost choked on the words near the end, her voice remained firm, steady, and loving.

During the entire brief ceremony, Mykella had barely glanced in the direction of Undercommander Areyst, except the one time in passing, not because she had not wished to do so, but because she felt that any favor she might show him might jeopardize his very life.

The honor guard re-formed below the steps of the mausoleum.

Joramyl turned to Mykella, a pleasant, but thoughtful look upon his face, an expression belying the mixture of anger and worry within him. "You were very . . . impressive today. I trust you will be equally supportive of your father's successor."

"I intend to be, Lord Joramyl. Like you, I am beholden to my father's legacy." She paused. "I apologize if my words are brief, but it has been a trying time." She did her best to offer an apologetic smile.

XXVI

Mykella wasn't certain exactly how she made it through the rest of the day, replying to all sorts of meaningless platitudes politely. She was just thankful when she could plead exhaustion after a light supper and retire to her chamber.

As she closed the door, she realized she was thirsty, and she walked toward the side table by the bed. The tumbler there was empty, but the pitcher beside it has been refilled by the staff., and she reached for it. Her hand stopped short. A purplish aura surrounded the pitcher—the exact shade of purple she'd perceived shrouding her father just before he died.

She bent over the pitcher and sniffed, but she could smell nothing.

For the briefest of moments, she thought about using the sight-shield to place the pitcher where Joramyl would use it, but that was not a good idea for two reasons. First, he had not moved into the palace and would not until after he was formally installed as Lord-Protector at noon the next day—far too soon,

Mykella thought, but no one had asked her. Nor would anyone. That, she also knew. Second, as Salyna had pointed out, Berenyt would make certain that she was blamed, and he would just become Lord-Protector sooner—and he probably wouldn't even have to marry Rachylana.

Mykella snorted. If she'd drunk the poison, doubtless Joramyl would have claimed a brain weakness ran in the family.

She did make sure that the door bolt was fastened before she put out the lamps and climbed into bed.

The faintest click awakened her from a restless sleep. She could sense someone outside her door, and she immediately reached for the greenish darkness deep beneath the palace, even as she slipped from beneath the covers and to her feet, waiting.

The door bolt slowly slid open, and the door opened. Despite the near pitch-darkness of the room, Mykella could make out that the slender but muscular figure who entered her chamber was garbed entirely in black, with even a tight-fitting black hood. She waited until he closed the door and edged toward the bed, a loop of something in his hand.

Using her Talent, she reached out and slashed at his lifethread node. Tiny threads sprayed away from him, and he pitched forward onto the stone floor. The thud was muffled by the old rug at the foot of the bed.

After cloaking herself and the dead man with her sight-shield, Mykella eased open her door. As she half suspected, none of the guards were anywhere in sight. Although she was no weakling, it did take her quite some time to drag his figure to the staircase, where she pushed the body off the top landing.

How far the dead assassin rolled down the steps she didn't know. Nor did she care.

She made her way back to her chamber where she rebolted the door, then took the desk chair from before her writing table and propped it under the door handle lever. While it might not hold against a determined assailant, anyone who could break it to get inside would definitely make enough noise to wake her.

She smiled grimly.

Her dear uncle was obviously worried. The fact that he was suggested that his support among the seltyrs and High Factors was not all that he might have liked. She hoped so.

XXVII

Mykella was the first in the breakfast room—for what was to be her last meal there, at least according to her uncle. Salyna and Rachylana entered just behind her.

"Did you hear?" asked Salyna. "They found an assassin on the stairway."

"How did they know he was an assassin?" asked Rachylana. "No one would claim that."

"He was dead," Salyna said. "That's what Pattyn said—he was the head of the guards on duty. The man was wearing assassin's black, and he had a dagger and a garrote."

"The guards killed him?" asked Mykella, sitting down at her place, all too conscious of the empty seat where her father had always seated himself. Her eyes burned, and she looked down for a moment, then swallowed before she raised her head.

"No one knows," Salyna replied. "Pattyn said he was dead, and there wasn't a mark on him." She poured herself cider.

The serving girl brought Mykella tea, but Mykella studied it for a moment, deciding it was safe, before taking a sip.

Rachylana glanced at Mykella. "There have been too many strange things happening, like the light that fell on you yesterday."

"It fell on Father's coffin," Mykella pointed out.

"And on you."

"She is the eldest, Rachylana," Salyna said. "What other heir does Father have?"

Mykella hoped her youngest sister hadn't guessed too much.

"Daughters can't inherit."

"Can't ... or haven't?" asked Mykella. "There's nothing in the charter or the archives that forbids it."

"You've looked? I would have thought as much," sniffed Rachylana. "Even if Joramyl and Berenyt didn't exist, just how much of the Southern Guard would accept a woman?"

"Rachylana ... that's ..." Salyna shook her head.

"Who would know?" asked Mykella. "There's always been a male heir."

"I still say that too many strange things are happening," Rachylana finally said, after swallowing some cider.

"Like the doors that opened in the palace with no one around," added Salyna quickly, clearly thankful not to have to discuss the possibility of a woman as Lord- or Lady-Protector. "One of the guards even found a silver in the middle of the lower corridor."

"Some factor probably dropped it. He wouldn't have missed it," pointed out Mykella. "Some people can't see what's before their faces."

Salyna gave the slightest of headshakes, and Mykella wished she could have taken the words back.

"What are you wearing today, Rachylana?" Mykella asked quickly.

"A new gown of light blue, I think . . ."

XXVIII

Salyna and Mykella walked down to the rotunda inside the main entrance to the palace at a half glass before noon. Rachylana was already there, talking with Berenyt, who wore the full dress uniform of a Southern Guard.

Rachylana looked at Mykella. "That long black cloak makes it look like you're still at the funeral."

"I can wear mourning garb if I wish," Mykella replied. "Joramyl said we were in mourning." Actually, under the cloak, Mykella had chosen what she wore with care—everything was black, except for the vest of brilliant blue—the Lord-Protector's color. While she appeared to be wearing a full skirt, it was actually a formal split skirt for riding, the difference not noticeable under the cloak.

"After the investiture," replied Rachylana.

Salyna glanced to Berenyt, as if to ask for an intercession.

"I heard about the assassin," said Berenyt. "You'll all be safer in the hill villa. I've asked Father to send two squads with you as guards."

More like gaolers, Mykella thought.

"You will visit, won't you?" asked Rachylana.

"I wouldn't think otherwise." Berenyt bowed. "I have to leave you now and join Father. He wouldn't wish his heir-apparent to be late."

"No . . . you should be with him," Mykella said politely, "especially today."

Salyna frowned for a moment but said nothing.

Berenyt smiled and turned, then walked briskly along the corridor, the sound of his boots echoing in the near-empty hallway, a space that normally would have held at least a score of people doing business with the Lanachronan functionaries housed on the main level of the palace.

"He's most elegant," observed Rachylana.

"He does look very handsome," Salyna replied.

"There's an old saying about handsome is as handsome does," Mykella said blandly. She still couldn't forget that Berenyt had been with the plotters at every meeting. That made him as guilty as his father.

Rachylana sniffed, and Mykella could sense her thoughts—You're just jealous.

Mykella wouldn't have wanted Berenyt on a silver platter, even if he hadn't been her cousin. He wasn't anywhere close to the man her father had been, nor a fraction of the man Undercommander Areyst was. She pushed that thought away for the moment.

"Ladies?" An undercaptain of the Southern Guard appeared, with Lady Cheleyza behind him. "It's time for you to take your places."

Mykella followed the undercaptain and Cheleyza, with her sisters behind her. They took their positions on the fourth step of the five low and wide stone steps that led to the main palace entry—the topmost one was empty, by tradition, because the Lord-Protector-select had to ascend that last step alone. Cheleyza stood on the left side of the open space that formed an aisle down the center of the steps, alone, and Mykella and her sisters stood on the right. The lower three steps held the various ministers and senior functionaries, and their families. The public crowds around the plaza were modest, with possibly fewer spectators than had attended Feranyt's funeral, but since the plaza was not that large, and since both Southern Guard companies assigned to the palace were drawn up in mounted formation, the plaza appeared full enough.

The investiture was a simple ceremony. Joramyl would ride in from the side, accompanied by Berenyt, dismount, and present himself to the three senior officers of the Southern Guard, waiting on the east side, then to the seltyrs and High Factors on the west. After making his statement and bowing to each group, he would slowly ascend the steps. Once he reached the top step, he would turn and offer the ritual statement. Then he would walk down, alone, mount, and ride off—if only to the rear courtyard.

A single trumpet heralded Joramyl's approach. Wearing the brilliant blue dress tunic of the Lord-Protector, he rode slowly down the open space before the arrayed Southern Guard companies and the palace. Behind him rode Berenyt in his formal dress uniform.

They reined up short of the senior Southern Guard officers and the seltyrs and High Factors, then dismounted and handed the reins to two waiting guards. Joramyl stepped forward and nodded to Arms-Commander Nephryt before turning and walking several paces toward the seltyrs and High Factors, to whom he offered the ritual question, "Will you accept me as Lord-Protector?"

Mykella sensed that the approval was somewhere between perfunctory and grudging.

After inclining his head to the seltyrs and High Factors, Joramyl slowly started up the stone steps toward the outer columns of the rotunda, columns clearly added later, because they had already become rounded and pitted in places, while the stone of the original structure looked as though it had been built within the past few years. The Lord-Protector-select was followed by Berenyt, as Joramyl's heir-apparent.

Although Mykella had begun to draw upon the darkness deep beneath Tempre as soon as Joramyl had ridden toward the steps, she waited until Joramyl reached the third step before dropping her cloak and stepping sideways and onto to the topmost step, where she looked down upon Joramyl.

"What . . . don't be a fool, Mykella," said Joramyl.

Blazing light flared around the Lord-Protector's daughter as Mykella focused those energies with which she had practiced and practiced.

"You killed my brother, and you poisoned my father."

Joramyl's mouth opened as Mykella's voice carried across the steps toward the crowd, amplified with her Talent—amplified and carrying the utter conviction of truth. "All this was done in shadows and silence. You cannot bear to have the truth come out, and that truth will kill you here where you stand!"

Without touching Joramyl—except with her Talent—she severed his lifethread node, and he pitched backward down the stone steps.

Behind him, Berenyt's eyes widened.

"You, Berenyt, plotted with your father so that you might become Lord-Protector in turn. The truth will kill you as well."

Berenyt's mouth opened, his face ashen, before Mykella cut his lifethread node. Like his father, he toppled silently.

"No . . ." murmured Rachyla.

In the stunned silence that followed, Mykella took the four steps down the stone stairs, decreasing the intensity of the light that surrounded her. Then she stopped and surveyed the three officers of the Southern Guard.

"Will you have a Lady-Protector of Tempre?" she asked more quietly. "Or will you try to hide treachery as well?"

"You? No woman will rule Tempre while I'm Arms-Protector." Nephryt's sabre slashed toward Mykella's seemingly unprotected shoulder.

His face turned ashen as the blade shattered against her unseen Talent-shield.

Mykella reached out with her senses and ripped his lifethreads from his body.

Nephryt's mouth remained open as he fell face-first onto stone pavement of the plaza, further scattering the fragments of the shattered sabre.

Mykella turned to the two remaining Guard officers. She smiled. "I believe that takes care of Arms-Commander Nephryt's objections."

Demyl looked from the fallen form to Mykella, then back to the body. He swallowed.

"You may leave Tempre this moment," Mykella said to Demyl. "If you do not, you will never leave."

Demyl glanced at the body on the plaza before him. "Much good it will do you."

"Go, traitor!" This time Mykella's voice rang across the plaza. "Be not seen in Tempre again, nor in Lanachrona!"

Demyl turned and walked woodenly toward the guard who held his mount. The crowd beyond the low stone wall watched as he mounted and spurred his mount out through the gates.

Mykella turned to the Undercommander.

Areyst looked to Mykella. "There has never been a Lady-Protector of Tempre."

"There's a first time for everything. Before Mykel, there had never been a Lord-Protector," she replied. "If I name you as Arms-Commander, will you serve me and the people of Lanachrona honestly and with all your abilities?"

Areyst inclined his head. "I can do no less, Lady-Protector."

Mykella sensed his feelings—both dismay and respect . . . and a grudging admiration.

Those would have to do. She doubted that Mykel the Great had gained any more at the beginning, either.

Then she turned and walked to the seltyrs and High Factors, inclining her head to the group of twenty-odd. She could sense the absolute fear radiating from them. "Honored Seltyrs, High Factors, will you have an honest and true Lady-Protector of Tempre? One who will not divert your tariffs or plot in secret and silence? One who will hold your liberties as dearly as her own?"

There was a moment of silence. Then Almardyn and Hasenyt exchanged glances. Hasenyt nodded to Almardyn. Almardyn cleared his throat. "Your father stood for us, and we would be unwise indeed to refuse a Lady-Protector of your power and his honesty."

Scarcely a ringing endorsement, but an endorsement. "You will have the benefit of all my Talent and all the honesty my father prized so dearly, even at the cost of his own life."

"We accept you as Lady Protector," replied the two.

After a long moment, a chorus followed. "We accept . . ."

Mykella inclined her head once more, then turned. Grudging as it was, they would honor it, and she would honor her pledge.

As she walked back toward the steps, she stopped before Areyst. "If you would follow me, Arms-Commander."

"I am no heir, Lady-Protector."

"For now, I have no other heir, and Tempre and Lanachrona deserve the best."

Areyst lowered his head. "I did not . . ."

Mykella smiled. "I know. Follow me."

Mykella turned and walked up the steps, sensing the approval sweeping the crowd—and the Southern Guard—of her designation of Areyst as heir-apparent.

When she stood on the topmost step and turned, she surveyed the plaza and those below for a long moment. She spoke firmly and quietly, though her voice carried to all, as she offered the ancient and original pledge that had not been used in centuries—and now, she knew why.

"I swear and affirm that I will protect and preserve the lives and liberties of all citizens of Tempre and Lanachrona, and that I will employ all Talent and skills necessary to do so, at all times, and in all places, so that peace and prosperity may govern this land and her people."

Her eyes flicked to the Arms-Commander-heir-apparent . . . who would be more, much more.

Palm Sunday

Ian Watson

Today was Saturday, and tomorrow would be Palm Sunday, when most people would gather in Grand Square to party, then all hold the palms of their hands up to the sky in celebration of life.

As Saturday dawn was approaching, Rootha left Pool's house. She and Pool had made love, then they had talked for at least an hour, lying together. Several times Rootha and Pool would say exactly the same thing at the same moment, so deep was their communion. Then they made love all over again—before sleeping for three hours, him holding her.

Three hours asleep was time enough for a person's hands to close up and for the patterns of the palms to reshape themselves, for a new fortune to impress itself on the flesh.

Once the sunlight was bright enough, the little cabins of the palm-readers along Riverfront and in Grand Square would open for business. New day, new fortune! Maybe merely a fortune similar to the day before. Business people especially would want their palms interpreted.

Dawn was in the east, violet and lilac, but the full moon still shone through dispersing streamers of raincloud, glinting upon puddles where the street's flagstones tilted. Thus Rootha could avoid soaking her shoes and the hem of her long gown. Joho, her husband, probably wouldn't return on the early steamferry from the capital, but you could never be sure. Don't arouse suspicions.

Yawning before sunset might seem suspicious too. Should she try to catch some extra sleep? Or should she stay awake to visit a teller? The teller might see a change in her destiny. How unfair to stay bound to Joho because he'd lent her parents so much money, when Pool was so perfect for her and she for him—like hand in glove, like glove on hand. When she first met Pool, going to his shop for a glove fitting, Rootha and he had *fitted* astonishingly. Both knew immediately.

The scent of nightblooms drifted from gardens as Rootha hurried through the deserted streets to a home that wasn't her true home. Joho's business was buying raw gemstones from the hills to the north, and cutting them. Usually he took his cut gems once a month to the capital on the coast. So only once a month, for some hours by night, could Rootha be her real self.

She must *not* resent her dad for his financial failure. Never. Never must she hint at her own sacrifice.

A few hours earlier Pool had told her, not for the first time, "We'll be together in a future life. Next time, we'll meet each other soon. It's destined because we're so like twins, you and I, like separate halves of the same person. And even in this life, who knows what may happen?"

Such as the ferryboat sinking and Joho drowning? Rootha didn't wish to curse her husband, for then she would feel even more guilt.

Later, as Rootha headed for Riverfront, now wearing brown boots and a violet gown, her coal-black hair pinned-up, a carriage overtook her. Fine lady going to have her hand read. Should I invite the mayor to my party, or not since I don't like him much? Should I wear green or gold? Decisions, decisions.

Rootha gazed at the new lines on her own right hand. She had read a pamphlet arguing that the moon and the sun and the world and the stars all pulled at people's mutable palms, just as the moon pulled tides. Nonsense! For if that was so, everybody in the same town ought to show almost identical lines. The science of reading palms was very complex. Apprentice tellers took three years to master the subject. In the past, centuries had gone into understanding the shiftings of destiny.

As she walked, she fiddled with her bronze binding band. The weld was almost seamless. After the ceremony, a young cousin had asked her, "Does it hurt, the soldering?" Of course not. Brides mustn't scream or whimper. A thin pad, slid between wrist and band, blocked almost all the heat. If only she could wrench the band from her wrist, and undo all her union with Joho.

Beyond the curving low-walled esplanade of Riverside the river was very wide and slow, almost a lake. Fishermen were out in their boats, lines baited. Aha, one man scooped up a big squirming catch in his hand-net. First of the day. He hallooed, knifed the fish loose from the hook, swung the net around and around his head—then hurled the fish towards the nearest boat, where another fisherman caught it in his hand-net. With a halloo, that man sent the fish onward. *Halloo-halloo* rang across the water as the tossed catch went this way and that till one man overreached and fell in. Merrily all the fisherman flourished an open hand. Lucky in its escape, unlucky in its wounded mouth, the fish would be swimming away, gasping water.

Rootha was drowning, living with Joho, now that she knew Pool existed. He was her air.

How was Pool not infuriated with jealousy? He was remarkable, unique, like no other man. True, Pool knew that Joho was very unlikely to give Rootha a child. Though lately Joho had been suggesting adoption. An adopted infant in the house would be an emotional responsibility, and Rootha's emotions were focused elsewhere. Rootha told her husband she only wanted a baby from out of her own body, not from someone else's. So she must bear Joho upon her often while he tried and tried, always in vain.

The fine lady's carriage stood by a vermilion cabin decorated with white palm-prints set at different angles. All of the thirty or so cabins beckoned differently. People tended to favor the same teller, consequently two or three people were waiting outside most cabins, none as yet outside a few. Rootha headed for one of the latter, which was blue with silver stars. She preferred variety and a certain anonymity. All tellers were sworn to secrecy. The punishment for telling tales outside the booth was drowning in a sack. But suppose a teller spied the *exact* details of her affair! What then?

This teller was a chubby, freckled woman gowned in grey. Charts of hand-lines covered all the wall space that wasn't window curtained by lace. Seating herself on the tripod stool, Rootha paid a little-silver coin, then placed both her hands, knuckles down, in the grooves on the telling table.

Scrutiny, and scribbling of symbols.

Much was insignificant, but finally the woman said, "You'll find out about otherlife today."

"You mean I'm going to die?"

Was Joho about to discover and kill her? If she died, when the news reached Pool would he kill himself, to join her immediately in rebirth?

"No, I believe you should visit a temple."

Well, a temple concerned itself with the migrations of the eternal soul. As regards temples, usually Rootha only attended special festivals where Pool would also be. Of course she couldn't approach Pool then, not with Joho accompanying her, yet at least she and Pool could glimpse one another, which was both comforting and taunting. Might today's destiny bring her a sense of an otherlife *with Pool*? People from early middle-age onward often experienced sensations from their previous lives. Never visions, only sensations. Rootha had tried to capture some, but hadn't succeeded. She was still too young.

The teller hadn't said which temple to visit, so Rootha went to the purplebrick temple close to her home which wasn't a true home. Usually a number of templegoers would be staring past candles at the twisting reflection of flames in warped circular mirrors mounted on tripods, to cause a trance of atunement. Unusually, this morning, a bearded young speaker was holding forth, compelling a lot of attention.

"What," the speaker was saying, "if our otherlives do *not* progess from the past through the present to the future, the way we assume? What if your immediately previous life occurred in what, to us, is the future? What if your very next life will occur in what, to us, is the past?"

His hand made a zigzag gesture, high up and low down—then it chopped low in a series of waves.

"What if several successive lives are lived in our past, yet in an opposite sequence to events in history? What if we do indeed advance towards perfection—however, our perfect life has *already* occurred previously?"

What he said was so utterly new and provocative. This explained why he was speaking so early in the day! Rootha could have wept. To think that she and Pool would be together in a future life, which would therefore be a perfect life, had been such a consolation. To hear that this perfect life of being with her twin soul might *already* have happened—and might even be the reason why they had recognized each other immediately the year before!—that was horrible. She had nothing to look forward to.

"No!" she cried out. "It can't be!"

As if her outburst was a signal, other listeners also began to shout *no* and *out* and *leave*.

A senior speaker intervened, holding up his wrinkled palms for peace.

"Even though this young man's wrong, we should at least hear him, not try to drown him with our voices!"

"No!" shrieked Rootha, covering her ears, cursing today's destiny written on her hand.

The senior speaker addressed the bearded man. "Does it matter if our different lives aren't chronological? We still live all of them!"

"And how many is *all*?" came the reply. "Our souls are twisted in time like a knot, or like a tangled serpent sucking its own tail. Perfection must be followed by imperfection, again and again endlessly—otherwise our souls would stop existing because they would have reached their culmination. What else," shouted the young man, "can come after perfection—except imperfection? Without this"—and his hands gyrated—"this cycle of repetitions, the soul could not be eternal!"

So even if Rootha gained Pool, she would lose him again! Distraught, Rootha couldn't bear to hear more. She rushed to the nearest mirror, thrust her hand quickly through the candle flame, pressed her palm against the mirror itself. Distorted reflections and twisted light dazzled her. She pressed harder, as if to push her hand right through the thick glass into an otherlife where Pool might catch her by the hand.

And the mirror toppled, and the candlestick too, and Rootha's unbalanced body followed, as the mirror broke into pieces beneath her and the candle extinguished itself. Already strong hands were lifting Rootha swiftly. For a moment she imagined those hands were Pool's.

"Pardon, lady!" A rough unfamiliar voice. Of a burly man. One of the templegoers. He smelled of fish.

"Can you stand on your own?"

When she nodded, the fisherman—or fishmonger—released her. The senior speaker was beside her now.

"I'm sorry," Rootha gasped. "Pay . . . the damage."

"You cut your hand," was all he said.

She stared at blood on her palm, and without thinking, like some animal she licked her wound. Salty the taste, like tears.

When Rootha left the temple, her little cut already staunched, a severe-looking greying woman—her neighbour, in fact, Lola Caprizon—followed and said to her, "You're very faithful. Your husband should be proud of you."

For a terrible moment Rootha thought that her neighbour had noticed her rare nocturnal excursions to be with Pool whenever Joho went away. But no; Lola Caprizon was referring to faith in otherlife as taught in temples.

"That certainly shut him up," Rootha's neighbour said with a grim satisfaction. "He ought to be sewn in a sack and thrown in the river for fate to decide, sink or float."

When Rootha woke beside Joho on the morning of Palm Sunday and went to the window, her right palm looked more intricate than ever before. Her left palm seemed much as usual.

As a teenager, Rootha had played the thumb-drums well enough to belong to a trio of drummer-women who performed at bondings and fates and even at the Palm Sunday festival. That was where Joho had first seen her and become enamored.

When she was younger, Rootha had even thought that drumming might be her whole life—the beat of the heart, the pulse of the blood—but presently passion for Joho prevailed. And within a few years that passion faded, just as she herself faded in Joho's shadow. She ought to have waited! Yet how could she ever have predicted Pool's existence? It was only a little over two years since he arrived here from the capital and set up shop.

Joho stirred and yawned loudly and stretched himself. He hauled himself upright, the weighty presence in her life, to which were attached the weight of her father too, and her mother.

"Today's our day," he said.

Rootha turned away from the window.

"How do you mean?"

"The day I first saw you. Can't you remember? You were drumming."

"Oh yes. Of course. Joho, I'll have my palms read before the festival starts."

"To decide how you'll dress? I'd have thought the purple gown."

Oh yes, she thought bitterly, to decide how I'll dress as your wife. However, she smiled.

"Probably the purple, but even so! And you?"

"My brocade suit, of course."

"I meant about visiting the teller."

"No need of that," said Joho. "Reed saw my hands before my trip. That's enough."

Joho always patronised the same elderly teller in Grand Square. Reed knows me like the front of my hand, Joho often said.

"Besides, we aren't made of money," Rootha's husband added. No doubt an allusion to his father-in-bond. Joho was like that. A heavy presence. Pool was an absence, ever present in her mind.

This time on Riverside, Rootha visited a yellow cabin decorated with bird emblems in blue and white. The teller was a short thin man with a beak of a nose.

"Never seen the like before!" he exclaimed as he gazed at her right palm. "I do declare it's more a *map* than a destiny. Lady, may I possibly copy it? Some inking on your palm, then press upon paper. Wash off easily."

Rootha tried to make her refusal lighthearted. Yet he was right. How could she not have realised? A map was on her hand. Instead of the lines of life and heart and head, and the islands and squares of restriction or protection, of escape or frustration, and the crosses of irritation, and the bars and arches all with their interplaying meanings: instead of these, a map.

"What's more, I swear it's like a map of this city, but at the same time it's not this city exactly. A bit different, as if say a fire burned parts, then they get rebuilt in a different way."

She thought of the candle flame.

"Mayn't I copy it merely to study?"

Rootha shook her head and closed her right hand, shutting within it her day's destiny.

✧　　✧　　✧

Guiding herself by her right palm, almost in a trance Rootha walked in the direction corresponding to where Pool's house should be. Presently she noticed a marble building she had never seen before. Then another. Fashions had altered. Women wore shorter robes and fanciful feathered hats. Lips were painted in many shades of red. A few people glanced at her curiously—as well they might at someone holding out her hand constantly as she walked along.

Presently she arrived at Pool's lane. The flagstones had been reset, all level, though the houses all looked much the same.

Heart thumping, she arrived at the door and clanged the bell.

Footsteps.

The man who opened the door was a blue-eyed stranger whose hair was long and fair, much longer and lighter than Pool's had been.

"Can I help you, lady?"

She gaped at him, without any of the instant thrill of recognition she had expected, even if his appearance was different in this otherlife of the future.

"I'm looking for Pool the glovemaker."

Yet of course, why should he be living in this particular house, and why should his name be Pool, and why should he even make gloves, except maybe that his talent had remained with him?

"Hmm, but I do seem to remember a Pool somewhere on the deeds of the house. It's an unusual name. I don't recall how long ago. How strange. I would think he'd be quite old or even dead by now." This occupant of Pool's house was intrigued. "My deeds are with the lender in Grand Square, though of course he's shut today for the festival. So even though I'm going to Grand Square this afternoon..." He flashed a palm at her amiably.

Palm Sunday! Almost everyone would be going to the festival, all gathered together in one place.

"Oh thank you for your help!" Rootha exclaimed.

"But I haven't—"

"You have!"

After a while, she passed a shop window and saw herself reflected, just as always. Oh yes, she was faithful! Faithful in the deepest sense. She must look eccentric, perhaps a bit of a mad lady.

A coin from her pocket bought her a meat bun and an apple juice and change from a vendor in Grand Square, where many youngsters were already gathering to enjoy a carousel and a house of mirrors and the other entertainments, some unfamiliar. Glancing back, she noticed the vendor admiring her coin, a grin on his face—that little-silver must have become rare.

Presently more and more townfolk were pouring into the square, dressed in their best. Rootha was walking around and glancing discreetly at every man until too many people were present and she felt panic, and redoubled her efforts. Could it be that Pool lived in another city or town, and she must travel from place to place—after first finding work for money, maybe as a drummer if her fingers were still nimble?

Yet she had the map on her hand, the map of this city, no other. She kissed her palm, where yesterday she had licked blood.

An hour passed. Two. What a throng. At last a senior speaker clad in white ascended the steps of the town hall, and spoke much as usual about destiny and otherlife.

Finally he raised his hands high, palms to the crowd, and a moment later everyone copied him, cheering.

It was then that Rootha saw *him* and forced her way through. Not the Pool who had been—but she *knew.*

And at last she faced him.

"Fate, I *know* you," he said. "It's as if . . . But where? *Who are you?*"

They talked and talked. She told him everything; and the truth seemed self-evident.

"Last year," he confessed, "I was going to bond, but at the last moment somehow she seemed wrong for me. As if only part of her matched me. I felt so sad breaking off because I made her so sad, but my palm was always ambiguous and a teller said *wait.*"

"Did you love her?"

He was honest. "Yes. For at least two years."

By now people were dancing to drummers in the streets leading out of the square. He took her by the hand. She realized that she didn't yet know his name in this otherlife; hadn't even asked.

"Come home with me."

So she went with him, by a way that was familiar, until they arrived at . . . the same house that hadn't been a home. Altered, yet so similar.

"I rent the upstairs," he told her.

The Necromancer in Love

Wil McCarthy

The young necromancer is a blight on the social landscape, because when his sweetheart meets with an untimely interruption of service (don't they all? don't they always?), he's bound to do something the rest of us regret.

Class, listen. This is important. Put down your pencils, close your laptops, shut off your recorders and listen; we'll get back to histopathology later. The information in this class can be misused, and we need to talk about that.

The necromancer is a person much like yourselves. Naive, desperate, he clutches at emotional straws while he sobs on his girlfriend's blouse. She isn't dead, he thinks, and there's more than just denial in this thought. It's the mitochondria, right? The power plants of the cell, these little bastards are obligate aerobes; a few minutes without oxygen will unravel them permanently.

All right, there are tissue-specific differences. Some tissues can be totally ischemic for hours and recover on reperfusion. Sadly, the brain and heart are not among these tissues, and when the power plants go belly up they also spill proteins that can trigger apoptosis, or cellular suicide. But executing that program also takes energy which, under the circumstances, the cell doesn't have. The influx of sodium and calcium ions, coupled with the efflux of potassium ions, has also caused neurons to swell but not burst. It's a bit of a mess.

But aside from these niggling problems the cell—every cell—is intact! The nucleus, the cytoskeletal transport networks, the endoplasmic reticulum dripping with ribosomal protein factories... That stuff won't rot for at least a day, even at room temperature. It isn't dead at all, any more than a city in the grip of a power failure is dead. Mitochondria take in oxygen, glucose, and a low-energy phosphate molecule called ADP. You've all had Biochem 210, right? You know mitochondria exhale CO_2 and a high-energy phosphate called ATP, which is fuel for everything else. If you don't know that, I suggest you start making alternate career plans.

Anyway. Everything else in the body is idled, sleeping, waiting for the kiss of energy to return it to life. *And it will*, vows the young man. By all he's ever held dear, it will.

Young, naive, he begins with the basics: a bath of the fuel itself in a saturated solution of lactated ringers. Smelling like gatorade and beef bullion, it flows over that beautiful face, that beloved body now stripped of its tattered clothing. When she floats, as of course she must, he ties her down with weights.

And nothing happens. Hear that? Nothing happens; this thin, slimy broth doesn't penetrate her openings, doesn't pierce her skin and flow through. How could it? Reluctant, torn with anguish, the young man violates her with tubes, forcing the stuff inside her. And still nothing happens, because the osmotic potential of the ATP is insufficient to drive it across a trillion cell membranes.

Finally, he begins to really think about the problem. He pressurizes the tank to three atmospheres, then backs it off slightly when its groaning and creaking start to freak him out. Gut-shot with a popped rivet, he'll be of no use to her, right? Next he switches on an ultrasonic cleaner, hoping the combination of vibration and pressure might force the ATP across some membranes.

Again nothing happens, but it's a different sort of nothing. Are there subtle changes in her pallor, her rigor, her *elan vital*? Does she look perhaps a bit less like a doll, more like a living creature in some deep, deep coma? Through the murky white fluid it's hard to say, and even in his raging grief he knows better than to trust his own judgment. He knows that much, yes.

But he's encouraged, and from where the rest of us are standing, that's a problem. No leash can hold him now.

For an hour he lets the potion work its way into her, and then he pops the tank seals and lifts her out. Apologizing, he hangs her from chains. First upside down, to drain the fluid from her lungs and stomach, and then in even less dignified ways, believing he must be thorough. There are so many places these chemicals don't belong!

When it's done he hoses her down with cold water and straps her to a table. The final touch: an electrical shock to kick-start the excitable membranes of the heart and nervous system. It's not a gentle thing—two hundred joules, minimum, probably a lot more—and it leaves visible burns on her chest and forehead.

Does he really expect this to work? If you asked him, he'd certainly say so. "God, it has to. It ought to, yes. I'm not aware of any reason why it wouldn't."

Why, then, does he shriek and pull away when she opens her eyes? Maybe it's just the look on her face—of shock, of bewildered agony and mute, animal fear. Has every pain nerve lit up? Has he created some unthinkable biohell inside that mortal shell? Her own scream is silent, and though she gasps in a single breath, the muscles of her face soon slacken, their fuel supply . . . depleted. She only absorbed a few seconds' worth. Not even long enough to lay down a memory of what's happened here.

"Holy crap," says the young necromancer, his heart thumping so hard he can hear it clicking wetly in his throat. He's seen her sad, excited, sleepy, bursting with pride and elation. He's seen her drunk and asleep and even dead, but until this moment he's never seen her in pain.

He takes her cold hand, presses his cheek against it earnestly. Gasping, sobbing, his eyes spilling over with tears. "I'm sorry, babe. I'm so . . . I'm sorry."

This is going to be harder than he thought.

In every case, this much is certain: the necromancer has medical training, like all of you, and unquestioned access to certain materials. He's known well enough by his peers that he can move around without drawing attention, but not so popular that people randomly poke their noses into his business.

Maybe he's flunked out of his residency for cutting too many corners, for doing too many things his own way. Some of you should be paying attention to this! If he were truly brilliant his teachers might have cut him more slack, but he's a creature of passion whose intellect runs hot and cold, or flickers like an old neon sign. Determination can only take him so far, and when he falls in love—really falls, for the first time in his life—something has to give. Spilled dreams pile up at his feet; he can't bear any further loss, or believes he can't. Won't try, at any rate, and that's the problem.

Maybe he works nights as a coroner's assistant and days at a biotechnology company. He really does live alone in a big house, or else in one of those spacious, unfinished lofts you don't see much anymore. The kind that actually are converted industrial space, not mahogany fakes custom built for urban yuppies.

His hobbies include sculpture and metalwork, and usually some kind of hands-on electrical thing. Could be ham radio, could be Tivo hacking, could be some exotic breed of digital photography. Thermal IR, Kirilian auras, something like that. Everyone has neighbors, everyone is seen, but this man's neighbors are accustomed to strange comings and goings, to loud noises and flashes of light.

"Oh, that guy," they say. "Yeah, he's always doing stuff like that."

Truthfully, whatever unease they feel about it is tempered with admiration and even envy, because the young necromancer is exactly the sort of rugged, handy, easy individualist every American is supposed to be, but few actually are. Sometimes he makes even his teachers feel inadequate, which is part of his problem. Eccentric and smug—not a good combination. Again, yes, some of you out there should be paying particular attention!

Computer people would call him a hacker. Scholars would call him a dilettante. To soldiers he'd be "goofball" or "yardbird" or "wiseass," and in politics or business he'd be a wildcard, a loose cannon. Not insulting terms, per se, but not trusting ones either.

Still. "He's got a real pretty girlfriend," the neighbors will tell you. "Must be doing something right."

Yes, the girl is always pretty, always charming, always possessed of that peculiar mix of innocence and sexual precocity that no man can resist. Human nature, right? If she were dumpy and timid he'd get over it, but this one is *the* one; he'll never do better, and he knows it.

Tragedies are always born of love.

It must feel strange to go out and leave her alone. His best girl naked, strapped to a table, not breathing! But he needs supplies, needs access to high-end equipment. Needs to show his face at work to avoid raising suspicion.

He's cool about it, too, or he wouldn't get far, and we wouldn't still be talking about him. He nods to his colleagues, says a few words to them here and there, maybe not smiling but certainly not catatonic with grief. He passes muster; nobody spares him a second glance, even when he pulls a bacterial sample vial out of cryostorage, thaws it, throws a few bugs under the microscope and starts jabbing them with micropipettes, injecting God knows what.

Satisfied after a bit of chemical testing, he puts the engineered bacteria in a petri dish filled not with nutrient agar, but with a growth medium composed of living cells. You're familiar? Yes? He tapes it shut, pulls it out through the glovebox airlock and slips it in his pocket, warm as any incubator. Rifling through cabinets, he pilfers drugs, needles, electronically operated valves, all sorts of things. He stuffs it all in a red nylon lunchbox and then, telling his disinterested coworkers he's not feeling well, leaves early.

Before he goes home, though, he stops off at a medical supply store to pick up a few more items, things they don't have at work or that he can't just smuggle out under his jacket. A respirator, for example. A few liters of polyheme blood substitute tagged For Veterinary Use Only. An automated chest compressor we used to call the Pumper. Have you worked with those at all? Like a seat belt threaded through an electric laundry wringer. We see a lot less of them than we used to—part of the growing disillusionment with chest compression. Anyway, he gets more than he needs, much more than his revised plans actually call for. He's partly impulse shopping, partly just making sure he's ready for anything. He wasn't a Boy Scout, but he does admire the ethic.

When he gets back home, his girlfriend looks exactly the same as when he left: cold, livid, extinguished. Shouldn't she?

Grimly, he begins his work: harvesting the bacterial colonies, dissolving them in saline, injecting her with them. Crudely restarting her heart, her lungs, forcing the blood to circulate, to spread the pathogens around.

What are mitochondria, after all? Aerobic bacteria, swallowed by some larger cell a billion years ago and somehow, randomly, put to work rather than digested. And from there sprang all the plants and animals of the world, eh? All the amoebas and slime molds, all the fungi and protozoa.

Maybe we swallowed the wrong bug. Silly, fragile little things, they die without oxygen, but there are similar bacteria still alive in the world that don't: the rickettsia, which burrow right into eukaryotic cells—living or dead—and set up shop. What if scrub typhus or Rocky Mountain spotted fever had its ATP production genes replicated ten times over? What if it found traction in a viable corpse? What if growth factors helped it multiply, spreading through all the cells of the body? Or most of the cells, or even some?

Only one way to find out, he thinks.

"Soon, baby. Just hang on a little while longer."

Is there a soul, and if so, at what point does it depart the body? Can it be prevented? Chained? Pickled in place with formaldehyde? Make no mistake, we live in an Age of Horrors, where all kinds of things have become crudely possible. In thirty years time necromancy may be a staple of emergency medicine. There may be textbooks and courses in it, warning against the unintended consequences of this or that. How to preserve the original personality, how to ward off impulse dysplasia and silence the Hungry Ghosts, how to avoid unleashing a zombie plague upon the land . . . Death may one day take its place with "vapors" and "dropsy" and other quaint little disorders people simply don't get anymore.

But we're not there yet, hmm? Indeed, today's education system errs on the side of suppression, of saying too little, of encouraging each young necromancer to believe he's the first, the smartest, the *only*. And so we see the same patterns unfolding, again and again.

Don't take notes, just listen.

Other things we know before we even meet him: he's between the ages of twenty-five and thirty-four. He plays chess but not football, although he's usually strong enough, and often quite agile. He may well keep an online dream diary, and show a keen interest in lucid dreaming and dream control. As a child he was given to sleepwalking—a disorder which sometimes lasts into adulthood—and he probably still takes sleep medications of some kind.

He's never homosexual, and rarely a smoker, but he has been convicted of, or pled guilty to, one criminal offense. Rarely two, for some reason. In more than fifty percent of cases, he also plays a musical instrument.

The Bureau of Justice Statistics home page logs fourteen instances of necromancy across the United States, mostly hidden away under "felony desecration of a corpse," with a smattering of reckless endangerments and some panicky overtones of attempted bioterrorism. Not so many, you might say, but the trend is definitely up, with six more cases expected this year alone.

Other things we know about *her*: She's between the ages of nineteen and thirty, though never more than two years older or seven years younger than he is. She's probably blonde or redhead, although it may come out of a bottle. She looks good in a tight sweater, and has the sort of infectious laugh that makes people in restaurants turn around and look.

Typical quote from him: "No croutons, babe. They interrupt the texture." Typical quote from her: "Because they shot him, sweetie."

They've been dating for less than six months—past the third-date and eight-week barriers, but not long enough to see each other at their worst. The honeymoon is decidedly not over. Not yet. And that's the problem.

Even an armchair medical sleuth can see the Achilles heel of the necromancer's plan right away: rickettsia infections are easily transmitted. Through close (though rarely necrophilic) contact with his dear departed, the necromancer is almost certain to suffer the bite of a chigger, a flea, a body louse in need of a warmer host. He contracts the illness himself, yes, unless he's taken steps to prevent it, or to treat it at the first sign of rash or fever or head-ache. And even if *he* somehow doesn't catch it, *she's* a carrier—a rich reservoir of the disease organism for whom a "cure" would be fatal. Or refatal, if you prefer.

So.

She sits up: groggy and confused. Gasps in a first uncertain breath, looks around her, looks at him. Tries to speak, and right away he can tell there's something wrong. Her voice is slurred, her lips drooping, her words unintelligible. She looks like a stroke victim and sounds like a mentally challenged drunk.

Wheezing, she gets off the table and shambles toward the door, ignoring his calls, his cries, his imprecations. Even the iron grip of his hands, attempting to restrain her.

Sometimes she gets away. Sometimes she infects others, with a mix of symptoms that don't occur in nature. Sometimes these other victims die right in front of their baffled doctors, only to rise again in an hour or two, like something out of a bad movie. Zombies, yes, the emerging contagion no one is talking about.

Don't write this down. Don't record this. You didn't hear it from me.

In any case, one thing she doesn't do is regain full consciousness. He grasps the reason, and communicates it to himself silently, in the voice of Scotty from Star Trek: "She needs more power, Laddie."

You don't know Scotty? All right, never mind.

The other thing she doesn't do is protect herself against the rickettsia's harmful effects, or against invading pathogens of any sort, or against the steady seep of her own hungry gut bacteria. How could she? As her immune system comes online the first thing it does is attack the pathogens keeping it alive. By the time he catches her, restrains her, straps her to the table for a thorough examination, he imagines he can already see the first signs of secondary infection, smell the first hints of carrion on her breath, feel the bruised-apple softness of injuries that will never heal. Acting in what he believes is her best interest, he's managed to turn his beloved into a deranged leper.

Weeping, possibly even howling in despair, he shoots her up with broad-spectrum antibiotics and apoptosis inhibitors, and drowns her in iced saline.

Sometimes he stops there. Sometimes she kills him and eats him. Sometimes he succumbs to the infection and loses interest in earthly affairs. Love doesn't always conquer all! But these halfway Harrys are no more noble, no less deranged than their brothers in sin, and this isn't their story.

Our necromancer—damn him!—dries his tears, wipes his hands, straightens his spine and gets back to work.

✧   ✧   ✧

The stages of grieving are anger, depression, denial, bargaining, and acceptance. Arguably, the necromancer experiences all but the last of these, all smooshed together into a single driving impulse: to do something about it. Our boy has had enough of failure.

In the icewater bath he can keep the body for a good long while—long enough to make some calls, do some web research, thumb through back issues of *Nature*, *The Lancet*, *NEMS Kinematic Review* and my personal favorite, the *Journal of Cerebral Blood Flow and Metabolism*, beloved of brain-death researchers everywhere. There are several overlapping problems in need of solution here; he needs a lot of information.

He puts in longer, more convincing appearances at work. He has to buy groceries, do laundry, pay bills. You think mad scientists don't have bills to pay? He waits in line at the DMV, just like you.

He also manages, somehow, to charm away suspicion; the police never search his basement or his attic, the back room of his loft for the missing woman. A week passes, then a month, and finally the better part of a season. He falls into a routine of self-maintenance—how could he not?—and despite his best efforts he begins to forget the angle of her smile, the furrow of her brow, the exact lilting tone of her giggle. Memory is not a hard drive or a box of old photographs; it's designed to show the past through the distorting lens of the present. In his dreams she smells of rot; her footprints are fetid black sponge marks along the floor. If he didn't take sleep medications before, he does so now. If he had the scrip already, he triples his dosage and still wakes up screaming, sweating, his stomach in knots.

But he hasn't been idle during this time. In the burgeoning literature of the nanotech industry he's found whole classes of machinery powered by ATP, whole companies dedicated to supplying it in various ways. There's even a mitochondrion-sized device called a Freitas cell that uses nanopellets of gadolinium—a radioisotope chemically similar to uranium, but lighter—to power an endless reconstitution of ADP into ATP. Tireless, robust, far simpler in design than the mitochondria they could reasonably be expected to replace. They'll do.

For ten thousand dollars the necromancer buys a hundred trillion of these, suspended in a solvent called toluene in a little vial of brown glass. He does other things as well, which I won't describe here for fear of spreading the memes in unnecessary detail. This is a warning, not a how-to session.

Long story short? Too late, yes, I know. But there comes a moment when she opens her eyes again. Looks at him, looks around her, feels the shackles holding her down. Remembers the moments leading up to her death, compares them against her current surroundings. Does the math.

"What have you done?" she asks him, with a cool, contemptuous anger. She speaks his name, then repeats the question.

Her voice is all wrong: strong yet oddly squeaky. She has no need to breathe. She could live a hundred years in a coffin without a single whiff of oxygen. Her eyes are wrong as well: too wide, too vivid, too glittery-cold. Her mind as sharp as a razor back behind them somewhere. If looks could kill . . .

"Darling," he tries.

But her flesh is stronger, too. If she feels pain, she masters it, bursting her restraints or possibly wriggling out of them, heedless of the skin on her wrists and ankles.

Does he try to reason with her? Crack a joke? Pull a gun? Even if he fires it, even if he punctures the heart, it won't stop her. She doesn't need a circulation, either. Ironically, a silver bullet lodged inside her might slowly poison the tiny power plants. A lithium bullet would work even better, or any of hundreds of organic toxins, especially in the brain. It hardly matters at that moment, though, because he's laid no real plans for putting her out of commission again. Not his sweet treasure! Not this time!

"I love you," he says. "Look what I've done, look at all I've sacrificed. For you. For us!"

But what's he really thinking? That they can get married, raise children? Are they even still members of the same species?

"Fool," she tells him, striking him dead with a backhand swat. "How many times have I told you not to cling?" And then of course she breaks through the wall to begin her rampage. Hell hath no fury, indeed.

The arc of each necromancer's tragedy seems preordained; even with differences as great as the similarities, the similarities are vast . . . and troubling. And I will ask each of you to consider this, and to look at your classmates and within yourselves for any symptoms of the disorder.

You are here for one reason: to help and heal and do no harm, so please believe me—especially you men, yes, are you listening? Believe me when I say that women don't come back to you once they've left. It's a problem mere science will never correct, and one that requires a bit of gentlemanly restraint. No slashing tires! No cheating death!

That's all for now, yes. Read chapter six tonight, submit a summary in the morning, and never speak of this again, to me or anyone else. One day we'll have the power to take on death with the finesse it truly demands, but I caution you: even then, the gift of love itself will remain fragile, and perhaps not so easily resurrected.

Sleep well for your exams. I'll see you in the morning. Young man? Yes, you. Mr. Taylor, isn't it? Please come with me. I'm afraid I have some bad news.